Harlequin Secret Babies Collection

Life is full of surprises, and sometimes the best come in tiny packages—as the men and women in this special 2-in-1 collection are about to find out!

These heroes think they have things all figured out...until a confession turns their worlds upside down and sends them hurtling into fatherhood. Suddenly our gorgeous, charming and irresistible bachelors need to figure out how to be daddies to these adorable babies—and fast!

Join us as our heroes and heroines beat the odds and come together to form the families they only ever dreamed about having!

If you enjoy these two classic stories, be sure to check out more books featuring secret babies in Harlequin Desire and Harlequin Special Edition.

USA TODAY bestselling author **Kathie DeNosky** writes highly emotional stories laced with a good dose of humor. Kathie lives in her native southern Illinois and loves writing at night while listening to country music on her favorite radio station. Visit her online at kathiedenosky.com.

Look for more books by Kathie DeNosky in Harlequin Desire—the ultimate destination for powerful, passionate romance! There are six new Harlequin Desire titles available every month. Check one out today!

USA TODAY Bestselling Author

Kathie DeNosky

and

Brenda Harlen

Suddenly a Daddy

Recycling programs
for this product may
not exist in your area.

ISBN-13: 978-0-373-60990-1

Suddenly a Daddy

Copyright © 2014 by Harlequin Books S.A.

The publisher acknowledges the copyright holders
of the individual works as follows:

The Billionaire's Unexpected Heir
Copyright © 2009 by Kathie DeNosky

The Baby Surprise
Copyright © 2010 by Brenda Harlen

This edition published by arrangement with Harlequin Books S.A.

For questions and comments about the quality of this book,
please contact us at CustomerService@Harlequin.com.

® and TM are trademarks of the publisher. Trademarks indicated with ® are registered in the United States Patent and Trademark Office, the Canadian Intellectual Property Office and in other countries.

Printed in U.S.A.

HARLEQUIN®
www.Harlequin.com

CONTENTS

THE BILLIONAIRE'S UNEXPECTED HEIR   7
Kathie DeNosky

THE BABY SURPRISE   157
Brenda Harlen

THE BILLIONAIRE'S UNEXPECTED HEIR

Kathie DeNosky

This series is dedicated to Charlie,
the love of my life.

And a special thank-you to my editor,
Krista Stroever.

Here's to new beginnings.

Chapter 1

"Hi, I'm Jake Garnier, the new owner of Hickory Hills."

From the corner of her eye, Heather McGwire saw the man stick out his hand in greeting, but she chose to ignore the gesture. She knew who he was and she'd just as soon have a snake crawl up beside her. Jake Garnier was the last person she wanted or needed to have to deal with this close to the big race. But now that he was the new owner of the thoroughbred farm she managed, there was no way of getting around it. She either had to get used to working for him or stick it out until after Stormy Dancer won the Southern Oaks Cup Classic, then look for employment elsewhere.

Besides, after what they'd shared, she took exception to the fact that he didn't even have the decency to remember her. The thought hurt more than she would have imagined or was comfortable with.

When she remained silent, he stared at her a moment as if trying to place her. "Heather?"

His smooth baritone caused her nerves to tingle and her heart to speed up, reminding her that a little over a year ago all it had taken was the rich sound of that voice to make her lose every ounce of sense she ever possessed. Now it only made her want to smack him for being the biggest jerk to ever draw a breath.

"Jake." She barely managed a short nod of acknowledgement.

Standing with her forearms resting on the white board rail surrounding the practice track, she concentrated on the stopwatch in her hand as Dancer passed the quarter-mile post and headed down the backstretch. The top contender for the prestigious Southern Oaks Cup Classic, the thoroughbred was on pace to break his own record.

"Come on, Dancer. You can do it." She glanced from the watch to the horse. "Just keep it up."

"I remember you mentioning that you worked at a thoroughbred farm, but I wasn't aware that it was Hickory Hills," he said, sounding a lot happier to see her than she was to be seeing him.

"For the record, I'm the manager here." As Dancer headed for the homestretch, she added, "The name of the farm and where it was located never came up. Besides, you weren't that interested in hearing personal details, were you?" She glanced his way, and it was apparent her hostility didn't set well with him.

"Heather, I don't know what you think I've done, but—"

"It doesn't matter now," she interrupted. She didn't care to be reminded of how foolish she'd been.

He was silent for a moment. "At the risk of pissing you off further, how have you been?" he asked tightly.

Like you really want to know. If you had, you wouldn't have refused to take my phone calls.

She shrugged. "I've been all right." She didn't bothering asking how he'd been because she had a fair idea of what he'd been doing since they parted ways and didn't particularly care to hear the specifics.

"Is that our contender for the big race?" he asked, pointing toward Dancer.

Doing her best to ignore the man beside her, she urged the jockey, "Let him have his head, Miguel. Turn him loose." She glanced at the silver stopwatch again, and clicked the button on the side as the big bay sprinted past them. "Fantastic."

"I take it that was a good run?"

When Jake leaned close to see the time, his arm brushed hers and a tiny jolt of electricity shot straight through her. "It was excellent," she said, gritting her teeth and backing away. Turning to make her escape, she added, "Now, if you'll excuse me, I have work to do." She barely suppressed the urge to run when he fell into step beside her.

"I'd like for you to give me a tour of the farm if you have the time."

"I'm sure you need to unpack first," she said. Thanks to the mansion's housekeeper, Clara Buchanan, Heather had received a phone call the moment he passed through the security gates at the end of the half-mile-long driveway leading up to the mansion.

She desperately tried not to notice how his outstretched arms caused his snug hunter green T-shirt to outline the muscles of his broad chest and emphasize his well-developed biceps when he stretched. "I've been cooped up in the car for the past four days on the drive from Los Angeles and it feels good to be out in the fresh air again."

"Mornings around here are pretty busy—we have our daily workouts and grooming," she hedged.

When they reached the stables, she grabbed a lead rope by one of the stalls, slid the half-door back, then eased inside to attach it to Silver Bullet's halter in an effort to escape Jake's disturbing presence.

"All right," he said, stepping back as she led the big dappled gray gelding out of the stall and down to the tack room. "This afternoon will be soon enough."

She shook her head as she tied the rope to an eye hook by the tack room door, attached another rope to the halter, then tied it to another hook on the opposite wall of the wide stable aisle. "That won't work. My schedule is pretty full today and to tell you the truth, tomorrow isn't looking all that good."

"Clear it for this afternoon." Jake's no-nonsense tone indicated that he was quickly running out of patience.

For the first time since he walked up beside her at the practice track, Heather met his irritated blue gaze full-on with a heated one of her own. "Will there be anything else, Mr. Garnier?"

Scowling, he stared at her for several long moments before he finally shook his head. "I'll be back after lunch." Turning to leave, he added, "And you might as well plan on working late this evening. After you show me around, I intend to meet with the other employees, then I want to go over the accounting records."

As she watched him walk away, a nudge against her leg had her glancing down at the big Bernese mountain dog that had sidled up beside her. "You could really use some work on your guard dog skills, Nemo. Instead of taking a nap in my office, you're supposed to keep varmints like him away."

The dog didn't act the least bit repentant when he looked up at her adoringly and wagged his thick black tail.

Returning her attention to the matter at hand, she released a frustrated breath as she picked up a brush and began grooming the gray. She had no idea how he'd managed to get his hands on Hickory Hills, but she'd told herself when she learned Jake was the new owner that she'd be able to handle seeing him again. That she could keep what happened between them all those months ago separate from their working relationship.

Unfortunately, that was going to be a whole lot easier said than done. The sound of his voice carried with it the memory of him calling her name as they made love.

Closing her eyes, Heather rested her forehead against the big thoroughbred's shoulder. Over the past year, she'd done everything she could to convince herself that Jake wasn't that good-looking, that her perception of their only night together had been clouded by loneliness and the haze of too much champagne. But she realized now that she'd been in deep denial.

Jake Garnier was well over six feet of pure male sex appeal and it was no wonder that he had an endless stream of women clamoring for his attention. With broad shoulders and narrow hips, he had the lean, muscular body of an athlete. When they'd met at the thoroughbred auction in Los Angeles, he'd been striking in a suit and tie, but today in jeans and a T-shirt, he was raw sensuality from his thick black hair to the soles of his outrageously expensive running shoes.

Sighing heavily, she went into the tack room, retrieved a saddle, then returned to place it on the horse's back. She tightened the saddle's girth, then bridling Silver, led him out of the stable toward the practice track.

As much as she'd like to forget what happened that night in L.A., she couldn't regret it. Jake was arguably the biggest player on the entire West Coast. But there was an earnestness to his charm that she'd found completely irresistible. And she was reminded of how captivating it was each and every time she gazed into her baby daughter's eyes. Eyes that were the same cobalt blue and held the same sparkle of mischief as Jake Garnier's.

Walking back up the path from the immaculately kept stables, Jake wondered what the hell had just taken place. He wasn't used to getting the cold shoulder from women and Heather's blatant snub didn't sit well.

There were only two things besides his siblings and highly successful law practice that caught and held his attention for any length of time and that was fast, flashy cars and shamelessly uninhibited women. And to his immense pleasure, the first frequently attracted plenty of the latter.

So why did one woman's obviously low opinion of him matter? He wasn't sure, but there had been a sparkle of hostility in Heather's eyes that had taken him completely by surprise.

Thinking back to the first time he'd seen her, he still couldn't believe how captivating she'd been. He'd attended a thoroughbred auction to personally see that the woman he'd represented in a bitter divorce sold the horses she and her husband had purchased as an investment. Jake had quickly lost interest in the parade of equine offerings and looking around spotted a pretty little filly of the human variety to divert his attention. And from the moment he introduced himself to her, he found Heather to be the most enchanting woman he'd ever had the pleasure of meeting.

They'd spent the rest of that day and one incredibly sensuous night together and over the course of the past year he'd come to the conclusion that he should have asked for her last name and a number where he could reach her. It was totally out of character for him and something he'd never contemplated before. Once he parted ways with a woman, he never looked back, never had the slightest regret about not contacting her again. At least he hadn't until Heather.

But surely she wasn't angry that he hadn't kept in touch over the fifteen months since. Besides the fact that he didn't know how to reach her, it was a well-known fact that he wasn't looking for a relationship of any kind and that none of his liaisons went any further than a good time.

He had no idea if that's what the problem was, but he had every intention of finding out and settling the animosity between them once and for all. If she was going to be running the horse farm that his newfound grandmother, Emerald Larson, had insisted he take over, it was essential that they get whatever had her panties in a twist straightened out so they could at least be civil.

In the meantime, he needed to unpack and put in a call to Emerald, Inc. headquarters to find out what the hell Emerald had up her sleeve this time. Given her track record of setting her grandchildren up to find their soul mate, he wasn't naive enough to think that she wasn't attempting to do the same thing with him. He wasn't sure how she'd done it, but she had to have discovered that, however brief it had been, that he and Heather had a bit of history.

But the old girl was in for a big disappointment if she thought her tactics were going to work with him. He wasn't looking to settle down with a wife, kids and the requisite canine. Nor was he inclined to trade his sleek little red Ferrari for a family-friendly minivan with car seats and clumps of dog hair.

With a plan of action to set down a few ground rules for both Emerald and his farm manager, Jake followed the path around the antebellum mansion to the circular drive in front where he'd parked his sports car. Just as he pressed the remote on his keychain to open the trunk, a teenage boy wearing stylishly ragged jeans, an oversize chartreuse T-shirt with It Is What It Is screen-printed on the front and a red baseball cap turned backward on his head came out of the house to greet him.

"Hi, Mr. Garnier," the kid said, crossing the veranda and bounding down the steps. He came to a sliding halt at the side of the car, then stood staring at it as if in awe. "Suh-weet."

"Thanks," Jake said, chuckling at the way the boy stretched the simple word into two syllables. "And you are?"

"Daily." He grinned. "My dad was a horse trainer before he died and talked my mom into naming me after the Daily Double at Churchill Downs." He reverently circled the car. "Dude, I have *got* to get me a ride like this when I get old."

Jake realized that the kid was talking to himself and meant no disrespect. But the comment reminded him that within a few short weeks he'd mark his thirty-seventh year and he supposed that in the eyes of a young teenager, he was probably considered a fossil.

Smiling, Jake reached into the trunk for the suitcase he'd packed for his short stay at Hickory Hills. But Daily jumped forward to grab the handle.

"I'm sorry, Mr. Garnier. I didn't mean to get so carried away looking at your car." He hoisted the suitcase out of the trunk. "My grandma sent me out to get your luggage and take it upstairs for you."

"You're Mrs. Buchanan's grandson?" Jake asked, following Daily up the steps of the veranda.

The boy nodded. "Grandma's in charge of the house and Heather is in charge of everything else." Daily's youthful face suddenly split into a wide grin. "Wait until you meet Heather. For an older chick, she's way hot. Having her to look at every morning makes my chore of mucking out stalls a lot easier."

When Emerald and her stoic assistant, Luther Freemont, had met with him to turn over ownership of the farm, they'd informed him that Clara Buchanan was the live-in housekeeper. But they hadn't said a word about Heather being the farm manager. That just reinforced Jake's theory that Emerald was definitely up to something. Why else would she mention the name of the housekeeper and leave out all reference to the woman who ran the majority of the farm?

"I've met Heather." The kid couldn't be more than fourteen or fifteen years old, but it seemed he already had an appreciative eye for the ladies. "And I agree. She's very pretty."

When Daily opened the double doors and stood back, Jake entered the foyer and immediately felt as if he'd taken a step back in time. Decorated with furniture he had no doubt were period antiques, he half expected to see a woman in a wide hoop skirt descend the sweeping circular staircase. Or more likely a Kentucky colonel dressed in a white suit and holding a mint julep come strolling out of the study.

"Grandma told me to take your luggage up to the west wing," Daily said, walking toward the stairs. "If you want me to, I can show you where your room is, Mr. Garnier."

"Lead the way." When they reached the top of the staircase, Jake grinned. "I'll bet sliding down a banister like this one is as close to being on a roller coaster as you get without going to an amusement park."

"Oh, dude, talk about a rush," Daily said, his voice enthusiastic. He stopped suddenly, a concerned expression crossing his youthful face. "Uh, you probably don't want me doing that because of scratching the finish."

"It's water under the bridge now." Jake shook his head. "But I'm not as concerned with a few marks on the wood as I am about you taking a fall. That's a long way down and you could be badly injured."

"You won't tell my grandma, will you? She'll kill me if she finds out."

Jake took pity on the kid. "As long as you don't do it again, I think we can keep it between the two of us."

Clearly relieved to hear Jake would be keeping his secret, the boy smiled. "Thanks. You're really cool, Mr. Garnier."

"I'll take that as a compliment." Every time Daily called him Mr. Garnier, he felt as old as dirt. "And while you're at it, why don't you call me Jake?"

After a delicious lunch, Jake strolled back down the path leading to the stables and couldn't help but wonder if he'd lost his touch with the opposite sex. He'd never had this much trouble with women in his entire life. If things didn't change, he just might end up developing a complex.

Emerald, for one, was purposely avoiding him and unless he missed his guess, she'd continue to do so for a while. She had to know he was on to her latest matchmaking scheme and no doubt wanted to avoid having him tell her to mind her own damned business.

But Mrs. Buchanan's sudden disappearance right after serving him lunch was a complete mystery. She'd been friendly enough when he first walked into the kitchen. But as soon as she put his plate in front of him, she'd apologized and rushed off to the housekeeper's quarters as if she thought he was contagious.

And then there was the chilly reception he'd received from Heather that morning. Her body language and obvious contempt let him know in no uncertain terms exactly how she felt about his reappearance in her life. But try as he might, he couldn't figure out why. He hoped for better luck with her during their meeting this afternoon, but he wasn't fool enough to count on that happening.

Entering the stable, he walked past several stalls to the opposite end of the structure where the manager's office was located. He wasn't the least bit surprised that Heather was nowhere in sight. Given her attitude toward him, he really expected no less. He wasn't, however, prepared for the very large black dog that got up from a blanket in the corner, walked over and stretched out on top of his feet.

"At least you're friendly," he said, reaching down to pet the dog's head.

Irritated that she'd obviously blown off his request to set up a meeting with the farm employees, he extricated his feet from beneath the animal and covered the short distance to where the broodmares were kept. He found Heather bent over a horse lying on its side in one of the stalls, and his mouth went completely dry. She was dressed in a pair of faded blue jeans and a pale pink T-shirt. With the denim hugging her shapely little bottom to perfection, he didn't think twice about taking in the delightful view.

As she straightened, an older man Jake assumed to be one of the grooms brushed past him to enter the stall and hand her a pair of rubber gloves. When she pulled them on they extended up to her shoulders.

"What's going on?" he asked, venturing farther into the enclosure.

"The stork is going to make it before the vet." She knelt down behind the horse in the middle of the oversize stall. "Jake, I want you to hold her head to keep her from trying to get up, while Tony and I take care of things on this end," she instructed.

Jake wasn't used to anyone issuing him orders, but something in Heather's tone had him kneeling down to carry out the directive. As he watched, the man she'd called Tony held the horse's tail, while she helped guide the foal from the mare. She quickly lifted a membrane away from the colt's nose, then vigorously massaged the animal's small, wet body with a towel.

"Is that to make sure it starts breathing?" He found her skill and efficiency to be very impressive.

Nodding, she pulled off the gloves and stood up. "He was doing pretty good on his own, but it never hurts to have a little insurance when it comes to foals this valuable." She smiled down at the weak little creature. "We may be looking at the next Triple Crown winner."

Rising to his feet, he moved away from the mare's head as she started to get her legs under her. "Do you have to do this sort of thing very often?"

Before she could answer his question, the cell phone clipped to the waistband of her jeans rang, and she stepped out of the stall to take the call.

Jake turned to the groom. "By the way, I'm Jake Garnier, the new owner here."

Grinning, the man nodded. "I figured as much. Welcome to Hickory Hills."

"I have to go up to the main house for a few minutes," Heather interrupted, stepping back into the stall. "If you have any questions about the broodmares, training schedules or the farm's daily routine, Tony can fill you in."

Jake walked over to stand beside her. "I think I'll go with you, then you can show me around."

"There's really no need." Her long golden brown ponytail swayed back and forth as she shook her head. "I'll only be a few minutes and there's no sense in you walking all that way just to turn around and walk back."

Had that been a hint of panic he'd detected in her soft voice? Why didn't she want him going with her?

"I don't mind at all," he said, placing his hand to the

small of her back to usher her along. There was no way she'd leave him behind now. "Afraid of a little exercise?"

Jake could tell she wanted to protest at his wisecrack, but clamping her lips together, she quickly stepped away from his touch and preceded him out of the stall. Neither spoke as they walked side by side up the path to the back entrance of the mansion and he couldn't help but wonder what she was trying to keep from him. And he had no doubt there was something. He hadn't been an attorney for the past twelve years without learning to recognize when someone was trying to conceal a secret.

When they entered the kitchen, Jake stopped short at the sight of Clara Buchanan with a crying baby in her arms. Never in a million years would he have thought the emergency calling Heather away from work would be a baby. But his astonishment was compounded tenfold when Heather hurried over to them and took the child from the housekeeper. The baby instantly calmed down and it was obvious that Heather was the child's mother.

"I think she might be running a little bit of a fever," Clara said, touching the baby's round little cheek.

Heather nodded. "I thought she felt warm when I got her up this morning." She tenderly pressed her lips to her daughter's forehead. "I think she might be trying to cut her first tooth."

"That's what the pediatrician said when I called her." The housekeeper smiled fondly at the tiny girl. "But I wanted to let you know and see what you thought about taking Mandy in to her office."

"It might not be a bad idea to have a doctor check her over," Jake said from behind her.

He knew even less about babies than he did about

horses. But he and his twin brother, Luke, had raised their ten-year-old sister after their mother was killed in a car accident and remembered that when a child had an elevated temperature it was always better to err on the side of caution.

"Just to be on the safe side, I think I will take her to see Dr. Evans."

"I'll get the diaper bag," Clara said, disappearing down the hall toward her apartment.

As she and Jake stood in uncomfortable silence while she waited for Clara to return, Heather felt as if her nerves had been stretched to the breaking point. Was Jake aware that he was standing barely four feet away from his own daughter? Had he noticed that Mandy had his blue eyes and dark hair?

Ever since she'd learned that he was taking over Hickory Hills, she'd wondered how she was going to break the news to him about the baby. But she hadn't anticipated him meeting their daughter before she had a chance to tell him about her.

He hadn't said anything. Maybe he hadn't noticed how much Mandy looked like him. If that was the case, she'd be able to explain everything in a much less rushed fashion. She hoped.

"Needless to say, I won't be giving you that tour of the farm this afternoon or holding the meeting you wanted with your employees," she finally said as she cradled the baby close.

He nodded. "That's understandable. We can reschedule for tomorrow morning or even the day after if she's still not feeling well."

When the housekeeper came back into the room, he

reached out and took the diaper bag from her. "I'll help Heather and the baby get to the car."

"Call me when you get back to let me know what you find out from the doctor about our little angel," Clara called after them as they left the house.

"Would you mind letting Tony know that he's in charge until I get back?" Heather asked as they walked the short distance to the carriage house.

Jake shook his head as he watched her open the back door of the older-model sedan parked in front. "No problem. I'll take care of it. Is there anything else?"

"Not that I can think of."

When Heather turned to put the baby in the car seat, the little girl looked at him over her mother's shoulder for the first time and he felt as if he'd been flattened by a steamroller. He couldn't have gotten his vocal cords to work if his life depended on it and simply stood back as Heather got into the car and drove away.

As he watched the vehicle disappear around the corner of the mansion and head down the drive toward the main road, his heart pounded against his ribs and he found it extremely hard to draw air into his lungs. The baby had dark hair and big blue eyes. Eyes the color of cobalt. The same color of cobalt that met his gaze when he looked into the mirror each morning to shave.

Chapter 2

That evening, when Heather answered the insistent knocking on her cottage door, she wasn't the least bit surprised to find Jake standing on the other side. In fact, she'd been expecting him. She'd known that once he saw Mandy it was just a matter of time before he put it all together.

"We need to talk." Instead of waiting for her to invite him in, he took hold of her elbow and propelled her back into the living room, kicking the door shut behind him. "I want answers and I'm not leaving here until I get them, Heather."

"It never crossed my mind that you would," she said calmly. She wasn't going to allow him to upset or stress her out in any way.

"That baby belongs to me, doesn't she?" he demanded, cutting right to be heart of the matter.

"*That baby* has a name—Amanda Grace. I call her Mandy. She's almost seven months old." Heather walked across the room to pull the nursery door closed to keep their raised voices from disturbing her daughter. "And if by belong, you mean are you her biological father? The answer is yes."

"What happened? I used protection."

Was he actually questioning that he was the father of her child?

"I'm well aware of that. It obviously had a defect." She raised an eyebrow. "Surely you're aware that nothing is one hundred percent effective except abstention. And if we'd gone that route—"

"We wouldn't be having this conversation," he finished for her.

"Exactly." She looked him directly in the eye. "But let me assure you, Mandy is your daughter."

He shook his head. "I wasn't questioning that. She looks just like me."

Heather watched a muscle work along his lean jaw as Jake stared at her for what seemed like an eternity. She could tell his anger was bordering on outrage, but that was just too bad. As far she was concerned, not knowing he'd fathered a child was his own fault and she wasn't about to let him turn the blame back on her.

"Did you even think about getting in touch with me when you discovered you were pregnant?" he finally asked, his voice low and menacing.

Heather had told herself that she wasn't going to let him get to her, but his accusatory tone angered her as little else could. "I really don't think you want to go there, Jake. Believe me, you won't like hearing what I have to say."

"Go ahead. Try me." He took a step toward her. "I told you I'm here to get answers."

"Then I would suggest you drop the intimidation tactics as well as the idea of being the wounded party in all of this because you're not." When she turned to walk into the kitchen to put a little more distance between them and the nursery, she fully expected him to follow.

He didn't disappoint her. "Did you or did you not consider letting me know that you were expecting my child?"

Turning on him, she took a deep breath in an effort to calm down. She had a lot to say and she was going to savor every second of it. She'd wanted this conversation for over a year, but never thought she'd have the chance to have her say. She wasn't going to allow herself to lose momentum by becoming overly emotional. She refused to give Jake that kind of power over her.

"I not only considered letting you know, I spent my first trimester leaving messages that I needed to talk to you urgently." She met his angry gaze head-on. "*You* never returned my calls, and I wasn't comfortable leaving that kind of information with your secretary."

"I—"

Holding up her hand to stop whatever lame excuse he came up with, she went on, "Then I spent the second trimester trying to convince myself that there had to be a reasonable explanation for you ignoring my requests to get back to me. It turns out I was wrong. There wasn't a good reason, other than you really are an insensitive, self-absorbed jerk who uses women, then casts them aside."

He opened his mouth to no doubt refute her assessment of his character, but she cut him off again.

"And somewhere during the course of my third trimester, I came to the conclusion that you really didn't deserve to know about our daughter and that we were both going to be a lot better off without you in our lives." She folded her arms beneath her breasts. "Any more questions?"

Heather could tell by the stunned look replacing the angry expression on his handsome face that she'd gotten through to him.

Rubbing the back of his neck as if to relieve tension, he shook his head. "I have my secretary—"

"Screen your calls so that you don't have to deal with uncomfortable situations with the women you've bedded," she interrupted. When he remained silent, she knew that her comment had hit a little too close to home. "And you don't have to worry, Jake. Mandy and I are just fine on our own."

His eyes narrowed. "You're going to try to cut me out of her life?"

Heather shook her head. "That's not what I said. I'm telling you that you're off the hook. You're free to go back to Los Angeles and resume your life as if nothing happened. I don't want or need your help—financially or otherwise. I'm perfectly capable of taking care of and providing for my daughter. I just thought you had the right to know about her."

"She's mine, too."

Having had her say, she suddenly felt drained of energy. "I'm relieving you of that responsibility, Jake."

"I think we need to get this straight once and for all, Heather."

He stepped forward to place his hands on her shoulders. The heat from his touch seeping through her

T-shirt and the determination she detected in his deep baritone sent tingles zinging straight up her spine. But when he used his thumb and forefinger to lift her chin until their gazes locked, the sensation danced across every nerve in her body.

"I accept that it was my own damned fault I didn't know about the pregnancy. But it doesn't mean that now that I'm aware I have a child I don't intend to be a big part of her life. And that will be much easier for me to do when I move you and Mandy into the mansion with me."

"That's not going to happen, Jake. We're very happy right here in the carriage house."

"We'll see about that."

Before she could protest or step away, his mouth covered hers and the feel of his firm lips once again caressing hers with such care caused her head to spin. She tried with all of her might to remain unaffected, but her traitorous pulse took off and a delicious warmth began to flow through her veins.

Placing her hands on Jake's wide chest, instead of pushing away from him as she intended, she reveled in the feel of his strength beneath her palms and the steady beat of his heart. This was total insanity. He'd used her, then cast her aside with little or no regard for her feelings. But when he traced the seam of her mouth with his tongue, she parted her lips without so much as a second thought and allowed him to deepen the kiss.

As he wrapped his arms around her and pulled her more fully against his large frame, he teased her with a tenderness that caused every fiber in her being to quiver to life and her stomach to flutter wildly. The excitement she'd experienced in his arms fifteen long months ago began to fill her from head to toe and it scared her as little else could. Losing herself to Jake's kiss was the very reason they found themselves in their current set of circumstances.

"Please…stop," she said, leaning away from him.

Jake immediately put a bit of space between them, but continued to hold her loosely in his arms. "All things considered, I probably shouldn't have done that." He gave her the same seductive smile that had been her downfall that night in Los Angeles. "But I'll be damned if I'm sorry I did. You have the sweetest lips I've ever tasted."

She shook her head. "Forget my lips. It's not going to happen again."

He stared down at her for endless seconds and just when she thought he was going to argue the point, Nemo chose that moment to come lumbering in through the doggie door. Finding the two humans standing face-to-face, he apparently took it as an open invitation to push his way between them and plop his big, bulky body on top of their feet.

"What's his deal?" Jake asked, staring down at the dog. "Every time he sees me, he traps my feet beneath him."

Thankful for the distraction Heather stepped back then knelt down to scratch the big gentle dog behind his floppy ears. "It seems to be a trait of his breed. I think they realize that they're too big to sit on your lap, so they lay on your feet to be close to you."

Jake bent down to pet Nemo's thick, black coat. "So I guess this means he likes me, huh?"

"It looks that way." Only inches apart, they stared at each other for endless seconds before she straightened to walk back into the living room to peek inside the nursery door.

She should have named the dog Benedict Arnold. Nemo was supposed to be loyal to her, not cozy up to the enemy like they were long lost friends.

"What did the pediatrician say this afternoon?" Jake asked from behind her shoulder. "Is she cutting her first tooth or is something else wrong?"

Unaware that he'd followed her, Heather jumped as much from the unexpected sound of his voice as from his close proximity. "Uh…yes, she's teething. The doctor said she has two that should be through her lower gum by the end of the week."

"She'll start feeling better after that happens, right?"

Heather nodded as she pulled the door to and moved away from him. The concern in his voice touched her and that was something she didn't like one bit. It was much safer for her to think of him as the shallow, uncaring man who refused to take her phone calls, than a daddy worried about the welfare of his baby girl.

"I think it would be a good idea if you leave now, Jake." She walked over to open the front door. "I have to be up by five in the morning and I really need to get some sleep."

Glancing at the gold watch on his left wrist, he nodded. "I have a lot to do tomorrow and need to be up early myself."

He walked over to her, then cupping her cheeks with both hands lightly pressed a kiss to her lips. As he raised his head, the determination she saw in his incredible blue eyes sent a shock wave all the way to her soul.

"If you and the baby need me before morning, don't hesitate to give me a call. You have my word that from this day forward, no matter what I'm doing or where I am, I'll always be available for you and our daughter."

Once the front door closed behind him, Heather squeezed her eyes shut against the tears of frustration threatening to spill down her cheeks. She'd known the former owner was looking to sell, but why did Jake Garnier have to be the new owner of Hickory Hills? What cruel quirk of fate had caused their paths to cross again? And why, after all that had happened, did she still find him to be the most handsome, irresistible man she'd ever met?

When he'd introduced himself at the annual thoroughbred auction in Los Angeles, he'd not only charmed his way past her defenses and swept her off her feet, he'd stolen her heart, as well. She'd always heard about love at first sight, but she'd never given it a lot of thought, never believed it would happen to her. Not until last year. Not until Jake.

Swallowing hard, she reminded herself of the disillusionment and emotional pain she'd suffered when he refused to return her calls and she'd realized she meant absolutely nothing to him. It had taken her a long time to move past that and no matter how drugging his kisses were or how wonderful it had felt to be in his arms, she wasn't about to put herself in that position again.

Besides, it wasn't just her emotions at stake anymore. She had Mandy's well-being to take into consideration, as well. And Heather wasn't going to stand back and watch her daughter bond with Jake, then be devastated when he moved on like the playboy he was.

As he walked down the long driveway toward the big wrought-iron entrance gates, Jake still couldn't quite wrap his mind around everything that had happened. In the span of a few hours, his life had changed in ways he could have never imagined. He had reconnected with the only woman he'd ever regretted not keeping in touch with, learned that by taking over Hickory Hills she'd become his employee and discovered that a little over six months ago she'd given birth to his baby.

Unbelievable.

But as he thought about Heather making several attempts to get in touch with him, his gut burned with anger. He deeply regretted that she'd been forced to go through the pregnancy alone. If his secretary hadn't become overly zealous about screening his calls, she wouldn't have. He'd have not only been there for Heather throughout the pregnancy and birth, he wouldn't have been cheated out of the first six months of his daughter's life.

His daughter.

Jake's heart slammed against his rib cage and he took several deep breaths. He had a tiny baby girl who looked just like him.

It blew his mind that he had a child. Fatherhood had been something he'd never expected to experience. And it wasn't because he didn't like little kids. He did. He'd just made a conscious decision years ago never to marry and have one of his own.

His own father had twice walked away after impregnating his mother, and even though Jake didn't think he was capable of doing something like that, he hadn't wanted to take the chance. What if he carried the same narcissistic gene that had caused his father to shirk his responsibilities to his children in favor of pursuing his next good time?

Jake shook his head. It was all a moot point now. He had a daughter. And even though it scared the living hell out of him to think that he might somehow let her down the way his father had his children, Jake was going to do everything he possibly could to be a good father.

Lost in his disturbing introspection, it took a moment for Jake to notice the shadowy figure climbing over the gates at the end of the drive. "Daily?"

The boy froze halfway over the gate. "Mr. Garnier, I…oh, dude, this probably doesn't look real good, does it?"

"No. It looks like I just busted you for sneaking out of the house." Stopping a few feet from where the boy was perched, Jake planted his feet and folded his arms across his chest. "You want to come down from there and tell me why you're out this late, as well as why you don't want to alert anyone up at the house that you're leaving by activating the gates?"

When Daily dropped to his feet in front of Jake, he seemed to take a great interest in the tops of his un-tied high-top tennis shoes. "It's kind of personal, Mr. Garnier."

Jake hid a smile. "Want to tell me what her name is?"

The boy's head snapped up so fast, Jake wouldn't have been surprised if Daily had suffered whiplash. "How did you know I was going to meet a girl?"

Jake did his best not to laugh out loud at the aston-ished look on the kid's face. "I know it's probably hard to believe, but I was fourteen once, Daily."

"I'll be fifteen in a couple of weeks," the boy said, straightening his skinny shoulders.

"That's still too young to be out this late. Not to

mention the fact that you don't have your grandmother's permission."

The boy's shoulders slumped. "Yes, sir."

"I think you'd better give your girlfriend a call and tell her that you won't be able to make it this evening," Jake suggested.

As he watched Daily whip out a cell phone and rapidly punch in a text message, a knot began to form in the pit of Jake's stomach. In about thirteen years some pubescent boy with more hormones than good sense could very easily try to set up a midnight meeting with his daughter.

He barely managed to suppress a groan. He'd already raised one girl through the teen years when he and his twin brother finished raising their younger sister, Arielle. And just thinking that he was going to have to do it all over again with his own daughter was enough to give him an ulcer. His only consolation was that this time he'd be sharing that responsibility with Heather, instead of his brother who had turned out to be as clueless as he'd been.

When the boy slipped his cell phone back into his jeans pocket, Jake motioned toward the tree-lined drive leading up to the mansion. "Come on, Daily. I think it's time we both called it a night."

They remained silent for some time before Daily asked, "Are you going to tell my grandma about me trying to sneak out tonight?"

Jake shook his head. "No, I'm not. But you are."

"Me?"

"Part of growing up is learning to accept responsibility for your actions," Jake said, reminding himself as much as Daily.

"I'm gonna be grounded for the rest of my life," the boy complained when they entered the mansion through the kitchen door.

"I doubt it will be that long," Jake said, chuckling. "But as long as you're going to be sticking close to home for the next week or so, there are a few things around here I'm going to need help with. Do you think you'd be interested in the job?"

"A real job? Really? Oh man, that would be awesome," Daily said, his voice suddenly filled with enthusiasm.

"You'll have to keep up with your other chores and check with your grandmother first, to make sure she has no objections." Jake gave the boy a pointed look. "Right after you tell her about what happened this evening and accept whatever punishment she deems necessary."

Daily nodded. "I will."

"Then you'd better get some sleep," Jake warned. "We have a big day ahead of us."

"Yes, sir."

As he watched the teenager hurry down the hall to his grandmother's apartment, Jake headed for the stairs. He'd made Heather a promise and he fully intended to keep it. While she oversaw Stormy Dancer's morning workout and attended to whatever else her job entailed, he and Daily were going to get her and the baby moved from the carriage house into the mansion. And once he accomplished that, he had every intention of spending the rest of his stay at Hickory Hills getting to know his daughter.

"Jake Garnier, how dare you?" Heather demanded when she found him sitting at the desk in the study.

She was angry enough to bite nails in two and it was all his fault.

His unrepentant grin when he looked up made her want to throw something at him. "I assume you're referring to the moving of the baby's things and yours from the carriage house to the rooms upstairs?"

"You know good and well that's what I'm talking about. You had no right to do that."

He walked around the side of the desk to stand in front of her. "I don't know why you're so upset," he said calmly. "I told you last night that's what I intended to do."

She couldn't believe his arrogance. "And I told you it wasn't going to happen. Mandy and I are perfectly fine in the carriage house. It's all she's ever known."

"I'm sure you're happy." He took another step toward her. "But you'll be even happier here. There's a lot more room. And besides, it will be more convenient for all concerned."

"You've got to be joking." Where did he come up with that idea? "It might be more convenient for you, but it certainly isn't for me."

He was a lot closer than she was comfortable with. But there was no way she was going to back away. That would only give him the satisfaction of knowing he still had an effect on her.

"I fully intend to be a big part of my daughter's life," he said, sounding so darned reasonable it made her want to punch him.

"We live less than a hundred feet away. How is moving to the big house going to change anything?"

He gave her a smile that caused her heart to skip a

beat. Just because he smiled at her it wasn't going to get him off the hook.

"I want to watch you put her to bed at night and get her up in the morning."

"You could do that at the carriage house."

"So you're telling me that you want me to move in with you and Mandy?" he asked, giving her that same charming smile.

"N-no. That wasn't what I said at all and you know it." She should have known he'd twist her objections around to suit his purpose. After all, he was an attorney. "You knew what I meant. You could stop by around those times, then leave."

He took the last step separating them, then lightly touched her cheek. She suddenly had to remember why she was angry with him.

"If Mandy wakes up in the middle of the night, I want to be able to get up with her." He shook his head. "If I'm here and the two of you are in the carriage house, I can't do that."

"Take my word for it, being awakened from a sound sleep is highly overrated," she said before she could stop herself.

"I'm sure that taking care of her by yourself and trying to work has been very tiring at times. Wouldn't it be nice for a change to have someone sharing that responsibility?"

When he looked at her the way he was doing now, Heather was lucky to remember her own name, let alone what he'd asked. "No. I'm fine with the way things are."

"I could get up with her while you sleep," he pressed.

The heat from his touch branded her and the scent of his aftershave made her want him to hold her, kiss her and… She swallowed hard. She needed to escape his presence before her traitorous body had her agreeing to go along with what he wanted.

"I—I don't mind at all being solely responsible for Mandy," she insisted.

"But you don't have to be, honey. Not anymore." He moved his hands down to her waist, then pulled her into his arms. "I'm here now and you don't have to do everything alone."

"Please, Jake," she interrupted. "Don't." Pulling from his arms, she somehow found the strength to back away from him. "I won't try to stop you from being part of Mandy's life. But I want you to keep a couple of things in mind before you take that step. First and foremost, it's all or nothing. You're either her father for life or not at all. I don't want her becoming attached to you, then you walk away when you get tired of playing daddy. And second, count me out. I'm not part of the package."

He stared at her for several long moments before he slowly shook his head. "You have my word that I will never do anything that isn't in her best interest or yours."

"Good. Because hurt my daughter and you'll have me to deal with." She could tell from his expression that he meant what he said—now. The only problem was, whether they intended to or not, people sometimes broke their promises and others ended up getting hurt.

"Now that we have your main concern out in the open and settled, are you and the baby going to stay here in the mansion?" he asked, seating himself back behind the desk.

"Jake, I don't think—"

"I've missed out on a lot with her already, Heather."

His chest rose and fell as he took a deep breath. "All I'm asking is that you give me a chance to get to know my daughter and build a relationship with her."

She knew if she and the baby did stay in the mansion with him, she would be taking a huge risk for both Mandy and herself. If she hadn't known that before he kissed her last night, she did now. No matter how much he'd hurt her or how hard she tried to resist his charm, she still found Jake to be six feet two inches of pure temptation. And that could very well prove to be disastrous for her if she didn't keep her wits about her.

But she'd told him she wouldn't stop him from trying to bond with Mandy and she couldn't, in good conscience, deny either of them the right to get acquainted. And while he was getting to know their daughter, she intended to learn more about him, his family and where he grew up. After all, she had the right to know about her daughter's father.

Heather sighed heavily. Unfortunately, now wasn't the time to put him through the third degree. Aside from the fact that she'd already put in a grueling day, she was still too angry. She wanted to be calm, rational and in complete control when she talked to him.

"We'll stay in the mansion as long as you're here at Hickory Hills. But only on one condition."

His eyes narrowed ever so slightly before he asked, "And what would that be?"

Walking to the door, she turned back. "I meant what I said about not being part of the equation, Jake. Don't count on me to be one of your…diversions when you get bored."

Chapter 3

Jake frowned as he watched Heather place their sleeping daughter into the small baby bed that he and Daily had set up earlier in the day. "Is that thing full size? It looks awfully small."

When she placed her finger to her lips, it was all he could do not to groan. He couldn't forget the kiss they'd shared the night before and wanted to once again taste her sweetness and feel the softness of her perfect mouth beneath his own. But he knew better than to push. She'd outlined her conditions and he had to admit it was probably for the best. It wouldn't be long before they had to address some very sensitive issues concerning shared custody and how they were going to raise Mandy. If they became involved, it could make doing that a lot more difficult. He just wished that the attraction between them wasn't as powerful now as it had been when they first met. That would certainly make things a lot easier.

"It's a mini crib," she whispered, drawing his attention back to his question.

He waited until she turned on the baby monitor, clipped one of the receivers to her belt and they'd both stepped out into the hall before he asked, "Why didn't you get a regular size bed for her?"

"The room I turned into the nursery at the carriage house is small and I wanted to save space," she answered as they started downstairs.

"What about when she gets a little older?" he asked, following her. He didn't like the idea of his child being in a room that was too small when she had every right to live in the mansion and enjoy the spaciousness of any one of the spare bedrooms. "How will you fit a regular size bed into that room and still have enough space for her to play?"

"When the time comes, I'll convert the room I use for a study into another bedroom." At the bottom of the steps, she turned to face him. "Why are you asking about this now? It won't be an issue for another year or two."

He smiled as the germ of an idea took root. "I was thinking that the two of you could live here in the mansion even after I go back to L.A."

"No. That's not an option," she said, shaking her head until her ponytail swayed back and forth.

"Why not?"

She started toward the hall leading to the kitchen. "Because it's not *my* home."

Reaching out, he took hold of her arm and the feel of her soft skin beneath his palm sent heat straight to the pit of his belly. He did his best to ignore it. "This is my house now and Mandy is my daughter. She has every right to live here."

Heather gave him a look that stated in no uncertain terms that she didn't like his idea one damned bit. "But it's not mine, Jake."

He knew as surely as he knew his own name that there was a good deal of pride holding her back from accepting his offer. "I'm telling you it can be, Heather."

"I work for you and living in the carriage house is part of my contract."

"I'm offering you an amendment to that agreement." Barely resisting the urge to pull her into his arms, he hastened to add, "You don't have to make a decision about the move being permanent now. But I would like for you to give it some serious thought." Unable to stop himself, he reached up to brush a wayward strand of hair from her soft cheek. "It would make life for you and Mandy a lot more comfortable than being cooped up in a space where there's barely room for one."

Before she could come up with any more excuses why she and Mandy shouldn't live in the mansion permanently, he reluctantly dropped his hand to his side and crossed the foyer to enter the study. If he hadn't put some distance between them, there had been a very real possibility that he would have acted on his first impulse to grab her and kiss her until she agreed to his proposal. And that would have been a huge mistake.

It would take a fool not to see that just like a magnetic force, the attraction between them was too strong to fight and impossible to resist. But at this point, she didn't trust him anymore than she would a snake coiled to make a strike. And until he proved himself to her and they worked out an agreement to raise their daughter, he had no other choice but to bide his time and no doubt end up taking more than his share of cold showers.

He sighed heavily as he lowered himself into the chair behind the desk and reached for the phone. As he punched in his brother's number, he thought about the irony of it all. The only woman he hadn't been able to forget was back in his life, was the mother of his only child and thought him lower than the stuff she scraped off her boots after a trip through the stables.

"My life is just about as freaking wonderful as it can get right now," he muttered sourly.

"As a matter of fact, mine is going pretty good, as well," Luke said, laughing.

Wallowing in his own misery, Jake had missed hearing his brother answer the phone. "Good to hear, bro. How are things in Nashville?"

"We couldn't be better. Haley has passed the point where morning sickness is an issue and we're just waiting for the sonogram to see if we're having a boy or a girl." His twin sounded happier than Jake could ever remember.

"Glad to hear my favorite sister-in-law is feeling better," he said, wondering if Heather had experienced a lot of problems with morning sickness when she'd been pregnant with Mandy.

They were both silent a moment before Luke asked, "So what's wrong, Jake?"

"What makes you think there's a problem?"

He wasn't surprised by his brother's intuitiveness. As with many twins, he and Luke shared a sixth sense where the other was concerned and instinctively knew when things weren't going right. But Jake wasn't entirely certain how to deliver the news that upon his arrival at Hickory Hills he'd discovered he had a daughter and avoid having to listen to the I-told-you-so speech that was sure to follow. Luke had been warning him for years that his "love 'em and leave 'em" ways were going to catch up to him one day.

"You're talking to the only person who knows you better than you probably know yourself." Luke paused. "So you want to tell me what's going on?"

"I have a daughter." Jake hadn't meant to deliver the news quite so bluntly, but once the words were out, he realized there wasn't any easier way to say it.

"Whoa! You want to back up and say that again?"

"You heard me," Jake said, wanting to reach through the phone and throttle his twin. "I have a six-and-a-half-month-old daughter named Mandy."

His brother was silent for so long, Jake wasn't sure they hadn't lost the connection. "And you found this out when you moved to the horse farm Emerald gave you?" Luke finally asked.

"Yeah." He took a deep breath. "Heather's the manager here at Hickory Hills. I'm betting when the old girl's investigators found us, they discovered that a woman I met at a thoroughbred auction last year had become pregnant from our one night together."

"That explains why you ended up in a place about as far removed from your life in Los Angeles as it's possible to get," Luke agreed. "Arielle and I wondered why you were given an enterprise that was totally out of your element when we were given businesses in our respective career fields."

"I don't know why Emerald didn't just tell me about Heather and Mandy instead of blindsiding me like this,"

Jake complained. "Didn't she think I would step up and do the right thing?"

His brother made a strangled sound. "You're getting married?"

It was Jake's turn to choke. "Hell, no. You know how I feel about marriage. It's not for me."

"Don't knock it until you've tried it," Luke advised. "I didn't think I was husband material, either, and look at me now."

"Whatever."

They were silent a moment before Luke asked, "Why didn't the baby's mother tell you about the pregnancy?"

"She tried, but my secretary didn't see fit to give me the messages." Jake made a mental note to call the woman the first thing in the morning and discuss her not bothering to give him a list of callers.

"Ah, if you'll remember, I told you—"

"Don't say it, bro."

Luke's laughter grated on Jake's nerves. "So when do we get to meet our niece and her mother?"

"That's the reason I called. How would you and Haley like to come up to Louisville for the Southern Oaks Cup Classic in a couple of weeks? The favorite to win the race came along with the farm."

"Sounds good," Luke said. "I assume you're inviting Arielle and Zach?"

"Of course, along with the rest of the clan."

A few months ago, when he and his siblings learned that the most successful woman in the corporate jungle was their paternal grandmother, they'd also been informed that they had three half brothers. After meeting them at one of Emerald's receptions and finding themselves in the unique position of being the unexpected heirs of one of the world's richest women, they'd become friends.

"And before you ask, I fully intend to invite our illustrious grandmother and her stiff-as-a-board assistant, too. She and I are going to have a little talk about her withholding information about my daughter," he added.

Luke snorted. "Good luck with that."

Making plans to talk again before the impromptu family reunion, Jake hung up, then called his other siblings to invite them to the gathering. With promises from all to attend, he walked into the foyer and ran right into Heather.

"Are you all right?" he asked, placing both hands on her waist to keep her from falling. A jolt of electric current as strong as a lightning strike shot through him and when she looked up, the awareness he detected in her aqua eyes let him know that she'd felt it, too.

"I—I'm fine."

"I'm sorry, I didn't see you," he said, filling his senses with her. The scent of her herbal shampoo and the feel of her softness beneath his hands sent heat coursing straight to the region south of his belt and his body's reaction was not only predictable, it was inevitable.

"I…was just…on my way upstairs." She sounded delightfully breathless and sent his blood pressure up a good ten points or so.

As if an invisible force held them captive they remained silent for so long, Jake finally forced himself to speak. "I…uh, was on my way to take a shower and call it an evening myself."

Still operating on West Coast time, he hadn't even

entertained the idea of calling it a night. But he did need a shower. A cold one.

She nodded. "Well…I guess I'll see you in the morning."

"What time does Mandy wake up?" he asked, still holding her at the waist.

"Early."

Finally forcing himself to step back, he motioned toward the staircase. "Then it would probably be a good idea if we call it a night."

As if awakening from a trance, she blushed suddenly and ducking her head, started walking toward the steps. "Good night, Jake."

"Night."

He stood in the foyer long after Heather reached the second floor and disappeared down the hall. The sound of her voice and the realization that she would be sleeping just down the hall from him had him fully aroused in less than a heartbeat.

Taking the stairs two at a time, he made a beeline for the master bathroom. By the time he reached his bedroom, he'd already stripped off his shirt and left a trail of clothing on his way to the shower.

As he stood there punishing his body beneath the frigid spray, he couldn't help but wonder how long Heather was going to deny the chemistry that flowed between them. They could fight it, try to run from it and argue that it even existed, but it was just a matter of time before they made love again. He had no doubt about that. The only question was when.

With a record-breaking crop of goose bumps and his teeth chattering like the wind-up ones found in a novelty store, he turned off the water. He grabbed a thick towel and began to vigorously dry off. They were going to have to work out the agreement for Mandy, and Heather had to come to her senses and accept the inevitable. He didn't particularly like shivering his ass off in a shower so cold he could spit ice cubes.

"Heather, I'm sorry, but I'm not going to be able to watch Mandy for you this afternoon. I forgot that I have an appointment with the high school counselor to get Daily enrolled and set up his freshman schedule."

"I suppose I could take her with me," Heather said slowly, wondering how she was going to attend a meeting at Churchill Downs with a baby in tow.

"We can change that to another day, Grandma," Daily offered, sounding hopeful. "I don't care. I'm not all that into school anyway."

"Young man, you'd better get 'into it' real fast," Clara said sternly. "You're in enough hot water as it is after that stunt you pulled the other night."

"Listen to your grandmother, Daily. If you want a car like mine when you get 'old,' you're going to need a good job. And that takes education."

"Yes, sir," Daily answered, shoveling a fork full of scrambled eggs into his mouth.

Looking up, Heather's heart skipped a beat as she watched Jake stroll into the kitchen and seat himself at the head of the table. Dressed in a light blue polo shirt that emphasized the width of his broad shoulders and a pair of jeans that hugged his muscular thighs like a glove, he wasn't just his usual good-looking self. This morning, he was white-hot. Busying herself with Mandy's breakfast, she tried her best not to stare.

"What time is the meeting?" Clara asked. "Maybe we'll be back before you have to leave."

Heather shook her head. "It's a luncheon meeting and probably won't be over until late afternoon." She spooned a bit of baby cereal into Mandy's eager mouth. "I'll just take her with me and hope she has a good long nap during the speeches."

"I can watch her," Jake spoke up as he took a couple of strips of bacon from the platter in the center of the table.

"That's okay. I'm sure you have better things to do." She wasn't at all comfortable leaving her daughter with a man who she was almost positive had zero experience babysitting an infant.

Smiling, he shook his head as he took a sip of his coffee. "I don't have anything going on this afternoon. Besides, it will give Mandy and me a chance to get acquainted."

"Really, it's not a problem," she said firmly. "I'll take her with me."

An ominous silence suddenly reigned throughout the kitchen as Jake put down his coffee cup and their gazes locked. "Don't be ridiculous, Heather. She's my daughter, too. I have every right to watch her while you're busy."

"No way!" Daily said, his eyes wide. "You're Mandy's dad? I didn't know that."

"Come on, young man," Clara said, removing the boy's plate from the table. "You can finish your breakfast in our apartment before you go down to the stables to muck out the stalls."

"But, Grandma—"

"You heard me," the housekeeper said, cutting him

off. "These two need to talk and they don't need you hanging on their every word. Now move."

Heather waited until Clara and a reluctant Daily left the kitchen before she turned her full attention back to Jake. "How many babies have you taken care of?"

"None."

"That's what I thought." When Mandy protested loudly, Heather spooned another bite of cereal into her mouth. "You don't have the slightest idea what to do with a baby."

His frown deepened. "I've got to start somewhere."

"My daughter isn't an experiment."

"She's *our* daughter." He placed his hand on top of hers. "I know you're worried I won't know what to do. But I promise, I'd never let anything hurt her."

She could tell from the sincerity in his voice and the look in his eyes that he meant every word he said. But he admittedly had zero experience with babies.

"I won't let her out of my sight the entire time you're away," he promised.

"Jake, I'm not at all comfortable with—"

"I'll even stay in the same room with her while she takes her nap," he interrupted.

"Have you ever changed a diaper?"

"No, but it can't be that hard to figure out. Besides, I'm a quick study," he said confidently. "You can show me how to put a new one on her before you leave."

She barely managed to hide a smile at his misguided self-assurance. He had no way of knowing that their daughter thought diaper changes were great fun and the perfect time to exercise her legs by kicking like a little karate champion.

"What about lunch?" she asked, beginning to realize she didn't have any other option. She couldn't get out of the meeting and it was no place for a baby. "Do you think you'll be able to feed her?"

"I watched you feed her breakfast and it didn't look all that difficult." He grinned. "Piece of cake."

Spooning the last bit of cereal into her daughter's mouth, Heather wiped the baby's face. "You'll call me if you have even the slightest problem?"

"Of course."

She lifted Mandy from the high chair and handed her to him. "Would you mind holding her while I wipe off the high chair and put it away?"

Jake had been too busy yesterday with the unauthorized moving of her things from the guesthouse to do more than watch her or Clara with the baby. It was time that father and daughter met officially. Besides, she needed to see how Jake was with Mandy before she agreed to him watching the baby.

He gently lifted Mandy to sit on his arm. "Hey there, Honey Bunny. I'm your daddy."

As Heather watched, the baby gazed at him intently for several seconds, then giggling, happily slapped her tiny hand against his cheek. But it was the look of awe and complete wonder that instantly came over Jake's handsome face that had her blinking back a wave of tears.

She wouldn't have believed it was possible to actually see it happen. But right before her eyes, Jake fell hopelessly in love with their daughter.

Chapter 4

When Heather returned from her meeting, she practically burst through the back door of the mansion. She'd tried several times on her drive from the Downs to call Jake on her cell phone, but he hadn't answered and with each passing second her concern increased. Searching the rooms downstairs, her heart began to pound hard against her ribs when she couldn't find either of them. Why had she let him talk her into allowing him to watch her baby?

But her anxiety turned to mind-numbing fear when she hurried up the staircase and entered the bedroom where Jake had set up the crib. The two were nowhere in sight.

In a near panic, she raced down the hall to the master suite. "If he's let something happen, I'll never forgive…"

Her voice trailed off as she came to a skidding halt

just inside the suite door and a knee-weakening relief washed over her. There in the middle of the king-size bed her daughter lay curled up on top of Jake. Both were out like a couple of lights.

Leaning against the door facing, her panic began to recede and as she stood there catching her breath, she couldn't help but be touched by the moment. Heather knew for certain she'd never forget the poignant sight of her tiny baby girl sleeping so trustingly on her daddy's wide bare chest. For the second time in a matter of a few hours, she found herself blinking back tears.

Quietly, so as not to disturb either of them, she gently lifted Mandy into her arms and, walking back to the bedroom where the crib was, placed the baby in the small bed. Turning on the monitor, she clipped the receiving unit to the waistband of her khakis and turning to leave, came face-to-face with a wild-eyed Jake.

"Dear God, Heather, why didn't you wake me up to let me know you were taking Mandy?" he demanded. "When I opened my eyes and she wasn't there, I—"

Heather placed her index finger to his lips to silence him when the baby moved restlessly and let out a little whimper. "I'm sorry," she mouthed. She motioned for him to follow her out into the hall. "You looked like you might be a little tired from babysitting and I thought I'd—"

"Give me a heart attack," he finished for her.

That's when she realized that he'd been as terrified as she had when she'd been unable to find them. "I really am sorry. I didn't mean to frighten you."

Running a frustrated hand through his thick black hair, he took a deep breath. "I've never been that scared in my entire life."

As they stood there, she couldn't help but stare at his bare chest. Every muscle was well-defined and as her gaze drifted lower, she had an almost uncontrollable urge to reach out and trace her fingers over each one of the ridges on his abdomen.

"W-what happened to your shirt?" she asked instead.

"Oh, that." He frowned. "Do you know how disgusting baby food spinach looks? And dear God, it smells even worse. But when it gets on clothes, it's just plain nasty."

She laughed. "It is pretty gross, isn't it?"

"It's horrible." He made a face. "I thought I was going to lose it a couple of times when Mandy decided to take a handful and rub it in her hair."

Heather couldn't stop laughing. "Don't tell me. You set the dish too close to the high chair."

Nodding, he chuckled. "By the time lunch was over, she had more food on her than in her. And I'm positive our daughter could hold her own in a frat house food fight."

"No doubt about it," she agreed, smiling. "Any other problems? How did the diaper changes go?"

"When I finally got her to hold still it went all right. Up until then, it was a little hazardous." He rubbed his flat stomach. "She's got a hell of a kick." His expression turned serious and he fell silent a moment before reaching up to touch her cheek. "Thank you, Heather."

The back of his knuckles stroking her skin sent a shaft of longing all the way to her toes. "W-what for?"

"For today." His voice took on a husky quality that stole her breath. "For giving me the chance to get to know my daughter."

Without a second thought, she closed her eyes and

leaned into his tender touch. She might have been able to resist had it not been for the sincerity in his tone and the genuine gratefulness in his amazing blue eyes. But no matter how much she tried to fight it, he was the man who had stolen her heart all those months ago and given her a precious baby daughter.

"I want to kiss you, Heather."

His whisper made her feel warm all over. "Th-that probably wouldn't be a good idea."

"Oh, I disagree, I think it's an excellent idea." His firm lips lightly grazing the shell of her ear and his warm breath feathering over her skin caused excited little shivers to course throughout her entire body.

She was flirting with danger. This was Jake Garnier, player extraordinaire. But even as she tried to reason with herself, she swayed toward him.

Apparently, that was all the encouragement he needed because the next thing she knew he wrapped his arms around her and pulled her close. She opened her eyes just in time to watch him slowly, deliberately, lower his head and when his mouth covered hers in tender exploration, she thought she just might melt into a puddle at his feet.

As his tongue stroked her lips apart, her eyes drifted shut again and the intensity of his kiss caused her head to spin. But when he coaxed, demanded and persuaded her to respond, every cell in her body tingled to life and Heather found herself holding on to him for support.

She should stop him. It wasn't smart to kiss the man who obviously hadn't wanted anything more to do with her until he learned that she'd given birth to his daughter. But the thought evaporated when Jake crushed her to him and she felt his hard muscles against her tightening nipples and his insistent arousal pressed into her lower belly.

Her knees threatened to buckle and a swirling hunger began to flow through her when he moved his hand to cup her breast, then chafed the hardened tip through the layers of her clothing. She wanted him with a fierceness that frightened her more than she'd ever thought possible.

Jake must have sensed the change in her because he slowly eased away from the kiss, but continued to hold her close. "We've got plenty of time."

She could deny that having him kiss her, that being in his arms and having his body entangled with hers wasn't what she wanted, too. But they'd both know it was a total lie.

"No, it can't happen, Jake." It was hard to be convincing when his large hand still covered her breast. But she couldn't seem to find the strength to pull free of his arms.

"I'm not going to stand here and argue. Right now, I have to take a shower."

As she watched him retreat to the master suite, Heather couldn't help but wonder if she shouldn't take her daughter and run as fast as she could back to the safety of the carriage house. It was obvious that no matter what she said, he wasn't going to listen to her. And living in such close proximity was going to make resisting him extremely difficult.

But thankfully with the Southern Oaks Cup Classic only two weeks away and all of the activities that preceded it, they were both going to become very busy in a very short time. If she could just hold out a few more days, everything should be fine.

She was going to have to attend to Dancer seven days a week and make sure that he was ready to run the race of his life. And as the owner of the favorite to win the Cup, Jake would be away at the almost non-stop receptions and balls that were held to celebrate the annual event.

With her going to bed early in order to oversee the thoroughbred's dawn exercises and Jake sleeping in after being out late with Louisville's social elite, their paths probably wouldn't cross more than a handful of times. And the few times they did, it would most likely be in a public setting for pictures and publicity for the race.

Then, by the time the festivities came to a close, Jake would no doubt be bored with the comparatively slower pace of Hickory Hills and more than ready to head back to his exciting life in Los Angeles. She and Mandy would move back into the carriage house and once again settle into their comfortable, familiar routine.

As Jake sat in the study thumbing through a pile of invitations to teas, receptions and balls being held in honor of the big race, he frowned. How the hell was he supposed to work things out and reconnect with Heather when he was going to have to attend a string of social events?

But staring at the elaborate print on one of the invitations, a slow smile curved the corners of his mouth. The words "and guest" had him rising from his chair.

"Clara, could you watch Mandy for a few minutes while I walk down to the stables to talk to Heather?" he asked when he entered the kitchen.

"No problem." She smiled when he handed her the

baby monitor. "How long has our little angel been down for her nap?"

"About a half hour." He checked his watch. "I'm not sure how long she sleeps, but I'll only be a few minutes."

"Take your time." Clara grinned as she motioned toward Daily seated at the kitchen table peeling a pile of potatoes. "We won't be going anywhere for at least the next two weeks."

"I keep telling you, Grandma. When somebody's grounded, it doesn't mean they have to do stuff like this," the boy complained. "It means they just can't go anywhere."

Jake hid a smile as he left the mansion and walking past the pool, started down the path toward the stables. Since his grandmother learned about his plan for a late night rendezvous, Daily had mucked out stalls, mopped floors, polished silver and performed any other menial task she could think to assign him.

In a few days, the kid would get a bit of a reprieve from doing household chores. Jake had already talked to Clara about having Daily help him with a few projects to improve the place. The housekeeper had readily agreed and expressed her gratitude for Jake's influence with the boy. It seemed that Daily was having a hard time adjusting to his mother remarrying after the death of his father and she'd sent him to Hickory Hills in an effort to keep him out of trouble.

Shaking his head, Jake couldn't help but wonder what his friends in L.A. would think of that one. With his reputation for partying and entertaining a different woman every night, he was the last person most people would want influencing their teenage boy. But since his arrival at Hickory Hills, Jake had found that he was enjoying the slower, laid-back pace and had started thinking less and less about getting back to the hectic schedule he'd kept for the past several years.

Maybe it had something to do with finding out he'd fathered a child. Or it could be that it was just so vastly different from his usual lifestyle the novelty hadn't worn off yet.

He frowned. So why didn't going back to L.A. sound all that appealing?

As he entered the stable, another thought occurred to him, but he dismissed it. He refused to believe that he might finally be ready to settle down. That was just ludicrous. Of course, he wanted to return to his condo and highly successful law practice. He'd be a fool not to want that.

Greeting Tony and another groom as they attended to one of the thoroughbreds, Jake relegated his self-analysis to the back of his mind. It was amusing to think that he owned over two dozen of the finest animals in the country and he'd never been on the back of a horse in his entire life.

"What's up?" Heather asked when he walked into her office. "Is everything all right?"

Jake nodded. "Mandy is taking a nap and Clara is making Daily rue the day he even thought about sneaking out to see his girlfriend by making him peel potatoes for dinner."

Heather's smile sent a shockwave of heat straight to the pit of his belly. "Poor Daily. I doubt that he'll be eager to try that again."

Jake barely managed to suppress his frustrated groan. He seriously doubted she realized just how pretty she looked with soft curls escaping her ponytail and her creamy cheeks flushed from the early summer heat.

But it was her coral lips that fascinated the hell out of him. Since kissing her outside of Mandy's room two days ago, all he'd been able to think about was doing it again and a whole lot more. And it was the "whole lot more" that was about to drive him over the edge.

"Jake, did you hear what I asked?"

"Uh…sorry." Lost in his own misery, he hadn't realized that she'd been talking to him. "What was that again?"

"I asked if you needed something," she said patiently.

Oh, yeah, he needed something all right. But she didn't want to hear what that was.

"As a matter of fact, there is something I need your help with." That was an understatement, he thought sardonically. Forcing himself to focus, he sat down in the chair in front of her desk. "I have a million receptions and a couple of balls over the next two weeks."

She nodded. "That's part of the Southern Oaks Cup celebration and as Dancer's owner, you're expected to make an appearance."

"From the number of invitations I've received, I'm beginning to realize just what a big deal this is," he said, choosing his words carefully. Over the course of the past several years, he'd gotten into the habit of attending parties without a date. Now, he couldn't believe how out of practice he had become at asking a woman out. "And I'd really like for you to go with me."

He watched her open and close her mouth several times before she found her voice. "You can't be serious."

He smiled. "I'm very serious. I wouldn't have asked you to be my date if I weren't."

"I…um, appreciate it, but I can't," she said, her eyes still wide with disbelief.

That wasn't the answer he wanted to hear. "Why not?"

"I'm going to be far too busy overseeing Dancer and preparing for the race to be able to attend." Her smile looked suspiciously relieved when she added, "I'm sorry, but you'll have to go without me."

It was perfectly clear to him why she was turning him down. The more time they spent together, the bigger the possibility she could no longer deny the pull between them. And that was the very reason he was going to insist that she go with him.

"But you would attend the various functions with me if not for your job, right?"

"Well…I…uh…since I'm not about to quit, it's not an issue," she hedged.

He knew he had her and if the look on her pretty face was any indication, she knew it, too.

Rising from the chair, he walked over and called for Tony to come to the office. When the man walked to the door, Jake smiled. "From now until the race is over, you're in charge of the stables. I want Heather free to concentrate on overseeing Dancer's training, preparations for the race and attending social functions."

The man looked as if he thought Jake might be joking. "Me?"

"Yes," Jake answered decisively. "Do you think you can handle the job?"

He watched the man's gaze cut to Heather, then back to him. "Sure. I can handle it, but—"

"Then it's settled." Jake shook Tony's hand. "If anything comes up, you're still to consult with Heather."

When he turned to walk back and lower himself into the chair in front of Heather's desk, she looked as if she might blow a gasket. "What do you think you're doing?"

"I'm relieving you of your other duties until after the race is over." He smiled. "This way you'll be able to focus on Dancer and the race and attend the social side of this thing with me."

"You can't do that to me," she said, standing up to pace back and forth behind the desk.

"Sure I can."

She stopped to glare at him. "I have a signed contract that says otherwise. You may own this place, but I run it. I'm in charge and I call the shots."

"You're still in charge, Heather." He hadn't anticipated that she'd get this upset.

"At least running this farm will look good on my résumé," she muttered.

He narrowed his eyes. "You haven't been looking for a position elsewhere, have you?"

"Not yet," she admitted belligerently. "But you just made the decision to start the search a lot easier."

Rising to his feet, he walked around the desk and took her into his arms. "Look, you're still in charge. You're still overseeing Dancer's racing career. That hasn't changed. I'm just making it easier for you to concentrate your efforts on him."

"Get real, Jake. We both know the reason you relieved me of the majority of my responsibilities was purely self-serving. You want me to attend the social events with you. That's the only reason you did this."

He took a deep breath. "That's the way it started out. But the more I think about it, the more it makes sense for Dancer to be your top priority now."

"I can't argue that," she grudgingly agreed.

"And won't it make the next two weeks easier if you can turn your sole attention to that goal?"

She slowly nodded.

"I'm sorry I usurped your authority, but I'm used to being the one in charge." He kissed the top of her head. "From now on, I'll consult with you before I make a decision about the stables."

She leaned back to look him square in the eyes and he could tell she was only slightly less furious with him. "You'd better, because if you interfere again, I'm out of here."

If he'd doubted how seriously she took her job before, he didn't now. "Understood. Now, will you please consider attending events with me. It would be nice to have someone I know at my side."

"There isn't a shy bone in your body. You'll do just fine without me."

He smiled as he brushed an errant strand of golden brown hair from her soft cheek. "Yes, but I want you with me."

"I told you, I'm not one of your diversions while you're here," she stated flatly.

She wasn't going to give in easily. But then he wasn't, either. "Would you at least think about going with me?" he whispered close to her ear.

Staring at him for what seemed an eternity, she finally nodded. "I'll consider it, but I'm not promising anything."

Satisfied that his plan to spend more time with her had a chance, Jake lowered his mouth to hers to seal the deal with a kiss. His blood pressure skyrocketed as he slowly caressed her lips with his, and he decided he could easily become addicted to her sweetness as he savored the taste of her.

When he traced the seam of her mouth to deepen the kiss, he took advantage of her soft sigh and slipped inside to stroke her tongue with his. Teasing and coaxing, he encouraged her to explore him, as well, and when she tentatively acquainted herself with him, Jake felt as if a fire had been ignited in the pit of his belly.

But it was the feel of her breasts pressed to his chest, her nipples scoring his skin through the layers of their clothing, that caused his body to harden so fast it left him feeling lightheaded. He moved his hands down her back to the flare of her hips. Pulling her forward allowed her to feel the effect she had on him, how she made him want her. She whimpered softly and sagged against him, letting him know without words that she desired him as much as he did her.

Unfortunately, his timing was lousy. They were in her office in the stable with several people close by. And going back to the mansion was out of the question.

Reluctantly easing away from the kiss, Jake took a deep breath as he leaned back to stare down at her. He didn't think he'd ever seen a more beautiful sight. Heather's porcelain cheeks were flushed and her eyes were glazed with the haze of unfulfilled desire.

"I suppose I should let you get back to work now," he finally managed to get out through his dry throat. Before she could gather her thoughts and tear into him over kissing her again, he released her and, walking to the door, added, "Our first reception is this evening. You can fill me in on our host and hostess on the drive over to their place."

Chapter 5

Heather accepted the hand Jake offered as she got out of his Ferrari in front of the home of John and Martha Wainwright, then waited for him to hand his keys to the valet. She was still upset with him over his disregard for her authority at the farm, but the more she thought about it, the more she realized attending these social events with him could work to her advantage. If she did have to look for a position elsewhere, the contacts she made at receptions like this one could prove invaluable.

"So tell me about these people," he said as he cupped her elbow and they walked the short distance to the tall, carved oak front doors of the estate.

"John Wainwright is president of the Southern Oaks Bank and Trust and Martha is the treasurer of the local ladies' club," she said, quickly filling him in on their host and hostess. "Neither of them have the slightest interest in horses or the Classic. But they would both have a coronary before they passed up an opportunity to host a reception for it."

"In other words, they're all about showing off with a big party and getting a mention in the society column."

"Exactly."

When he handed the doorman their invitation, the man smiled broadly and swung one of the entry doors wide. "Welcome to Waincrest, Mr. Garnier." He nodded and gave her a wink. "And Miss Heather."

"Hi, Hank. How is Mae?" she asked, smiling.

The man's grin widened. "She's doing just fine, Miss Heather. Thank you for asking."

As they followed his directions past a sweeping staircase and out a set of French doors onto the terrace, she felt as if she'd stepped into a fairy tale. The place was decorated with a canopy of tiny white lights, white wrought-iron patio furniture and huge bouquets of red and white roses in marble urns. Clearly, the Wainwrights had spared no expense in transforming their lawn into a very elegant cocktail party.

"That's our host and hostess," she said, discreetly nodding toward a couple standing by the bar.

"This is why I needed you with me," Jake said, leaning close. "You know who all these people are and what role they play in all of this hoopla."

She rolled her eyes. "Like you wouldn't have figured it out on your own."

When a waiter carrying a silver tray with glasses of champagne stopped in front of them, Jake removed two of the flutes, then handed one to her. "If I remember correctly, I think this is how we met."

She swallowed hard when his fingers lingered on

hers a little longer than necessary and a feeling of déjà vu swept through her. He'd walked over to her, handed her a glass of champagne and the rest was history.

He leaned close. "Do you think the evening will end the same way it did that night?"

"With me pregnant?"

Jake's teasing smile faded. "I didn't mean *that*. But I'll be damned if I'm sorry it happened. We wouldn't have Mandy if it hadn't."

She could tell he was completely sincere, and she had to agree. "She's brought more joy into my life than I could have ever imagined."

Before either of them had a chance to say anything further, John Wainwright walked over to greet them. "You must be the owner of Stormy Dancer," the man said, turning up the wattage on his smile. Almost as an afterthought, he nodded at her. "Miss McGwire."

Wainwright wasn't interested in talking to her and she knew why. His bank handled the accounts for Hickory Hills and he wasn't going to waste his time with a lowly farm manager when he could schmooze with the owner of one of the premier stables in the entire country.

As the man engaged Jake in a conversation about becoming a member of the local country club, Heather quietly excused herself and started to walk away.

Jake put his hand on her arm to stop her. "Where do you think you're going?"

Smiling, she pointed toward the buffet table. "I'll be over there."

She could tell he wasn't happy with the way John Wainwright had dismissed her as insignificant. But she really didn't mind being excluded from their conversation. She was far more comfortable talking to the Wainwrights' staff than she was mingling with people who thought they were better than everyone else.

"Dear, would you mind helping me?" a small, elderly woman asked politely. With a cane in one hand and a mint julep in the other, the poor woman had no way of carrying her plate of appetizers.

Smiling, Heather shook her head. "I don't mind at all. Where are you sitting?"

"As far away from these pompous asses as possible," she replied, her expression so sweet that Heather thought she might have misheard.

"Excuse me?"

"You heard right, dear. I called them pompous asses," the older woman repeated proudly. "I've finally reached the age where I speak my mind and don't give a fig what people think. Now, come. Let's find a place to sit and get acquainted."

When Heather followed the elderly lady to an empty table away from the majority of the crowd, she helped the woman get settled. "Is there anything else you need, Mrs…"

"Wainwright." The old lady shook her head disgustedly. "My son is the windbag who snubbed you in favor of kissing up to your young man." She patted the chair beside her. "Sit, dear. I need someone to talk to who doesn't act like they're something they're not." She gave a disgusted snort. "I just hate when John and Martha throw one of these receptions. They put on such airs, it's a downright disgrace."

Heather didn't know what to say. But she couldn't help but like the elderly woman and her candid observations.

"It's all right, dear." The old woman patted Heather's

hand. "I have no illusions about how important most of these people *think* they are. And my son and daughter-in-law are the two biggest ducks in the puddle."

"Well, your son is the president of Southern Oaks Bank and Trust."

"Pish posh. It doesn't matter what job somebody ends up with, they should never forget where they came from." Mrs. Wainwright grinned. "I'll bet you didn't know that John grew up the son of a tobacco farmer who was land rich and dirt poor." She pointed an arthritic finger toward Jake. "But your young man seems to be different. You can tell he's got money, but he doesn't appear to act like he's better than everyone else. I'll bet he hasn't forgotten who he really is and where he came from."

Heather stared at Jake. She still knew very little about him. Busy getting ready for the race, she hadn't had the opportunity to ask where he grew up, about his childhood or his family.

Were his mother and father still alive? Did he have siblings? Could Mandy have family that Heather knew nothing about?

She didn't have a clue. But she had every intention of finding out.

As Heather continued to think about it, she had to admit that Mrs. Wainwright was correct in her assessment of him. Jake had never made her or anyone at the farm feel as if they were beneath him. Even Clara had commented that he went out of his way to make everyone feel comfortable.

Heather had watched him with the grooms and stable boys and he never failed to greet them by name or stop and talk to them for a few minutes. And he was probably the only billionaire she'd ever heard of who sat at the kitchen table to eat his meals with his housekeeper, her teenage grandson and his farm manager.

"Are you ready to thank our host and hostess for a nice evening and head home?"

Heather jumped. Lost in thought, she hadn't realized that Jake had ended his conversation with the bank president and crossed the lawn to join her and the man's mother.

Introducing him to the elderly Mrs. Wainwright, she smiled. "It was nice chatting with you."

"It was my pleasure, dear." Mrs. Wainwright placed a bony hand on Heather's arm and motioned for her to lean close. "You hang on to your young man," she said in confidence. "Mark my words, he's the real deal."

"Thank you, Mrs. Wainwright." She smiled. "I'll try to remember that."

After bidding the Wainwrights a good evening, Jake waited until he and Heather were seated in his car before he apologized. "I'm sorry, honey."

"What for?" She looked thoroughly bewildered and so damned beautiful it was all he could do to keep from stopping the car and taking into his arms.

"Wainwright had no right to ignore you the way he did." When the man dismissed Heather as if she didn't exist, a protectiveness he'd never known he possessed had consumed him and Jake had wanted to punch the bastard in his big pretentious nose.

They fell silent for some time before he felt Heather staring at him. "What?"

"Tell me more about yourself."

Glancing her way, he frowned. "What do you want to know?"

"Everything. Where did you grow up? Do you have siblings?" She laid her soft hand on his thigh and he had to concentrate to keep from steering the car into the ditch. "Does Mandy have an extended family?"

"What brought this on?" he asked, covering her hand with his to keep her from moving it. He liked when she touched him.

"Jake, we have a child together and beyond the fact that you're a successful divorce attorney in Los Angeles, I know very little else about you," she said quietly.

"There's no big mystery. My siblings and I were born and raised in San Francisco. I have an identical twin brother named Luke—"

"My God, there are two of you?" She sounded truly shocked.

Grinning he nodded. "But don't worry. He's always been the quiet, more serious one of us."

"In other words, your exact opposite." She looked thoughtful. "Is he married?"

"As a matter of fact, he just got married a few months ago. He and his wife, Haley, are expecting their first child in about six and a half months." To his surprise, Jake found that he liked sharing details about his family with Heather. "And we have a sister, Arielle. She's ten years younger. She got married last month and is five months pregnant with twin boys."

Heather was silent so long, he thought she might have fallen asleep. "I'm so happy that Mandy is going to have aunts, uncles and cousins." She paused. "What about grandparents? Are your parents still alive?"

"No, our mother was killed in a car accident when

Luke and I were twenty." He took a deep breath. No matter how long it had been, he still missed the woman who had give him and his siblings life.

"I'm so sorry. What about your father?"

He snorted. "We only met our father once. After he made our mother pregnant with me and Luke, he took off and she didn't see him again until we were almost ten. That's when he showed up, stuck around only long enough to make Mom pregnant with Arielle, then took off again." It was his turn to pause. "We recently got word that he was killed in a boating accident a couple of years ago."

"Who finished raising your sister after your mother died?" she asked, sounding genuinely concerned.

"Luke and I were in college and managed to work out a pretty good system. He would work one semester and take over most of Arielle's care while I went to school. Then I'd lay out the next semester, get a job and I'd be responsible for her while he attended classes."

"My God, Jake, that had to have been so hard for both of you." She turned her hand, palm up, to clasp his. "Did you try to get in touch with your father to see if he would send money to help out with your sister?"

Stopping the car at the entrance to Hickory Hills, he used the remote Clara had given him to open the wide iron gates. "We tried, but it proved to be impossible. We didn't even know his real name."

Her mouth dropped open. "He lied about who he was?"

Jake nodded. "We didn't find that out and who he really was until we were told he was dead."

When he drove the car through the gates, he pushed the button to swing them shut and as they traveled the long oak-lined drive, he decided to omit his newly discovered grandmother's name. Emerald Larson was Mandy's great-grandmother but he still wasn't comfortable with the fact or with the way she manipulated her grandchildren.

"Mandy does have a great-grandmother," he said, watching Heather from the corner of his eye. "We learned about her at the same time we found out about our father's death."

She smiled. "It's nice that you finally found each other."

"More like she found us." He shrugged. "She knew how wild and unsettled her son was and after he died, she had a team of investigators search to see if he had any children so that she could set things right with all of us."

"That's when she got in touch with you and your siblings?" Heather asked, seemingly fascinated with what he was telling her.

"Among others."

He could tell from her expression that Heather was thoroughly shocked. "You mean…he fathered more children than just you and your siblings?"

"It turns out our father took the biblical passage where it says 'Be fruitful and multiply' to heart." He smiled as he parked the car in the circular drive in front of the mansion. "He also fathered three other sons by three different women in the ten years between fathering me and Luke and Arielle."

Her eyes grew even wider. "Wow! He certainly was…um, active."

"To say the least."

Jake got out of the car and as he walked around to

open the passenger door for her, he couldn't help but see the parallel between the way he'd been living his life and the way his father had. And he wasn't overly proud of it. But he was different from his father in one very important way. Jake was going to be there for Mandy where his father had failed his children in every way possible.

When Heather got out of the car to stand in front of him, he didn't hesitate to put his arms around her. "I know it seems like I've been living my life a lot like my father did, and maybe to a certain extent, I have. But let me assure you, I'll always be there for Mandy… and for you."

"Jake—"

"I mean it, Heather. I'm not the irresponsible jerk my father was."

Deciding that enough had been said about his notorious father and atypical family, he let his gaze travel from her silky hair swept up into a stylish twist, down the length of her black strapless cocktail dress, to her impossibly high, black heels. In L.A. they had a colorful phrase for those kind of shoes and he seriously doubted that she realized some women wore them to send a message that they were open to a night of unbridled passion.

Groaning, he raised his head to rest his forehead against hers. "Do you have any idea how sexy you are? How beautiful?"

Before she had the chance to speak, Jake teased and coaxed her mouth with his own until she granted him the access he sought. But he was completely unprepared and not at all disappointed when Heather took control of the kiss and touched her tongue to his.

At first tentative, her shy stroking sent electric sparks to every nerve in his being. As she gained confidence and engaged him in a game of advance and retreat, the sparks touched off a flame in the pit of his belly that quickly had him wondering if he was about to burn to a cinder.

The reaction of his body was instantaneous. He hadn't become aroused this fast since his teens.

With his knees threatening to buckle and his head swimming from a serious lack of blood to the brain, he reluctantly broke the caress. If he didn't put an end to the kiss, and right now, he was in real danger of making love to her right there on the steps of the veranda.

"Honey...I can't believe...I'm going to say this." He stopped long enough to draw some much needed air into his lungs. "Unless you're ready to go upstairs with me—to my room, my bed—we'd better call it a night."

He watched her passion-flushed cheeks turn a deep shade of rose a moment before she shook her head. "I'm sorry...I...not yet." She suddenly clamped her mouth shut, then took a step away from him, then another. "I mean...no. That's not going to happen."

When Heather turned and fled up the steps, across the veranda and disappeared into the house, Jake reached up to unknot his tie and unbutton the collar of his shirt. Then, stuffing his hands in his pants pockets, took off at a brisk walk back down the long drive toward the entrance gates.

He couldn't believe how the evening had turned out. He wasn't in the habit of divulging personal information to the women he dated. It kept things from becoming complicated when he went his way and they went theirs.

But Heather was different. For reasons he didn't care

to contemplate, he wanted her to know all about him. And he wanted to learn everything about her. What had inspired her to choose her career? Did she have siblings? Were her parents still alive?

Shaking his head, he fell into a steady pace as he started back toward the house. He had no idea what had gotten into him. Yet as he got better acquainted with his only child, he had every intention of getting close to her mother, as well.

Checking on her daughter sleeping peacefully in her crib, Heather crossed the hall and, entering the bedroom she'd been using since Jake moved her and Mandy into the mansion, closed the door. What on earth had possessed her to take control of that kiss? And why had she the same as told him that at some point she would be ready to make love with him again? Had she lost her mind?

As she removed her heels and unzipped her dress, she thought about the details he'd shared with her about his family. There was a lot more to Jake Garnier than first met the eye or that he allowed people to see.

He was a self-made man who hadn't always had an easy life. He'd been there right along with his twin brother to step in and accept the responsibility of raising their younger sister, while still managing to complete his education. That had been a monumental undertaking and she could tell that he wouldn't have considered doing it any other way. He and his siblings had struggled to stay together and they'd made it. That certainly wasn't something a self-indulgent playboy would do.

She slipped out of her dress and hanging it in the closet, took down her hair and changed into her nightgown. When she climbed into bed, she closed her eyes and hugged one of the pillows tightly against her.

The more she learned about Jake, the more she admired him. Considering she was finding it almost impossible to resist him, that was extremely dangerous. She couldn't afford to let go of her preconceived notion that he cared little or nothing about anyone but himself. If she did, there was a very real possibility that she and her daughter would both end up getting hurt.

Lying there hugging the pillow, she must have drifted off to sleep because the next thing she knew, her daughter's cries coming through the baby monitor awakened her. She tossed the pillow aside and, getting out of bed, reached for her robe. But the sound of Jake's voice stopped her.

"What's wrong, Mandy? Did my little honey bunny have a bad dream?" He must have taken the spare receiver to his room before he turned in for the night.

As she listened to him comfort their daughter, tears filled her eyes and spilled down her cheeks. It was clear from the tone of his voice that he loved Mandy, and Heather knew as surely as she knew her own name that he would be just as committed and protective of their daughter as any father could possibly be.

Without a second thought, she quietly opened her door and tiptoeing across the hall, watched Jake gently cradle Mandy to his bare chest. She waited until he put their sleeping daughter back in the crib, then walked out into the hall. "I appreciate your trying to let me sleep."

Running his hand through his thick hair, he shook his head. "Too bad it didn't work out."

When they both fell silent, Heather found it hard not to stare. Dressed in nothing but a pair of navy silk pajama bottoms, he looked absolutely…yummy. She suddenly felt warm all over.

"Heather, are you all right?"

"I…um, yes." She needed to make her escape while she still had the presence of mind to do it.

His slow smile said that he knew exactly what she'd been thinking. "I like the way you look, too." Reaching out, he traced one of the thin spaghetti straps of her gown with his index finger. "You make turquoise look real good, honey."

"I thought that was supposed to be…the other way around," she said, realizing that she'd forgotten all about her robe when she'd heard Jake talking to the baby. "Isn't the color supposed to complement the person wearing it?"

"Not in your case, Heather." He trailed his finger down the strap to the gown's rounded neckline. "You make everything you wear sexy."

A shiver flowed through her when the tip of his finger lightly grazed the slope of her breast. "I'm…going back to…my room."

He took her into his arms. "I'd rather you stay with me."

"Out here in the hall?"

Staring up at him, she knew she was playing with fire. The feel of him holding her and the rich sound of his voice lowered to an intimate timbre caused an ache that she knew for certain only he could ease.

"I was thinking more like my room." His seductive smile sent her pulse into overdrive.

What she wanted was to go with him. What she needed was peace of mind. And that would be in serious jeopardy if she let her heart overrule her head.

She took a deep breath as she summoned every ounce of strength she possessed. "I want you to go to your room and...I'll go to mine."

"Are you certain that's what you really want, Heather?"

They both knew she was telling a huge lie. The last thing she wanted was to go back alone to the big empty bed across the hall. But making love with Jake would only add another wrinkle to their already complicated situation, not to mention pose a serious risk to her heart.

"Y-yes." Turning to go across the hall to her room, she wished she'd sounded more convincing. "Good night, Jake."

When he placed his hand on her shoulder to stop her, the look in his amazing blue gaze caused her heart to beat double time. "You can only run from this—from us—for so long." He leaned forward to kiss her with such tenderness she thought she might do something stupid like give in. "Sleep well, sweet Heather."

As she watched him stroll down the hall toward the master suite, she had to lean against the door frame to keep her knees from folding beneath her. How on earth was she ever going to be able to resist such blatant sexuality?

She somehow managed to walk into the bedroom and close the door. If it was just a matter of physical attraction, she was pretty sure she'd be successful. But the more she learned about Jake and the more she saw how much he cared for their daughter, the closer she came to listening to her heart. And that was something she couldn't let happen again.

She climbed into bed and hugged the pillow close again. There was no doubt about it. If she intended to survive Jake's visit to Hickory Hills, she was going to have to keep her emotions in check. She was in danger of losing a lot more than her heart if she didn't. They still had yet to discuss how they were going to raise Mandy, and considering the high-handed way he'd relieved her of most of her duties, she might end up losing her job.

But as she lay there thinking about how it felt when he touched her, held her, she knew that keeping her wits about her was going to be all but impossible to do. She was falling for him all over again and there didn't seem to be anything she could do to stop it.

Chapter 6

"Where's Heather?" Jake asked when he walked into the kitchen and found Clara feeding the baby breakfast.

"Tony called. There was a problem down at the stables with one of the horses and he wanted her to come down to assess the situation." The housekeeper shook her head. "He knows Heather would never forgive him if he hadn't let her know about it."

Jake frowned. He'd put Tony in charge to free Heather from having to deal with this sort of thing until after the race. "Is there something wrong with Dancer?"

"No. I think she said one of the other studs has a really nasty cut on its pastern." She spooned a mouthful of cereal into Mandy's open mouth. "Heather's almost as good as a vet when it comes to taking care of horses and I'm pretty sure Tony wanted her to take a look at the injury to see how bad it is."

Clara might as well have been speaking a foreign language for all he understood about where the horse was injured. "How did she learn so much about horses?" he asked as he grabbed a mug from the cabinet, then poured himself a cup of coffee.

"Bless her heart, she learned from the best," the housekeeper said, smiling fondly. "Before he died five years ago, her dad, George, was the manager here. From the time she was old enough to walk, she followed him around like a shadow and soaked up everything he knew about horses."

Fascinated by the details he was learning about Heather, Jake leaned against the kitchen counter. "What about her mother? Is she still around?"

Clara snorted. "No, and I say good riddance. She was a wild one, always looking for a good time. She took off when Heather was six and they never heard from her again."

It sounded to him like Heather's mother and his father were a lot alike—narcissistic and completely irresponsible. "I think I'll walk down to the stable and see what's going on. Would you mind watching Mandy until Heather and I get back?"

"Not at all." Clara grinned as she wiped the baby's face. "Take all the time you need. The only thing I have to do this morning is come up with another list of chores to keep Daily busy after he finishes mucking out the stalls."

Chuckling, Jake wondered how much longer the woman was going to make the boy suffer for his lapse of judgment. "I have another project that I'd like his help with. Do you think you could pencil that in on the schedule for tomorrow?"

Clara nodded. "Will you need him all day?"

"Probably several days. Will that be a problem?"

"Not at all." She smiled. "What have you got up your sleeve this time?"

"When we moved Heather and the baby, I noticed the carriage house could use a fresh coat of paint and some new carpet."

As Jake left the house and walked the distance to the stables, his thoughts returned to Heather and he couldn't help but wonder how she'd slept the night before. If he was taking bets, he'd wager that she hadn't gotten any more sleep than he had.

Entering the stable, he followed the sound of a loud commotion. What had been so important that Tony felt the need to call Heather?

"Hold him while I get him tranquilized."

Jake automatically turned at the sound of Heather's voice inside one of the stalls and it felt as if his heart came up into his throat. As he watched, she, Tony and another groom jumped back just in time to keep from being kicked by a very large, extremely agitated horse.

"Heather, get out of there." He tossed the coffee cup onto a pile of straw and reached to open the stall's half door.

"Don't you dare open that door," she warned. "Just stay back. We've got this under control."

It didn't appear that they had everything in hand. It looked as if someone was about to get seriously hurt. The thought that it might be Heather had his heart hammering so hard that he thought he'd surely end up with a few cracked ribs.

When Tony and the other man finally caught hold of the thoroughbred's halter, Heather moved swiftly to jab a long needle into the animal's shoulder. The horse lurched to one side, then kicked the back of the stall with a blow that Jake knew for certain would have killed someone had it connected with one of the humans inside the enclosure. But just when he thought all hell was going to break loose, Heather and the grooms managed to open the half-door and escape.

Fear ignited an anger in him that quickly flared out of control and he was itching for a confrontation. "What the hell do you think you were doing in there?" he demanded when she stood safely in front of him.

"The job you pay me to do."

He stubbornly shook his head. "I pay a veterinarian to attend injured horses. And if the size of his bills are any indication, I pay him quite well."

As he and Heather glared at each other, Jake noticed Tony and the other man hurrying toward the far end of the barn. They apparently decided that retreat was the better part of valor.

"For your information, the vet *is* on the way." Her aqua eyes sparkled with anger and he didn't think he'd ever seen her look prettier.

"Then why were you in the stall? Why didn't you wait for Dr. Pennington to get here?"

"Because Magic needed a sedative immediately," she shot back. "We couldn't run the risk of him making the injury worse."

"I don't care," he said angrily. "You could have gotten yourself killed."

"I've been around horses all my life and I know what I'm doing," she insisted. "Besides, that horse is a full brother to Dancer and almost as valuable as he is. His stud fees alone are going to make you a fortune once he's retired from racing."

Reaching out, Jake took her by the shoulders. "Don't you understand? It's not about the money, Heather. Your safety is far more important to me than any money I could make off of a damned horse."

She stared at him for several long seconds before her stormy expression began to ease a bit. "Honestly, I really wasn't in as much danger as it might have seemed, Jake."

He crushed her to him. "Even the slightest chance of you being hurt in any way is one chance too many, honey."

As his heart slowly returned to a more normal beat, he couldn't get over the fear that had coursed through him when he saw the horse come so close to kicking her. It had rivaled the feeling he'd experienced a few days ago when he'd awakened to find his napping daughter missing from where she'd fallen asleep on his chest.

Before he could analyze what that might mean, he lowered his head to cover Heather's mouth with his. He told himself that he needed to reassure himself that she was indeed all right. Yet the truth of the matter was he'd become quite good at looking for reasons to kiss her.

Soft and pliant, her lips immediately fused with his as she wrapped her arms around his neck. But when she used the tip of her tongue to invite him to deepen the kiss, her eager response to the caress sent blood surging through his veins and his body hardened so fast it made him dizzy.

As he slipped inside and teased, he slid his hands from her back to her delightful little blue jeans-clad bottom and tried to pull her even closer. But an insistent nudge against his legs had him breaking the kiss to look down at the big dog trying to work his way between them.

"Thank God Nemo came along when he did." Heather's cheeks colored a pretty pink as she glanced down the wide aisle to see if anyone had been watching.

"I thought you were supposed to be man's best friend," Jake groused when he bent to pick up his discarded coffee cup. He scratched behind the big dog's ears. "How would you like it if I interrupted you and one of your female friends?"

"Since he's been neutered, I doubt he'd care," she said dryly.

"Nemo, buddy, I'm so sorry to hear that," Jake said sympathetically.

She looked confused. "Why are you sorry he's been neutered?"

"It's a guy thing." Jake shook his head. "You wouldn't understand."

"The vet just arrived," Tony called from the opposite end of the stable, drawing their attention back to the matter at hand.

"Heather and I are going back up to the house," Jake said before she could answer or find an excuse to stick around. "You assist him with whatever he needs."

"No problem, boss."

"I'm not going anywhere," she stated. "My job is to stay right here and see to Stormy Magic's welfare."

"Dr. Pennington has arrived and Tony will see that he takes good care of whatever treatment the animal needs." Turning her, Jake put his arm around her shoulders and started walking them from the stable. "Besides, if you'll remember, we have a dinner meeting with a couple of the other owners and then the Southern Oaks Ball to attend this evening."

"You could go without me."

"Nope. You agreed to be my date for these things. It's too late to back out now."

She shook her head. "It was more like you pulled rank and told me I was going."

He chuckled. "Whatever. You'll need to start getting ready early."

"Why? We're not meeting the other owners until seven this evening."

"I was contacted this morning by the television network carrying the race. They want to interview us before dinner and get some footage for their *Meet the Owners* pre-race segment."

"I don't own Dancer. You do. There's no reason for me to be included in that." She shrugged from beneath his arm and stopping, glared at him. "Right after he was named the favorite to win the Classic, they showed up here to tape his daily exercises and grooming. They interviewed me then and I told them everything there is to know about Dancer." She shook her head. "This particular fifteen minutes of fame is all yours."

When Jake helped her out of the back of the limousine, Heather felt as if she'd stepped right into the middle of a three-ring circus. Cameras whirred and reporters called out questions as they walked along the carpeted runway toward the entrance of one of the oldest and most prestigious hotels in Louisville.

"This is just like a Hollywood premiere," Jake said, placing his hand to her back to guide her.

"And the very reason I would have preferred staying at home," she muttered. They'd spent an hour and a half before dinner being interviewed by the television network as well as a couple of reporters from the print media. She was more than ready to escape the spotlight.

"What was that, honey?" he asked, leaning close.

"It's not important." She wasn't surprised he hadn't been able to hear her. The noise was almost deafening.

Thankfully they left most of the chaos behind as they crossed the lobby to enter the Grand Ballroom. She waited while Jake presented the doorman with his invitation, then walking into the ornate room, looked around. The light from the massive crystal chandeliers caused the gold accents on the pristine white walls to take on a rich glow and complemented the heavy floor-to-ceiling red velvet drapes. As she continued to scan the room, she spotted a few of the same guests that had attended the Wainwrights' reception along with several well-known celebrities and foreign dignitaries.

"Is that who I think it is?" Jake asked as a sheikh and his entourage strolled past them.

She nodded. "That's Sheikh Kalid Al-Kahra. He owns Dancer's biggest competition."

"Do you think we have anything to worry about?" Jake asked.

"Not a chance." She couldn't stop her smug smile. "The sheikh's jockey has a tendency to take the horses he's riding to the lead right out of the gate and doesn't let up. By the time they reach the homestretch, the horse has nothing left for the sprint to the finish."

"I'm glad that jockey is riding the sheikh's horse and not ours," Jake said, grinning.

"The previous owner of Hickory Hills demanded the best. That's why we have Miguel Santana wearing our silks." She nodded toward a group standing off to the side of the orchestra. "See that distinguished-looking gentleman over there with all the medals and ribbons? He's the Crown Prince of Marunda. He owns the long shot."

"The Wainwright affair was small potatoes compared to the company we're keeping this evening," Jake said, accepting champagne for both of them from a passing waiter. "There are some very impressive pedigrees here this evening."

"I suppose you could say that." She accepted the sparkling wine he handed her and took a sip. "But I'm more impressed by the horses than I am with the people owning them."

He looked thoughtful. "You really mean that, don't you?"

She nodded. "Owners like the sheikh and the prince were born into their positions in life. They didn't have to work to get where they are. But every horse starts out the same. They may have impressive bloodlines, but they still have to work and prove themselves on the track. That's something to be admired."

They fell silent for several moments before she felt him watching her.

"Is something wrong?"

"Not at all." His smile caused her pulse to speed up. "Do you realize you're the most beautiful woman here tonight?"

"I really hadn't given it much thought," she said truthfully.

She had, however, thought a lot about how handsome *he* was. Dressed in a tuxedo she knew for certain hadn't come off of a rack, he looked absolutely amazing.

When a beautiful young woman stepped up to the microphone in front of the orchestra and began to sing the song "At Last," Jake set both of their glasses on a nearby table. "Let's dance."

He took her hand and leading her out onto the dance floor, took her into his arms. The awareness suddenly arcing between them was spellbinding. Gazing into the other's eyes, neither spoke as the orchestra played and the young woman sang about finally finding love. Jake held her close, and swaying in time to the music, Heather knew that she'd remember the moment for the rest of her life.

When the song ended, the orchestra immediately played the beginning notes of another slow, dreamy love song and he pulled her more fully to him. Resting her head against his broad chest, she closed her eyes. She'd never felt more cherished, more secure than she did at that very moment in Jake's arms.

"Honey, I want you more right now than I've ever wanted anything in my entire life," he whispered close to her ear.

His warm breath caused a shiver to course through her. She could deny that she didn't want him just as much, but she was tired of lying. From the moment he arrived at the farm, she'd fought what she knew now to be the inevitable. Jake's touch, his drugging kisses and being held in his arms had worn down her defenses, and she'd lost the battle she'd waged with herself. She wanted him just as much now as she had the night they'd conceived Mandy.

Leaning back to stare up at him, the heat in his cobalt gaze stole her breath.

"How long are we expected to stay at this thing?" he asked.

Her heart sped up. "We've put in an appearance. That's all that's expected."

"Then what do you say we call it an evening and go home?" The promising look he gave her sent excitement coursing through her veins.

Before she could answer, he led her off the dance floor and out of the ballroom straight to the concierge desk. Requesting that their limousine be sent to the front entrance, Jake helped her into the backseat. He raised the window between them and the driver, then gathered her into his arms.

Touching her chin with his index finger, he smiled when their gazes met. "You do know what's going to happen when we get back to the farm?"

Her smile robbed him of breath. "Yes."

Crushing her to him, he covered her mouth with his and it suddenly felt as if the temperature in the car went up a good ten degrees. As she put her arms around his neck, she parted her lips and he didn't hesitate to deepen the kiss.

Her eager response sent blood surging through his veins and he didn't think twice about slipping his hand inside the low cut neckline of her evening gown. Caressing her breast, he touched the beaded tip with his thumb. Her moan fueled the fire building in his belly, but when she moved her hand upward from where it rested on his thigh, the rush of heat tightening his groin made him feel as if the top of his head might just come off. He would have liked nothing more than to strip her of the sexy dress and make love to her right then and there. But he hadn't made out in the backseat of a car since he was in his teens and he'd forgotten just how uncomfortable it could be.

Breaking the kiss, Jake breathed in some much needed oxygen as he removed his hand, rearranged her dress, then tucked her to his side. As much as he needed her at that moment, he didn't want their lovemaking to be rushed. He wanted their first time together again to be special.

When she snuggled against him and rested her palm on his chest, he covered her hand with his. The ride to Hickory Hills seemed to take twice as long as it should have and by the time the chauffeur stopped the limo in the circular drive in front of the mansion, Jake felt as if he had enough adrenaline running through his veins to run a marathon. Without waiting for the driver, he opened the door and helped Heather out of the car.

Neither spoke as they walked the short distance to the veranda and climbed the steps. Opening the door, Jake stood back for Heather to enter and once they stood inside the foyer, he put his arms around her.

"Is Clara babysitting Mandy in her quarters for the night?"

She nodded. "She volunteered and since I wasn't sure how long we would be out this evening, I took her up on the offer."

Kissing her until they both gasped for breath, he slipped his arm around her waist. "Let's go upstairs, honey."

When they climbed the stairs and started down the hall toward the master suite, he forced himself not to pick her up and sprint the short distance. He wanted her with a driving urgency. But he focused his entire attention on taking things slowly and refreshing her memory of how good they'd been together in Los Angeles.

Entering his bedroom, he guided her over to the side of the bed, then turning on the bedside lamp, gathered her into his arms. He kissed her forehead, her eyes and the tip of her nose.

"I'm going to kiss you all over and by the time we're finished there won't be a single inch I haven't loved."

As he nibbled his way from the hollow behind her ear down her delicate throat to her collarbone, he reached behind her to unzip her cream-colored sequined gown. When the garment lay in a glittering pool at her feet, his heart stalled at the sight of her white lacy garter belt, sheer nylons and spike heels. He didn't know a man alive who didn't have some sort of fantasy about a woman wearing one of those little scraps of lace and a pair of impossibly high heels.

"If I'd known you were wearing this, we'd have left after that first dance," he said, meaning it.

Her sultry smile sent his blood pressure off the charts as she stepped away from the gown. "When I get dressed to go out, I like feeling feminine."

He grinned. "We'll have to start going out more often."

Releasing the garters, Jake bent to slowly slide his hands down one of her thighs, taking the sheer hose past her knee and down her slender calf. He lifted her foot to remove her shoe, then pulled the nylon off and tossed it to the side. He did the same thing with her other leg and as he straightened, he leisurely ran his hands up along her thighs, enjoying the feel of her smooth skin beneath his palms.

As he raised his head to capture her mouth with his,

he unfastened the garter belt and added it to the growing pile of clothing. Her soft, moist lips clung to his and he knew he'd never tasted anything quite as enticing.

He broke the kiss and holding her gaze with his, made quick work of unhooking her strapless bra. When it fell to the floor, his breath lodged in his lungs at the sight of her perfect breasts. Taking the weight of them in his palms, he watched her close her eyes and a blissful look come over her as he chafed the tips with his thumbs.

"You're so beautiful, so perfect."

"So are you," she said, bringing her hands up to slip them beneath the shoulders of his tuxedo jacket. Sliding them down his arms, she took his coat with her and it soon joined her clothing on the floor.

His heart hammered hard against his ribs as she toyed with the studs on the front of his shirt, then slowly released them one by one. When she parted the linen to place her hands on his chest, her delicate touch caused him to harden to an almost painful state.

"I've wanted to do this since returning from my meeting at Churchill Downs the other day," she admitted as she explored him.

"Not as much as I've wanted you to, honey."

He closed his eyes and enjoyed her fingers tracing the pads of his pectoral muscles and the ridges of his belly. But when she traced the line of hair from his navel all the way down to the waistband of his slacks, his eyes snapped open as a shaft of heat shot straight through him.

Quickly reaching to stop her, he shook his head. "I love the way your hands feel on my body, but I'd rather not start this party without you."

She raised her gaze to meet his and the need he detected in the aqua depths robbed him of breath. "It's been so long," she said breathlessly.

"I know, honey."

He kissed each one of her fingertips before he placed her hands on his shoulders, then brought his to rest at her waist. Staring down at her, he ran his index finger along the waistband of her panties and watched her eyes darken with desire.

Without a word, he slipped his fingers beneath the elastic and sliding his hands down, bent to remove the scrap of satin. When she stepped out of them and he straightened to face her, his heart stalled at the look she gave him just before she reached out to unfasten the waistband of his trousers.

Before she caused him to have a coronary, he stepped back and made quick work of removing his shirt and pants. But when he reached to remove his boxers, she stopped him.

"Do you mind?" The sound of her voice slid over him like a fine piece of silk.

"Not at all, honey," he said, grinning. "You're doing just fine."

Their gazes remained locked as she slid them from his hips and down his legs. Kicking them aside, he stepped forward and took her into his arms. The feel of her soft breasts crushed to his chest, her hardened nipples pressing into his skin, had his body feeling as if he'd go up in flames.

A shaft of need knifed through him when she skimmed her hands over his back and down his flanks, but when her slender fingers found him, Jake felt as if the intensity of pleasure would knock his knees right out from under him. As she gently measured his length and girth, he leaned down to capture one of her puckered nipples between his lips and worried it with butterfly flicks of his tongue.

Her soft moan was his reward and raising his head, he kissed her smooth cheek. "I think we'd better get into bed, honey. Otherwise, I'm not sure I'll have enough strength left to get there."

When she turned toward the bed, he reached into the nightstand drawer to remove a small foil packet, then placing it under his pillow, stretched out beside her. Gathering her to him, he covered her mouth with his and let his kiss tell her how much the moment meant to him, how much he wanted her.

He'd never wanted to please a woman as much as he wanted to please Heather. "Honey, I'd like to take this slow, but I'm not entirely certain that's an option," he said hoarsely.

Heather gave him a look that sent liquid fire rushing through his veins as she wrapped her arms around his neck. "And I've wanted you just as much, Jake."

He'd been positive that she was experiencing the same desire, but having her confirm his assumption caused a fever within him that threatened to send him up in a blaze. Kissing her parted lips, he brought his hand up to cup her breast and tease the beaded tip.

When he took her nipple into his mouth, then sucked on it gently, a tiny moan escaped her lips and running her fingers through his hair, she held him to her. "That feels so…good."

Kissing his way down her smooth, flat stomach, Jake slid his hand along her side to her hip, then down her slender thigh to her knee. She shivered against him and he knew her excitement was building. He wanted to bring her to even greater heights and, trailing his fingers along the inner part of her thigh, teased the sensitive skin as he went.

"Jake, you're driving…me crazy," she softly gasped.

When he parted her and found her hot, wet and ready for him, he was the one feeling as if he might go insane. Just knowing that she needed him as much as he needed her sent blood racing through his veins and he had to use every ounce of his concentration to keep from losing the slender thread he still held on his control.

He wanted nothing more than to bury himself deep inside of her, to bring them both the completion they desired. He took a deep breath and forced himself to slow down. He was an accomplished lover and never failed to satisfy his partner. But it was more important to him than ever that he ensure Heather's pleasure above his own.

"P-please…Jake."

Apparently, she was feeling the same urgency because she suddenly moved to find his arousal, then taking him into her delicate hand stroked him intimately. A white-hot haze began to build deep within him and he had to fight with everything that was in him to keep from plunging over the edge.

"Just a moment, honey," he said, reaching for the packet beneath his pillow. Quickly rolling their protection into place, he nudged her knees apart and settling himself in the cradle of her hips, entered her with one smooth stroke.

Gritting his teeth at the mind-blowing tightness surrounding him, he leaned down to capture her lips with his as he slowly began to move within her. But the tension building between them was like a wildfire, untamed and out of control. Each movement, each kiss, fanned the flame and drove them ever closer to being consumed by the passion.

When Heather suddenly arched up to meet him and he felt the immediate tightening around him, felt her feminine muscles cling to him, he deepened his strokes. He held her close and watched in awe as the ecstasy overtook her and she let go.

With his own release close, he moved into her again. He felt Heather suddenly tighten around him one more time and cry out his name. The mind-numbing realization that he'd brought her to a second release sent him over the edge. As he surged into her one final time, shock waves so strong they reverberated throughout his entire being shook him.

Easing to her side before he collapsed on top of her, he gathered Heather close and held her to him as they both tried to catch their breath. Shaken by the intensity of what they'd shared, Jake knew for certain that he'd never experienced anything as meaningful as their lovemaking. But even though he wasn't at all ready to try to put a name to what he was feeling, he wasn't fool enough to try to deny that it existed, either. And that should have made him nervous enough to jump out of his own skin. It was a mystery to him why it didn't.

"Are you all right?" he asked, kissing the top of her head where it rested on his shoulder.

"Mmm. That was incredible."

"I couldn't agree more." When she yawned and snuggled against him, he smiled and tightened his arms around her. "Why don't you get some sleep, honey? It's been a long day and the week has just started. We have about half a dozen more parties and receptions to attend before all of this is over."

"That many?"

"Unfortunately."

When she started to get up, he tightened his arms around her. "Where do you think you're going?"

She tilted her head up to look at him. "My room."

"I don't think so." He reached over to turn off the bedside lamp. "I want you right here."

"But—"

"I want to wake up with you tomorrow morning and make love again." He brushed her lips with his. "I can't do that if you're in one room and I'm in another."

She nibbled on her lower lip and he could tell she was waging an internal debate with herself. "Jake, I'm not sure this is such a good idea."

He knew she was afraid of getting in over her head. Hell, he was in uncharted waters himself.

"Please spend the night with me, honey," he pressed. "Then we'll take this one day at a time and see where it goes."

She stared at him for what seemed like forever before she finally nodded. "I'll stay tonight, but that's it. And when your family arrives in a few days, Mandy and I are going to move back into the carriage house."

"Why?"

"Because by my calculations, you're going to need our bedrooms to accommodate everyone."

"This suite is huge," he said, thinking fast. "We can move Mandy's crib in the sitting room and you can sleep with me."

She stubbornly shook her head. "I told you, I'll only

stay with you tonight. And we will move back to the carriage house in a few days."

He could tell she wasn't going to concede the issue. But he didn't like the idea of not having her with him, in his house, in his bed.

"All right," he finally agreed.

Apparently satisfied that he'd given up, she laid her head on his shoulder and in no time he could tell that she'd drifted off to sleep.

As he lay there holding her and staring at the ceiling, determination filled him. Hickory Hills was her and Mandy's home and they belonged right where they were. And he was certain he could come up with some reason for them to stay in the house. All he had to do was find it.

Chapter 7

"Heather isn't gonna like this," Daily said, looking uncertain.

Jake gave the boy an encouraging smile as they carried the sofa from the carriage house and loaded it onto a truck. "You let me worry about Heather. Just make sure you don't drop your end of this thing."

After she, Clara and the baby had left to go into Louisville for lunch and shopping, Emerald had called, prompting him to enlist Daily's help in emptying out the carriage house. Heather was probably going to throw a fit about it, but once he explained everything, she'd surely understand. The place needed to be repainted and recarpeted, and it wouldn't hurt to have some of the furniture replaced. He'd intended to make some of the renovations for her anyway, just not quite this soon.

But when Emerald finally returned his call to tell

him she was accepting his invitation to attend the race, she'd asked for downstairs rooms for herself and her assistant, and in doing so handed him the perfect excuse to keep Heather and Mandy in the house with him when the family descended upon them in a few days. Due to Emerald being somewhere in her mid-seventies and her assistant, Luther, being every bit as old, she'd reminded him that climbing the staircase in the mansion might not be a good idea for them. That's when he'd come to the conclusion that the one-level carriage house was the perfect solution.

"How long before the painters get here?" Daily asked, interrupting his thoughts.

As they turned to go back inside for the last pieces of furniture, Jake checked his watch. "They should be here any time. We'd better get the rest of this stuff loaded on the truck and take it to the storage unit, so the men can get started." He was having to pay double the normal rate to get everything done in time. But in the end, it was going to be well worth it.

Daily looked almost as nervous as the night he'd tried to sneak out to see his girlfriend. "Have you figured out how you're going to keep Heather from finding out what's going on until everything's finished?"

"I'm not." Jake laughed at the boy's horrified expression.

"She's gonna kill both of us when she finds out," Daily said, shaking his head. "It's been nice knowing you."

"Don't worry. I'll take the heat with Heather," Jake assured. "You're just doing what I asked you to do."

An hour later, he and Daily had the carriage house emptied and the furniture unloaded into the storage unit. The painting crew had just finished taping the woodwork and were laying down drop cloths when Heather, Clara and the baby drove up in Heather's old sedan. "Jake, what's going on?" she asked when she got out of the car.

"I'm having the place renovated," he answered, hoping her reaction wasn't going to be as dire as Daily had predicted.

"What do you mean by that?" she demanded, her voice reflecting her displeasure.

"I'm having it painted and re-carpted."

She propped both fists on her shapely hips. "What did you do with my furniture and all of my things?"

"I stored the furniture until the work is finished and put all of your personal effects in your room in the mansion." He'd contemplated moving them to his room, but abandoned that idea after some careful thought. He'd reasoned that she'd be irritated enough that her plans to move back into the carriage house had to be changed, and there was no sense adding more fuel to that particular fire.

"You can't do this, Jake." Her voice shook with anger as she walked up to stand toe to toe with him. "I liked everything the way it was."

"You're on your own, dude," Daily said, taking off down the path toward the stables like the hounds of hell chased him.

"I'll go ahead and take Mandy into the house," Clara offered as she quickly moved to get the baby out of the car seat.

Jake waited until Clara crossed the patio and entered the house with Mandy, before he turned his full attention on Heather. If he was going to get himself out of the hole he'd dug with her, he figured he'd better do some fast talking.

"Before you become too upset, let me explain."

She folded her arms beneath her breasts. If looks could kill, he figured he'd be a dead man in nothing flat. "This had better be good."

"I received a call from my paternal grandmother this morning. She's going to join the rest of the family here for the race this weekend."

"And?"

"She and her assistant are both elderly." He wasn't about to tell her that Emerald and Luther were two of the spryest septuagenarians he'd ever met and that he strongly suspected Emerald's request was another ploy to control the situation. "There isn't an elevator in the mansion and I don't think it's a good idea for them to climb the stairs to get to their rooms. At their ages, a fall could be disastrous."

He could tell by her sudden frown that she was giving his reasoning consideration. "I can understand your concerns, but you should have discussed this with me first, instead of taking it upon yourself to start changing things." She pointed to the front door of the carriage house. "That's my home and I should have something to say about what goes on with it. You had no right to get rid of my furniture."

Reaching out, he pulled her into his arms. "Honey, this whole farm is your home. And your furniture will be moved back in as soon as the work is done. I promise the only thing different will be the color of the walls and carpet."

He lowered his head and kissed her until they both gasped for air. "If you decide later to move back into the carriage house, won't it be nice to have those things already done?"

"There's still a problem of not having enough bedrooms in the house when your family arrives."

"I'll have it all worked out by the time they get here." He was just glad she wasn't still glaring daggers at him. "Now, let's go into the house so you can show me the hat you bought for the race and explain to me why all of the women wear them."

After dinner, Heather sorted through the boxes Jake had moved from the carriage house. She should have anticipated him finding a way to get her to stay in the mansion while his family visited. But she had to admit he did have a valid reason. There was no way she'd subject two elderly people to the perils of climbing all of those steps. She'd never forgive herself if one of them fell and was seriously injured.

"What are you doing in here, honey?" Jake asked from the door.

"I'm trying to organize and find a place to put everything until after your family leaves and Mandy and I can move back into the carriage house," she answered without looking up.

He walked over to sit on the bed beside her. "I meant it when I told you that I want you and Mandy to feel free to live in the mansion whether I'm here or not."

She sighed heavily. "Do we have to go over this again? It doesn't belong to me and I wouldn't feel right—"

"We'll cross that bridge when the time comes," he interrupted. "Right now, I have something I want you to see."

"This is the only free evening we've had in the past few days and I'd really like to relax." When she'd discovered they didn't have a reception to attend, she'd looked forward to a quiet, uneventful night.

Taking her hand, he pulled her to her feet. "Trust me, you're going to like this."

She allowed him to lead her down the hallway to the stairs. "Let's get this over. I have a date with the Jacuzzi a little later."

His grin caused her to feel warm all over. "Want company? I'll wash your back if you'll wash mine."

The thought of being in the bubbling water with him caused a delightful fluttering in the pit of her stomach.

"We'll talk about it later." She stopped as he led her toward the front door. "I forgot the baby monitor."

"Don't worry about Mandy," he said, opening the door. "I asked Clara to watch her." He covered her eyes with his hand. "Now, follow me."

"But she has been babysitting so much the past few days." She let him lead her out onto the veranda. "I hate to take advantage of her."

"Clara volunteered." She could hear the smile in his voice as he helped her down the steps. "I think she knows we both need some down time. Besides, she told me the other day that it's a lot easier to grandmother a baby than a teenager."

Nodding, Heather laughed. "I've seen Daily turn as red as a beet when she kisses his cheek, whereas Mandy loves it."

"Are you ready for the surprise?"

"I suppose so." She couldn't imagine why he was being so secretive.

He removed his hand. A shiny royal-blue minivan

with the farm logo sat in the driveway. "What do you think?"

"Who does that belong to?" she asked cautiously.

"The farm. But it's primarily for your use."

She turned to stare at him. "Why?"

He pulled her along as he circled the car and opened the sliding side door. "I saw how cramped the backseat of your car is with Mandy's car seat and you can definitely use the room. Besides, it's not fair for you to drive your car for the farm business."

He handed her a set of keys. "Try it out."

She bit her lower lip. It was such a pretty car and would save her from having to put a lot more miles on her aging Taurus. "I'll only use it to go to meetings and to pick up things for the farm."

"Honey, I want you to feel free to use it whenever you like. I'd feel better if you and Mandy were in this than a car that could break down and strand you somewhere." He urged her to get behind the wheel, then walked around to close the side door. But before he slid it shut, Nemo jumped in and sat down on the bench seat in the back. "What the hell?"

"He likes to go for rides," she said, laughing.

Jake patted the big dog's head, then closing the door, got into the passenger seat. "I guess we'll take Nemo for a ride."

By the time they drove several miles down the road and back to the mansion, Heather had fallen in love with the new car. "This is wonderful," she said when she parked it and they coaxed Nemo out of the backseat.

"I'm glad you like it," he said, smiling warmly as he picked up a clump of dog hair from the leather seat, then tossing it to the ground, closed the door. "I'll install a car seat tomorrow and you'll be good to go."

As they walked hand in hand into the house, she started to go back upstairs, but he stopped her. "Where do you think you're going? The evening has just started."

"What do you have up your sleeve this time?" she asked, smiling.

Leading her into the den, he motioned for her to sit on the sectional couch in front of a large flat-panel television. As she sank into the plush cushions, she noticed a bowl of popcorn and a couple of soft drinks on the coffee table.

"I thought we could watch a movie together," he said, sitting beside her. He picked up a remote control, pushed a button to start the movie, then put his arms around her shoulder and pulled her close. "We've been on the go so much lately, I figured it might be a good way to relax."

Settling back into his embrace, Heather munched on popcorn and watched the comedy he'd selected for them. She briefly wondered if Jake felt as happy and content as she did. This was her idea of the perfect evening, but she wasn't sure about him. He seemed to be enjoying the quiet evening at home. But he could very well just be marking time until he could get back to the fast-paced lifestyle he led in Los Angeles. After all, he was used to going out every night and partying until the wee hours of the morning.

"What's running through that head of yours?" he asked, startling her. He switched off the television.

"Why do you ask?"

"Because you look pensive and you're not paying attention to the movie." He used his index finger to brush a strand of hair from her cheek. "Otherwise, you would have laughed. Especially at that last part."

She stared at him for several seconds before she voiced her thoughts. "I was just wondering if you're bored yet."

He frowned. "Where did that come from?"

Shrugging one shoulder, she met his confused gaze. "You've been here a week and other than the sedate receptions and the ball last night, you haven't gone out to any of the clubs. And you've had more than enough time after you brought me home to go back out. But you didn't. I would have thought by now you'd be climbing the walls."

"Honey, I haven't missed that scene one time since I've been here." He looked thoughtful as if he couldn't quite believe it himself. "In fact, I don't find the idea of going clubbing the least bit appealing."

"Are you feeling all right?" she asked before she could stop herself.

He unbuttoned his shirt, then taking her hand in his, placed it on his bare chest. "You tell me."

Her pulse sped up. "I think you feel pretty good. Wonderful actually."

Pulling her onto his lap, he cradled her to him as he tugged her shirt from her jeans and slipped his hand under the hem. When he cupped her breast, he rested his forehead against hers. "You feel pretty awesome yourself."

A delicious warmth began to flow through her veins and she closed her eyes as she lost herself to the sensation of his hand on her sensitive skin. Was it possible that he really didn't miss his old lifestyle? Or when the first opportunity presented itself, would he revert to his old ways?

Jake covered her mouth with his and she gave up all speculation. She didn't want to think about what tomorrow would bring. At the moment, she was in his arms and that was all that mattered.

"Let's go upstairs, honey," he said, ending the kiss. "I think your suggestion about our having a date with the Jacuzzi is an excellent idea."

Putting her arms around his shoulders, she smiled. "I thought that was *my* date."

His mischievous grin caused her heart to skip a beat. "Do you mind if I make it *ours?*"

"Not at all."

When he set her on her feet and stood, she didn't think twice about placing her hand in his and walking out of the den and up the stairs. As they entered the master bedroom, he ushered her into the sitting area and over to one of the chairs.

"Stay right here," he said a moment before he disappeared into the bathroom. A couple of minutes later, he walked back into the room and smiling, leaned down to kiss the tip of her nose. "Come with me, Heather. I have a surprise for you."

Doing as he requested, when he led her into the bathroom, she couldn't believe her eyes. The flicker of white candles in all shapes and sizes lit the otherwise dark room and the filled bathtub was already bubbling.

"When did you do this? There wasn't enough time—"

"I set the candles out and filled the tub earlier. The thermostat kept it warm for us." He took her into his arms. "I just lit the candles."

She wrapped her arms around him and laid her head against his chest. "This is perfect. Thank you."

"Let's get undressed and see if it's as relaxing as it looks," he suggested.

Taking turns removing each other's clothes, Jake stepped into the Jacuzzi and eased her between his thighs. The feel of his body against hers when he pulled her back to lay against him sent electricity skipping over every cell in her being.

"This feels so good," he said as he tightened his arms around her.

"Yes, it does." She blissfully closed her eyes. "The water is just right."

His low chuckle caused goose bumps to shimmer over her. "I wasn't talking about the water." A shiver of excitement coursed through her when he kissed her shoulder at the same time his hands covered her breasts. "Tonight is all for you, honey. I'm going to love you so well that there won't be a doubt left in your mind how much I desire you."

The sound of his deep baritone promising a night of passion and the feel of his rapidly hardening body against her backside caused her to feel as if she never wanted to be anywhere else but in his arms. And that's when it hit her. She'd told herself that it wasn't happening and tried her best not to do it, but she'd fallen hopelessly in love with him.

If she'd had the chance, she might have been frightened beyond words. There was a very real possibility that she would get hurt again. But Jake didn't give her the opportunity. His hands were moving over her body with precision care and robbed her of all thought.

When he slid his palm down her abdomen to the apex

of her thighs, then gently parted her to stroke the tiny nub nestled within, Heather felt as if a spark ignited in her soul. The intensity of the sensations coursing through her caused her body to hum with a need stronger than anything she had ever known.

"Jake, please."

"What do you want, Heather?"

"Y-you."

She turned her head to look over her shoulder at him. "Please make love to me."

His deep groan vibrated against her back. "Turn around, honey."

When she did as he commanded and straddled his thighs, he lifted up to meet her and entered her in one smooth motion. The feel of his hard body nestled inside of her and the hunger darkening his blue eyes stole her breath.

She watched him tightly close his eyes as he struggled for control and she knew his need was as great as hers. Without hesitation she wrapped her arms around his neck and slowly moved against him. His eyes immediately snapped open and placing his hands on her hips, he helped her set a steady pace.

Feeling more cherished than she had in her entire life, she bit her lower lip to keep from crying out at the intensity of emotions swirling through her. She loved Jake with all of her heart and soul.

As the knowledge filled her, an undeniable tension built inside of her and she rapidly began to climb toward the peak. Jake must have sensed her readiness and deepening his thrusts, sent her over the edge. As her body clung to his, waves of pleasure flowed through her and almost immediately, she felt him tense, then give into the force of his own climax. His tremors rocked them both and she held him close as they rode out the storm together.

When they slowly drifted back to reality, Jake's heart suddenly pounded so hard against his ribs, he wasn't entirely certain it wouldn't jump out of his chest. "Dammit all to hell."

"What's wrong?" Heather asked, clearly startled by his outburst.

He set her away from him and moved to get out of the Jacuzzi. "I wanted you so much, I didn't even consider protection."

She smiled. "Oh, that."

Why was she taking it so lightly? They already had one baby they hadn't planned. And although he loved Mandy more than life itself, he didn't think having another was going to help an already complicated situation.

"Let's get out of here and dry off," he said, wondering if he'd lost his mind. As he got out of the bathtub, he handed her a plush towel, then dried himself off with another.

There was no question about it. He didn't want to make her pregnant again. Hell, he didn't know if he was a good father to one child yet, let alone two.

He shook his head in an attempt to clear it. There hadn't been one time in his life that he'd failed to use protection. Even as a teenager, he'd been conscious of the implications and responsibilities attached to an unplanned pregnancy.

"Jake, are you listening to me?" she asked, wrapping the towel around her.

He'd been so distracted, he hadn't realized she was

trying to talk to him. Securing the towel at his waist, he motioned toward the door. "Let's go into the bedroom, honey. We need to talk."

"But I'm trying to tell you—"

He placed his index finger to her lips. "Not until I've had my say."

She looked thoughtful for a moment before she nodded and walking into the bedroom, sat down on the side of the bed. "I'm listening."

Unable to stand still, he paced back and forth in front of her. "There's no excuse for my forgetting to protect you." He stopped and ran his hand over the tension building at the base of his neck. "But I want you to know that if you do get pregnant because of my carelessness, I'll be there this time." He knelt in front of her and took her hands in his. "I promise you won't have to go through everything alone like you did when you were pregnant with Mandy. This time I'll know, and I give you my word that I'll be there for you, Heather."

"Are you finished?"

He couldn't believe her lack of concern. Did she want to become pregnant again?

Nodding, he drew in a deep breath. "Yes, I think that about covers it."

"You can stop worrying. I'm not going to get pregnant." She shrugged one bare shoulder. "There was an issue of my being regular after Mandy was born, so the doctor put me on the Pill."

Instead of the relief he should have felt, disappointment settled in the pit of his belly. Had he really wanted to make her pregnant again? Had he lost what little sense he had left?

Of course not. The thought was ludicrous. But he

couldn't seem to chase away the let-down feeling that accompanied her announcement.

"Why didn't you tell me?" he asked.

"The subject never came up. And besides, it really wasn't any of your business."

She was right, of course. But what he couldn't understand was why he wanted it to be.

Reaching out, she touched his cheeks with her soft hand, then leaned forward and gave him a kiss so sweet it robbed him of breath. "You wouldn't have gotten so worked up if you'd only let me explain. You really could use some work on your listening skills, Mr. Garnier."

Two hours later, after making love to Heather again, Jake held her close as she slept and thought about his uncharacteristic emotions. Not quite two weeks ago, he'd been a carefree, commitment-shy bachelor with nothing more on his mind than paying a visit to his newly acquired horse farm, sticking around for the big race and then he was supposed to be back on the road to L.A. But all that had changed with the discovery that he'd not only found the one woman he'd regretted not staying in touch with but also that she'd had his baby.

Why did he all of a sudden want all of the things he'd spent most of his adult life trying to avoid?

Tightening his arms around her, he pulled her close and tried to relax. But as sleep began to overtake him, Jake couldn't help but feel that he was walking a fine line. And once crossed there would be no going back.

"How's my little angel?" Heather asked as she picked the baby up from the crib. "Did you have a good nap?"

Mandy's happy grin as Heather changed her diaper revealed a small white place on her lower gum.

"Your tooth has broken through." Kissing her daughter's soft cheek, Heather picked her up from the changing table and walked out of her bedroom toward the stairs. "We'll have to find your daddy and show him. He's been worried about when it was finally going to stop bothering you."

Shortly after awakening to find herself alone in Jake's bed that morning, she'd gone in search of him and found that he had moved the crib into the room she'd been using. He'd explained that with his grandmother and her assistant staying in the newly decorated carriage house there would be plenty of rooms for everyone when they descended on them later in the day.

Hearing voices when she reached the bottom of the steps, she crossed the foyer and entering the den, found several people taking their turns hugging Jake. It appeared that his family had arrived.

"Heather, I'd like you to meet the clan," Jake said when he noticed her standing just inside the door. Walking over he lifted Mandy onto his arm and put his other arm around her shoulders. "This is my daughter, Mandy, and her mother Heather."

"Please let me hold her," his sister, Arielle, said reaching for Mandy. Almost six months pregnant, she and her husband, Zach, had just learned they were expecting twin boys. "She's absolutely adorable. And she looks just like you, Jake."

As everyone greeted her and made a fuss over the baby, a bittersweet feeling filled her chest at the pride in Jake's voice. She only wished he could love her half as much as he did their baby.

When he finished making the introductions, Heather couldn't help but notice how much Jake and his half brothers were alike. All of them were quite tall, had the same athletic build and bore a strong facial resemblance. They even shared some of the same mannerisms. When his brother Hunter O'Banyon talked about the stress of being an air medevac pilot, he ran his hand over the back of his neck, which Jake had a habit of doing, too.

"Where's your twin and his wife?" she asked, noticing their absence.

"Haley had a doctor's appointment," Jake answered. "Luke said they'd meet us at Churchill Downs before the race tomorrow."

"Heather, I hear you're the one in charge of the winning horse," Nick Daniels said. "Jake told us you raised him from a colt."

Smiling, she nodded at the rancher from Wyoming. "Actually, I was responsible for choosing his bloodlines as well as helping the mare foal when the vet couldn't get here in time."

"Hang on to her, Jake," Nick advised. He put his arm around his pretty wife, Cheyenne. "Take it from me. You can't go wrong with a woman who knows her horses."

"I'll remember that," Jake said, smiling.

"Heather, do you have time to go shopping with us?" Caleb Walker's wife, Alyssa, asked. "I've heard that it's a tradition for all of the women to wear a hat to the race."

"I got a new one a couple of days ago and I'd be more than happy to take all of you to the shop where I bought it," Heather offered. "They have a great selection, in all colors and styles."

Callie O'Banyon sighed. "A shopping trip without little ones in tow sounds like heaven."

"By the way, where are your children?" Jake asked.

Caleb chuckled as he pointed to his brothers. "We all decided to leave them with the babysitters and enjoy spending a little alone time with our wives."

"If everyone's agreeable on the shopping, we could go right after I take a nap," Arielle suggested, yawning. She handed Mandy to Alyssa, then with her husband's help, rose to her feet. "Could you tell me where our room is, Jake?"

"I'll be happy to show you where you'll be staying," Heather spoke up, earning a warm smile from Jake.

When they climbed the stairs and Heather showed the pretty young woman where she and her husband, Zach, would be sleeping during their stay at Hickory Hills, Arielle motioned for Heather to follow her into the room. "Are you up for some girl talk before I crash?"

Heather liked all of Jake's brothers and sisters-in-law, but there was something about Arielle that told Heather if given the chance they would become very good friends. "Of course."

Lowering herself to the side of the bed, Arielle smiled. "I just wanted you to know how thrilled I am that someone has finally tamed Jake. I couldn't be happier for both of you."

Heather frowned. "I think you must have gotten the wrong impression. Jake and I are just—"

"Don't tell me you're just friends," Arielle interrupted. "I've seen the way my brother looks at you and there's a lot more to the way he feels about you than friendship."

Heather wasn't quite sure what to say. She wasn't going to lie to the woman. But she wasn't certain there

was anything more going on for Jake than a strong attraction and undeniable desire.

"It's...complicated," she finally said, settling on the
truth. Whatever was going on between them was going
to take some time to sort out. They still hadn't discussed
how they were going to handle raising Mandy together
with so much distance between their residences. Jake
had talked about going back to Los Angeles and leaving her and Mandy the run of the farm, but that didn't
mean the custody issue was settled. He could still come
up with demands for equal time.

Arielle placed her hand over Heather's. "You love
him, don't you?"

She didn't even think to hesitate. "Yes."

"Trust me, Jake may not realize it yet, but he's in
love with you, too," Arielle said, smiling. "I've never
seen him like this. He can't keep his eyes off of you."

"It's not like he has much to choose from here,"
Heather said dryly. "Besides the housekeeper, Clara
Buchanan, who's sixty if she's a day, I'm the only other
woman here at Hickory Hills."

Arielle laughed. "How many times has he been out
since he's been here?"

"Other than the receptions and ball we've had to attend, he hasn't," she admitted.

"I rest my case." Arielle hid a yawn behind her hand.
"I know my brother. If he didn't have some very strong
feelings for you, he would have been out every night."

"I wish you were right, but—"

"I am." The young woman yawned again. "Now,
why don't you go downstairs and get to know the others
while I take my nap. When I get up we'll all go shop-

ping and buy some wildly expensive hats we'll probably never wear after the race tomorrow."

Heather gave Arielle a hug, then walked out into the
hall and quietly pulled the door shut behind her. She'd
give almost anything for Jake's sister to be right. But
she couldn't trust that Jake had changed for good. Before coming to Kentucky, he'd been perfectly content
being the irresponsible bachelor with no children and no
commitments. And once he was back in his element in
Los Angeles, around friends who enjoyed partying all
the time, he just might find that he'd missed that non-
stop excitement and revert to his old ways.

Chapter 8

"Heather, I'd like for you to meet my paternal grand-mother, Emerald Larson," Jake said, wondering how she'd take the news that he was the grandson of one of the richest women in the world.

The one thing that Emerald had respected and taken great pains to protect was her grandchildren's right to privacy. She left it entirely up to them when and to whom they revealed the relationship. And as if by un-spoken agreement, all six of them had been discreet and managed to keep the news fairly quiet.

As he watched, Heather's aqua eyes widened a mo-ment before she recovered and shook Emerald's hand. "It's nice to meet you, Mrs. Larson."

"I see Jake has taken his cue from the rest of my grandchildren," Emerald said, patting Heather's cheek.

"Don't worry, dear. None of the others revealed my identity until they had to, either."

"If you'll excuse me, I was just on my way to the paddock to see if Tony has everything under control," Heather said, rising from her seat.

As she started past him, Jake caught her hand in his. "Will you be back in time for the race?"

Her smile lit the darkest corners of his soul. "Absolutely. I wouldn't miss this for anything."

"Where's your assistant?" he asked Emerald as he watched Heather disappear into the crowd.

Since Emerald never went anywhere without the distinguished-looking gentleman, Jake knew he couldn't be too far away. He just hoped he didn't have to go looking for Luther in the sea of people. Churchill Downs had a record crowd and he'd probably never find the poor old guy.

"Luther is placing a small wager for me on your horse, Jake," Emerald said as she found a seat in the box section he'd reserved for the family to watch the race.

Unless she'd changed her ways, Emerald never did anything on a small scale. No telling how much she'd had Luther put down on Stormy Dancer. But it wasn't as if she couldn't afford it. She could probably buy the entire race track with all of the horses and not even scratch the surface of her bank account.

"This is such a festive atmosphere," she said, looking genuinely excited. "And I love that all of the ladies have such decorative hats." She touched the brim of her own elaborate headwear. "I think it's sad that these aren't called for on more occasions. I can remember a time when all the women wore hats for every occasion."

Jake paid little attention to what she was saying as

he scanned the crowd for Emerald's assistant, Luther Freemont. When he finally spotted him, Jake breathed a sigh of relief. The man was slowly making his way through the crowd to the box section with a mint julep in each hand and a bet slip sticking out of the breast pocket of his suit.

"Mr. Garnier." Luther nodded a greeting in his usually stiff manner, then handed one of the glasses to Emerald. "Your julep, madam."

"Thank you, Luther." Emerald patted the seat beside her and the man lowered himself into it. "I'm so glad we're right here in front of the finish line. We'll be able to see Jake's horse win."

As the bugler played the call to race, his brothers and their wives began to file into the box. Jake checked his watch. Where the hell was Heather? She should have been back from checking on Dancer down at the paddock by now.

Just as the horses began their parade past the grandstand on their way to the starting gate, he saw her hurrying up the steps. "Was everything all right?" he asked, when she reached him.

"Dancer was a little more skittish than usual," she said, sitting down beside him. "Thoroughbreds are high-strung by nature—he can sense this is the race of his life."

"Which one is Stormy Dancer?" Caleb asked from behind them.

"That's Dancer," Heather spoke up, pointing to one of the bays. "Our silks are red and blue with a white stripe cutting diagonally across the jockey's chest. When they're running along the backstretch or packed up, look for the colors and you'll be able to keep track of him during the race."

"Thanks for the tip," Caleb said, picking up a set of binoculars.

"There's a lot to remember in this business," Luke said, laughing as he sat down on the other side of Jake.

"Tell me about it, bro." Glancing at his twin, he felt as if he looked into a mirror. Lowering his voice, he admitted, "I couldn't have gotten through these past couple of weeks without Heather. Every time a question was asked about Dancer or his training, she'd tell the reporters and sportscasters what they needed to know."

Luke looked thoughtful. "When's the wedding?"

"How many mint juleps have you had?" Irritated, Jake shook his head. "If I were you, I'd lay off for a while."

Luke shrugged. "Still in denial, huh?"

Before he could tell his brother to mind his own damned business, they started loading the horses into the starting gate and everyone jumped to their feet. As soon as the last horse was guided into place, the front of the chutes flew open at the same time the announcer shouted, "They're off."

The roar of the crowd made it impossible to be heard, and when the horses raced past the grandstand, Heather grabbed his hand and squeezed it until his fingers went numb. He barely noticed. He was too busy watching her. Her cheeks had colored a pretty pink and he didn't think he'd ever seen her look more breathtaking. With sudden insight, he realized that he'd underestimated how much it would mean to her if the horse she'd raised won. She'd chosen his bloodlines, overseen his development and this race was her validation—the culmination of her work.

The horses entered the backstretch and Jake noticed that the sheikh's horse was way out in front, just as Heather said he would be. Picking up the binoculars he'd brought with him, Jake searched for Dancer and found him in the middle of the pack. As they rounded the turn and headed for the homestretch, their jockey must have turned Dancer loose because he suddenly shot to the outside and made his way to the front. And as Heather predicted, the sheikh's horse started slipping back into the pack and Dancer took over the lead. By the time he sprinted across the finish line he was five or six lengths ahead of his nearest challenger and there was no doubt he'd won the race.

"We won!"

With enough adrenaline flowing through his veins to lift a freight train, Jake caught Heather up in his arms and kissed her like a soldier returning from war. He knew his level of elation had nothing to do with the their horse winning and everything to do with the relief that she hadn't been disappointed with the results of the race.

When he set her on her feet, she grabbed his hand. "We need to get down to the track. After Miguel weighs in with the saddle, they'll want you in the winner's circle."

Jake shook his head. "They want *us* in the winner's circle, honey. I may be the owner on paper, but Dancer has always been your horse and always will be."

Tears filled her eyes and she raised up on tiptoes to lightly kiss his cheek. "Thank you, Jake. That means a lot to me."

* * *

After posing for endless pictures and helping Jake get through the required interviews with the media, Heather called Clara to check on Mandy. Then, leaving orders with Tony to give Dancer an extra scoop of oats to celebrate, she joined Jake and his family for an elaborate dinner at the hotel where the Southern Oaks Ball had been held.

Once their waiter had popped the cork on a bottle of outrageously expensive champagne, Jake stood up and raised his glass. "To Heather, her excellent instincts and expertise. Today was the culmination of your hard work and the realization of a dream. May Dancer be the first of many winners under your expert management."

As everyone added their congratulations, Jake sat back down beside her. "Thank you," she whispered, blinking back tears. His recognition of her accomplishment meant more to her than he'd probably ever know.

"You deserve all of the credit and accolades for the outcome of today's race, honey." His hand found hers beneath the table and he gave it a gentle squeeze. "And I couldn't be happier for you."

When the waiter served the main course, conversation turned to catching up on what was going on in the various lives of Jake's siblings, and Heather found it heartwarming that in spite of their unconventional relationship, they'd all become good friends.

"What's up next for you, Jake?" Hunter asked. "Any more big races on the horizon?"

"I'm leaving that up to Heather," he answered. "I called a Realtor yesterday to put my condo on the market and have her find a house along the beach in Malibu for me."

As the group left the private dining room and entered the Grand Ballroom for the victory party, Heather didn't have time to dwell on what Jake might have planned as she noticed several celebrities milling around the bar. All of them had notorious reputations for partying and she couldn't help but wonder if some of them were Jake's friends.

When a singer started singing the song they'd danced to at the ball, Jake turned to her, smiling. "I think they're playing our song, Heather." Leading her out onto the dance floor, he wrapped his arms around her. "Are you happy, honey?"

She stared up at the man she loved with all of her heart. "Are you?"

"Let's see. Our horse won the Classic. The family all made it for the big race. I have a sweet baby daughter with a new tooth who loves to throw baby food at me. And you're in my arms." He brushed his lips over hers. "What more could a man ask for?"

She wanted to believe that all of that would be enough for him. Unfortunately, she knew it wasn't. If he'd already started looking for a house along the beach in Malibu, where she was certain several of his acquaintances had property, he wasn't considering leaving the wilder side of life behind.

The song ended and the orchestra immediately began to play the other tune they'd danced to. Looking up into his cobalt eyes, she blinked back tears. "You arranged for those songs to be played back to back, didn't you?"

His smile made her feel warm all over in spite of the disappointment filling her. "They will always remind me of you and a very special night we spent together."

He tenderly kissed her forehead. "You're so beautiful and I want you so much right now."

She loved the way his body felt against hers. "I want you, too. But—"

"I know. You don't have to say it." He shook his head. "Do you think I can charter a jet to take my family all back to their homes tonight?"

She shook her head. "I don't think that would be a good idea."

"I do."

When the music stopped and he led her off the dance floor, her earlier speculation was answered about the celebrities in attendance being his friends when a tall, dark-haired man she recognized as one of Hollywood's baddest bad boys walked toward them. "Jake Garnier, I heard you owned the horse that won today. I hoped you'd stop by this evening." The man grinned from ear to ear, showing off a mouthful of capped teeth. "Now I know this little bash is going to rock."

"What are you doing here, Cameron?" Jake asked, smiling at his friend.

"One of the actresses in my latest film is part owner in one of the nags that ran in the big race and she asked me to come along with her to watch." The conspiratorial wink he gave Jake set Heather's teeth on edge. "You know me. If a woman asks, I'm always up to the challenge." Turning his attention her way, the man's grin evolved into an outright leer. "And who do we have here?"

She felt the arm Jake had draped around her waist, stiffen. "Heather McGwire, this is the infamous Cameron Strombeck."

"Jake!" a tall willowy redhead called as she made her

way across the dance floor toward them. "Congratulations. I'll bet you'll be out all night. Be sure and save a dance for me, darling."

As the celebrities continued to gravitate toward them, Heather felt increasingly more uncomfortable. It appeared that instead of having to go back home to pick up his life where it left off, Los Angeles had come to him.

"I think I'll join your family," she said, slipping from his arm before he could stop her.

She walked over to the table where the women were gathered as they waited for their husbands to return with their drinks and sank into an empty chair beside Arielle. "I hope you don't mind my joining you."

"Not at all," Callie O'Banyon said, smiling warmly.

"You and Jake looked amazing out there on the dance floor." Arielle reached over to hug her. "Congratulations, I'm so happy for you."

"Thank you. Dancer's win was definitely exciting." She knew that wasn't what the woman meant, but it was easier to change the subject than to accept good wishes for something that was never going to happen.

When the orchestra started playing again, the volume made conversation impossible and they all fell silent. Heather glanced at Jake several times and her heart broke a little more each time. He looked as if he was having the time of his life with his friends from Tinseltown. As she watched, the redhead melted against him on the dance floor. He didn't seem to mind in the least.

"I hope you don't mind but I think I'll call it a night," she said, rising to her feet.

"Heather, wait," Arielle said, placing a hand on her arm to stop her.

"I'm…um, really pretty tired. I'll see you all in the morning." She had to get out of there before she humiliated herself by dissolving into a torrent of tears. She'd done the very thing that she'd told herself she couldn't let happen. She'd started to believe that Jake might be content staying with her and Mandy. But she knew now that wasn't going to happen. He would soon be leaving Hickory Hills to return to his life in L.A. and the sooner she accepted that, the better off she'd be.

Hurrying across the hotel lobby, when she stepped out onto the sidewalk, she found Mrs. Larson and her assistant waiting on their limousine. "What's wrong, dear?" Mrs. Larson asked, clearly concerned.

Heather forced a smile. "It's been a full day and I'm going back to Hickory Hills before I collapse."

"Would you like to ride with us?" Mrs. Larson offered. "It's past our bedtime and we'd like to get a good night's sleep before we fly back to Wichita tomorrow."

"I would appreciate it. Thank you."

She'd intended to get a cab, but she was going to have to watch her money for a while. There was no way she could continue working for Jake after what she'd just witnessed. Effective the first thing tomorrow morning she was going to resign her position as farm manager and find employment elsewhere.

"Back off, Lila," Jake demanded, setting the woman away from him. Aside from the fact that he wanted nothing to do with the woman, he didn't want Heather getting the wrong idea.

"I thought you'd be open to having a little fun for old times." Her expression turned to a pout that he was certain she'd practiced for years. He couldn't for the life of him remember why he'd ever found her attractive.

"I'm with someone else. Besides, if you'll remember, that ship sailed a long time ago. We went out a total of three times. You've got to move on."

Her lips curled into what could only be described as a snarl. "You don't know what you're missing."

"Oh, I think I do." He started to walk away, then turned back. "And don't worry. I'm sure you'll find someone to help you have a *good time* this evening. Have a nice life, Lila."

He glanced over at the table where his sister sat and breathed a sigh of relief. At least Heather hadn't been around to witness Lila's brazen move.

"Hey, Jake, would you like to go see what the clubs around here have to offer?" Cameron asked, stopping him halfway across the room. "This is dull. We want a lot more action than what this horse crowd has to offer."

As he stared at the man, Jake couldn't believe he'd ever considered him a friend. A pleasure-seeker from the word go, Cameron Strombeck was about as shallow and self-absorbed as a human could possibly be. His disdain for the fine people of the racing industry—for people like Heather—grated on Jake's nerves as little else could.

"No, I'm fine right where I'm at. But you might want to check with Lila Dixon. I happen to know she's looking for a little excitement."

"Really? That could be interesting. I'll catch you when you get back to L.A., then," Cameron said, turning to find Lila. "Give me a call."

"Don't hold your breath on that happening," Jake muttered. Continuing on to the table where Arielle sat, he noticed that she looked ready to tear him in two. "What's wrong?"

"Sit."

"Where's Heather?"

"I said sit!" He didn't think he'd ever seen his sister look as determined as she did at that very moment.

"Where's Heather?" he repeated, desperately searching the ballroom for her. He saw his brothers and their wives on the dance floor and his brother-in-law, Zach, over by the bar. But Heather was nowhere in sight.

"She left." Arielle shook her head. "And I don't blame her. How could you do that to her, Jake? What were you thinking?"

"What the hell are you talking about? I didn't do anything."

When he started to get up, Arielle stopped him. "Stay right where you're at, big brother. I have something to ask you."

"It's going to have to wait, Arielle. I need to find Heather."

"You and Luke have made me listen to both of you all of my life, now you're going to hear what I have to say." He'd never known his sister to be this upset with him.

"Could you make it quick?" he asked impatiently. "I've got to get to Heather and find out why she left."

Arielle looked thoughtful a moment. "She's extremely important to you, isn't she, Jake?"

"Yes."

"You love her, don't you?" Arielle pressed.

"I wouldn't go that far," he said stubbornly. He knew he had deep feelings for Heather, but he wasn't comfortable with the word *love*.

"Oh, Jake." Arielle's voice softened as she reached

out to put her arms around him. "You're frightened, aren't you?"

"That's ridiculous, Arielle." He hugged her back. "I can't think of one single thing I need to be scared of."

Leaning back, she smiled sadly. "How about losing Heather? Aren't you afraid of that?"

His chest tightened painfully at the thought of never holding her, loving her, again. "You don't understand, I..."

When his voice trailed off, his sister nodded. "That's exactly what's going to happen if you don't take the chance, Jake. I don't know what's holding you back, but whatever it is, you've got to let it go."

As he stared at his younger sister, he knew that she was right. He'd avoided making a commitment for fear of turning out to be as irresponsible as his father. But he was nothing like Owen Larsen and never would be.

No other woman incited the degree of passion in him or made him want her the way Heather did. And he'd never met any other woman who made him want to be a better person. Not until Heather.

Taking a deep breath, he rose to his feet and kissed Arielle's cheek. "For a kid, you're pretty damned smart."

"What's going on?" Zach asked when he walked up to the table.

"I have to go find Heather and do some serious explaining," Jake answered, turning to leave.

"Stop by a sporting goods store first and get a set of knee pads," Zach called after him. "If Heather is anything like Arielle, you're going to need them when you're on your knees begging her to give you another chance."

* * *

After checking with Clara to see if she could watch Mandy for the rest of the evening, Heather barely managed to make it to her room upstairs and close the door before the tears she'd been holding in check spilled down her cheeks. How could she have let herself think there was a chance that Jake was different now than he'd been over a year ago? How could she have been so stupid?

Collapsing on the bed, she hugged one of the pillows. She should have known better than to think that he had changed. Jake was Jake. He couldn't be someone he wasn't, couldn't be the man she wanted him to be. Seeing him with his friends tonight and hearing his plans to buy a house in Malibu had been all the proof she needed to see that she and their daughter weren't enough for him.

She wasn't certain how long she lay there sobbing against the pillow, but when she finally managed to stop crying, she gathered the scraps of her broken heart and got up. There were things she needed to do before she faced Jake tomorrow morning.

Going into the bathroom, she washed her face, then took off the evening gown she'd changed into for dinner and put on a pair of jeans and a T-shirt. She needed to pack her and her daughter's things and take them down to her old car, then draft her resignation.

As she opened the dresser drawers and started pulling out clothes, the sound of a car coming to a screeching halt in front of the mansion caused her to jump. Almost immediately she heard the front door bang back against the woodwork.

Hurrying to the top of the stairs to see what was

going on, she stopped short at the sight of Jake, stand-ing in the open doorway staring up at her.

"Heather, honey, we have to talk."

Chapter 9

"I don't *have* to do anything," Heather stated flatly.

She watched him release a frustrated breath. "Would you please come down here? I need to tell you something."

"Where are your friends?" she asked as she slowly descended the steps.

"Damned if I know and damned if I care." He closed the front door, then walked over to stand at the bottom of the staircase.

"I would have thought you'd be out celebrating with them," she said, drawing on every bit of strength and pride she could muster.

"That's one of the things we need to discuss." When she descended the last step, he started to take her by the hand, but she sidestepped him. He stared at her for a moment before he motioned toward the study. "Please follow me."

"I don't really want to discuss anything right now, Jake." Did he think hearing that he was leaving her and Mandy would make everything all right?

She walked over to the fireplace and traced her finger along the frame of a snapshot that he'd had Clara or Daily take of himself holding their daughter. Just like the photograph, she was never going to be a part of the picture. The thought caused an ache so deep inside, she had to look away to keep from crying out.

When Jake put his hands on her shoulders to turn her to face him, she backed away from his touch. "Please don't."

"Heather, honey, you have to listen to me."

"You don't have to make excuses or explain," she said, surprised that her voice remained steady. "You're an adult. You can do as you please."

"But I'm going to tell you anyway," he interrupted. "Now, will you stop arguing with me and start listening?"

Sighing heavily, she walked over to sit in one of the chairs. "Let's get this over with. I have things to do."

He stared at her for several long seconds. "What do you have to do at this time of night?"

"I need to pack."

He folded his arms across his broad chest. "Are you going somewhere?"

"I suppose now is as good a time as any to tell you that I quit effective immediately." She had to pause before she could finish. "You'll have to find someone else to manage Hickory Hills and oversee your horses."

A dark scowl wrinkled his forehead. "You can't do that."

"Watch me." A sudden anger swept through her and she started to get up.

He quickly stepped forward to block her. "I won't let you quit and I don't want you leaving."

"You can't stop me," she said, settling back in the chair.

"Dammit, Heather, Hickory Hills is your and Mandy's home." He pulled another armchair over to sit in front of her. "You belong here."

"Not anymore, I don't." She glared at him. It was much easier to let her anger build than to give into the misery of a broken heart. "You're going back to your life in L.A. and I'm staying here. But do you honestly think I want to be here when you bring a woman with you for your next visit? Or wait for you to return so that I can be a diversion while you're here?"

He shook his head. "That's not going to happen."

She watched him close his eyes as if garnering his patience. When he opened them, there was a determined spark in the cobalt depths.

"If you'd stuck around long enough you'd have seen me decline Cameron's invitation to go barhopping with him and a few others I know from L.A."

"Didn't you want to reconnect with your friends?" she asked.

"Those people wouldn't know how to be a friend if their lives depended on it. They're too self-centered, too shallow." He sat back in his chair. "You probably won't believe this, and I wouldn't blame you if you didn't, considering my track record. But I've been tired of the party crowd for quite some time. I just didn't realize it."

"That is pretty hard to believe," she said, tamping down a tiny bubble of hope.

Sitting forward, he reached out to take her hands in his. "Honey, I'm not going to pretend that I've been a saint since you and I were together in Los Angeles. But I can tell you that after you left, I realized that something was different about me. I suddenly felt like I wanted more out of life than being part of that scene."

"So you're telling me that I caused you to have some grand revelation about yourself?" she snorted.

He laughed. "I'm a little more thickheaded than that." His expression turned serious as he stared down at their entwined hands, then looked up to capture her gaze with his. "It's not an easy thing for me to admit, but all of my adult life I've been afraid to risk my heart, afraid to love. Deep down I was afraid I'd turn out to disappoint a woman the way my father had my mother. So I ran from it. I went out to clubs and dated more than my share of women to keep from becoming too involved."

Was he telling her he was incapable of loving?

Without warning, he reached over to lift her onto his lap. "But then I met you and all that changed."

"In what way?" It felt so wonderful to be in his arms, but she couldn't let herself believe that everything was going to work out between them. When she tried to get to her feet, to escape the temptation he posed, he tightened his arms around her.

"I couldn't forget your laughter, your smile. I couldn't forget you." He nuzzled her hair with his cheek. "I found myself lying in bed at night regretting that I hadn't learned your last name, where you were from and how I could keep in touch with you. And that's something that had never happened to me before."

"Never?" She had a hard time believing that he'd been able to forget every other woman he'd ever gone out with, but her.

"It's the truth, honey." He kissed her cheek. "I never thought I'd ever say this to a woman, but I think I've loved you ever since I spotted you standing there at that horse auction."

Tears welled up in her eyes as the hope within her burst free and spread throughout her being. "You love me?"

"With all of my heart, Heather." He cupped her cheek with his palm. "And I'm tired of running, honey. If you can find it in your heart to forgive me for being so thick-headed, I want it all. You, marriage, brothers and sisters for Mandy. I even want the minivan filled with car seats and clumps of dog hair."

"Are you sure?" she asked cautiously.

"I've never been more certain of anything in my entire life." His smile caused her heart to skip a beat. "I love you, Heather McGwire. Will you marry me?"

"Oh, Jake, I love you, too." The tears spilled down her cheeks. "But—"

"That's all I need to hear," he said, capturing her mouth with his.

Tracing her lips with his tongue, he deepened the kiss and she knew she had to take the chance. She loved being held by him, kissed by him. And knowing that he wanted to spend a lifetime showing her how much he cared for her caused her heart to swell with more love than she'd ever thought possible.

When he finally broke the kiss, he leaned back to gaze at her and the love she saw in his eyes stole her breath. "There's something else we need to talk about," he said, smiling.

"What would that be?"

"Where we're going to live."

She worried her lower lip for a moment. She'd never imagined herself living anywhere but in the heart of Kentucky's horse-racing country. But as long as she, Mandy and Jake were together, she could live anywhere.

"I've never lived in a huge city." She took a deep breath. "But they have horses in California, too."

Giving her a smile that made her feel warm all over, he shook his head. "Don't get me wrong, I love California. It's one of the most beautiful places on earth. But I think I'd like to live right here."

"Really? Why?" She couldn't have been more surprised. "You told Hunter you were looking for a house in Malibu."

"That will be our vacation home. I want you to be able to continue making a name for yourself in the racing industry," he said. "You have a real knack for choosing bloodlines and producing champions. I want you to have the opportunity to build your reputation as the best in the business."

"I could do that in California."

He nodded. "That's true. But you've already made Hickory Hills a force to reckon with. Why not continue to build it into a racing empire?"

Loving him more with each passing second, she laid her head on his shoulder. "What about your law office? It's in Los Angeles and quite successful. Are you sure you want to give all of that up?"

"Honey, I can practice law anywhere." He shrugged. "But to tell you the truth, I'm tired of helping people end their marriages." He paused a moment. "I think I'd like to give being a gentleman farmer a try and help my wife raise her champion thoroughbreds." He laughed. "Besides, having me around all of the time is going to save you and Clara a lot of grief."

She sat up to stare at him. "I don't understand."

"Mandy can practice her food-fighting skills on me, instead of you." He smiled. "And Daily's a good kid, but he's a lot like I was at that age."

"Heaven help us," Heather said, rolling her eyes.

His low chuckle sent a shiver coursing through her. "No kidding. I think Clara is going to have her hands full when he gets a little older and could use the help."

"I know she'll appreciate it."

Content with being in each other's arms, they remained silent for some time before he spoke again. "You never did give me an answer, honey."

"About getting married?"

He nodded. "You said you love me, but you haven't officially accepted my proposal. Will you marry me, Heather McGwire?"

"Yes."

"How soon?" His grin was bright enough to light a small city. "We've already wasted a year being apart and I'd like to make you mine as soon as possible."

Before she could tell him that she wanted that, too, the sound of the front door opening and several people entering the house intruded.

"It appears that your family has made it back from the victory party."

"Good." He set her on her feet, then rose to take her by the hand. "Let's go share our news with them."

When they walked out of the study arm in arm, everyone fell silent and turned to look at them expectantly.

His eyes never leaving hers, he announced, "I've asked Heather to marry me and she said yes."

Apparently shocked by the news, silence reigned, then everyone seemed to start talking at once.

"I'm so happy for you both," Arielle said, rushing over to give both of them a hug.

Luke laughed. "I told you so, Jake."

"Have you set a date?" Hunter wanted to know.

Smiling, Heather shook her head. "We haven't gotten that far."

Jake kissed the top of her head. "It can't be soon enough for me. If I had my way, we'd be standing in front of a minister right now."

"Me, too," Heather said, gazing up at the only man she'd ever love.

"Do you mean that?" Alyssa asked, stepping forward.

When they both nodded, Heather watched the women exchange a brief look a moment before Arielle spoke up, "We can do this, girls."

"Absolutely," Callie agreed. "Would tomorrow evening work for both of you?"

"Yes, but we can't possibly get ready in time," Heather said, disappointed. "Tomorrow is Sunday. We can't even get a marriage license until Monday."

"Don't underestimate this bunch," Haley said, laughing.

"Let's make a list." Cheyenne reached into her purse for a notepad and pen. "Nick, go get Emerald and Luther. We're going to need their help with this."

"Yes, ma'am," Nick said, his grin wide as he left the house.

When he returned with the elderly pair, Emerald breezed into the room in her satin and chiffon robe to hug Jake and Heather. "This is wonderful. I can't tell you how happy I am for you." Then, before Heather's eyes, the woman turned from a doting grandmother into a decisive, corporate giant on a mission. "Luther, find out who we know in the Louisville city government and get them to open the clerk's office first thing tomorrow morning so the kids can get their license."

Distinguished-looking even in his slippers and robe, the older gentleman gave a stiff nod. "Consider it done, madam."

Turning back to the group, Emerald continued, "Caleb, Hunter and Nick, call your nannies and baby-sitters and tell them my corporate jet will pick them and the children up by noon tomorrow. I want the entire family to be here for this. Luke, you and Zach are assigned to helping the girls with whatever they need to pull all of this together."

"Wow!" Heather could understand why Emerald Larson was the highly successful businesswoman she was. Seeing her in action was like watching a battlefield general direct his troops.

"Heather, dear, would you prefer the ceremony be performed here or do you have somewhere else in mind?" Emerald asked, smiling.

There was no question in Heather's mind. "Right here."

"Excellent. Indoors or outside?"

"I've always dreamed of coming down that staircase

to meet my groom at the bottom of the steps," Heather answered, pointing toward the sweeping structure.

Jake gave her a tender smile. "And I'll be there waiting for you."

"Another excellent choice," Emerald approved. Turning to Heather's soon-to-be sisters-in-law, the woman grinned. "Divide up the list and get started first thing in the morning, girls. We have a wedding to get ready for tomorrow evening."

When Jake walked out of the master suite the next evening, Luke was waiting for him. "Are you ready to take the plunge?"

"I never thought I'd ever hear myself say this, but it can't be too soon," Jake admitted as they descended the stairs.

Taking his place at the bottom of the steps, he looked around. He'd never loved or appreciated his family more. They'd all worked hard to pull a wedding together on the spur of the moment and everything was picture-perfect. Heather was going to love it.

When the string quartet began to play, Jake's attention was drawn to the top of the stairs and the sight of his bride robbed him of breath. Heather was absolutely stunning. Her golden brown hair lay in soft curls around her bare shoulders and the white lace and antique satin wedding gown emphasized her enticing figure. But it was her radiant smile that he knew he'd never forget as long as he lived.

As she came down the circular staircase, he heard the baby start fussing, and walking over to Clara, took Mandy from her. Then, with his daughter in one arm, he extended his other to her beautiful mother and together they walked over to stand in front of the minister to exchange their vows and become the family he wanted with all of his heart and soul.

"Oh, Luther, I was so afraid this day might never happen," Emerald said as she dabbed her eyes with her linen handkerchief. "I was worried that Jake would turn out to be like his father and remain an irresponsible philanderer for the rest of his life."

"There was that possibility, madam," Luther agreed, nodding.

As she watched the minister pronounce Jake and Heather husband and wife, Emerald couldn't help but feel a bit sad. The investigative team she'd hired to find all of her grandchildren had concluded their search and they'd reported back that there were no more heirs to be found. Her family was finally complete.

When the group gathered in the foyer for pictures, Emerald motioned for Luther to join her. "You need to be in the picture, too, Luther. You've been instrumental in helping me find my heirs."

"It was my pleasure, madam," he said, walking over to stand at her side.

"You know, I'm going to miss helping my grandchildren find their soul mates," she whispered wistfully as the photographer tried to get the children to stand still for the picture.

"You've done a fine job with that task, madam," Luther said, keeping his voice low as he patted her hand. "They've all made good matches."

"After all of the unhappiness that my son caused, I'm pleased that we were able to make everything right and give them all their rightful place in Emerald, Inc."

Clasping his hand with hers, she gave it a little squeeze. "Now, I can concentrate on trying to find my own bliss."

He squeezed her hand back. "I don't think you'll have far to look, madam," he said gruffly.

Turning, she gave him a happy smile. "Neither do I, Luther. Neither do I."

Epilogue

One year later

"Do any of you have the slightest idea why we've been summoned to Wichita?" Jake looked at his brothers and brother-in-law expectantly as they sat in the family room at Emerald's Wichita mansion. When they all shook their heads, he shrugged. "Me neither."

"All she told me was our presence was mandatory," Luke said, setting the baby bottle down and shifting his six-month-old son to his shoulder to be burped.

"Yeah, I told her I had plans to go to a cattle auction in Denver and she told me to cancel it," Nick added.

"Arielle has become pretty close to Emerald," Hunter said, looking thoughtful. "Does she know anything, Zach?"

"If she does, she didn't tell me," he said, glancing

over to check on his eight-month-old twin boys sleeping peacefully in their baby carriers beside his chair.

"When are she and our wives supposed to return from their shopping trip?" Caleb asked. "All of the kids will be waking up from their naps pretty soon and it'll turn into a three-ring circus again."

Hunter grinned. "Yeah, with ten kids between us, it does get a little hairy sometimes."

"This time next year, there'll be eleven," Jake said proudly. "We just found out Heather is pregnant."

"Make that an even dozen," Nick said, laughing. "Cheyenne is pregnant again, too."

"More like a baker's dozen," Caleb added, grinning like a fool. "Alyssa is close to entering her second trimester."

As they all congratulated each other, Emerald, Luther and their wives walked into the room. "I would imagine you're all wondering why I've asked you here for the weekend," Emerald said, smiling.

"It's crossed our minds a time or two," Luke said dryly.

When Heather walked over to sit on the arm of the chair beside him, Jake put his arm around her waist and gazed up at her. He couldn't believe how happy he'd been in the past year. Marrying her was the best thing he'd ever done. He loved her more with each passing day.

"I have a couple of announcements to make that will have a direct impact on all of you," she said, seating herself in an empty armchair.

"You have our attention," Jake said, watching Luther move to stand beside Emerald. Something was definitely up. Normally as stiff as a board, Jake had never seen the old gent look so relaxed.

"I'm retiring," Emerald said without preamble.

Jake was certain he could have heard a pin drop in the suddenly silent room. The first to find his voice, he asked, "When?"

"Next month." She paused to let the information sink in, then added, "And I'm appointing all of you to the Emerald, Inc. board of directors. I'll maintain ten percent of my stock, but the other ninety percent will be divided equally between my six grandchildren."

"Are you sure you want to do this?" Arielle asked, clearly concerned. "You started out with a home business fifty years ago and built Emerald, Inc. into a corporate empire. It's been your life."

Emerald smiled serenely. "I'm getting ready to enter a new chapter in my life."

"What are you up to this time?" Hunter asked, grinning.

Jake watched her glance at Luther and for the first time since he met the older man, Luther grinned.

"Your grandmother is going to do me the honor of becoming my bride," Luther said, placing his hand on her shoulder.

"We'll be getting married right after we both retire," Emerald said, placing her hand on Luther's. "Then we intend to take an extended honeymoon and travel the world. So I'm counting on all of you to see that Emerald, Inc. remains solid and the gold standard for corporate excellence."

After everyone expressed their surprise and promised not to let their grandmother down, Jake spoke up. "I think I speak for all of us when I say we wish you every happiness. If not for you and Luther, I might never have found Heather and Mandy."

Each of his siblings agreed that if not for Emerald and her matchmaking they might not have found their spouses and true happiness.

"Is there anything we can do to help get ready for your wedding?" Haley asked.

Jake didn't think he'd ever seen a brighter smile on his grandmother's face. "As a matter of fact, there is, dear. You all did such a wonderful job with Jake and Heather's wedding that Luther and I were wondering if you'd all like to plan ours."

"I think that's our cue to retire to the media room, boys," Hunter said, rising to his feet. "The Astros are playing the Cardinals this afternoon."

"If you don't mind, I'd quite like to join you," Luther said, surprising all of them. He kissed Emerald's cheek. "If you'll excuse me, my dear. I think I'll attempt to 'bond,' as the younger generation are so fond of saying, with my future grandsons."

"There just might be hope for you yet, Luther," Jake said, standing to shake the older man's hand.

To his surprise, Luther actually winked. "I have twenty that says the Cardinals win. Anyone want to place a little wager?"

As Emerald watched her grandsons and the man who had stood by her side for over forty years leave to watch the ball game together, she smiled contentedly. In her day, children born out of wedlock had been considered illegitimate and in some cases went unclaimed by their families. But she'd never considered her grandchildren illegitimate. She'd searched high and low to find them and now her life was filled with more happiness than she'd ever thought possible.

She'd done everything in her power to help each one of them discover their own happiness, and to her immense satisfaction they had.

* * * * *

THE BABY SURPRISE

Brenda Harlen

For Courtney & Terri—
representatives of the new generation
of romance readers.
Thanks for being such loyal fans
(and for Zach's name).

Prologue

Paige Wilder had less than zero experience with kids, but when Olivia Lowell, a friend and coworker at Wainwright, Witmer & Wynne, asked if she would be her birthing coach, she didn't know how to say no to the single-mother-to-be. And despite her initial apprehension, the event of Emma's birth was the singular most amazing experience of Paige's entire life.

So when, several months later, Olivia asked her to watch the baby overnight, Paige had agreed. With both Ashley and Megan—her cousins and two best friends—now in the early stages of pregnancy, she figured it was a good time to get some babysitting experience and that she was up for the challenge.

A decision she was fervently regretting by 5:00 a.m. when she laid Emma in her crib and fell facedown on the narrow bed in Olivia's guest room. Around midnight, she'd finally set aside the pretrial memorandum she'd been working on and decided to go to sleep. About the same time, the usually-charming infant woke up screaming like a banshee, and she'd repeated the performance almost every hour on the hour since then.

If nothing else, the experience reminded Paige why she'd never thought about having a child of her own. She was simply in awe of any parent who could deal with a crying child through all hours and still manage to get up and go to work the next morning.

As she finally drifted to sleep, she sent up a weary prayer of thanks that this babysitting assignment was only for one night.

Three days later, she found out otherwise.

Owen Wynne, the senior partner who had hired her to work at the firm almost six years earlier, set aside the pages from which he'd finished reading and looked across the desk at her.

Paige, still reeling from the shock that her friend had been killed in a car accident, struggled to comprehend the words he had spoken. "But what does that mean?"

"It means that you are now Emma Jane Lowell's legal guardian," he said patiently.

"That can't be right," she said, her tone tinged with equal parts desperation and disbelief.

Owen frowned. "I'd assumed, when Olivia came to me about drafting her will, that she'd already discussed this with you."

She could only shake her head.

"Well, then, you're certainly entitled to deny her request," he assured her.

And Paige knew what would happen if she did—

nine-month-old Emma would end up in the system. It was possible that the baby would be adopted by a wonderful couple and loved as if she was their own. Or she might bounce from one foster home to another until she'd reached an age where the state was no longer concerned with her care.

Either way, Olivia's daughter would never know anything about her mother; she would never know how much she had been loved.

But still Paige hesitated. "I don't know anything about kids."

"Neither did I, when I first became a father," Owen admitted.

"What about Emma's father?" she asked, clearly grasping. "Are you sure Olivia never mentioned his name?"

"Not to me."

Not to Paige, either, other than to insist that she'd had no contact with him since she'd told him she was pregnant. Her friend had always been a private person, but Paige had worried that, in this instance, she'd been so tight-lipped because the man already had a family.

"You don't have to make a final decision today," Owen told her.

Except that the decision had been made for her when Olivia named Paige as her daughter's legal guardian. Why Olivia had chosen her would probably always be a mystery, but she couldn't disregard her friend's final wishes.

"Yes, I do," she said. "I want this settled, for Emma's sake."

Paige wanted to ensure that Olivia's baby had the

kind of stable childhood that she herself had never known.

But when the papers were signed and she walked out of Owen's office with Emma in her arms, she felt anything but settled. And she couldn't shake the feeling that even the best-laid plans could go awry.

Chapter 1

Five months later

As a little girl, Paige had never really felt as if she had a home, as if there was anywhere she truly belonged. Growing up as the only child of a divorced Army colonel, she'd left too many homes and too many friends to count, an experience that had taught her early on not to get too attached to anyplace or anyone.

When she was fifteen, her father had decided that Paige was too much trouble to keep with him and had sent her to live with his sister and her family. Even then, Paige had mostly kept to herself. In fact, for the first six months she'd refused to put her clothes in the dresser of the room she'd been told was her own, certain she would need to pack up and leave again as soon as she felt settled.

But six months had turned into a year and then two, and Paige found herself growing close to Ashley and Megan, the two sisters who were her cousins and now also her best friends.

Still, her aunt's residence had never felt like home so much as a house that she was visiting. Even when Paige moved into her own condo in Syracuse, it was little more than a place to store her belongings and lay her head. But there was a house on Chetwood Street in Pinehurst, New York, that Ashley and Megan had purchased a few years earlier, and Paige felt more at home there than anywhere else she'd ever lived. So maybe it wasn't surprising that it was where she went when her life fell apart.

She had called both of her cousins to let them know that she wanted to come home for a while and to make sure they didn't mind if she stayed at the currently empty house. Megan had been the first to move out, when she'd married Gage Richmond the previous year, followed by Ashley, who had vacated the premises only a month ago, after her wedding to Cameron Turcotte. The sisters had decided to list the house for sale but hadn't yet taken any steps in that direction, so Paige had proposed that she rent the property for the summer.

She really wasn't sure how long she intended to stay. Her career as a family-law attorney usually kept her too busy to allow for anything more than a long weekend, and even then she usually worked extra hours both before and after in order to make up for the time away from her office. As for an actual vacation, she honestly couldn't remember the last time she'd taken one, although she had taken more than the occasional day here and there over the past five months—a fact that had not gone unnoticed by the partners who were now concerned about her apparent lack of commitment to her clients and the firm.

It was the reason for this hiatus, which came with the recommendation that she take the time to think about what she wanted for her future. As if having full-time care of a fourteen-month-old baby allowed one time to think.

At first she'd been so shocked by the suggestion that she hadn't known what to say or do. Her immediate instinct had been to insist that she wanted what she'd always wanted—a partnership at the firm. It was what she'd been working toward for the past half-dozen years. But when she'd picked Emma up from the sitter after work, she'd accepted that a lot had changed in the past five months, that taking care of Emma had changed her.

And if it really came down to a choice between having her name stenciled on the wall behind the reception desk at Wainwright, Witmer & Wynne or providing an orphaned little girl with some semblance of family, well, there really wasn't a choice to be made. Because she loved that little girl with her whole heart.

That realization had been a simple one, but it was followed by some tough questions. Most notably, if she chose at this point in her life to walk away from the career she had only recently started to build, where would she go? What would she do?

It was these concerns that had directed her toward Pinehurst, New York.

Unfortunately, almost a week later, she still wasn't any closer to figuring out if she could balance her professional obligations and personal responsibilities, or even if she wanted to.

It was difficult enough to accept that Emma would never know her mother or father, but the demands of Paige's career required that she leave the child with a babysitter for ten hours a day. Of course, Annabelle was a wonderful caregiver who had been chosen by Olivia to take care of her daughter, but that knowledge did little to alleviate Paige's feelings of guilt.

These thoughts were weighing on her mind Thursday night when she was startled by a brisk knock on the door. A quick glance at the glowing numbers on the front of the DVD player revealed that it was 8:12 p.m., but because Emma had been fussing for so long and had only just fallen asleep, it felt much later.

She pushed herself up from the chair, careful not to jostle the baby, and hurried toward the door. She'd spoken to both Ashley and Megan earlier in the day and neither had made mention of any plan to stop by, and because both of them had keys to the house, it was safe to assume that someone else was knocking.

Shifting Emma to her other shoulder, she hastily tugged open the door before the uninvited guest could knock again.

She noticed his eyes first. Dark blue, intensely focused and strangely familiar. And when those eyes locked on her, she felt an unexpected surge of heat through her veins, an unwelcome sizzle in her blood.

Then she noticed the uniform, and everything inside of her went cold.

"Are you Paige Wilder?"

His voice was deep and sexy, and she felt that sizzle again. But ignored it.

"I am," she admitted. "Though I don't know why my

identity would be of any interest to a lieutenant colonel in the United States Air Force."

His brows lifted, as if he was surprised by her accurate reading of his uniform insignia, and she was struck again not just by the intensity of his gaze, but also the rugged handsomeness of the whole face. His skin was tanned and taut over his sharp cheekbones and strong jaw. His hair was dark and glossy and short. He was well over six feet—probably six-three, she guessed—and his shoulders were broad, his torso long and lean, his legs even longer.

The overall effect was one that any woman could appreciate, and Paige was no exception. Apparently fifteen years as an army brat hadn't inoculated her against the effect of a handsome man in uniform, but five years as an attorney had taught her the wisdom of looking beneath the surface.

"I'm not here in an official capacity," he assured her.

"Then why are you here?"

"I'm Zach Crawford—" his gaze shifted to the baby curled up against her chest, then back to her "—Emma's father."

Emma's father.

The words echoed in Paige's mind, the implications sweeping through her with the chilling intensity of a bitter winter wind, numbing everything inside of her despite the warmth of the late-May evening. She instinctively tightened her hold on the baby in her arms and took a step back, away from this stranger's outrageous claim.

The man standing on the porch interpreted her action as an invitation and moved forward. She shook her head and stood rooted in his path.

"Emma doesn't have a father," she told him.

Amusement glinted in those all-too-familiar eyes.

Emma's eyes.

She desperately pushed that thought aside, trying to convince herself that his eyes were simply blue and any perceived resemblance was nothing more than that.

"Are you really that unfamiliar with basic biology, Ms. Wilder?" he asked.

She felt her cheeks heat in response to the unexpected teasing note in his deep voice. "Olivia told me that Emma's father wasn't interested in being a father," she clarified.

"Then she lied," he said bluntly.

Paige shook her head again. "She named me as Emma's guardian because she had no other family. Because Emma had no other family."

"Except that's not exactly true, either."

She couldn't believe it—didn't want to believe it. Why would Olivia have lied about something like that? And, more importantly, what did this man's presence here now mean for the little girl sleeping in her arms?

"Look, I can see that this has caught you off guard," he said. "And I'm sure we both have a lot of questions that, if you let me come in, we could discuss without the neighbors watching."

A quick glance across the street confirmed that Melanie Quinlan, an attractive young divorcée who made no secret of the fact that she was on the hunt for husband number two, was in her front yard, garden hose in hand to water the flowers she'd just finished planting. Except that her attention was on the uniformed stranger, so she was actually watering her porch rather than the colorful blossoms in the bed in front of it.

Paige lifted her free hand to wave, and the other woman smiled and waved back enthusiastically, not even trying to hide the fact that her attention was riveted to the scene playing out in front of her—or at least on the man who was part of that scene.

"If I said no, would you go away?" Paige asked Zach. "No."

She sighed and stepped away from the door. "Just let me put Emma down."

She wasn't sure why she thought he might protest, why she thought he might want to hold the child he claimed was his own—or at least take a closer look at her—but she was undeniably relieved when he let her go without a word. She felt his gaze on her, though, the weight of that intense stare heavier than the child in her arms, and wondered why it made her feel all hot and tingly inside.

She worried over that as she carefully laid Emma on her back in the crib and bent to touch her lips to the baby's soft cheek. She inhaled the scent of baby shampoo and felt tears sting her eyes. She'd started to take this nightly ritual for granted, and now the appearance of a stranger at her door threatened not just this special time she shared with the little girl, but also the whole future she'd envisioned for them together.

She'd never thought about having a child of her own. Even when it was all her friends and family had been talking about, she'd been too busy with her career to spare a single thought to motherhood. But then Emma had come into her life, and suddenly stepping into the role wasn't a choice but a necessity.

She'd had to make a lot of adjustments when she learned that Olivia had named her as Emma's guardian, and not without resistance, at least in the beginning. But it hadn't taken Paige long to realize that Emma hadn't just changed her life, she'd enriched it. The little girl's presence made her think about things she hadn't thought about before. Playing the part of her guardian made her appreciate what it meant to be a mother when that wasn't something Paige had ever considered.

But through all of the transitions and adjustments, Paige had never imagined that someday someone might turn up in her life and lay claim to the child, as Zach Crawford had just done.

Olivia had always been stubbornly closemouthed about the man who had fathered her child. It was the only topic about which Paige had ever really argued with her friend. She didn't care about the identity of the man except insofar as she believed he should bear some responsibility for the child he'd helped create.

She'd been frustrated by Olivia's stoic determination, but her friend had always maintained that she could do it alone—and she wanted to. She knew that there were people who whispered about her situation—not because she was an unwed mother-to-be but because they knew that having to shoulder the responsibility on her own would limit the professional opportunities available to her. She would no longer be able to schedule late-night meetings or quick out-of-town trips for the convenience of a client, and at Wainwright, Witmer & Wynne, imposing such limitations was akin to career suicide.

The few female partners at the firm had done everything but handstands to prove they deserved to be there. And any woman who happened to be a mother *and* a lawyer was even more suspect because—God forbid—she might put her family responsibilities ahead of her obligations to the firm. Karen Rosario had waited until she'd made partner to start a family and gave birth to her first baby at age forty-two. And then she hired a live-in nanny to raise the child she'd supposedly wanted so much.

When Paige decided to go into law, she hadn't considered how difficult it might be to someday balance her career with a family. But she'd thought about it a lot after Olivia told her she was pregnant, and the more she'd thought about it, the angrier she'd become thinking that Olivia was making all of the sacrifices while the man who'd gotten her pregnant—whoever he might be—had simply walked away from his responsibilities.

Maybe it was the lawyer in her, but Paige had wanted to track him down and slap him with a paternity suit to ensure that he at least shared financial responsibility for the baby he'd helped make.

"It's a lot of responsibility to handle on your own," Paige said to her friend, cautiously broaching the topic she'd avoided for the past several months because she'd been certain Olivia would tell her about the baby's father when she was ready. But so far, she'd volunteered nothing.

"I know."

"Are you sure you have to do it alone? Maybe the father—"

"No," Olivia interrupted quickly. "This has nothing to do with him."

"You're an attorney—you know better than that. Whether you like it or not, it's his baby, too, and that means he has both legal rights and responsibilities."

"He has enough responsibilities without adding a child—especially one that neither of us planned—into the mix."

The comment gave her pause, but Paige finally asked, "Is he married?"

She was relieved when Olivia laughed at the question.

"Married? No, he's not married. And he's not the kind of guy who would cheat on his wife if he was."

"But he's the kind of guy who would abandon the woman who's pregnant with his child?" she challenged.

Her friend looked away. "Drop it, Paige. Please."

Because she could tell that Olivia was still hurting, and because she knew better than anyone that a man couldn't be forced to feel something for a child he didn't want, she'd dropped it.

And Olivia had never told her anything else about her baby's father, not even his name, which meant that Paige had a lot of questions for Lieutenant Colonel Zach Crawford.

She headed back downstairs now, determined to get some answers.

Zach was still standing in the hallway where she'd left him, his feet shoulder-width apart, his hands clasped behind his back. Paige recognized the military stance but, in conjunction with the uniform, it left her feeling anything but "at ease."

She moved toward the kitchen, and he fell into step behind her. She'd spent countless hours in this room, usually with Ashley or Megan or both, and she'd never felt as if the space was small. But something about Zach's presence made her feel...crowded. She was far too aware of him—his impressive height, his obvious strength, his overwhelming masculinity.

She glanced at him as she reached for the empty carafe from the coffeemaker, and she swallowed hard when she found those intense and stunningly blue eyes on her. The tug of attraction came again, and she found herself as annoyed as she was baffled by it.

Of all the times for her body to suddenly decide it had been in stasis for too long, now was not a good one. And even if it had been a good time, Zach Crawford was definitely not a man she should ever find herself attracted to. Not just because of the uniform, but because he had once been intimately involved with one of her best friends.

It occurred to her that the uniform might have been why her friend had never told her about the man who had fathered her child. Because Olivia knew something of Paige's history with her father, she knew Paige would question her decision to get involved with a man who could never make her or their daughter a priority in his life.

She was considering this as she turned on the tap to fill the carafe. "Do you want coffee?" she asked Zach.

"I've been on the go since oh-five-hundred," he told her. "I would love coffee."

She'd been up since oh-five-hundred herself—5:00 a.m. to nonmilitary people—and she would have preferred to skip the coffee and sink into her mattress and into the oblivion of sleep as peacefully as Emma had finally done.

But she knew she wouldn't get any sleep tonight—not until she had some answers to the questions that had been swirling through her brain since Lieutenant

Colonel Zach Crawford had spoken the two words that continued to echo in her mind.

Emma's father.

If it was true, if Lieutenant Colonel Zach Crawford really was the father of Olivia's baby, that simple fact would change everything.

Paige worried over the possibility as she put a filter in the basket and measured out the grounds.

It was easy to see how Olivia might have been attracted to the man. Over and above the fact that he was six feet three inches of mouthwatering masculinity, he moved with a sense of purpose and carried himself with an aura of command that were as much a part of who he was as those blue, blue eyes.

She reached into the cupboard for two mugs and filled them from the carafe.

"Cream? Sugar?" she asked him.

"Just black, thanks."

She handed him one of the mugs and added a splash of milk to the other.

He waited until she'd taken a seat at the pub-style table in the dining room, then sat down across from her.

"I understand you worked at Wainwright, Witmer & Wynne with Olivia?"

She nodded.

"You were good friends?"

"Since our first year at law school together," she told him.

"She never mentioned you to me."

"She never mentioned you to me, either," she told him. "In fact, she never said anything about Emma's father."

He raised an eyebrow. "Nothing at all?"

"The only thing she ever told me, and only when I asked where the baby's father fit into the picture, was that he wasn't interested in playing any role in his child's life."

He scowled at that. "I might not have been thrilled by the news of her pregnancy, if she'd ever bothered to tell me, but she had to know there was no way in hell I would abandon my child."

"If Olivia never told you she was pregnant, how did you find out? And how do you know that you are Emma's father?"

"Well, at this point, I'm not one-hundred-percent certain," he admitted. "But I have a letter from Olivia that says I am, and I have no reason to disbelieve it."

"You just said Olivia lied."

"She lied to *you*," he clarified, "if she told you that I didn't want to know my child. Because the truth is, I didn't know about the baby. Not until I got home from Afghanistan and found the letter she'd left for me."

"Olivia died five-and-a-half months ago," Paige told him, with an ache in her heart that was more for the child who would never know her mother than for the premature end of her friend's life.

A shadow—grief? regret?—momentarily clouded those stunning blue eyes, but then it passed and he nodded. "I found that out when I went to your law firm to find her. The receptionist told me about the accident."

"No one knows why she was in New Jersey," Paige admitted.

He sipped his coffee, then set the mug down again. "I live in Trenton," he told her. "Or maybe it would be more accurate to say that I have an apartment about five minutes from the base, which is where I sleep when I'm in town."

"She went...to see you?"

He nodded, confirming another fact that seemed to give credence to his claim of paternity. Of course, Paige wasn't going to take his word for it, nor was she simply going to hand over a child on the basis of his say-so.

"My landlord told me a young woman stopped by looking for me early in the new year. When he told her I was overseas, she left a letter for me."

"Do you have the letter?"

He took it out of the inside pocket of his jacket and passed it across the table to her.

Apprehension whispered through her as she picked up the envelope. Her fingers trembled as she lifted the flap and pulled out the single page.

Zach,
I'm sure you're wondering why you're hearing from me now, after so much time has passed, especially since I was the one who asked you not to contact me, so I'll get straight to the point. You have a daughter...

Chapter 2

Paige sucked in a breath, startled to see the words clearly written there, supporting this stranger's claim to the little girl in her care. She wanted to crumple the letter in her fist, to stuff the paper back in the envelope and tell Zach to take it away, to tell him to go away—far away from Emma. But she forced herself to read on.

When she was done, she refolded the letter and tucked it in the envelope again, then slid it across the table to him. She picked up her half-empty coffee cup then set it down without drinking, her stomach churning.

"With all due respect, I have no intention of giving up custody of Emma just because you showed up on my doorstep with a letter that claims you're her father."

"A letter written by her mother," he pointed out.

She couldn't be one-hundred-percent sure that Olivia

had actually written the letter. In an age of computers and e-mail and text messaging, she honestly didn't recognize the handwriting as her friend's. However, why would this man be here now if he didn't believe it was true?

"Even so, Olivia never identified you as the father on Emma's birth certificate," she reminded him.

"Did she name anyone else?"

She ignored his question. "I was Olivia's birthing coach—I went to prenatal classes with her and I was in the delivery room when Emma was born. And through it all, Olivia never once mentioned your name. And, contrary to what is in that letter, she claimed that Emma's father knew of the pregnancy but wanted no part of his child."

"That was the lie," he said again.

And the contents of the letter he carried certainly bore that out. But she wasn't ready to give up, she wasn't ready to have her heart torn out of her chest, and she knew that was what would happen if he took Emma away.

"Still, I think the best course of action right now would be to have a paternity test."

He frowned into his empty mug, then pushed back his chair to refill it. "Fine," he said. "How soon can we get that done?"

"I can make some calls tomorrow," she told him. "But probably not until sometime next week."

His scowl deepened.

"And you're going to need a lawyer," she told him.

"Aren't you a lawyer?"

"Yes, but I'm not going to represent you."

"Why in hell do I need representation?"

"Because…" She hesitated, not wanting to give him any ideas about seeking custody if that wasn't a course of action he'd already considered. Maybe he didn't want Emma with him—maybe he just wanted to meet the little girl he believed was his daughter. So all she said was, "Because you should make sure you understand all of your rights and responsibilities."

"I'm aware of my rights and responsibilities," he assured her. "And I intend to be a father to my daughter."

Which still didn't tell her whether he was looking for full custody or standard every-other-weekend noncustodial parent access or occasional visits during his periods of leave.

"For how long?" she asked.

He frowned at the question. "What do you mean?"

"When do you have to report back for duty?"

"July seventh."

Which was actually longer than she'd expected and still not nearly long enough if he was serious about building a relationship with Emma. "So why are you even here?"

"What do you mean?"

"I mean, why did you bother to come all this way, feign an interest in being a father to the child you claim is your own, if you're going to go wheels up again in a few weeks?"

"I'm not feigning an interest," he said. "And I'll go wheels up again because that's my job."

"And if Emma is your daughter, who will take care of her while you're doing your job?"

Zach was taken aback, not just by Paige's question—which demonstrated the glaringly obvious fact that he hadn't thought very far ahead when he'd embarked on this journey—but by the disapproval in her tone.

Okay, so maybe he didn't have all of the answers. Maybe he didn't have *any* of the answers. But he was determined to do the right thing and, as far as he could tell, being a father to his daughter was the right thing.

"I don't know," he admitted. "But I'll make arrangements."

"You mean day care," she guessed.

"Didn't you have her in day care?"

"Olivia had found a babysitter who lives close to the office. It's a more personal environment than a day care and Emma's happy there."

"That's great," Zach said. "Except that I live in New Jersey."

Paige dipped her head, her coppery hair falling forward to hide her face, but not before he saw the tears that filled her eyes.

He silently cursed himself for his insensitivity. Because he knew that as much as he'd been completely blindsided by the news that he had fathered a child, this woman had been just as shocked to find him standing at her door. For the past five-and-a-half months she'd been raising Emma. She'd been responsible for the day-to-day care of his child and, with a few simple words, he'd threatened to destroy the foundation of that relationship.

He impulsively reached across the table and touched a hand to her arm.

She jolted at the unexpected contact. Or maybe she'd been startled by the electricity that suddenly crackled in the air. It had sure as hell startled him.

She looked at him now, and he saw both wariness and awareness in the depths of her dark brown eyes.

He'd expected her to have green eyes to go with the red hair. Instead, they were the color of rich, dark chocolate and sinfully tempting. His gaze dipped to her mouth, to lips that were naturally pink and sweetly curved, and he found himself wondering if they would taste as good as they looked.

Whoa—totally inappropriate thought there.

This woman was the legal guardian of his daughter, and it was unlikely he would gain either her trust or sympathy by making a move on her within two hours of meeting her. But he couldn't deny he was tempted.

Of course, he'd been overseas for the past year and a half and hadn't been with a woman for even longer than that. In fact, he hadn't been with anyone since the last weekend he'd spent with Olivia…likely the weekend their daughter had been conceived.

Thinking of Emma reminded him why he was there, and he dropped his hand from Paige's arm. But the air continued to crackle, the tension continued to build.

"I don't want us to be adversaries," he said at last.

"I don't see how we can be anything else, not if it's your intention to disrupt Emma's life."

"I want to get to know my daughter. How is that disruptive?"

"The disruption will come when you disappear from her life as abruptly as you appeared in it."

She spoke with such conviction he guessed it was likely that she'd grown up with a father who was a transitory presence, too. He knew he had no hope of defending himself against her personal demons, so he only said, "Maybe we should continue this conversation tomorrow."

"Why?"

"Because I just got home last night, I read Olivia's letter this morning, then drove from Trenton to Syracuse to Pinehurst, all the while trying to get my head around the fact that I have a fourteen-month-old child I didn't know anything about before today."

"I thought you'd be going back to New Jersey tomorrow, if not sooner."

"You mean you wished I was."

She didn't deny it.

"I'm not going anywhere until we figure this out," he assured her.

"Unless duty calls," she guessed.

"I have almost two months."

But the skepticism in her eyes warned that she knew it was a promise he couldn't make and confirmed that Paige's apparent disapproval of his career was about more than the possibility of his deployment interfering with his ability to get to know Emma.

"Then I guess I'll see you tomorrow," she said.

"What time is good?"

"Not oh-five-hundred," she warned.

He smiled. "How about oh-nine-hundred?"

"A much more civilized hour."

Zach wished her a good-night and made his way to the door.

His first meeting with Paige Wilder hadn't gone as well as he'd hoped. But nothing had gone quite as he'd expected since his plane had touched down at McGuire Air Force Base twenty-eight hours earlier. From the shocking news revealed by Olivia's letter to his unexpected and undeniable reaction to Paige Wilder, his life was suddenly FUBAR.

Yet, as he made his way to his SUV, he realized he was whistling and already looking forward to tomorrow.

Zach had spotted a couple of hotels on Main Street when he'd driven through town earlier, so he started to retrace his route, figuring he would check into the first one that he came across. He found "Hadfield House— A Bed-and-Breakfast" first. The sign outside promised private baths and hot breakfasts, but Zach only cared that there was an empty bed because he was too exhausted to go much farther.

Thankfully he always traveled with a duffel bag packed with a change of clothes and some basic toiletries—he certainly hadn't planned on staying overnight. He hadn't planned on being gone more than a few hours—just long enough to make the trip into Syracuse, talk to Olivia, demand an explanation for the letter and her silence, and try to figure out what the hell they were supposed to do now.

The news that Olivia was dead had been as much a shock as her revelation about the baby. And although he grieved the death of the vibrant young woman, he was also frustrated by the realization that he wouldn't ever have the opportunity to confront her and demand answers to the questions that crowded his mind.

Early that morning, when he'd read Olivia's letter— and reread it over and over again, as if doing so might somehow change the words that were written—he'd tried to call her, but both her home and cell numbers were out of service. At the time, he'd been more annoyed than concerned by the realization, but he'd decided that the conversation they needed to have should be face-to-face, and he'd driven to the apartment building she'd lived in while they were dating.

When he got there, he found that her name was no longer on the tenant directory and his inquiries of the landlord only revealed that she no longer lived there. His next stop was the law firm where she worked, and when he walked through the heavy glass doors of the law offices of Wainwright, Witmer & Wynne, he'd been confident that he was getting closer to the answers he sought.

It was the receptionist—Louise Pringle, according to the nameplate on her desk—who'd told him, with tears in her eyes, that Olivia had been killed in a motor-vehicle collision more than five months earlier.

He'd had to swallow around the lump of guilt and regrets that had lodged in his throat before he could ask, "Did she have her baby with her?"

"Oh, no. Paige was babysitting the little angel, and thank the good Lord for that."

Relief shuddered through his system, assuring him that, although the news about the baby had rocked him to the very core, he wanted a chance to know his child, to be a father to his little girl.

"Paige?" he prompted.

"Paige Wilder. She's another one of the attorneys here. She has legal custody of Emma now."

"Is it possible for me to see Ms. Wilder?"

"She's out of town," the efficient Louise had said, consulting the schedule on her computer. "But Victoria Lawrence might be able to squeeze you in around two o'clock tomorrow."

"Thanks, but I really need to see Ms. Wilder," he

had said. "Do you have a number where I could contact her?"

The older woman had started to shake her head, but then she eyed the uniform again and paused. "I really can't give out that kind of information," she said. "Maybe if you left your name and number and the reason you want to speak with her, I could contact Paige and ask her to get in touch with you."

"It's a personal matter."

The furrow in her brow deepened, but when she looked up at him again, her eyes suddenly widened. "Oh, I didn't realize."

"Didn't realize?" he prompted.

"You're Emma's father."

Her matter-of-fact assertion had taken him aback. Although he had originally gone to the law offices to see Olivia about that possibility, he'd been completely unprepared to hear a stranger echo his short-term girlfriend's allegation.

"What makes you say that?" he asked, as wary as he was curious.

"She has your eyes," Louise told him.

"Crawford blue" was how his mother had always referred to the color that each of her children had inherited from their father.

Although blue was a common eye color, he'd had enough people comment on the unique shade of his to realize that "Crawford blue" was distinctive. But he couldn't say for certain whether or not Olivia's child had the same color eyes because she'd been asleep when he arrived at Paige Wilder's door.

He hadn't looked at her closely enough to see if there was any other resemblance. Maybe he hadn't wanted to. He was willing to do the right thing by his child, if Emma was his child, but, if he was honest with himself, he wasn't sure he was prepared to tackle fatherhood and everything it entailed at this point in his life. He hadn't thought much about having kids at all, except in the vaguest of terms and somewhere in a still-distant future.

He was thirty-seven years old, long past the age when most of his contemporaries had settled down with a wife and kids. Some of them were even on their second or third wives, which was not a path he had any desire to follow.

But if he'd fathered a child, as Olivia claimed, he *would* be a father to that child.

And so he'd taken the address Louise had discreetly slipped to him and he'd found Paige Wilder and Emma.

He'd found his daughter.

And seeing the baby in Paige's arms had absolutely terrified him.

He'd seen and experienced some unbelievable things during his years in the Air Force, all without batting an eye. But the sight of that beautiful little girl, so small and vulnerable and completely dependent, had nearly knocked him on his ass.

After Zach left, Paige stood beside Emma's crib, tears streaming down her cheeks as the truth of the situation sank in. She could try to block Zach Crawford at every turn, she could stall him with all kinds of legal maneuvering, but her efforts would only delay the inevitable. Because she knew too well that the interest of a previously unknown father was a significant change in circumstances that could—and would—successfully challenge her custody decree.

And losing Emma would break her heart.

Why did you do it, Olivia? Why did you lie about Emma's father?

Of course, her friend couldn't answer her questions now, and Paige found herself cursing in frustration. And then she felt guilty for cursing a woman who had died so young and so tragically—a woman who had been one of her closest friends and yet, in retrospect, a woman she wasn't sure she had really known at all.

If I'd known, I would have been prepared for the possibility that Emma's father might show up someday. Instead, you let me fall in love with this child, never guessing that Zach Crawford might show up and want to take her away.

She had no doubt that was what he planned to do. A man who had risen to the rank of lieutenant colonel was undoubtedly dedicated, honorable and trustworthy—definitely not the type of man to walk away from his own child.

But maybe Emma wasn't his child. Maybe, despite Olivia's letter, her friend was mistaken about the baby's paternity. Because aside from the eye color, she really hadn't seen any resemblance between Zach and Emma. The man was a complete contrast to the child. He was so solid and strong and—

The mental image was so vivid that her heart actually skipped a beat, and Paige cursed herself for the uncharacteristic weakness. She wasn't usually the type of woman to get all fluttery and tongue-tied over a handsome man, and letting her imagination run wild with respect to Zach Crawford wasn't just futile—it was dangerous.

I don't want us to be adversaries.

But they were, and she needed to remember that and forget that the lieutenant colonel had stirred feelings she hadn't felt in a very long time.

Chapter 3

Zach didn't usually dream. Or maybe it would be more accurate to say that he didn't usually remember his dreams. But when he bolted up in bed early the next morning, the details were fresh in his mind and his heart was pounding hard and fast from the adrenaline that had surged through his system.

He scrubbed his hands over his jaw, blinked away the last remnants of slumber and reminded himself that it had only been a dream.

But it had felt so unbelievably and terrifyingly real.

He was flying an F-22 Raptor in enemy skies when the jet suddenly started to spin. He couldn't get the plane under control and he was dropping fast. He swore and he prayed, then he reached for the ejection handle.

But he felt no relief when he successfully punched out, only an escalating sense of panic when the para-

chute failed to deploy. Then he glanced down and saw
that there was a baby sitting in his lap. A tiny little girl
who looked up at him with wide, trusting blue eyes.
And all he could do was hold on to her and fervently
pray as they plunged toward the ground.

He pushed himself out of bed and strode toward the
bathroom. A quick flick of his wrist had the shower
running, and he stripped away his briefs and stepped
under the pounding spray, desperate to clear the lingering shadows of the dream from his mind.

He didn't need a psychiatric assessment to know
that learning he was a father had sent his whole world
spinning out of control. What worried him more was
to think that maybe the dream hadn't simply been a
manifestation of his own fears but an omen—a warning that his sudden appearance in Emma's life could
tear her away from the safety and security of the life
she had with her legal guardian.

And suddenly an image of Paige Wilder filled his
mind.

The gleaming coppery hair, the dark chocolate-
colored eyes and the distinctly feminine curves packed
quite a punch. There was no denying that he'd felt an
immediate jab of purely sexual attraction the moment
she'd opened her door. But it was more than her obvious
physical beauty that tugged at him. It was the stubborn
tilt of her chin, the determined glint in her eyes and the
realization that this woman was as fiercely protective
of the little girl who had been placed in her care as a
mother bear would be of her cubs.

But Zach wasn't going to be scared off by anything
she said or did because that little girl was his daughter.
He was sure of it. And he suspected that Paige was sure

of it, too, but she was going to drag things out, hoping that he would have to go wheels up again before anything was resolved.

If that was the case, Paige Wilder was in for a surprise because Zach wasn't going anywhere without his daughter.

Emma was still sound asleep when the sun started to peek over the horizon, but Paige crawled out of bed anyway. Oh-nine-hundred was definitely a more civilized hour, but she knew that the promise of French toast would be enough to summon her cousins for a quick breakfast meeting before Zach arrived.

Ashley was a first-grade teacher who'd never wanted anything more than she'd wanted a family, and in the past year she'd ended her engagement to a cheating fiancé and then married the high-school sweetheart who had moved back to town. Now she was stepmother to his darling little girl and expecting a baby of her own in just about three months. Megan was the vice president of research and development at Richmond Pharmaceuticals, married to the company president's youngest son and in her ninth month of pregnancy.

The three of them had traditionally met once a month for Sunday brunch and, occasionally, on Friday nights just to hang out together. It used to be that their social gatherings included as much wine as conversation, but that had changed in the past year since first Megan and then Ashley got pregnant and Paige learned she'd been entrusted with custody of Emma.

But the camaraderie they shared and their trust in one another hadn't changed, and Paige knew they never would. And that was why she'd come home—to be with these women who knew her better than anyone else ever had, who understood her hopes and dreams, and who would understand how confused and conflicted she was feeling right now.

As if on cue, Ashley was at the door with her seven-year-old stepdaughter just as the coffee finished brewing and Emma woke up.

"I hope you don't mind that I brought Maddie," she said. "I figured she could help keep Emma busy while we talked and then she and I can leave for school directly from here."

"Of course I don't mind," Paige said because, aside from the fact that she was grateful Ashley was there, she absolutely adored Maddie.

"Do you like French toast?" she asked.

The child's eyes sparkled as she nodded her head enthusiastically. "I *love* French toast."

"Then you get the first piece," Paige decided, dipping a slice of bread into the egg batter, then dropping it into the hot pan.

Her cousins were the reason she'd come back to Pinehurst when the proverbial rug had been pulled out from beneath her feet. Of course, she'd had no idea then that things were going to get a lot worse before they got better—and she was keeping her fingers crossed that they would get better—but she knew she could count on Ashley and Megan to stand by her and support her whatever she decided to do.

"Mmm, I smell French toast," Megan said, waddling into the kitchen a few minutes later.

"I promised you breakfast," Paige reminded her.

"So you did," Megan agreed. "But you know we would have come even without the bribe."

Paige nodded, tears stinging her eyes as she slid the spatula under the bread and flipped it in the pan.

And although she knew her cousins had to be curious about the reason for her frantic phone calls last night, they didn't press her. Instead, they worked around one another in the kitchen—Paige making the toast, Ashley serving it up for the kids, Megan brewing the herbal tea her sister had always preferred while sipping half a cup of coffee generously doctored with milk for the benefit of the baby she was carrying.

When Maddie had finished her breakfast and washed up, she took Emma into the living room to play with her, and the three adults sat down with their plates.

"Is this about the hunky guy Melanie saw you with last night?" Ashley asked.

"When did you see Melanie?" Paige countered.

"What hunky guy?" Megan wanted to know.

"Melanie was walking her dog when Maddie and I were on our way over here. She told me that there was a tall, dark-haired and very handsome man at your door last night and that you invited him inside. But not for very long, she assured me. Just about long enough for a cup of coffee, and then he was on his way again."

Paige shook her head. "Remind me again why I decided to stay here."

"Because you wanted to take some time to figure out your future, because you wanted to be closer to Megan and I, and because it's a great neighborhood where the residents look out for one another."

"Is that another way of saying 'spy on one another'?"

"Who cares about the neighborhood?" Megan said. "I want to hear about the hunky man."

Paige swirled a piece of French toast in syrup, then

set her fork down again without eating it. Even the coffee that was as necessary to her system as oxygen in the morning wasn't sitting comfortably in her stomach, and the breakfast she'd prepared held even less appeal.

"The hunky man is Lieutenant Colonel Zach Crawford of the United States Air Force. He claims—"

She thought she could get through this without any more tears, but the moisture that filled her eyes proved otherwise.

"He claims to be Emma's father."

"Emma's father?" The shock in Ashley's voice echoed Paige's initial response to Zach's announcement.

She nodded.

"Did he have any proof?" Megan demanded. As a successful research scientist, she was skeptical of anything that couldn't be proven.

"He had a letter…from Olivia."

Megan reached across the table and squeezed her hand. "Olivia named you as Emma's guardian."

"I know. But if it turns out that he is her father—"

She couldn't finish the thought.

But she didn't need to. When Ashley reached for her other hand, she knew that they understood the bond she'd formed with Emma. It didn't matter that she hadn't carried the child in her womb or given birth to her— she'd taken prenatal classes with Olivia, coached her through the birth and, after the doctor and the mother, she'd been the first to hold the newborn baby.

Still, it was more than that. It was the realization that when Olivia died, the child had no one. And admittedly, there had been more than a few moments when Paige had cursed her friend for naming her the baby's guardian, moments when she'd fervently wished Olivia had chosen someone—anyone—else.

But now things were different. They had a routine, and a connection. When Emma cried, Paige instinctively knew whether she was wet or hungry or tired or just wanted to be held. And she'd found that nothing comforted her so much as offering comfort to the baby she'd grown to love as if she were her own.

"If he'd shown up five months ago—heck, maybe even five weeks ago—I might have jumped at the opportunity to turn Emma over to him. But now…I can't imagine my life without her."

"You're the expert on custody matters," Ashley reminded her. "So all I'll say is, whatever you need, we're here for you."

"Absolutely," Megan agreed.

Paige knew it was true, and their unwavering support meant the world to her. "Thanks. At this point, I don't know what I need, what he plans to do. I got the impression that he discovered the letter from Olivia when he got home from an overseas tour, tore off to confront her, found out she'd been killed and that I had custody of the baby, and raced out here without really thinking about what he planned to do when he finally came face-to-face with the child that he believes is his own."

"Poor man," Ashley murmured sympathetically. Then her gaze flew to Paige's. "Not that I'm taking his side. Of course not. I just can't help thinking that the news must have thrown him for a loop."

"You mean like when Paige found out she'd been named Emma's legal guardian?" Megan asked her sister.

Ashley nodded. "But at least Paige knew the baby existed. This guy didn't even know he'd had a child."

"If she's even his baby," Paige felt compelled to interject.

"You don't think he is Emma's father?"

"I don't know what to think, why Olivia never told anyone about him. Any time I tried to get information about her child's father, she stonewalled me. And yet, if I believe him, if I believe she wrote the letter he showed me, then she had a change of heart and decided to tell him about the child. She wanted him to be a part of her daughter's life."

"What do you want?" Ashley asked gently.

"I want *him* to have a change of heart—to have woken up this morning and, in the light of day, realize that he's not ready to take on the responsibility of being a father and just disappear as unexpectedly as he appeared."

But she knew it wasn't going to happen.

A fact that was confirmed when Zach's SUV pulled into the driveway while she was saying goodbye to Ashley and Maddie a few minutes later.

Ashley paused on the step, obviously wanting to hang around and meet him. But Maddie tugged on her hand, a silent reminder that they both had to get to school, and with a last wave, she was gone.

Unfortunately, Megan was still inside. But Paige had invited Zach to come by, so she gestured for him to follow her into the house.

As she was introducing Zach and Megan, she heard the soft slap of the baby's hands on the ceramic tile floor as she crawled toward the sound of familiar voices. When she rounded the corner and spotted Paige, those big blue eyes lit up and her mouth curved in a wide smile.

Beside her, she heard Zach's breath catch.

Emma heard it, too, because she looked over at him, then actually scooted back a step. And the little girl, whose exposure to the male species had been limited and who had certainly never met anyone as big and imposing as the man in front of her now, started to cry.

Paige wanted to scoop the child into her arms, to hold her and hug her and promise her that the big scary man would go away and everything was going to be okay. But it was a promise she knew she wouldn't be able to keep, so she stood motionless, helpless, while Zach squatted beside the teary child.

He murmured softly to her, so softly that Paige couldn't hear the words that were said. But despite the soothing tone, Emma turned away, tears tracking down her cheeks as she crawled over to where Paige was standing. Grabbing hold of her pant leg, she pulled herself up and hung on, peeking at the stranger from behind the shelter of Paige's leg.

Zach stood, too, and sighed wearily.

"She's a little wary of strangers," Paige told him.

She expected he would again claim that he was her father, but he seemed to understand that even if that was true, he was also a stranger.

"But she warms up quickly," Megan interjected, as if to reassure Zach. Then she ruffled Emma's soft curls. "Don't you, Em?"

The little girl looked up at her and smiled shyly. Then, apparently bored with the adult conversation, she dropped down to the floor again and crawled back to the living room.

"I want to get the paternity test done as soon as possible," Zach told Paige.

"All right," she agreed, biting back a more elaborate retort that would have let him know in clear terms that what she wanted was for him to descend into the fiery underworld.

Megan sent her a look that warned her cousin that she knew what evil thoughts were lurking in her mind, then she turned to Zach and asked, "What are you going to do in the meantime?"

"I had originally planned to fly out to California tomorrow, but finding out about Emma changed those plans."

"Having the responsibility of a child changes everything," Paige felt compelled to point out.

He nodded. "That's why I've decided to stay in Pinehurst until we've established Emma's paternity."

He planned to stay in Pinehurst?

Oh, this is not good, Paige thought.

At the same time, Megan said, "That's great."

Paige frowned at her, but her cousin refused to meet her gaze.

"Because caring for Emma has been a big responsibility for Paige to tackle on her own," Megan continued.

"I'll gladly help in any way that I can," Zach said.

Paige didn't need or want his help and the steely-eyed glare she sent in his direction told him so. But he wasn't looking at her but at Megan, who rewarded his evident compliance with a smile.

"And it would probably help ease Emma's shyness if she got used to seeing you around," she continued. "She's in the living room playing, if you wanted to hang out in there."

"Do you mind?" he asked Paige, as if her opinion actually mattered.

She forced a smile through gritted teeth. "No. Go ahead."

Paige waited until Zach had left the room to turn to her cousin. "I can't believe you just did that."

"What I just did was ensure that Zach Crawford will see firsthand how good you are with Emma, how much she's bonded with you, and realize how difficult it would be for her if he tries to take her away," Megan said.

"So I'm supposed to believe that you did this for me?"

"You know that Ashley and I love that baby, too. Maybe not the way you do, but none of us want to see you lose her."

"Yet you just invited the enemy to essentially set up camp here."

"It's not as if you could force him to leave town before he's ready, and this paves the way for a cooperative, rather than an adversarial, relationship," Megan said reasonably.

"If he is Emma's father, he could take her away from me, so forgive me for not wanting to cooperate with him."

Megan sighed. "You are one of the most rational people I know, but you're being completely irrational about this."

Paige knew it was true, but she wasn't quite sure how to explain it.

"Something about him just sets off my radar," she finally admitted.

Her cousin's eyebrows lifted. "Your I-don't-trust-this-guy radar? Or your I-don't-trust-myself-around-this-guy radar?"

Paige frowned.

"Because I may be happily married and eleven months pregnant—" she glanced down at her enormous belly "—but even I couldn't miss the fact that Zach Crawford is seriously hot."

"He's a lieutenant colonel in the United States Air Force."

"Which, for a lot of women, would only further enhance his appeal. Yummy good looks, perfectly sculpted body, strong moral character and dedication to his country."

"None of which qualifies him to assume the care of a fourteen-month-old baby, even if she is his daughter."

Megan nodded slowly. "Now I get it."

"What do you get?" Paige asked warily.

"That this isn't about Zach at all."

"It's about Emma."

"Maybe," her cousin acknowledged. "And maybe it's about the fact that Colonel Phillip Wilder was a respected military leader but a complete screwup as a father."

"It's about Emma," Paige insisted.

And although there was no disputing that Paige was genuinely concerned about the child's well-being, it was obvious to both of them that there were more issues to be dealt with than the custody of one little girl.

Zach stayed through the morning, just hanging around while Emma played. Sometimes Emma approached Paige, wanting her help with some task or another, and although she cast frequent curious glances in Zach's direction, the little girl kept a careful distance between herself and the stranger.

To his credit, Zach didn't push to engage her in play or conversation and he didn't hover. He just stayed in the background, silently observing. Paige knew it was ridiculous, but she couldn't help feeling that her every word and her every action were being monitored by the man who claimed to be the little girl's father.

When it was time for Emma's lunch, she felt compelled to offer to feed him, too. And he responded with such genuine appreciation, she felt guilty for making the offer so begrudgingly.

They munched on sandwiches while Emma tackled cooked noodles and vegetables with her six teeth.

"She'll go down for a nap after lunch," Paige told him, as she cleared their plates away.

Hint, hint.

"I guess that's my cue to head out," he said.

"I try to use the time when she's asleep to catch up on e-mail and other business matters."

"I thought you were on vacation."

She shook her head. "I'm actually on a leave of absence right now."

"Why?"

"Because I didn't realize the firm frowned upon an attorney giving closing arguments in a trial with a baby strapped to her chest in a Snugli." Not so long ago, she would have been horrified by the thought of putting a baby carrier on over one of her favorite Armani jackets, but almost six months with Emma had changed her perspective—and her priorities.

His lips curved. "Did you really?"

"I didn't have a choice," she explained. "The day before, when I picked Emma up from Annabelle's—that's her sitter—she warned me that one of the other kids she looks after had been throwing up. So I kept an eye on Emma for any signs of lethargy or fever, but she was fine. Unfortunately, though, Annabelle caught the bug and she called at six o'clock the next morning to tell me that she wouldn't be able to take Emma that day."

"This is six o'clock the same morning that you're due in court?"

Paige nodded. "And I didn't have a backup plan. Nothing like this had ever happened before. And because no one was available to watch Emma while I went to court, I took her with me."

"What did the judge think of that?"

"Both the judge and opposing counsel were understanding, and Emma slept through the whole process. Which, by the way, ended with my client maintaining custody of her four kids and her degenerate ex-husband's access being restricted and subject to supervision."

"So what was the problem?" Zach wondered.

"The problem came when Emma let it be known that she wasn't quite so happy at the office," Paige told him. "And it wasn't as if I intended to move her playpen beside my desk—I just went in to ask Rebecca to reschedule my appointments and to pick up some files so that I could work at home. But Carson Wainwright was meeting with the CEO of one of our biggest clients, who happens to be the doting grandfather of seven grandkids and who couldn't help but be drawn away from their meeting in the conference room by the sound of Emma's crying."

"And that didn't go over well with Mr. Wainwright," he guessed.

"Right again," Paige agreed. "Of course, he didn't

say anything at the time, but while the CEO was busy cooing over the baby, he was shooting daggers at me across the room. And when Emma was back at Annabelle's the next morning and I returned to my office, I was summoned into a meeting with all three of the senior partners, who suggested that I needed to rethink my priorities if I expected to have a future at Wainwright, Witmer & Wynne."

"They threatened to fire you?" Zach sounded as stunned as she had been.

"I don't think it will come to that," Paige admitted. "Owen Wynne immediately jumped up, urging everyone not to be too hasty, and suggested that I should take some time to think things through.

"So that's where I am—trying to figure out whether I can successfully juggle my professional obligations and personal responsibilities—or if I want to."

"You mean you might leave Wainwright, Winter and...Whatever?"

Her lips curved, just a little. "Wainwright, Witmer and Wynne. And I haven't made any final decisions yet."

She lifted a sleepy Emma out of her high chair. He stood up.

"Speaking of decisions, you never said when or where we should have the paternity testing done."

Emma rubbed her face against Paige's shoulder.

"I've used PDA Labs before," she told him.

At the lift of his brows, she felt her cheeks flush. "I'm an attorney," she reminded him. "I've had to deal with this issue for several of my clients."

"So how does it work?"

"We find a doctor to conduct the test, then contact

the lab to have them courier a kit to the doctor. Then it's just a swab of the inside of Emma's cheek and yours and waiting for the results."

"Do you know any doctors in town?"

"Cameron Turcotte, my cousin Ashley's husband, is a doctor."

He nodded. "How soon can we get it done?"

"I'll call him and the lab this afternoon."

He must have sensed her reluctance, because he said, "I would think you'd be as anxious as I am to have the matter of Emma's paternity settled once and for all."

Anxious didn't begin to describe what she was feeling. Her emotions were too intense and conflicted to be so simply categorized.

She felt helpless and scared, but she was also determined. Even if Zach was Emma's father, Paige didn't intend to quietly slip out of the little girl's life. No, she would make sure that any decisions made about the future were made not on the basis of DNA but considering what was best for Emma.

"Except that establishing paternity may only be the beginning," she warned.

Chapter 4

Zach thought about Paige's words as he drove back to his room at Hadfield House.

She was right, of course. Confirming Emma's paternity was only a first step, but neither one of them could really move forward with their plans until that first step had been taken.

Of course, at this point, he really didn't know what his plans would be, how he could fit a child into his life, but he knew that he would find a way. Because, while Paige insisted that a paternity test was needed to prove that he was Emma's father, he'd agreed solely to appease her. He didn't need a cheek swab to confirm what he already knew—Olivia's little girl was his daughter. And he had no intention of walking away from the child or the responsibilities that being a father entailed.

Maybe he and Olivia hadn't known everything about

one another, but she had to have known that. Although they'd only been dating for a few weeks, they'd spent a lot of time together during that period.

When he'd first read her letter, and her claim that he'd fathered a child, his first instinct had been to deny the possibility. He had never been careless about birth control and he certainly hadn't been with Olivia. But even as he'd recalled that fact to reassure himself, he'd heard the echo of his father's voice in the back of his mind: *the only birth control that is one-hundred-percent effective is abstinence. If you're going to play, be prepared to pay.*

He'd heard that same warning too many times to count during his teenage years and, although he hadn't always abstained, he'd always been careful.

Obviously not careful enough.

Okay, so finding out about Emma had definitely been a surprise, but he would never say that she was an accident or a mistake. He believed that everything that happened in life happened for a reason, even if the reason wasn't readily apparent. He certainly couldn't fathom any noble purpose for the accident that had not only ended Olivia's life tragically and prematurely but had also left an innocent child without her mother.

But even after her death, Olivia had ensured that her daughter was taken care of, and although he might wonder why she'd chosen to name Paige Wilder as Emma's legal guardian, he couldn't fault her choice. Because what he'd seen in the young attorney's interactions with the child was a woman who was both attentive and affectionate, who anticipated and responded to the child's every need. And a woman who had no intention of accepting that he was Emma's father until he'd jumped through all kinds of hoops.

Well, he would show her that he was more than ready to jump through those hoops and take responsibility for his child. And if he had to spend time in Paige's company in the process, well, he didn't think that was going to be much of a hardship.

Zach came back the next morning, and the morning after that. He wasn't obtrusive and he didn't get in her way, but Paige was all too aware of his presence, of his eyes following her every move, of her own response to him.

She was attracted to him. It was pointless to deny that fact when every nerve ending in her body fairly hummed whenever he was near. It was even more pointless to think that anything could ever come of that attraction when their goals were so diametrically opposed. He wanted to be Emma's father and she had no intention of letting him take the little girl away from her.

Megan had given her the name of a friend who worked at PDA Labs, and she'd contacted Walter Neville directly to inquire about the DNA testing. He'd promised to send a test kit to Dr. Turcotte's office right away and assured her that he would give the package priority when it was returned to the lab. He was so willing and helpful that Paige didn't know how to tell him that she didn't want the package to be given priority, that she would actually prefer if it disappeared into a crack somewhere in the lab.

She did tell Zach that Cameron would let her know when the package was received so that they could go in for the test. He seemed satisfied with that information, but she knew that he was eager to have the question of paternity settled.

On the fourth day after Zach's arrival in town, he called in the morning to tell her that he had some errands to run but would stop by after lunch to spend some time with Emma then. But when Paige opened the door after she'd settled the little girl down for her nap, she found Megan on the porch instead.

"This is a surprise," she said, stepping away from the door so her cousin could enter.

"I hope you don't mind," Megan said, waddling in. "I was up a few times in the night with a backache and Gage was threatening to cancel a meeting today to stay home with me, but I told him I would spend the afternoon with you so he didn't have to do that."

"I don't mind at all," Paige assured her. "In fact, I'm grateful for the company." And for the buffer that her cousin's presence would provide when Zach showed up later.

"Is that coffee I smell?" Megan was already moving toward the kitchen.

"Yeah, but I thought you gave it up for your pregnancy."

"I did, aside from half a cup in the morning," her cousin agreed. "But that doesn't mean I can't drink in the luscious scent."

Paige smiled. "I can make you a cup of tea."

"That would be great." Megan eased herself onto one of the stools at the breakfast counter while Paige filled the kettle and set it on the stove to boil. "Where's Em?"

"Sleeping."

"Which means I'm intruding on the only quiet time you have during the day."

"Sometimes it's too quiet," Paige said.

"Has Zach been here already today?"

She shook her head. "He said he wanted to come this afternoon, to go with Emma and I on our daily trek to the park."

"I know you're not thrilled with him hanging around," Megan said, "but you have to applaud his effort. The man is definitely trying."

"I know he is," Paige admitted. "And Emma is starting to warm up to him. Yesterday she threw a block at his head."

Megan's brows lifted. "That's warming up?"

"Before that, she completely ignored him."

"Then I guess that's warming up," her cousin agreed.

"But enough about Zach," Paige said, wanting to talk about anything but the man who seemed to occupy far too many of her thoughts already. "Tell me about this backache that had you up in the night."

Megan shrugged. "I've had twinges for a few days. Which probably isn't surprising, considering that I'm hauling around an extra twenty-four pounds and I'm three days past my due date."

Paige smiled as she turned off the kettle and poured water into a mug. Her cousin's obvious disgruntlement confirmed that she'd expected her baby to pop out precisely on schedule and was none too pleased with the delay. She set a box of lemon cookies in front of the expectant mother along with the tea.

"Didn't I just say that I've put on twenty-four pounds?" Megan demanded, but she was already opening the box.

"You did," Paige agreed. "But I happen to know that those are the baby's favorites."

"Which probably explains twenty-two of those pounds," her cousin mumbled around a mouthful of cookie.

They chatted and ate cookies while Megan drank her tea and looked longingly at Paige's cup of coffee. But before her tea was finished, Megan slid off the stool.

"Are you okay?" Paige asked.

Megan shrugged. "I can't sit for too long, or stand for too long, or do anything without feeling restless and…oh."

Paige was immediately on her feet and beside her cousin. "Meg—what's wrong?"

The other woman's face was pale, her eyes wide. Paige wasn't sure how it was possible, but her cousin somehow looked both excited…and terrified.

"I think…my water…just broke."

"Ohmygod."

Megan just nodded.

Paige's brain scrambled. She'd been through this before, when Olivia had gone into labor with Emma, but at the moment she couldn't remember what to say or do. "Okay. Um. What are we supposed to do now?"

"I don't know about you," Megan said, sounding fairly calm, "but I'm going to call Gage."

"Oh. Right. Good idea." Paige turned to reach for the phone on the counter but stopped when Megan grabbed her arm, hard. "Contraction?"

Her cousin nodded.

"Are you breathing?"

Megan nodded again.

And then, as if Paige wasn't already frazzled enough, the doorbell rang.

She handed the phone to Megan before she went to answer the door.

"Oh, Zach. I'm sorry, but this really isn't a good time."

"But I called this morning and you said—"

"This morning my cousin wasn't standing in my kitchen in the beginning stages of labor," she told him. "But now I have to get Emma up from her nap so we can take Megan to the hospital—"

"Or I could stay with her," Zach offered.

"With Megan?"

He smiled, and even in the midst of all the chaos and confusion, her heart gave a giddy leap. "With Emma."

"Oh, of course." But she hesitated.

He was offering an obvious and easy solution. But her brain was still scrambling, and while her hormones were urging her to take whatever this man was offering, she wasn't quite ready to trust him alone with the little girl who had been entrusted to her care—even if he was Emma's father.

"Paige!"

She whirled away from the door, summoned by her cousin's impatient demand.

Zach stepped into the foyer behind her. Holding back a sigh of frustration, Paige chose to ignore him and focus on Megan.

"Gage said he'll meet us at the hospital, but he's going to be a while."

Knowing how devoted her cousin's husband was to his wife and how excited they both were about the baby, Paige was more than a little surprised by this response.

"He's in Manhattan," Megan explained.

"Manhattan?"

Megan nodded, her eyes filling with tears. "He's supposed to be here."

"He will be here," Paige promised, almost certain it was true. After all, it was only a three-and-a-half-hour drive from Manhattan, and Megan would undoubtedly be in labor a lot longer than that. "But in the meantime, we should get you to the hospital."

"I need my bag."

"I can get your bag after I get you to the hospital."

"I need to take my bag to the hospital," Megan insisted.

Paige knew her cousin's insistence wasn't as much about the bag as it was about the fact that Megan didn't want to go to the hospital without Gage, because she didn't want to have her baby without the baby's father by her side. So Paige took her hands and squeezed gently.

When Megan looked up, Paige simply said, "Breathe."

Megan drew in a lungful of air, then exhaled it slowly.

"Better?"

The mother-to-be nodded. "But I still want my bag."

"Honey, your house is in the opposite direction from the hospital."

"I could take Megan to the hospital and you can go pick up her bag when Emma wakes up from her nap."

Until he spoke, Paige had almost forgotten Zach was there. Or maybe she hadn't actually forgotten so much as she'd wished she could forget. In any event, she was as protective of her cousin as she was of Emma, and she had no intention of letting him intrude on her life any more than he already had.

"That's not necessary—" she began, only to be interrupted by Megan's hopeful request, "Are you sure you wouldn't mind?"

"Of course not," Zach assured her.

"I'm leaking," the laboring mother-to-be warned.

To his credit, Zach paled only a little, and his response was a casual, "Leather seats."

"Thank you." Megan turned back to Paige. "My bag's beside the door in the nursery. You have a key and the code for the alarm?"

"Yes, but—"

"Great."

"It's not great," she felt compelled to protest, but her cousin was already hustling—as much as she could hustle in her current condition—down the driveway toward Zach's Jeep, leaving Paige to stare after their retreating forms.

Through the baby monitor, she heard Emma stirring in her crib, and she pushed aside her annoyance and frustration to focus on the baby. Once she'd dealt with the waking child's immediate needs, she'd go get Megan's damn bag.

When Paige arrived at the hospital about an hour later, Megan still hadn't been admitted. Instead, she was pacing the waiting room with Zach beside her. Paige's pulse jolted when she saw him. He wasn't the first man whose appearance had affected her in such a way, but it was more than his dark good looks and long, hard body that made her belly quiver this time. It was the realization that a man so big and strong could be so gentle, as he was being with Megan right now.

She couldn't hear what they were talking about, but she saw her cousin smile in response to something he said. The smile slipped and she reached toward the wall to brace herself as another contraction hit. But Zach was right there, taking her hand, talking her through the pain.

Paige paused in the doorway—caught for a moment in the memory of doing the same things during her friend's labor, of keeping Olivia focused on her breathing while trying to distract her from the pain and silently cursing the man who had impregnated and then abandoned her friend.

Watching Zach with Megan, she was struck by the contradiction between what Olivia had told her about the baby's father and what—after only a few days—she knew about the man who was Zach Crawford. And she couldn't help but wonder how different things might have been for Olivia and Emma if he'd known about the pregnancy.

If Zach was Emma's father.

She shifted the still-sleepy baby to her other shoulder and acknowledged that even she was getting weary of her incessant protests about something everyone else seemed willing to accept as fact. Maybe she was being difficult. Maybe she was stubborn. But she wasn't ready or willing to simply let Zach step into the role of Emma's father without any concrete proof. She wasn't ready to lose the little girl she loved with her whole heart.

Gage arrived at the hospital only a short while after Paige, causing her to speculate that he'd either been on his way back from Manhattan already when Megan called him or he'd challenged land-speed records in his haste to get to his wife's side. In any event, Megan had finally been admitted, Gage's parents had shown up and Ashley had come by after school with Maddie.

Paige hovered in the background, reading some of Emma's favorite books to her and observing the scene. This part was unfamiliar to her. With Olivia, things had been mostly quiet and low-key—her friend had told no one but Paige when she'd gone into labor. She'd had no family hovering in the wings and no visitors had shown up until the day after Emma's birth. Of course, Paige hadn't thought too much about it at the time because she hadn't had anything to compare it to, but now that she did, she couldn't help but feel both sad and sorry that her friend had been so alone.

She smiled at Cameron when he came in to give his sister-in-law a quick pep talk and a hug before taking his daughter—despite her vehement protests and heartfelt pleas to stay until her new baby cousin was born—to her grandparents' house. Ashley stayed, almost as excited about the impending arrival of her niece or nephew as she was about the birth of her own baby due in another couple of months.

Because the waiting room was still rather crowded and Megan was pacing the halls and didn't seem as if she was going to have the baby anytime soon, Paige decided to take Emma down to the cafeteria for a snack.

Although she hadn't invited him to come along, Zach followed them into the elevator and, after he'd been so great with Megan, Paige couldn't bring herself to tell him to get lost. And even if she did, he probably wouldn't listen to her anyway.

Of course, he then insisted on paying for their coffee and Emma's snack, which made her feel even guiltier for wanting to ditch him. But when they were settled at a table and Emma was happily squeezing cubes of red Jell-O in her fists—and occasionally stuffing one into her mouth—she had to ask, "Why are you still here, Zach?"

He shrugged. "I'm curious."

"About what?"

"The whole process, I guess. I never had a chance to experience any of the stages of pregnancy or childbirth with Olivia because I never even knew that she was pregnant."

"And if you had known, you still would have been in Afghanistan while she was having your baby in Syracuse."

"I could have asked for leave."

"But there's no guarantee you would have got it, is there?"

"No," he admitted, sounding so genuinely regretful, Paige felt her heart softening toward him.

"She was in labor nineteen hours," she told him.

Zach's head swiveled toward her. "That's right—you were her birthing partner."

She nodded. "I was surprised she chose me. I mean, we'd become pretty good friends at law school and were both pleased when we got hired on at Wainwright, Witmer & Wynne, but I thought there must have been someone else she was closer to."

"She was an only child born late in the lives of both of her parents," Zach remembered. "And she lost them both the year after she graduated."

Paige nodded again and wondered why she was surprised that he knew those details. Obviously he and Olivia had engaged in conversation *and* sex—which was definitely not a path she wanted her mind to be wandering down, because just thinking of Zach and sex in the same sentence made her blood heat and her pulse race.

The attraction she felt for him was purely physical—and not entirely unexpected, considering how long it had been since she'd been with any man and that she'd never known a man who oozed testosterone the way Zach Crawford did. She also knew her feelings were wrong—and self-destructive. Unfortunately, that knowledge didn't give her any more control over them, but it did help her refocus her attention on their conversation.

"I was hesitant at first," Paige said, referring to the childbirth classes she'd attended with Olivia. "Or maybe it's more accurate to say that I was terrified that I would screw up or somehow let her down. But I finally agreed.

"Every week on our way to class, she would thank me again, telling me how grateful she was for my support, as if I was doing her this huge favor."

"To her, you were."

"Maybe," she acknowledged. "But I realized, as her pregnancy progressed and the date of Emma's birth drew nearer, that I was the one who was grateful. Because the whole process of growing a baby really is a miracle and I was thrilled to share in it."

"Did Olivia know she was having a girl?"

"Yeah. She didn't like surprises, and she was determined to know the baby's gender so that she would be better prepared for her arrival."

Zach finished his coffee. "Was she happy?"

"She was thrilled," Paige said. "I'm not sure that was true in the very beginning. As far as I know, she struggled through the early stages of oh-my-God-I'm-pregnant-what-do-I-do-now? on her own. She didn't even tell me until she was through her first trimester, and then it was a very matter-of-fact 'I'm pregnant. Yes, I'm keeping the baby. No, the father isn't going to be involved, and will you go to prenatal classes with me?'"

"I'm glad that she didn't seem to have any doubts about having the baby—if a little surprised," he admitted. "She seemed so completely focused on her career. During the time that we were together, she certainly never said anything to me—she never even hinted—about wanting a baby."

"I don't think she had thought about it, not until she realized she was pregnant. But she was a wonderful mother." Tears stung her eyes as she thought about Olivia with Emma, how much her friend had loved her baby and everything Emma had lost when she'd lost her mother. "She was so patient with the baby. Sure, she got overwhelmed and frazzled on occasion, but she never took it out on Emma. She simply and completely loved her little girl."

"Tell me about when Emma was born," he said.

"You really want the details?"

"Yeah."

Paige shrugged. "Her water broke at three o'clock in the morning, so she knew that labor would be starting soon, but she figured she had time to shower and shave her legs first—as if the ob-gyn cared about her razor stubble."

"I can see Olivia worrying about something like that," Zach said and smiled.

"Yeah, well, she took a chunk of skin off her ankle bone because she had the razor in her hand when the first contraction hit."

He winced. "Ouch."

"And that was only the beginning."

"When did she call you?"

She thought back, trying to remember. So many details of that day were permanently etched on her memory. Others were less clear. "It was around four, I think. She'd managed to finish her shower and dry her hair and get dressed, but the contractions were coming every fifteen minutes or so, and she knew she wouldn't be able to drive herself to the hospital."

"Which proves that she'd considered it," he noted.

Paige nodded. "Thankfully, I only lived a few blocks away, so we were at the hospital before five. Of course, her doctor didn't show up until seven, and even then, he wasn't ready to admit her because the labor hadn't progressed very far.

"Anyway, long story short, Emma was born just after ten p.m. that night."

"Why do I get the feeling that you skipped over a lot of stuff?"

"Because I didn't think you wanted to hear about the contractions stalling and the baby being in distress and finally being delivered by emergency C-section."

Nor did she want to think about those complications—and the accompanying terror—while Megan was in labor. Of course, she was confident her cousin could handle just about anything. Because from the minute she'd learned that she was pregnant, Megan had been reading everything she could find on pregnancy and labor and childbirth. In fact, Paige wouldn't be surprised if the mother-to-be couldn't teach the doctor a thing or two.

Still, Paige would feel a lot better once the baby was actually born. Because although it was true that women had been having babies since the beginning of time, it was also true that even with all of the progress in modern medicine, there were still occasions when things went wrong. And although Paige knew it was both silly and futile, she crossed her fingers under the table, hoping that nothing would go wrong for Megan or her baby.

"Yeah," Zach finally responded to her comment. "It's hard enough to think about how differently things could have turned out fourteen months after the fact. I can't imagine what she—and you—went through at the time."

"Olivia was a trooper throughout the whole thing," she told him. "But when they finally pulled the baby out, we both cried right along with Emma."

"Thank you," Zach said softly.

Paige looked over at him, surprised. "For what?"

"For telling me," he said. "But especially for being there, for Olivia and Emma."

"It was my pleasure—and an absolute thrill to hold Emma in my arms when she was only minutes old." She glanced at Zach again and felt an unexpected twinge of guilt, as if she'd stolen an experience that should have been his. But then she remembered the point she'd made earlier—that even if he had known about Olivia's pregnancy and wanted to be there for the birth, things might not have played out any differently.

Except that there would have been no question about the baby's custody when Olivia died. Or maybe the accident never would have happened, because Olivia wouldn't have driven to New Jersey to tell Zach about the baby because he would already have known. But it was pointless to play "what if" at this stage. All they could do now was move forward, even if neither of them knew exactly what direction was forward.

Emma wriggled, trying to get out of the high chair, just wanting to move. Cubes of Jell-O were scattered on the tray and on the floor, but clearly she'd had enough of her snack and was ready to escape her confinement. Paige glanced at her watch and frowned. "I can't keep her here all night."

"I could—" Zach began, then snapped his jaw shut.

She sighed. "I know I'm being unreasonable. I just can't seem to stop myself."

"And I don't know what to say or do to reassure you that I'm not going to disappear with her."

Paige put her empty cup on the tray beside his. She didn't know if it was the eagerness with which he'd listened to the story of Emma's birth or the attentiveness she'd observed in his interaction with the child, but she decided that it was time—maybe past time—to give him the benefit of the doubt. "Would you trust me with your Jeep?" she asked him.

His brows rose. "Is there any reason I shouldn't?"

She responded by digging her car keys out of her purse. "Leave me yours and you can have mine to take Emma back to my place. It's easier than trying to move her car seat," she explained, then couldn't resist adding, "That and I have anti-theft tracking, so if you take off with the baby, the cops won't have any trouble finding you."

"Thanks for the vote of confidence," he said drily, as he unhooked the tray from the high chair.

Desperate for freedom, Emma flung herself forward. Paige had a flash of panic as she remembered that she hadn't fastened the grimy safety strap around the little girl's waist, but Zach—obviously having anticipated the move—blocked her easily with a hand.

Emma frowned and opened her mouth to protest, but before she could make a sound, Zach had deftly plucked her from the seat and set her on her feet. She looked up at him, grateful but still wary, and took a few tottering steps toward Paige.

"Pawk?" she said hopefully.

It was her new favorite word and her favorite place. There was a small park at the end of the block where they lived in Syracuse and a bigger park even closer to the house on Chetwood Street, and Paige had gotten in the habit of taking Emma there after her nap. The little girl had been most displeased to be going in the car instead of to the park when she woke up today and clearly hadn't forgotten.

"You're going to go home with Zach," Paige told her.

Emma stole a cautious glance in his direction, then shook her head. "Pawk," she said again.

"I can't today," Paige said.

"But I can," Zach said.

Emma stole another glance at him, but continued to cling to Paige.

"What's your favorite thing at the park?" he asked. "The swings or the slide?"

Emma seemed to get what he was saying and her love of the park apparently outweighed her lingering uncertainty about this new man who had suddenly appeared in her life, because she looked right at him this time and said, "Pawk?"

He nodded.

Emma released her hold on Paige and held out her arms to Zach.

Chapter 5

When Paige returned to the maternity-wing waiting room, she found that Gage's brother, Craig, and his wife, Tess, had joined the party. There were also two other, older couples, who she figured were the prospective grandparents of some other baby.

She slid into the vacant chair next to the sofa where Ashley sat close to her husband. Her head was on his shoulder, and his hand was on the curve of her belly. The baby must have kicked because Cam's hand snapped back and Ashley laughed.

"You'd think I'd be used to that by now," he murmured.

"You'd think," Ashley agreed.

Paige felt an unexpected pang of envy as she watched them interact. She couldn't be happier for both of her cousins, even if she'd never thought she wanted what they had. For certain, she'd been shocked and panicked when she'd learned that she had been named Emma's legal guardian. And in that moment, she'd been certain that she did *not* want the responsibility of an infant.

Of course, her feelings had soon changed. Now she couldn't imagine her life without Emma and she refused to worry what Zach's presence could mean for the status quo she'd established with Olivia's baby, or what it could mean to the idea that had only recently begun to take root in her mind and her heart of someday having a baby of her own—a brother or a sister for Emma.

Ashley looked over at her. "Where's Emma?"

"She went home with Zach." She glanced at her cousin for reassurance. "Please tell me I haven't made a very big mistake."

"You haven't made a very big mistake," Ashley said obligingly.

The words did little to alleviate her concerns. She chewed on the edge of a thumbnail, as she sometimes did when she was worried, but she didn't realize she was doing it until Ashley gently tugged her hand away from her mouth.

"He hasn't been alone with her before," she said, trying to explain the origin of her concern.

"Then it's probably time he was."

"She's going to be wanting dinner soon," she suddenly realized. "And I didn't tell him what to feed her."

"I'm sure he'll manage," Cam told her.

But Paige wasn't nearly as certain.

"Do you remember the first time you babysat Emma?" Ashley asked her.

She nodded. "I didn't have a clue."

"And Emma couldn't say a word to tell you if she was hungry or thirsty or tired."

"She doesn't say much now," Paige noted.

"Well, Zach looks to me like a man who's capable of figuring things out. But if you're really not comfortable with the situation, why don't you go home, too?"

"Because I want to be here when Megan's baby is born."

"Well, if you're determined to stay, then stop chewing your nails. You're making me nervous."

She flushed and pulled her hand away from her mouth again.

Baby steps, Zach reminded himself as he sat Emma on top of the toddler slide.

He had to be patient, to give both Paige and Emma time to get to know him and feel comfortable with him. Unfortunately, that might take more time than he had.

His heart had torn wide open the first time Emma looked at him and started to cry. As ridiculous as he knew it was, he felt as if she'd rejected him. Just the latest in a string of women who had done so.

Heather was the first. Of course, he'd been a lot younger then and his emotions much more vulnerable. She'd been a model, stunningly beautiful, and he'd been blinded by lust. They'd dated for almost two years, and she'd seemed happy enough to be with him so long as he worked around her schedule. She'd even told him that she loved him. But when Zach got his first overseas assignment and their relationship was no longer convenient, she'd unceremoniously dumped him.

The first heartbreak had been as bitter as first love had been sweet, and losing Heather had taught him a valuable if painful lesson. Since then, he'd guarded his heart.

He'd had relationships with other women, of course, but because of his career, none were long-term or serious. His relationship with Olivia had been no different, despite the fact that a baby had been born of it. And yet it hurt to realize that Olivia had rejected him and any efforts he would have made to be a father to their baby by refusing to even tell him about her pregnancy.

Yeah, she'd changed her mind—too many months later—but that knowledge failed to appease him. And although he knew it served no purpose, he couldn't deny that he was angry with Olivia—furious at the way she'd first cut him out and then blindsided him with the information that he was a father.

Emma slid down the gentle slope, her face split with a wide grin, her blue eyes sparkling. When she giggled it was the purest and happiest sound he'd ever heard. And in that moment, looking at the beautiful little girl Olivia had given birth to, all his residual anger was washed away by a tide of joy and love so huge it took his breath way.

He caught her at the bottom of the slide and it was only when she wriggled that he let her go. He wanted to gather her in his arms and lavish her with all the love and attention he hadn't been able to give her in the first fourteen months of her life. Of course, he had to get past not just Emma's uncertainty but Paige's wary protectiveness first. Definitely not an easy task.

However, he'd never been one to shirk from a challenge.

Except when that challenge was a phone call from his

youngest sister, he amended as the phone in his pocket trilled again and Zach ignored it again.

He'd never admit it to her face, but he missed her like crazy and, more than anything when he'd come home from Afghanistan, he'd been looking forward to going out to California and seeing not just Hayden but his whole family again. He hadn't actually canceled those plans so much as he'd delayed them, and he didn't want to delay for much longer.

Emma had an extended family who wanted to meet her.

Or they would, when he finally figured out how to tell them that he was a father.

It was past midnight before Paige finally left the hospital, and despite her pleasure at seeing both her cousin and the brand-new baby doing well, she felt tense and uncertain as she drove toward home. She didn't realize it was worry over Emma that had lingered with her until she got close enough to the house to confirm that her car was in the driveway. She didn't have to go much farther than that to find both Emma and Zach.

The baby was curled up on one end of the sofa, her favorite blanket clutched in one little fist, the thumb of the other hanging out of her mouth. Zach was on the floor, his back against the sofa. His legs were out straight, his head was tipped back, and one of his hands was resting protectively on the sleeping child's back. At any other time, the peaceful scene might have warmed her heart, but she was too busy gaping at the chaos around them to fully appreciate the serene image of man and child.

She took another slow and careful survey of the

room, stunned. Okay, so maybe she'd wondered how he would fare on his own with the little girl, and maybe she'd even hoped that Emma wouldn't make things too easy for him. She hadn't expected the living room to look as if a Category 4 hurricane had torn through it.

But that was exactly how it appeared to Paige, with toys and plastic bowls and sippy cups and clothes and diapers—she sent up a quick prayer that they were at least clean diapers—strewn absolutely everywhere.

She must have gasped because Zach was immediately awake and on his feet, every muscle in his body on alert. He was so tall, so strong, so completely and undeniably male that, for a split second, the disaster zone faded away and there was only Zach.

His eyes locked on her, the air crackled, her skin prickled. The intensity of her reaction—the unexpected force of the attraction she felt—startled her enough that she looked away, breaking the seductive spell of those blue, blue eyes and reminding her of the chaos she'd stepped into.

"What the heck happened?" she asked, keeping her voice low so as not to wake the sleeping child while she attempted to hold her churning hormones firmly in check.

He tore his gaze from hers to glance around and winced as if he was seeing the room for the first time. "Hurricane Emma," he muttered.

His explanation was so close to what she'd been thinking that she might have smiled if the condition of her living room didn't make her want to cry. Instead, she just shook her head. "I need a cup of coffee."

"Wait—"

She paused in midstep. "You're going to tell me that the kitchen is just as bad, aren't you?"

"Probably worse," he admitted.

"As long as I can find the coffeepot."

Zach took hold of her shoulders to steer her away from the kitchen, and when his hands came down on her, she jolted as if she'd been zapped by a live wire. His hands dropped away. "Why don't you take Emma up to her bed while I make the coffee?"

She decided it was probably good advice and, ignoring the tingles that coursed through her veins in response to his touch, turned back to the sleeping child in the living room.

By the time she'd returned to the kitchen after checking Emma's diaper and tucking her into her crib, the coffeepot was gurgling away.

"Boy or girl?" he finally asked, passing a mug across the counter to her.

For the first time since walking into the disaster zone that had once been her house—at least for the summer—she smiled. "Boy," she answered. "Marcus Allan Richmond—for both of Megan's and Gage's fathers. Eight pounds ten ounces, twenty-two inches with big blue eyes and gorgeous blond curls."

"And how's the new mommy doing?" Zach lifted his own mug to drink.

"She's great. Amazing. Overjoyed. And Gage was so thrilled with both his wife and new baby, he actually cried."

"I'll bet you did, too," he guessed.

"Just a little," she admitted.

"When did all of this finally happen?"

"11:47."

Zach glanced at his watch. "You obviously didn't hang around for very long after."

"Long enough to congratulate the new mommy and daddy and steal a quick cuddle with the baby. But they had more than enough company to keep them busy through half of the night."

"And—despite the fact that you called four times from the hospital—you were worried about Emma," he guessed.

"Obviously with good reason."

He shook his head. "Nah, she was in complete control. If you were going to worry about anyone, it should have been me."

She smiled again. "I do appreciate you staying with her," she said, and realized it was true. "It would have been a nightmare trying to keep her entertained at the hospital all night."

"Instead, you came home to a nightmare."

She closed her eyes and held a hand to her mouth to stifle a yawn. "I'm trying not to think about that right now. Hopefully by morning I'll have the energy to tackle the mess."

"You look exhausted," he noted. "Why don't you head up to bed and I'll load the dishes in the dishwasher before I head out?"

"Don't worry about it," she said. "You have to be at least as tired as I am."

"I had a nap," he reminded her.

"Yeah, you looked as if you were resting comfortably when I came in," she noted drily.

"Believe me, your living-room floor is like a premium mattress in a five-star hotel compared to some of the places I've had to sleep." Zach grinned and her heart hitched.

Honestly, the man's smile was a potent weapon, and because Paige knew she was too weary to continue to fight, she opted for retreat. "Well, I'm looking forward to my real bed," she said, taking her empty cup to the dishwasher.

"Go ahead," Zach said. "I'll lock up when I go."

She hesitated, still not entirely sure she trusted him and yet all too aware that he'd given her no reason not to. And if he was willing to make a dent in the kitchen, she was certainly willing to let him. "If you're sure," she began.

"I'm sure. Good night, Paige."

"Good night."

Emma was, as usual, awake by six the next morning, which meant that Paige was, too. After changing the baby's diaper, Paige tucked her against her hip and started down the stairs. When she stepped into the living room, she had a moment to wonder if she'd only dreamed the disaster she'd come home to the night before because the room was absolutely immaculate. Continuing on to the kitchen, she found that the same was true there.

She settled Emma in her high chair with a cup of juice and set about making a pot of coffee. Emma banged her sippy cup on the tray.

"Yes, I know you want breakfast," she said soothingly, "but I *need* my caffeine kick in the morning."

Emma banged her cup again but was somewhat appeased when Paige sprinkled a few Cheerios on her tray. She put the cereal box back in the cupboard and opened the fridge to retrieve the eggs and milk. When she closed the door again, the note tacked to it fluttered.

Please don't call the police. I didn't steal your car—I simply borrowed it to get to the B and B because you still have the keys to my Jeep. I'll be back early in the a.m., but please call my cell (201-555-4757) if you need your car before then. Zach

She set the eggs and milk on the counter before she retraced her steps to the living room, peering out the front window just in time to see her car pulling into the driveway beside the Jeep that was still parked there.

The driver's side door of the Audi opened and Zach stepped out.

His blue eyes were shaded from the sun by dark glasses and he was casually dressed in a Just Do It T-shirt that stretched across his broad chest and a pair of well-faded jeans that hugged his narrow hips. He truly was an exceptional specimen of masculinity and—judging by the speed with which Melanie Quinlan raced down her walk, practically dragging her Chihuahua behind her—she obviously wasn't the only woman who thought so.

Though Paige couldn't hear what Melanie said, she knew her neighbor had called out to Zach, because he turned to respond. But he didn't chat with her for very long, since he was almost at the front door when Paige pulled it open.

Zach smiled and her pulse leaped.

"I'm not too early, then?" he said by way of greeting.

"No. Emma is an early bird."

"And you're not," he guessed.

"I never used to be, but I've learned to adapt."

"I didn't mean to intrude on your morning," he said, "but I wanted to get your car back before you needed it."

"I was just going to make some eggs if you wanted to join us."

"I didn't come over here to be fed," he protested, though not very vehemently.

"And if I wasn't already planning on making breakfast, I wouldn't have offered to feed you," she told him.

"In that case, I'd love some eggs," he replied, and followed her into the kitchen.

Emma's face lit up when she saw him, and Zach's heart melted. "Ack!" she said, which was apparently her interpretation of his name and which she followed with her favorite word, "Pawk."

He smiled and ruffled her hair. "Maybe later," he told her, then, "Mmm, that coffee smells great."

"You know where the mugs are," Paige said. She dug his keys out of her purse and set them on the counter. "I completely forgot we'd switched vehicles last night."

"Not a problem," he assured her, reaching around her to open the cupboard door.

As he did, he caught a whiff of her scent. It was subtle, with just the slightest hint of vanilla, which made him think it was probably a lotion rather than perfume. Of course, that brought to mind images of Paige smoothing lotion over her naked skin, running her hands up her long legs, down her slender arms, over her—

"Scrambled?"

The question jolted Zach out of his fantasy. "What?"

"Your eggs." She continued breaking them into a bowl. "Do you like them scrambled?"

"Sure," he said and filled his mug from the pot.

She splashed some milk into the bowl with the eggs, added a dash of salt and pepper and picked up the whisk.

Zach sipped his coffee.

Paige poured the mixture into a frying pan. "Did you bring in a cleaning crew after I went up to bed last night?"

"Not necessary," he said. "It looked a lot worse than it was."

"Forgive me if I'm a little skeptical about that."

He grinned. "Okay, it was pretty bad, but my mother taught me to always pick up after myself."

"Well, it was a pleasant surprise to wake up this morning and not have to face the chaos I saw last night."

"If you were impressed with a little tidying, you should see what I can do with a bed."

The inadvertent innuendo cracked between them, sizzling in the air like the eggs in the pan.

Paige's cheeks turned pink, confirming that she had taken the same mental detour he had. And he found himself wondering if her thoughts had drifted in that direction even half as often as his had. And if they had—if they were both feeling this tug of attraction—what the heck were they going to do about it?

Nothing. He answered his own question firmly. Definitively.

He cleared his throat. "I meant that I can make up a bed so tight that a quarter tossed down on the middle of the mattress will bounce six inches," he explained.

Paige just nodded and kept her focus on the eggs in the pan, while he tried to block out the mental image of bouncing on a mattress with her. Because how completely inappropriate was that? And why did he, even knowing it was completely inappropriate, find the idea so damned appealing?

He pushed the thought out of his mind and asked, "Can I help you with anything?"

"You can butter the toast," she said, just as it popped out of the toaster.

Zach was grateful for the task because it gave him something to do with his hands so that he couldn't give in to the urge to reach for her and determine once and for all if the attraction he felt was mutual.

Unfortunately, the task didn't keep his mind as occupied as his hands, and his thoughts continued to wander. And although he couldn't deny that several of those thoughts touched upon plans for getting Paige naked, he found himself simply enjoying the morning routine. Working with Paige to put breakfast on the table, retrieving the sippy cup Emma kept throwing to the ground, dodging the bits of toast and egg that she threw at him, then helping Paige tidy up the kitchen again when they'd finished their meal.

Their conversation was easy—although they were both careful not to make any mention of Emma's paternity—and he found himself relaxing in her company. Not that he was completely relaxed—how could he be when he was so keenly aware of her presence, her every movement and every breath?

No doubt about it—twenty-three months was a long time for a man to go without the pleasures of female companionship, yet he hadn't been aware of how very long it had been, and he certainly hadn't felt so acutely deprived until he met Paige. Which meant that he didn't want sex as much as he wanted Paige.

And that, he knew, was a big complication.

After the kitchen was cleaned, Paige left Zach with another cup of coffee while she took Emma upstairs to get her washed up and changed. When they came back down again, he pushed away from the table.

"I have to check out of Hadfield House," he said. "The clerk wasn't at the desk when I left this morning."

"You're leaving?" Paige wasn't sure why she was surprised or why his words caused something that felt like a pang of disappointment. After all, ever since he'd shown up at her door she'd been hoping he would turn around and leave again. But she'd started to get used to having him around; she'd started to believe he actually planned to stay. Of course, she should have realized that as soon as she began to count on someone, it was a cue for him to leave.

"Just leaving the B and B," he told her. "When I first checked in, I didn't know how long I would be staying and the clerk didn't think to mention that they were booked for the holiday weekend."

"So where are you going?"

"I'll try one of the hotels in town."

So he wasn't leaving town after all, she realized, strangely relieved by that fact. Maybe he would turn out to be a man that she—that *Emma,* she hastily amended—could count on. Still, Paige hesitated a moment before she said, "There's a spare room here."

Zach paused with his hand on the door. "Are you just sharing information or offering to let me stay with you?"

She hadn't intended to invite him to stay, but she felt guilty for attempting to thwart his every effort. Or maybe she felt that she owed him because he'd been so great with Megan the day before, not to mention that he'd cleaned up her house.

Yes, he'd been at least partially responsible for the mess in the first place, but his efforts were commendable. And he really did seem to want to get to know Emma and to be willing to take things slowly for the little girl's sake, and Paige found that she couldn't—in good conscience—continue to stand in his way.

Whatever her reasons, she simply shrugged, as if her offer wasn't a big deal. "You seem intent on hanging around here most of the time anyway."

"I'd be more than happy to get out of your hair, but you panic any time Emma is even out of your sight."

She couldn't deny it was true. "I don't know you well enough to trust you yet," she reminded him. "Maybe staying under the same roof will change that."

"Then I'll accept the offer," he said. "Because I know you have no reason to want to help me and all kinds of reasons not to."

"I'm doing it for Emma," she said. "Because if it turns out that you *are* her father, I want her to have a relationship with you."

"Do you really still doubt that I am?"

"It doesn't matter what I think. It only matters what the DNA test reveals."

"How long did you say it would take to get the results?"

"Because we're using a private lab, probably not more than a week or ten days."

"When did you say we can get it done?"

"Cameron said he can squeeze us in right after lunch on Monday."

"That would be good," Zach said.

For him, maybe. Paige would prefer to do the test… never. But that was an emotional and selfish response. This wasn't about her and the potential repercussions for her life—it was about Emma, and she truly did want what was best for Olivia's daughter.

"I'll head over to the B and B now to settle up and be back here in about an hour. Then—" he glanced at Emma, who was sitting in an Elmo chair and turning the thick pages of a favorite book "—maybe I can take Emma to the p-a-r-k."

Although Paige knew logically that a fourteen-month-old with a very limited vocabulary couldn't possibly spell, she also knew that Emma had an unerring instinct about some things, which she proved when her head shot up in response to Zach's comment. "Pawk?"

Zach's brows lifted. Paige shrugged.

"Later," he promised.

Later, when Zach and Emma had gone to the park, Ashley brought a plate of frosted brownies over to Paige.

"I had a craving," she offered the explanation along with the squares.

"Thank you." Paige's mouth was already watering and her gratitude was sincere. "But how does your craving lead to me getting brownies?"

Ashley followed her into the kitchen. "Because I satisfied my craving, and because it will be something completely different that I have to have tomorrow, I thought I would share."

Paige peeled back the plastic wrap and snuck a square out from under the cover.

"You could offer me a cup of tea in exchange for the goodies," Ashley suggested, settling at the table.

"Oh. My." Paige's eyes closed as she bit into the chocolate and pure bliss exploded on her tongue. "All you want is a cup of tea? I'd be willing to give up one of my kidneys for chocolate this good."

Ashley smiled. "Been a while since you had some?"

They both knew she wasn't referring to chocolate. Paige popped the rest of the brownie into her mouth as she turned on the tap to fill the kettle. "I'm not even sure I could tell you how long."

Her cousin removed the cover from the plate. "Dig in."

Paige tossed teabags into the pot and retrieved a couple of mugs from the cupboard before she helped herself to another brownie.

"Speaking of sex," Ashley said. "Did I see Zach come in here with a duffel bag?"

"I'm not sure I follow your segue," Paige said cautiously.

Her cousin smirked. "You look at Zach Crawford the way a sexually deprived woman looks at a plate of double-chocolate fudge brownies."

Paige turned away from her cousin's knowing gaze to pour boiling water into the teapot. "Hadfield House was booked for the weekend and because Zach is spending most of his time here anyway, it made sense for him to take the spare room."

"I don't think it's a bad idea," Ashley said. "I'm just…surprised."

"Surprised that I could be reasonable?"

Her cousin's lips twitched, as if she was fighting against a smile. "Well, you haven't exactly been reasonable since Zach showed up."

"Can you blame me?"

"No," Ashley admitted, her hand moving instinctively, protectively, to cover her rounded belly. "Because I know you wouldn't love that little girl any more if you'd given birth to her, and because I know I would fight to my last breath against anyone who threatened to take my baby."

"Speaking of babies," Paige said, eager to change the subject. "Have you seen Marcus today?"

"I just came from the hospital," Ashley said. "And though I wouldn't have thought it possible, he's even more beautiful than he was yesterday."

"And the new mommy?"

"Radiant but exhausted. Apparently the baby woke up every two hours in the night to nurse."

Paige winced. "I can't imagine."

"Gage offered to give him a bottle so she could sleep, but Meg is determined to ensure that Marcus has the best start and she believes breastfeeding is crucial to that and giving him a bottle at this stage could create nipple confusion and—as you can imagine—after a few more minutes of listening to her exceptionally detailed reasoning, Gage's eyes started to glaze over."

But Ashley only looked wistful, and Paige knew her cousin was now even more anxious to hold her own baby in her arms.

"Only a couple more months and you can debate the benefits of cloth diapers versus disposables until Cam's eyes glaze over."

"We've already done that one." Ashley said and

helped herself to a brownie. "Now getting back to Zach."

"Why?" Paige asked warily.

"Because I guess what I'm really surprised about is that you invited this guy—this stranger—to live with you."

"First of all, he's not exactly a stranger—he's the man that Olivia believed was Emma's father. Second, we're not living together—he's only staying with me until the question of Emma's paternity has been answered. Third, you were the one who told me I should cooperate with him."

"It seemed like a good idea at the time," Ashley mumbled.

"And why doesn't it seem like a good idea now?"

"Because there's a...vibe...whenever you and Zach are in the same room together."

"A vibe?"

Her cousin nodded. "Like I said, you look at him like he's a chocolate brownie, and he looks at you like... like you're a woman he really wants to get naked with."

"I'm sure you're misinterpreting something."

"I don't think so."

"Even if that's true—and Zach hasn't said or done anything to suggest that it is—you have to know that I would never fall for a guy just because he looks good in uniform." And she figured her cousin, who was all too aware of the tumultuous relationship Paige had with her own father, would understand that better than most.

"I'm not worried that you'd fall for Zach because of his uniform but in spite of it," Ashley clarified.

"There's no need to worry at all," Paige assured her. She only hoped she sounded more confident than she felt because the truth was, the more time she spent with Zach, the more she forgot about the uniform and focused on the man. And she knew that could undermine all of her plans.

Chapter 6

Paige had seen enough in her family law practice to know that there were good parents and bad parents and some who were simply indifferent. She also knew that some mothers and fathers emulated the parenting practices they'd grown up with, and others consciously chose to distance themselves from same.

Paige didn't remember her mother. She remembered, too well, her father. His apparent lack of interest in and affection for his daughter, his complete disregard of her wants and needs, his callous dismissal of her love. For years, she'd believed that she only had to try harder, be better, study more, or look prettier, and if she succeeded, then he might actually see her, maybe even care about her.

After her thirteenth birthday, she'd realized how delusional she'd been. And she'd decided that if she wanted any attention from her father—and as foolish as she knew it was, she still did—she was going to have to take drastic action to get that attention.

That was when she'd started hanging out with the older kids on base, breaking curfew and, when she was grounded, sneaking out at night to go to parties. And then she'd met Second Lieutenant Matthew Sanders. She'd known he was older—that was part of the attraction for her. Not old enough that anyone would accuse her of looking for a father figure, just old enough to shock her own father, if he ever noticed that she was with him.

Of course, Colonel Phillip Wilder hadn't noticed— not until she'd taken her rebellion further than she'd intended, until it was too late to go back and undo what had been done.

She shook off the memories and the regrets and reminded herself that she'd learned an important lesson from her father—how *not* to parent.

She'd thought, when she first saw Zach in his uniform, that he would be like her father. After knowing him only a few days, she'd realized she was wrong. Zach was nothing like the colonel. His determination to be a father to Emma was proof of that, and Paige knew that she couldn't continue to interfere with his efforts.

So when they got back from their appointment at Cam's office and Zach suggested a trip to the park, Paige surprised him as much as herself by suggesting that he and Emma go on their own. And she took advantage of the unexpected time to herself to enjoy a book and the quiet outside in the sunshine.

If Zach knew nothing else about Emma, he knew that she loved the park. And since he'd started accom-

panying her on her daily excursions there, she seemed
to be willing to transfer some of that happy feeling in
his direction. But today, she wasn't nearly as pleased
with their outing as usual.

When he took her over to the swings, she seemed
more interested in playing in the wood shavings that
were spread on the ground. Which was okay until he
caught her trying to put them in her mouth. He told her
"no" and forced her to unfurl her fists to brush the chips
away, which of course caused her to express her displeasure at the top of her lungs with huge tears thrown
in for dramatic effect.

After she'd finally finished crying, she decided that
she wanted to go on the swings, but as soon as he settled her in and set it in motion, she was squirming to
get out again. So he took her to the slide instead, then
she ran to the climber then back to the swings.

He tried to be patient, but it seemed that nothing
he did was making her happy. When she started rubbing her eyes, he finally figured out that she was tired.
She'd gone down for her nap at what he now knew was
her usual time, but she'd been awakened early so they
could make their appointment for the DNA testing. Although she'd seemed happy enough then, he was paying for it now.

When he got her back to the house, Paige was in the
kitchen, pouring herself a glass of iced tea.

"You look exhausted," she commented. "Both of
you."

"Why do you find that amusing?" he asked, inex-
plicably irritated by the hint of a smile lurking at the
corners of her mouth.

She shrugged, not denying that she did. "Because

I know what you were thinking when you waltzed in here that first day."

He had never "waltzed" anywhere in his life—except on a dance floor—but he ignored that fact for the moment to ask, "What is it you think I was thinking?"

"That considering your extensive military training and the ability to maneuver an F-16 jet, taking care of a baby would be a piece of cake."

"I'm not sure I thought it would be a piece of cake," he denied. "But I certainly didn't expect it to be this hard."

"She's teething," she reminded him.

"She's crankier than a constipated general," he grumbled.

Paige broke a Popsicle in two, gave one half to Emma and put the other half back in the freezer for later. Emma immediately began gnawing on the icy treat.

"How is it that you instinctively know what she wants?"

"It's not instinctive," she denied. "Or not entirely. Mostly it's practice. Five-and-a-half-months ago I was as ill-equipped as you are now."

"I find that hard to believe."

She lifted a brow. "Because I'm female, you assume I was more automatically prepared to deal with a child?"

"No, because you're obviously so good with her."

She was somewhat mollified by his response. "As I said, it's practice. I've been around her since Emma was born, so I learned to read her signals. You'll figure it out, too, if you stick around long enough."

He leaned back against the counter, folded his arms over his chest. "You do that a lot, you know."

"Do what?"

"Take those not-so-subtle digs at me."

"I'm not trying to be subtle," she told him. "I want to make sure that you realize what kind of commitment parenthood requires."

"I'm getting a pretty good picture," he assured her.

"And how do you think child care is going to fit in with your career?"

He ignored her question to ask his own. "What branch of the military was your father in?"

"Army," she answered automatically, then glared at him as if it was his fault she'd revealed information she obviously hadn't intended to share. "But we're not talking about me, we're talking about Emma."

"Except if your concerns about her future stem from your personal history," he guessed.

"They don't," she said, but he knew it was a lie.

When Zach suggested that he wanted to try to put Emma down for another nap, Paige willingly went back outside to her book and the sunshine. She'd only read a few pages when she realized she'd forgotten her drink, so she set the paperback on the table and traipsed back into the house again.

She didn't return to the house intending to spy on him. But when she went into the kitchen to retrieve her glass, she heard his deep voice through the baby monitor on the counter.

"Do you think I can't handle a challenge?" he was saying, apparently to Emma, who, of course, didn't respond. "Do you think I can't manage to change one poopy diaper just because you're pumping your legs and flailing your fists?

"I know Paige thinks I can't handle it. In fact, she's

probably counting on me giving up on the whole fatherhood thing. But I've got news for both of you," he continued, still speaking in the same even tone. "I am a lieutenant colonel in the United States Air Force and there's no way I'm going to let a fourteen-month-old baby see me crumble, no matter—

"OhmyLord, child, what did you eat that turned into *that?*"

Paige smiled, picturing the look of complete horror on his face that she heard in his voice.

For a few minutes, she heard only background noises. The whisper of wipes being tugged out of their container, some muted gagging, the click of the latch on the diaper disposal, the crinkle of a new diaper being unfolded, a quiet gurgle of appreciation, the snap of buttons being refastened. Then Zach spoke again.

"We've already made progress, haven't we?" he was murmuring softly to her now. "Only a few days ago, you would have rather screamed than smiled at me, and although we might have had a little setback at the park, now you're snuggled in my arms and your eyes are drifting shut."

He was right, Paige realized. He had made a lot of progress with Emma in a short time, so much so that the little girl looked around for him when she heard his voice and smiled when he came into the room. And she wondered, not for the first time, if she'd made a mistake in inviting Zach to stay with them.

Because Paige was beginning to realize that not only had he made progress with the little girl he was currently rocking to sleep, he was making progress with her, too. She was actually starting to *like* him, and that wasn't just foolish, it was potentially dangerous.

"I said 'your eyes are drifting shut,'" Zach repeated, and Paige smiled, easily picturing Emma's big blue eyes stubbornly wide open, staring up at him as he tried to coax her to sleep.

She wondered what his air force buddies would think if they could see him now, attempting baby hypnosis. But the silence from the baby monitor told her that he'd not only attempted but succeeded, forcing her to accept that there probably wasn't anything the man couldn't do.

Considering that he might seek custody of the little girl, the realization was hardly reassuring.

With a sigh, she picked up her glass and went back outside.

Four chapters later, Paige realized that Zach hadn't made an appearance since he'd gone upstairs to put Emma down for her nap. Curious, she went back into the house and made her way up the stairs.

She found him when she peeked into Emma's room. The baby was finally asleep in his arms and Zach looked as if he was sleeping, too. She hesitated in the doorway, tempted to leave them undisturbed. But she knew that Emma would sleep better and longer if she was settled in her crib, and Zach would likely end up with a stiff neck if she left him as he was with his head tilted back in the chair.

She slid one hand beneath Emma's head and the other under her legs, but as she started to lift the sleeping child, Zach's grip instinctively tightened. Paige had no intention of playing tug-of-war with the baby, but now her hands were trapped.

She could feel the heat emanating from his body, and

her own started to tingle. She swallowed and tried to ease away, but his hold on the baby held her just as fast.

She drew in a breath and inhaled his warm masculine scent. Oh, he smelled good. And looked even better.

His T-shirt stretched across his broad shoulders and molded to his pecs, and his jeans hugged his long, lean legs. Had he shown up at her door dressed as casually as he was now, she likely would have melted in a puddle at his feet. But the uniform had made her cautious, urged her to maintain a safe distance. She tried to picture him in that uniform now, but her mind insisted on wanting to undress him instead.

She swallowed, hard, recognizing that she was in big trouble here.

"What are you doing?"

Her gaze flew to Zach's face.

His eyes were open now, alert, and focused intently on her.

"I, uh—" Oh Lord, his eyes were so blue and so intense that she nearly lost her train of thought. "Emma," she suddenly remembered. "I was going to put Emma in her crib."

"I can do it," Zach said.

"Oh. Of course," she agreed. "But I was walking by and it looked like you were sleeping, too, and—"

"I just closed my eyes for a minute."

Paige nodded and tugged her hands free.

Zach rose from the chair with the baby in his arms. "I wouldn't have dropped her, you know."

She nodded again because she knew it was true. Because she knew that Zach wouldn't do anything to harm Emma, and the obvious evidence of his affection for the child was seriously undermining Paige's resolve to keep him at a distance.

He settled Emma on her mattress, pulled the blanket up over her. "I would protect my daughter with my life."

Yeah, she'd realized that, too. And how was she supposed to resist a man who so clearly loved the little girl? But she had to ask, "Are you really that convinced— or are you just so stubborn that you can't consider the possibility, any superficial physical resemblance aside, that she might not be your daughter?"

"Did Olivia sleep around?"

"No," Paige responded immediately, firmly, in defense of her friend.

"Was she dishonest?"

"No," she said again, because even though she could see where he was going with these questions, she couldn't lie to him.

"Then why would I question her claim that I am the father of her child?"

Paige sighed as she followed him out into the hall. "Because most men probably would."

"I'm not going to lie and say that I was filled with joy and anticipation when I read Olivia's letter," he told her, starting down the steps. "The truth is, I was stunned and more than a little panicked. And maybe my first instinct was to deny the possibility. But once I'd had a chance to think about it, I knew that Olivia wouldn't lie about something like this."

"I know you're right," Paige admitted. "But what if Olivia wasn't lying but was simply mistaken? It's not beyond the realm of possibility to think that she had a brief fling with someone else and didn't consider that the baby might be his."

"Well, I guess we'll know the truth soon enough."

"I guess we will," she agreed.

"In the meantime…" He paused at the bottom of the staircase and turned to face her.

Because she was still standing on the last step, they were eye to eye. Her fingers curled around the newel post; her breath caught. His gaze dropped to her mouth, as if he wanted to kiss her. Paige started to sway forward, as if she wanted him to kiss her.

Then Zach took a quick step back. "In the meantime, I wanted to talk to you about something."

She exhaled an unsteady breath. "What's that?"

"I want to take Emma to California."

It was a good thing she was still holding on to the post, because his words nearly knocked her feet out from under her. "You've got to be kidding."

She stepped down, moving past him as she tried to get her head around what he was saying. "Don't you think that's a little premature?"

He shook his head. "My parents are expecting me in California next week," he admitted. "I didn't know what to tell them about Emma. I wasn't going to tell them anything until the test results came back, but I know she's mine, Paige. And you know she's mine. And I want my parents to meet her."

"You can't honestly think I'm going to let you take her across the country with you."

"Of course not," he acknowledged drily. "But I thought you could come, too."

She almost laughed out loud at the absurdity of the suggestion. "I can't just pack up and take off for California."

"Why not?"

She frowned, realizing that she didn't have a ready answer to his question, that there was no legitimate reason to refuse his request. And yet, her instincts warned that going anywhere with Zach Crawford was a bad idea. So all she said was, "I'll think about it."

It was hardly the most promising response, but given that Zach had been prepared for an outright refusal, he was willing to accept it. At least for now.

He could understand why she might have some reservations, especially considering the chemistry that had been simmering between them since the beginning and seemed to be moving toward a full boil.

He knew she wasn't oblivious to it. At first, he hadn't been so sure. In fact, she'd seemed so cool and polite and distant, he'd thought the tug of attraction he felt whenever he was near her might have been entirely one-sided.

But recently, he'd noticed the way her gaze would drop away from his, as if she was afraid to maintain eye contact. Or the way she jolted whenever he touched her—even if that touch was the most casual or accidental brush of his hand against her arm. No, she definitely wasn't oblivious.

He only hoped her wariness wouldn't prevent her from agreeing to make the trip. He really wanted her to meet his family, to show her that he had parents and sisters who would love and care for Emma because she was part of their family, too.

In the almost ten days that had passed since he'd first come to Pinehurst, he'd barely heard her mention her own family—aside from Ashley and Megan, of course. And remembering Megan's earlier comment about Paige taking care of Emma on her own, he suspected that she didn't have a support system. That might be the reason why she was so reluctant to entrust him with any real responsibility where Emma was concerned—because she was just so accustomed to doing everything on her own that she didn't know how to accept help when it was offered.

Whatever the reasons for her resistance, he knew he didn't have very much time left to change her mind. His flight was scheduled to leave on Wednesday, and he'd already booked seats for Paige and Emma to go with him.

Paige couldn't sleep. She'd taken a hiatus from the law firm to figure out her plans for the future, but since Zach had shown up at her door, she now had to consider the possibility that Emma might not be part of that future. Because as much as Zach seemed to appreciate the role she'd played in the little girl's life, the reality was that if he got custody of Emma and was posted to Florida or Arizona or California—which was apparently where his family lived—it wasn't likely that she would ever see her again.

With that thought weighing heavily on her mind, she gave up even trying to close her eyes and instead pushed back the covers.

She made her way quietly down the stairs to the kitchen, where she found a bottle of her favorite merlot in the wine rack and poured herself a glass. Tucking the receiver for the baby monitor under her arm and carrying the glass in her hand, she slipped out through the patio doors onto the back deck.

The night was dark and quiet, but the sky was bright

with stars. She set the monitor and the wine on the table and stretched out on a teak lounger.

She'd had second and third thoughts when she'd packed up everything she could fit in the trunk and backseat of her car and brought Emma to Pinehurst for the summer. She'd thought she would miss her work, her colleagues and clients, and the usual frenetic pace at the firm. She'd thought she would go crazy after only a week in this quiet town where she'd spent the last of her teenage years.

But the town wasn't as quiet as it used to be. Or maybe it was her own maturity that allowed her to appreciate the slower lifestyle now, that made her see what a wonderful place it would be to raise Emma.

Paige knew she could find work here, if not at one of the firms in town, then by hanging out her own shingle. She was a good attorney and there were always clients who needed representation. The more difficult challenge might be finding a care provider for Emma.

She sighed and reached for her glass of wine, refusing to consider that care for Emma might not be an issue.

A light breeze rustled through the leaves and goose bumps rose on her skin, reminding her that she'd forgotten her robe. The cotton boxers and ribbed tank that were her summer pajamas had seemed warm enough inside, but the early June evening was several degrees cooler than her bedroom. Still, she wasn't overly concerned about her state of dress—until the patio door slid open again and Zach stepped out into the moonlight.

She hadn't turned on the outside lights, but enough illumination spilled over from the neighbor's yard that she could see his heated gaze rake over her, and her skin tingled everywhere it touched.

She was suddenly conscious of her half-dressed state and even more conscious of his. Because Zach was wearing nothing but a pair of jeans that weren't even buttoned. Without a shirt, she could see that his shoulders were even broader than she'd imagined and perfectly sculpted. And his stomach really did look like a washboard with all of those rippling muscles. As Paige's eyes skimmed over him, her mouth actually went dry.

If it was shallow to respond in a purely sexual manner to such a well-toned physique, well, then, she was shallow. She was also very close to whimpering.

She swallowed a mouthful of wine instead. "I, uh, thought you were sleeping."

"I was," he told her. "Until I heard the patio door slide open."

His protective instincts were obviously very finely honed—or at least a lot more so than her father's. Phillip Wilder had never noticed when his fourteen-year-old daughter snuck out of the house, or maybe he'd just never cared.

Regardless, she should have remembered that she wasn't alone in the house and put on a robe. Of course, it was Zach's presence that had kept her awake—and while she might have excused her inability to sleep as a result of her concerns over Emma's custody, she knew that was only part of the reason for her restlessness. The other—and maybe even the bigger part—was her awareness of this man.

She was definitely aware of him now. Aware and wanting and fervently cursing her hormones for not having the sense to realize how perilous wanting him could be.

She set down her glass and tucked her legs up against her chest so he couldn't see the hard peaks of her nipples pressing against the thin cotton of her shirt, so he wouldn't guess how desperately she wanted him to touch her, kiss her, take her.

She ignored the heat that coursed through her veins and said, "I didn't mean to disturb you."

He dropped down onto the lounger beside hers but sat so that he was facing her. "You definitely disturb me."

Paige thought it was probably wiser not to respond to the blatant innuendo, and so she said nothing. Not even when he reached for the wineglass she'd set down.

He lifted it to his nose, sniffed. His brows rose and he tipped the glass to his lips. There was something strangely intimate about him drinking from her glass, putting his mouth where hers had been.

He swallowed, and his lips curved again. "Stonechurch Vineyards merlot. The silver label Special Reserve."

"You saw the bottle on the counter," she guessed.

He shook his head. "My parents run the winery. Or maybe I should say that they used to run the winery. My sister, Hayden, took over most of the operations a few years back."

The revelation that she was drinking wine his family had made was as surprising as the realization that he had a family. It just wasn't something she'd thought about until he'd mentioned wanting to take Emma to California.

It was difficult enough to admit that this man might be the little girl's father, that he would have a legitimate legal claim to custody of the child who had taken complete hold of her heart, but she'd never considered that he might be able to offer her so much more than his name. That he had parents who could be Emma's grandparents, a sister who could be her aunt and maybe even an extended family who would want to be part of her life.

But all she said was, "I didn't know you had a sister."

"Three of them, actually," he told her.

"You're one of four kids?" She thought about how busy she was just chasing around after Emma. "Wow, that must have kept your parents busy."

"I always tease Hayden—she's the youngest—that they didn't have more than they could handle until she was born because that's when they finally quit."

"What is her response to that?"

"That the real reason they stopped having children was that they'd finally had the perfect one."

It was the affection she heard in his voice as much as his response that made her smile. "She's the one who works at the winery?"

He nodded.

"What do your other sisters do?" she asked, genuinely curious about the siblings she'd only just realized he had.

"Lauryn is a doctor and Jocelyn is a college professor."

"And you fly planes," she noted, thinking that his parents definitely hadn't raised any slackers.

He nodded. "It's all I ever wanted to do."

"Why the military?"

"I heard a rumor that chicks dig a guy in uniform."

She smiled because she knew it was the response he

expected. And because she didn't doubt for a minute that he'd found himself the object of countless affections, though she wouldn't assume that had anything to do with the uniform. Because even out of uniform, in only a pair of unzipped jeans, he was all too appealing.

She took back her glass of wine and swallowed a long, bracing gulp.

"What about you?" he asked. "Did you always know you were going to be a lawyer?"

"No," she said. "In fact, I was in my second year studying geology when I had to vacate the apartment I was renting because it flooded. I ended up staying with a friend and the landlord took me to small-claims court to sue for nonpayment of rent.

"Of course, there was no way I could afford a lawyer to defend against the claim, so I started researching the law myself. In the end, I countersued for breach of contract, pointing out that I couldn't be expected to live in an apartment that was eighteen inches underwater."

"And you won," he guessed.

She nodded. "That's when I decided to go to law school."

He shifted so that his knees were almost touching the side of her chair. The denim looked faded and worn and a lot softer than the rock-hard muscle that flexed beneath the fabric. Good Lord, just looking at the man's quads had her heart pounding inside her chest and her fingers itching to touch. Instead, she curled them tighter around the glass.

She finished off her wine and stood up so that the lounger was between them. "And that's where I met Olivia," she reminded him—reminding both of them—

of her close friendship with the woman who had been
his lover and had likely given birth to his child.

"I cared about Olivia," Zach told her, standing to
block her access to the door. "I wouldn't have been involved with her otherwise. But I wasn't in love with her,
and she wasn't in love with me."

She lifted a shoulder. "Your relationship with Olivia
really isn't any of my business."

"And yet you keep throwing her name out whenever
the topic of conversation touches on anything remotely
personal, as if you're deliberately putting up barriers
between us."

"She was one of my best friends."

"Are you afraid that she would disapprove of my
being here?"

She shook her head. "According to the letter you
showed me, she wanted you to have the chance to get
to know Emma."

"I'm talking about my being here with you."

"You're not here with me," she denied.

He smiled at that.

"I mean—you're here and I'm here," she explained,
conscious of the heat suffusing her cheeks. "But we're
not together."

"What if I want to change that?"

She shook her head again. "I don't think that would
be a good idea."

He took a step closer. "Well, apparently, we have a
difference of opinion."

She lifted a hand to ward him off and sucked in a
breath when her palm came into contact with his bare
flesh. He was every bit as solid and warm as he looked,
and she wanted—more than anything—to lean closer,

to press herself against him, to feel the hard length of his body against hers.

"Zach." She'd meant to speak his name as a warning. Instead, it sounded like a plea.

He took the empty wineglass from her hand and reached around her to set it back on the table. Then he lifted his hand to her face and gently cupped her cheek. The gesture was so unexpected, so tender, she nearly sighed.

"I just want to kiss you," he said and brushed his thumb over the curve of her bottom lip, slowly, sensuously.

"Definitely not a good idea," she said, all too aware that the breathless tone of her voice contradicted her words.

"Another difference of opinion," he said easily, and lowered his mouth to hers.

Chapter 7

She should pull away.

Paige knew that would be the smart thing to do. But Zach's hands were on her face, gentle but firm, holding her immobile beneath the sensual onslaught of his lips. And even if she'd been able to move, the truth was, she didn't want to.

His kiss was as gentle as his touch—and temptingly seductive. He kissed as she imagined he would make love—because yes, she had imagined not just kissing him but a whole lot more—slowly, deeply and incredibly thoroughly.

With a soft sigh, she parted her lips, meeting his tongue with her own. He tasted of the wine they'd both drank, but somehow his flavor was stronger, richer and even more intoxicating. As if of their own volition, her hands slid over the hard planes of his chest, over the tight muscles of his shoulders, to link behind his neck.

His fingers trailed down her throat, skimmed across her collarbone, then traced along the line of her spine, moving slowly downward until they curved around her bottom and pulled her closer. She felt the hard press of his arousal at the juncture of her thighs and moaned.

His kiss wasn't so gentle now. It was hot and hungry and so fiercely passionate that it made her shiver. Not because she was afraid, but because her own desire was just as powerful and overwhelming.

She was hardly a virgin, but nothing in her experience had prepared her for being kissed by Zach Crawford. The kiss went on and on, and with each racing beat of her heart, the wanting inside of her grew stronger.

She didn't know how far things might have gone if he'd wanted to push for more. But he didn't push at all. In fact, he was the one who eventually eased away.

"I think you should go back up to bed now," he whispered.

Her blood was still churning, her pulse pounding, her knees weak, but when he spoke, his voice was level and so carefully controlled that she might have thought the bone-melting kiss they'd just shared had no effect on him. Until she looked up at him, and the fire that continued to burn in his eyes proved otherwise.

To be wanted so much by such a man was…exhilarating. To want him so much that she couldn't think about anything else was…terrifying.

She ordered her trembling legs to move and stepped toward the door. "Good night."

* * *

Zach watched Paige slip back inside the house, and it took every ounce of his willpower not to follow. But he knew that what he needed right now was space—distance from the far-too-tempting woman who had him all tied up in knots.

Damn. He never should have kissed her.

If he hadn't, he'd still be in the fantasy stage of wondering if her lips were as soft as they looked, if her taste was as sweet as he imagined. But the wondering had been driving him to distraction, and so he'd stopped speculating and started kissing—and the jolt of heat had seared him right down to his toes.

Chemistry between a man and woman was an unpredictable thing. Sometimes it was there, sometimes it wasn't. He'd been attracted to other women before, and he'd learned that sometimes the chemistry sparked and sometimes it fizzled. With Paige, it was positively explosive.

A man had to be crazy to walk away from that kind of heat. Except that, in this case, Zach was all too aware that his efforts to stoke the flames between them could very well result in his getting burned.

And as much as he wanted Paige, he wouldn't do anything that might jeopardize his relationship with the daughter he'd only just found. If he hadn't already done so.

Because while he'd told himself it was "just a kiss"—and told *her* the same thing—they both knew it was a lie. There was nothing "just" about the kiss they'd shared. It wasn't a simple touching of lips that was over and done. No, the kiss they'd shared had been a prelude to and a promise of so much more.

And she'd been an equal participant in the kiss. Yeah, maybe he'd started it—but within a few seconds, she'd been just as involved in the lip-lock as he and making just as many promises.

Thankfully, he'd learned a long time ago about the dangers of trusting in a woman's promises, and he wouldn't let himself get sucked in again.

Ever.

Paige had promised Zach that she would think about going to California with him, but the more she thought about it, the more she was sure that traveling across the country with him wasn't a good idea. Unfortunately, she wasn't prepared to share with him the real reason for her apprehension—namely, that she had a hard enough time resisting temptation in her own backyard without giving him the home-field advantage.

But by Monday, Zach was really pressing for a response to his invitation, and when Paige continued to hedge, he asked, "Is it because I kissed you?"

"Of course not," she lied, because to admit otherwise would be to give the kiss far more significance than she was willing to acknowledge.

"Because we won't be alone there," he told her, as if he understood the real reason for her hesitation despite her denials.

She lifted her chin. "I'm not worried about being alone with you."

Zach's gaze dropped to her mouth. His own curved.

"Then what are you worried about?" he challenged.

"Emma," she said immediately. "She's already been through one recent move, and I'm not sure how she'd tolerate traveling all the way to the West Coast."

"I'm sure she'll be fine."

"And have you ever traveled with a baby?" she asked, because she was sure the answer would be "no." "Do you have any idea how much stuff we would have to haul with us? There's her porta-crib and her booster seat and her car seat and—"

"My sister Lauryn has two kids," he told her. "When Regan, her eldest, was born, my parents redid Lauryn's room as a nursery, so they have a crib and a change table and a rocking chair and a high chair and one of those exersaucer things and more toys than you could imagine."

"I just think, at this time, it makes more sense for you to make the trip on your own," she suggested.

But Zach shook his head. "If you and Emma won't go with me, then I won't go at all."

She shouldn't care whether he went to California or not, but she knew that his family did. He'd been overseas for the past two years and during that time, he'd been in contact with them only via e-mail and the occasional phone call.

Aside from how much she knew Zach wanted to see them, she knew what it would mean to them to be able to see him in person—because she knew what it had meant to her every time her dad had returned from an assignment. But that was ancient history.

"The test results should be in next week," she hedged. "Maybe we should wait until then."

"I've already changed my flight once," he reminded her.

She sighed. "You're talking about a flight that's leaving in two days. I might not even be able to get a ticket—"

"I'll take care of that," Zach told her.

Still she hesitated.

"Please, Paige."

It was the entreaty in those blue, blue eyes even more than the plea in his words that tipped the scales. "All right," she finally agreed.

But two days later, as their plane touched down in San Francisco, Paige wasn't feeling any more certain about her decision.

"I'm really not sure this is a good idea," she told him.

Zach reached into the overhead bin for her carry-on. "It's a little late now to be having second thoughts."

"I've had them since you first mentioned this trip," she reminded him, setting Emma on her feet. "They're just a lot more insistent right now."

"Everything's going to be fine."

"I just think this is a little premature. I mean, what if it turns out that you're not Emma's father?"

At first, Zach had seemed both baffled and frustrated by her continuing denials of Emma's paternity. Now, he just seemed amused.

"Then at least you'll have had a chance to explore California wine country with a native," he said easily.

"Is it really that simple for you?"

"No," he admitted. "But I've never been the type to worry about 'what ifs.'"

"Not even when you're flying?" she asked, genuinely curious.

"*Especially* not when I'm flying. The absolute last thing you want when you're in control of a fifteen-million-dollar plane is for your mind to be wandering."

"I guess that makes sense," she acknowledged. "But—"

Whatever she was going to say was forgotten when she caught a glimpse of the tall, stunning blonde who suddenly appeared and threw her arms around Zach.

"I can't believe you're finally home." She kissed first one cheek, then the other, then hugged him tight again.

Zach cast a guilty glance in Paige's direction. "What are you doing here, Hayden?"

"You haven't been home in two years," the blonde reminded him. "I was worried that you might not remember the way."

"I told you I didn't need a welcoming committee at the airport."

"I'm not a committee, I'm your sister. And since when have I ever listened to you?"

He sighed. "Good point," he acknowledged, then turned her around to face Paige and Emma. "This is my sister, Hayden."

But before he could introduce them to his sister, Hayden's eyes grew wide. "Ohmygod."

And in that moment Paige knew that he had just sprung a big surprise on his sister and all her doubts and uncertainties about this trip multiplied tenfold. When he'd insisted that he wanted his family to meet Emma, she'd figured that they knew about her. Hayden's reaction proved otherwise.

"This is Paige," he continued. "And the little girl she's holding is Emma."

Hayden shifted her attention from the baby to Zach. "She's yours."

It was a statement, not a question, but Paige felt compelled to interject. "We're still waiting for the DNA results from the lab."

"She has Zach's eyes—Crawford eyes," Hayden pointed out.

She reached out a hand, as if to touch the little girl's cheek, but Emma turned away, burying her face against Paige's shoulder.

Hayden's hand dropped back to her side, and when she looked at Paige now, her own blue, blue eyes were as hard and cold as ice. "Why would you deny it? You obviously got pregnant to trap my brother—"

"Hayden," Zach interrupted sharply.

The blonde shifted her annoyance to him.

"Paige isn't Emma's mother." He spoke again before she could.

But the furrow that creased her brow suggested that his words added to rather than detracted from his sister's confusion. "Then why is she here with you?"

"Emma's mom was killed in a car accident several months ago, and Paige has been taking care of the baby since then."

"Oh." There was both embarrassment and apology in Hayden's voice now. "I'm sorry," she said to Paige. "I shouldn't have jumped to conclusions."

"It's okay," Paige assured her. "I didn't realize that Zach hadn't explained who I was." She shot him a glance that let him know she wasn't pleased by that fact.

"Zach didn't explain anything. He just said he was coming home," she explained. "He didn't mention that he was bringing anyone with him, and when I saw the baby, well, I just assumed—obviously mistakenly— that she was yours."

"Olivia, Emma's mother, was a good friend of mine."

"I'm guessing there's a story here," Hayden said.

"And one that I don't intend to repeat more than

once," Zach told her. "So you're going to have to wait until we get home to hear it."

"How about a preview?" his sister asked, taking one of the suitcases from him and starting toward the exit.

"No," he said firmly.

Paige, carrying Emma, struggled to keep pace with him. Although she could understand his sister's curiosity, she had her own concerns.

"You didn't tell anyone we were coming?" She whispered the question behind Hayden's back.

"It wasn't something I felt comfortable trying to explain to my parents on the phone," he admitted.

"So we're going to show up at their home unannounced and uninvited?"

"It's my parents' home—I don't need to be announced or invited."

"What about Emma and me?"

"You're my guests," he said simply.

"Unannounced and uninvited guests," she muttered, more convinced than ever that coming to California had been a mistake.

Paige's apprehension increased throughout the drive.

Within a few minutes, Emma had fallen asleep, leaving Paige to her own thoughts. She watched the countryside as it passed outside the window, but she was too worried about how Zach's mother and father would react to their arrival to fully appreciate the beautiful scenery.

She didn't even realize they'd turned off of the highway until she spotted the sign that announced Stonechurch Estates Winery. Farther down the long, winding drive was a stunning two-story stone building with dozens of gleaming windows and wrought-iron balconies surrounded by gardens already spilling over with colorful blooms.

"Is that where you grew up?" she asked Zach and Hayden, thinking it looked more like a five-star hotel than anyone's home.

Hayden chuckled as Zach half-turned in his seat to respond to her question. "No. That's the château, as my mother likes to call it."

"To the rest of us, it's the winery," his sister informed her.

"That's some winery," she mused.

"The building also houses the tasting bar, wine boutique and gift shop, café and three private event rooms," Hayden continued. "Outside the gift shop, although you can't see it from this side, is an enormous pergola that shades half a dozen picnic tables. We get a lot of tourists who like to eat their lunch—either purchased from the café or brought from home—outside."

"Don't get her started," Zach warned. "The winery is her baby now."

"And not a surprise I sprang on Mom and Dad," Hayden teased.

Zach shot her a quelling glance.

The knots in Paige's stomach tightened.

In retrospect, Zach would have to agree with Paige that springing a baby and the baby's guardian on his parents with no warning might not have been the best idea he'd ever had. However, his mom and dad responded to Emma precisely as he knew they would— they fell in love with her at first sight.

They were a little more reserved with respect to

Paige. Of course, Hayden didn't help the situation any when she blurted out the introductions.

"Zach brought company," she announced to their parents. "The baby is his. I'm not sure if Paige is, but she's not Emma's mother."

"Well, thanks for clearing that up."

Hayden grinned unapologetically in response to her mother's dry remark.

"I'm Kathleen," Zach's mom said, offering her hand and a smile to Paige.

Paige shifted Emma's weight slightly to shake her hand, then that of the man standing behind her.

"I'm Justin."

"Paige Wilder," she told them. "And, as Hayden already mentioned, this is Emma."

At that, Emma opened her eyes and glanced around. Then she let out a huge yawn, and her lids drifted shut again.

"She's beautiful," Kathleen said softly.

"And she's definitely not a newborn," Justin commented, looking questioningly at his son.

"Any chance we could get a cup of coffee?" Zach asked.

He knew he was going to have to answer their questions—and face their wrath—and he desperately wanted a hit of caffeine before he had to do so.

"Hayden," his mom began.

"I'm on it," his sister acknowledged, already moving toward the front door.

"Why don't you come on into the kitchen while the men unload the luggage?" Kathleen suggested to Paige.

Paige cast him a worried glance, as if she was afraid

she'd have to face the inquisition alone. "I should help Zach with the bags."

"I'd say you already have your hands full," Kathleen noted, indicating the baby in her arms.

"I'll just be a minute," Zach assured her.

With a last desperate look, Paige followed his mother into the house, and Zach followed his father back to Hayden's car.

Kathleen Crawford led Paige through the front door and into an enormous foyer with numerous entrances into other rooms and a wide, curving staircase that led to the upper level. She headed down the tiled hallway and into an enormous kitchen that looked as if it could be photographed for a spread in a decorating magazine. Several of the glossy mahogany cupboards had glass doors that displayed what she imagined were the everyday dishes. Solid wood chairs were set around an oversize table on which sat a lovely glass bowl filled with apples so green and so shiny Paige couldn't tell if they were real or decorative.

"What a gorgeous kitchen," Paige told her.

"We remodeled last summer, and I have to admit I'm pleased with it," Kathleen said, "But I'll warn you that other parts of the house are still works in progress.

"The original foundation of the home was laid nearly a hundred and fifty years ago. Of course, there have been several additions put on since then, and we've done a lot of updating and remodeling, but there's still so much yet to do."

"I love old houses," Paige confessed. "They have so much character."

"A dozen or so years ago, when we were building

the château, Justin and I talked about building a new house, too, but neither one of us had the heart to tear this one down."

"I wouldn't, either," Paige told her, then exhaled a silent sigh of relief when she heard heavy footsteps in the hall.

A moment later, Zach and his dad stepped into the room.

"I just got a message from Emilio," Justin said to Hayden. "Asking if you could check in with him when you get a chance and before the three-o'clock tour, if possible."

She glanced at her watch, swore softly.

"Hayden," her mother admonished.

"Sorry," she muttered automatically. Then, to her father, "Do I have to go now?"

"Why are you asking me?" Justin countered, as he settled himself at the table. "You're the CEO now."

His daughter sighed. "I hate when you pull out the CEO card, because then I feel like I have to live up to the title."

"That's why we gave it to you," her father admitted.

She filled a mug from the freshly brewed pot and carried it toward the back door. "It was nice meeting you, Paige," she said over her shoulder. "And I'll look forward to hearing all of the details later."

"I'm not telling you anything," her brother answered, pouring coffee into the other four mugs she'd taken out earlier and set on the counter.

"Yes, you will. Because if you don't, I'll make up my own version," she warned just before the door closed at her back.

Justin shook his head. "They've been like that with each other since they were children," he told Paige.

"They're still our children," his wife reminded him. Then she turned to her son. "And speaking of children…"

Zach took the mugs to the table and, while they drank their coffee, he explained the situation as he'd become aware of it, with Paige filling in the occasional detail and some of the history and his parents interjecting with questions every now and again.

By the time all of their inquiries had been satisfied, Paige was yawning.

"I'm sorry," she apologized, trying to stifle yet another yawn.

"Emma had a rough night," Zach explained to his parents. "So neither Paige nor I got much rest before we had to head out this morning."

"She's teething," Paige explained.

"So you two are—" Justin cleared his throat, as if he was uncomfortable even asking the question "—living together?"

"No," Paige responded quickly, firmly. "Zach has been staying with me so that he could spend some time getting to know Emma."

"Oh, well, I guess that makes sense," Kathleen said, looking to her husband for confirmation, although she didn't sound entirely convinced herself.

"I'm living in Pinehurst, New York, right now," Paige explained. "Which is a significant distance from where Zach lives. He's been sleeping in the spare room so that he doesn't have to drive back and forth all the time."

"So it's just an arrangement of convenience," Zach's father concluded.

"Yes," Paige assured her.

"So who has custody of Emma now?" Kathleen asked.

"I do," Paige told her. "Because Olivia named me her legal guardian and the father was listed as unknown on her birth certificate, the court had no reason not to approve my application."

"And what will happen when you get the DNA test results?"

"We'll figure that out then," Zach said.

His mother didn't look happy with that response, but she only said, "I can show you to the guest room, Paige, if you want to rest before dinner."

"I would love to," she said gratefully.

"Do you want me to take Emma?" Zach asked.

Paige knew he was simply offering to look after Emma only while she caught a quick nap, but his choice of words rekindled the terrifying fear that had only recently started to ease.

Spending time with Zach and Emma, she'd actually begun to hope that they might find a way to work together. But being here with him now, with his family, made her realize that he didn't need her help. And that he probably wouldn't want it, either.

"No, I've got her," she said, and followed his mother back through the kitchen to the foyer and up that winding staircase she'd admired.

"This used to be Jocelyn's room," Kathleen explained. "We redecorated when she moved out, but that was quite a few years ago now. There's another guest room down the hall that was redone more recently, but this one is closer to the nursery and I thought you'd prefer to be near Emma."

"I would," Paige agreed. "And this is beautiful, really."

"It has a great view, anyway," Kathleen said, moving across the room to the window. "That is, if you like looking at grapes."

Paige smiled. "I do, thank you."

Kathleen moved back to the door, hovered there for a moment. In the end, all she said was, "Let me know if you need anything," and then she was gone.

Paige didn't manage to squeeze in much of a nap before Emma woke up from hers and demanded her attention. But it had revived her enough so that she was happy to explore the backyard with the toddler. Zach must have been watching for them because only a few minutes after they'd ventured outdoors, he came to join them.

He gave them an impromptu tour of the grounds, including some history of the area, a discourse on the life cycle of the grape and a crash course in the process of making wine.

Later, they had a quiet meal with just his parents since Hayden had an important business dinner she couldn't miss. Her recent bouts of crabbiness apparently forgotten, Emma was her usual charming self at dinner, and Paige could tell that both of Zach's parents were immediately enchanted by her.

On the whole, Paige thought the day had gone better than she'd anticipated, but when she settled back into bed later that night, she acknowledged that her feelings about Zach Crawford were now more confused than ever.

The first day, when he'd shown up at her door in uniform, she'd been sure she knew exactly who and what he was. But she'd been looking at him through her own experience and prejudice, and she'd finally begun to realize how very wrong she'd been.

He was a military man, but unlike her father, there was so much more to him than just that. He was a family man—a son, a brother, an uncle. Maybe a father. Emma's father. And the more time she spent with him, the more she was beginning to realize that having Zach for a father might not be a horrible experience for Emma. In fact, he'd been nothing short of wonderful with the little girl.

Sure, he had a lot to learn, but he was tackling the challenges of fatherhood with enthusiasm and determination. He wasn't afraid to admit that he didn't know everything, and he wasn't too proud to ask for help. And when Paige watched him with Emma, her heart just melted.

He was interested and attentive and patient, and he seemed to genuinely enjoy spending time with her. And Emma absolutely doted on him. Once she'd gotten over her initial trepidation, she'd fallen head over heels.

Paige couldn't blame her. What experience did the toddler have that would enable her to resist his effortless charm and easy affection? Paige herself had all kinds of reasons for being wary and even she wasn't completely immune to Zach.

The kiss they'd shared—the way it had singed every nerve ending in her body—proved that. And if she hadn't been hyperaware of him before that kiss, she certainly was now.

But Zach hadn't made a move since then. Maybe

he'd only been curious, and that single kiss had been enough to satisfy his curiosity. It had only piqued hers.

If he could make her feel so much with just the touch of his lips to hers, what would happen if he ever *really* touched her? If he ever made love with her?

She shoved those questions—and the almost-painful yearning—aside and pushed out of bed.

Although she hadn't heard a peep from the baby monitor, she decided to check on Emma. It was the little girl's first night in a strange place, in an unfamiliar bed, and she wanted to ensure that she was settled in okay.

Paige was reaching for the doorknob when she remembered being caught by Zach in her pj's once before and detoured back to get her robe. Her heart pounded with the memory as she shoved her arms in the sleeves and wrapped the belt around her waist.

Using the light in the hall to guide her, Paige tiptoed into Emma's room, only to confirm that the baby was tucked in with her favorite blanket and sleeping peacefully.

She had just turned back to the door when Zach stepped into the room.

"I thought I heard Emma stirring," he explained.

"It was probably just me," Paige told him. "She's fine."

"Can't sleep?"

Can't stop thinking about you, Paige thought, but of course, she didn't speak the words aloud.

"Just feeling a little restless," she said instead.

"Want a glass of wine to help you settle?"

"No," she responded quickly. Too quickly.

He smiled knowingly, and she knew then that he hadn't forgotten about the kiss. When his gaze dropped to her lips, she knew that he was thinking of kissing her again.

She took a step back—a retreat that was as much emotional as it was physical.

"I'm afraid that I may have given you the wrong idea," she told him.

"About what?"

"My reasons for agreeing to this trip."

"You made it clear that you're only here because I wanted my family to meet Emma."

"That's true," she acknowledged.

"But I wanted my family to meet you, too," he told her.

She was surprised by the statement, and more than a little unnerved by the way he was looking at her. "Why?"

"Because you're the most important person in Emma's life right now." His gaze caught hers, and even through the shadows, she felt the heat of his stare, causing an answering warmth to spread through her veins. "And because you're important to me, too."

"Because of Emma," she said.

"For a lot of reasons I'm not entirely sure I understand myself," he told her.

"Don't make this any more complicated than it already is," she pleaded softly.

"Do you think I chose for this to happen?" he asked, the husky tone of his voice making the words feel as intimate as a caress.

"There is no *this*."

He took another step closer. "Are you saying that if I touched you now, you could just walk away?"

"I *would* walk away," she insisted.

And she did just that before he could prove her wrong.

Chapter 8

Zach let Paige go.

He could have stopped her. He didn't doubt that for a minute. He could have blocked her path and made her face not just him but the feelings that were between them. Feelings that he knew she wasn't ready to acknowledge.

Feelings that he wasn't sure *he* was ready to acknowledge.

That was why he let her go. And why he wouldn't get any sleep right now knowing that Paige was in her bed just across the hall.

So he headed to the kitchen instead, and found his mother there with a cup of decaf coffee and a slice of leftover lemon meringue pie.

Her brows rose when he walked into the room.

"I can't believe you're not exhausted," she said.

"I *am* exhausted," he admitted. "I just can't sleep."

"I guess it's not surprising that you would have a lot on your mind."

He found the pie in the refrigerator and cut himself a piece. "I'm sorry I didn't tell you about Emma."

"If you'd known that your girlfriend was pregnant and didn't tell us, I'd be kicking your ass," she told him. "But under the circumstances, there's no need to apologize."

Her no-nonsense attitude and unconditional love were only two of the things he loved about her, and as he sat down across from her and scooped up a forkful of tangy lemon filling, he thought about how truly lucky he was to have been given such wonderful parents.

But then she asked, "Did you love Emma's mother?"

And he remembered that, wonderful though she was, she didn't always understand the concept of boundaries.

He winced as his fork clattered against the plate. "Mom—"

"I know love isn't always necessary—or even desired—for two people to be intimate," Kathleen said. "I just wondered about your feelings for the woman who had your child."

"I cared about her," he said at last.

"But you love Paige," his mother guessed.

He'd only recently admitted—and only to himself—that he had feelings for Emma's guardian. He wasn't yet ready to put a label on those feelings, and he certainly wasn't ready to make that emotional leap.

So instead of admitting or denying her claim, he said, "I've never known anyone like her. She's beautiful and smart, compassionate and caring. She's ready to change her life for Emma—in a lot of ways, she already has."

Unlike Heather, who'd claimed to love him but hadn't been willing to make the slightest compromise for their future together. So long as he'd been in training in California, everything had been great. The minute he'd been posted out of state, she'd turned her back on him.

"So maybe it's not surprising that you'd fall in love with her," his mother noted. "But how does she feel about you?"

"You mean you haven't got that all figured out?"

Her lips curved in response to his teasing, but the smile quickly faded.

"She's guarded," she said, her tone reflecting her worry. "She's wonderful with Emma and it's obvious that she loves that little girl, but it's not easy to know what she's thinking or feeling about anything else."

"I guess you have her figured out," Zach mused.

His mother shook her head. "She's even more guarded around you, and I can't figure out if that's because of Emma or if there's some other reason for her caution."

"She has issues with my career," Zach admitted.

His mother frowned. "What kind of issues?"

"I don't know exactly. I know her father was in the military and she had something of a transient childhood."

"And she doesn't want that for Emma," she guessed.

He nodded.

"I can understand why that would be a concern."

"I thought you'd be on my side."

"I want what's best for my granddaughter."

He smiled. "And you don't have any doubts that she is your granddaughter, do you?"

"Not from the first minute she opened her eyes."

"I felt the same way when I saw her. I was stunned, more than a little panicked, but absolutely certain that she was mine."

"But Paige still isn't convinced."

"I think Paige doesn't want to acknowledge that Emma is my daughter because she's worried about the repercussions from a legal standpoint."

"You know, if you let Paige know that you want to be with her as much as you want to be with your daughter, you might alleviate a lot of her worry," his mother suggested.

"I'm working on it," he admitted.

"Then I have no doubt you'll succeed."

The next night there was a family dinner to celebrate Zach's homecoming, which gave Paige the opportunity to meet the rest of his siblings.

His sister Lauryn showed up with her husband, Sam, and their two kids, four-year-old Regan and two-and-half-year-old Shane. She remembered Zach telling her that Lauryn was a doctor and she learned through conversation that her husband was an anesthesiologist and that they'd met, not surprisingly, at the hospital.

Zach's middle sister, Jocelyn, looked more like a cover model than a college professor, although her boyfriend, Luke, definitely looked like the accountant that he was. Or maybe Paige just had a chip on her shoulder as far as his profession was concerned because Ashley's cheating ex-fiancé had been an accountant, too. Of course, everything had worked out for her cousin in the end, so she decided she would make a conscious effort not to hold Luke's choice of career against him.

Hayden was the last to show up, which was surprising because she was the only one who still lived at home. Paige was in the kitchen, chopping vegetables for the salad, when Zach's youngest sister finally arrived.

"Something smells good," she said, and leaned over the stove to kiss her mother's cheek.

"Chicken Parmesan," Kathleen told her.

"Mmm. One of my favorites."

"Anything's your favorite, so long as you don't have to cook it," her mother noted.

"True enough." Hayden snagged a slice of cucumber from Paige's chopping board.

Her mother slapped her hand. "You can wait until we sit down to eat like everyone else."

"When will that be?" Hayden wanted to know.

"We'd be eating now if you'd been here earlier to help," Kathleen told her.

"I'll put the rolls on the table," Hayden said and, taking a basket in each hand, ducked out of the kitchen to do just that.

Kathleen sighed. "Sometimes I wonder where I went wrong with that girl."

Paige dumped the veggies into the enormous bowl of lettuce that had been washed and torn earlier. "I only hope I can do half as good a job raising Emma as you've done with all of your children."

Zach's mom smiled. "I know I don't really have cause to complain, but as a mother, I can't seem to stop worrying about her—worrying about all of them, actually." She glanced over at Paige. "Of course, I'm sure you've learned that with Emma already."

Paige shrugged. "I'm not really Emma's mother," she felt compelled to remind her.

"You are now, in every way that matters," Kathleen told her, then went to call the rest of the family for dinner.

Dinner was, as Crawford family gatherings usually were, a noisy event. It was also a belated surprise celebration of Emma's first birthday, although Zach hadn't told Paige what he'd planned because he'd wanted it to be a surprise for her, too.

"I know it's not really her birthday," Zach said, watching as Emma grabbed for a big pink frosting flower from the top of the enormous cake his mother had baked and decorated. "But because I wasn't around when it was, I wanted to do something special for her."

"I'd say you succeeded," Paige told him.

"She does look like she's having fun."

"Are you kidding? She's the center of attention and her whole body is revved up on sugar—of course she's having fun."

Zach noted that while Paige continued to watch Emma, her own plate of cake sat untouched beside her.

"I know she's too young to remember this day," she said a few minutes later, "but it says a lot that you went to the effort."

"It wasn't a big deal."

"Are you kidding? The balloons and party hats and the cake. Not to mention the presents that you and your parents and your sisters all lavished upon her. Now I know what your mysterious errands were all about this morning."

"Well, what kind of a first birthday would it be without a party?" Zach asked.

Her lips curved a little in response to his question,

but he noticed that the smile didn't quite chase the shadows from her eyes.

"Will you promise me something?" she asked him.

"Sure," he agreed easily, ready to promise her anything.

"Promise that you won't ever forget her birthday."

"Of course I won't," he said, stunned that she would even suggest such a thing.

"I mean it, Zach. I know there will be times that you won't be able to celebrate with her, but wherever you are, whatever you're doing, try to at least give her a call, let her know you're thinking about her."

Something in the earnestness of her tone warned Zach that Paige wasn't just thinking about Emma now, and although he'd suspected that she had some unresolved issues with her father, it was even more apparent to him now that she was still carrying the scars of his disinterest and neglect.

"I promise that Emma will never have cause to doubt how important she is to me," he told her.

Paige nodded, apparently satisfied.

Zach was anything but, and his curiosity about her past—and her relationship with her own father in particular—had definitely been piqued.

The day after Emma's birthday party, Paige decided to take Hayden up on her offer of a tour of the winery. But when Zach's sister was summoned to participate in an overseas conference call, Justin Crawford stepped in to take over.

The first time Paige had met him, she'd realized she was looking at the man Zach would be about twenty-five years in the future. Justin was as tall as his son and solidly built, with a little more gray sprinkled through his hair and deeper lines at the corners of his blue eyes. But he was still a very good-looking man and absolutely charming.

He easily picked up where his daughter had left off, but whereas Hayden had stuck to the facts, Justin liked to mix family history in with details about the wine-making process.

"Hayden is the fourth generation of Crawfords to make wine at Stonechurch Estates Winery," Justin informed her proudly.

"It must be nice to have a legacy to pass on to your children," Paige commented.

"It's as much a responsibility as a legacy," Zach's father told her. "And for a while, Kate and I weren't sure any of the kids wanted it.

"From the time he was knee-high, Zach was determined to fly airplanes, Lauryn was born to be a doctor and Jocelyn always wanted to be a teacher. As for Hayden, well, let's just say that Kate and I went through a period where we thought our youngest daughter's sole goal in life was to turn our hair gray.

"And then, just when we were convinced she would never find her focus, she came home from college one day and said 'I want to make wine.' At first, I wasn't sure she meant it. And for a long while, I worried that she'd taken it as the easy route."

"Hard to imagine, considering how passionate she is about the business," Paige noted.

"And I'm grateful that she is. I hated to think that almost a hundred years of making wine would be lost when I retired."

"You spend an awful lot of time in the winery for someone who is supposedly retired."

He chuckled. "You've been talking to my wife."

"I have," she admitted. "But from what I can see, she's just as busy as you are."

"It's hard to cut yourself off from something that was your life for so long," he said, just as Hayden returned to the office to retrieve some files.

"No one's asking you to cut yourself off," his daughter said. "But a little easing away would be appreciated."

"We'll be out of your hair for two whole weeks in November," he reminded her.

"If I haven't pulled it all out by then," Hayden grumbled.

"Where are you going in November?" Paige asked.

"Kate and I are escaping on a Mediterranean cruise to celebrate our fortieth anniversary," Justin replied.

"Forty years," Paige mused. "That definitely sounds like something to celebrate."

"If he lives that long," Hayden muttered. "I might bludgeon him with a wine bottle and stuff his body in an oak cask before then."

"You wouldn't do such a thing," her father said confidently. "You wouldn't risk contaminating the wine."

His daughter's smile was grudging. "True enough. And I wouldn't do it before the *San Francisco Chronicle* Wine Competition because I want to see you eat your words when Hayden's Reserve gets rave reviews from all of the judges."

"I'll happily do so, as long as I have a nice glass of Stonechurch Estates merlot to wash them down with."

Hayden shook her head, tucked the files under her

arm and walked out, Justin's chuckle following behind her.

"Did I miss something there?" Paige asked.

"She's been experimenting with a new vintage," Justin explained.

"And you disapprove?"

"On the contrary—I'm both pleased with and proud of what she's done, but when Hayden first developed the wine, she wanted me to take the lead with it.

"I wanted her to have enough faith in it to put her name on it, and now she has. Now she's as much a winemaker as Zach is a pilot," he said. "Of course, a career shouldn't completely define a person, but the right career is an important key to a happy life."

"The first time I met Zach, he was in uniform," Paige told his dad. "And I thought that uniform completely defined who he was. But seeing him here, with his family, I've realized it's only a part of the whole."

She'd also realized that she liked the man he was. His obvious attachment to and affection for his family, his sense of loyalty and responsibility, his sense of humor. There was a lot more to him than she'd originally thought, and her feelings for him were getting more and more complicated.

Since taking custody of Emma, she hadn't had the time or energy to pursue any kind of personal relationships. Nor had she missed the casual flirtations and meaningless hookups that were so prevalent in the dating scene. And truthfully, she'd never had a relationship that was anything more than that. Not since she'd gotten over her infatuation with Matt Sanders, anyway.

Her feelings for Zach were already stronger and deeper than anything she'd ever felt for any other man, and she knew that if she wasn't careful, she could fall for not only Zach but his whole family.

"Just as, I'm sure," Justin continued, drawing her attention back to their conversation, "being a lawyer is only part of who you are."

"And a lesser part than it used to be," Paige admitted.

Justin nodded his understanding. "I can't imagine how difficult it's been for you to juggle child care with a demanding career."

"There are days when I wish I'd chosen corporate law instead of family law," she admitted. "Because I go home to Emma and I just can't understand how some parents get so caught up in their personal grievances and demands that they lose sight of what's best for the children."

"Do you know much about other kinds of law?" he asked curiously.

"Why—are you looking for some legal advice?"

He smiled. "No, but I have a friend whose son is looking to take a new partner into his firm."

Paige was humbled by the suggestion that he might recommend her. "But...I'm not even licensed to practice in California."

"How do you get licensed?"

"I'd have to write the state bar exam."

"Is that a big deal?"

"Yeah, it's a pretty big deal," she told him.

"Well, I just thought I'd put the idea out there," he said. "Because we'd sure love to be able to see more of you and your little girl."

After her tour of the winery, Paige spent some time playing in the pool with Emma. Zach's mom returned from a luncheon meeting with a customer just as they were drying off. When she saw an obviously sleepy Emma rubbing her eyes, she asked if she could take the little girl inside to get her ready for her nap. Because Kathleen had been nothing but gracious and helpful, Paige didn't see how she could refuse.

So she sat alone with her thoughts—and still in her two-piece bathing suit—when Zach came down to the pool a few minutes later. She glanced over at the chair where she'd left her towel but knew that going out of her way to cover up her body would only draw more attention to it. Besides, the black halter-style top and boy-short bottoms were actually quite modest.

Or so she believed until Zach's eyes skimmed over her in a way that made her feel as if she was completely naked.

"You've been in the pool," he noted.

She nodded. "Emma loves the water."

"Where is Emma?"

"Napping."

He sat down beside her, nudged her shoulder gently with his own. "Wanna go skinny-dipping?"

"No. But thanks for the offer," she said drily.

"I didn't mean right now," he said. "I was thinking maybe later, when it's dark and—" The teasing glint faded from his eyes when he saw the glimmer of tears in her. "What happened, Paige? What's wrong?"

She hastily swiped at the lone drop that had slipped onto her cheek. "Nothing."

"I realize I don't know you very well, but I don't think you're the type of woman to cry over 'nothing.'"

She sighed. "It's your parents—"

She didn't get any further than that before he interrupted.

"What happened? Did one of them say something to upset you?"

His willingness to immediately and automatically defend her against some imagined slight made her smile, though her eyes were still blurred with tears. "No, no one said or did anything. Your parents are… wonderful."

He frowned. "Then what's the problem?"

"That *is* the problem."

"Okay, now I'm really confused."

"Your whole family is wonderful."

"Well, I've always thought so," he agreed, a little hesitantly.

"And they absolutely dote on Emma."

"She's family."

His response was both simple and heartfelt and she knew that it was true. From the minute both Kathleen and Justin had set eyes on the little girl, she had been theirs, completely accepted and unconditionally loved.

"It's really that easy for them, isn't it?" she asked, marveling over the fact.

"Why do you sound so surprised?" he asked.

She shrugged. "Not everyone places such high value on blood ties." Certainly not anyone in her experience.

Her mother had walked out when she was seven, her father had turned her out when she was fifteen, and though his sister had taken her in, Paige had always worried that her aunt Lillian's actions had been motivated solely by a sense of responsibility rather than any real affection.

"I'm guessing we're back to your father again," Zach said.

"My dad never made any secret of the fact that his first loyalty was to the military," she told him, and hoped he would leave it at that.

But of course, he didn't, asking instead, "Are you ever going to tell me what happened?"

"When?"

"When you went to live in Pinehurst."

"What makes you think anything happened?" she challenged. "Maybe my father just decided it was time I had a more stable environment and more structure in my life than he could provide."

"Is that all it was?"

She sighed. "No."

He waited, and his quiet patience gave her the courage to speak the words she'd never shared with anyone else before. "I was found in a compromising position with a second lieutenant. To put it more bluntly, we were caught naked together by his captain, who threatened to not only write up the officer for conduct unbecoming, but also to file criminal charges because of my age.

"Then my father stepped in. And he said he wasn't going to ruin a promising career because I was a slut and a tease and not smart enough to know when I was letting things go too far."

She pushed herself to her feet and went to retrieve her towel. She wrapped it around her body, tucking the end between her breasts. But she still felt exposed—not so much physically as emotionally. And even more so when she sensed Zach standing behind her.

"How old were you?" He asked the question through clenched teeth.

She ducked her head, staring intently at the tangerine polish on her toes. "Fifteen."

He tipped her chin up, forcing her to meet his gaze. "How old was he?"

"Twenty-two." Her response was barely a whisper.

Zach's eyes shot furious blue sparks. "And your father blamed *you* for what happened?"

"I wasn't an innocent bystander," she told him.

"You were a child."

In retrospect she knew it was true. But at the time, she'd thought she was both womanly and wise, and she'd been so high on the thrill of knowing that this sought-after twenty-two-year-old officer was interested in her.

"I was a rebellious teenager," she told him, because it was true. And because she still hadn't managed to shake the feeling that she was responsible for everything that had happened with Matt as well as the deterioration of her relationship with her father.

"Desperate for your father's attention," Zach guessed.

"Well, I finally got it," she said.

"And then he sent you away."

She nodded, the ache in her heart as real as it had been fifteen years earlier.

"What happened to the second lieutenant?" he wanted to know.

"After my father was satisfied that Matt understood the dangers of jeopardizing his career for a piece of ass—and yes, that's exactly what he said—" though her cheeks burned with shame at the memory, she didn't mince words "—he was promoted."

"I hate to say it," he said, not sounding at all remorseful, "but your father really was a bastard."

"He is a highly decorated colonel in the United States Army," she informed him.

"That doesn't make him any less of a bastard."

His assessment was so unequivocally supportive and his understanding so wholly unexpected that, to her complete mortification, Paige began to cry.

Not silent tears or quiet sobs—no, she started to bawl as she'd wanted to when she was fifteen years old and her father had followed up his verbal lashing with a sharp backhand. But she hadn't cried then. She'd refused to give him the satisfaction of her tears.

She couldn't stop them now. And Zach didn't even try. He didn't hush her or whisper useless platitudes. He simply held her until the storm of weeping had run its course.

"No one else knows what happened that day," she finally told him. "Not even Ashley and Megan. I didn't ever tell anyone. I couldn't. I was afraid they'd think it was my fault, too. Or maybe I was afraid that it was."

"And now?" he asked gently.

"Now..." She was relieved to have finally shared the story, to have unburdened some of the guilt and the grief, and weary from the emotions that had been weighing her down for so long. "Now I know that it was a mistake—no more and no less than that. But even if I could go back and change my actions, I wouldn't. Because it was that final confrontation with my father that resulted in me going to Pinehurst to live with Aunt Lillian and Ashley and Megan."

"I'm still sorry that you had to go through hell to get there," Zach said.

She managed to smile at that. "You know, when I first met you, I really wanted you to be a bastard, too."

His brows rose. "Why?"

"Because then I could feel righteous and justified in my determination to maintain custody of Emma," she admitted.

"You're doing what you think is best for Emma—that *is* righteous and justified," he told her.

She looked up at him, wondering if it was possible that he really did understand her motivations. "Even if that puts us on opposite sides of the courtroom?"

Every time Zach managed to take a single step forward on a personal level with Paige, she brought up the issue of Emma's custody and set them back two. But this time, he wasn't going to let it happen.

"Why don't we forget about that for a while?" he suggested to her now.

Her brow furrowed. "I'm not sure that we can."

"We can try," he insisted. "In fact, I have an idea that should help."

"What kind of idea?" she asked warily.

"It occurred to me that you haven't had a chance to see anything beyond the gates of the estate since we got here."

"We've only been here a few days," she reminded him. "Besides, the purpose of this visit was for Emma to meet your family, not for me to play tourist."

"Still, I'd like to take you out tonight."

"Out?"

She sounded so baffled by the offer, he had to smile. "For dinner," he said. "Without the rest of my well-intentioned but undeniably interfering family and without Emma banging her cup and spoon on the tray of her high chair."

"You mean—just the two of us?" She sounded a little less baffled now, a little more wary.

He nodded. "My mom and dad will be happy to watch Emma."

"Why?" she asked cautiously.

"Because she's a great kid."

She rolled her eyes. "I mean, why do you want to take me out to dinner?"

"Because I think we both deserve a few hours to ourselves. And because I know of a really fabulous restaurant that I think you would like."

"I can't remember the last time I had a night out," Paige finally admitted.

"Then I'd say you're overdue," he told her.

"I'd feel guilty about leaving Emma."

"My parents *want* to spend time with her," he insisted. "And they'll take good care of her."

"I know they will, but—"

"Let me do this, Paige."

He took her hands, linked their fingers together. His touch was warm and strong and somehow reassuring even as tingles of awareness spread through her.

"To show my appreciation for everything you've done for Emma, for making sure she felt loved instead of abandoned when she lost her mother."

"Everything I did, I did for Emma," she reminded him.

"I know," he agreed. "So let me do this for you."

Still she hesitated. Not because she didn't want to accept his offer, but because she was afraid she was starting to want so much more than what he was offering.

"All right," she finally said. "What time do you want to go?"

Chapter 9

Paige assessed the contents of the closet in which she'd hung her clothes and realized that her options for dinner with Zach were definitely limited. She had a pair of dark gray slacks and a wrap-style blouse that would be a distinct improvement over the jeans and T-shirts that had been her unofficial uniform since she'd arrived, but her gaze kept drifting to the lone dress hanging by itself.

She still wasn't sure why she'd let Ashley talk her into packing it, but because she had and because it was there, Paige figured she might as well wear it.

Her heart was pounding hard inside her chest as she slipped the garment from the hanger. It had been a long time since she'd dressed for a night out with a man, and though both she and Zach had been careful not to refer to their dinner plan as a date, there was really no other word for it. And she was filled with both excitement and trepidation as she tugged the dress over her head.

It was a sheath style with a square neckline and a straight skirt that fell to her knees. Simple. Elegant. With just a hint of sexy.

She didn't bother with pantyhose but slipped her bare feet into a pair of strappy sandals that Ashley had tossed into the suitcase along with the dress. Then she added a touch of makeup—a sweep of eyeliner, a hint of mascara, a swipe of gloss over her lips.

She came down to the foyer at ten minutes to seven. Her life was too tightly scheduled to worry about being fashionably late, and besides, she wanted to steal a few minutes with Emma before she left with Zach. When she saw him waiting for her with the little girl in his arms, she felt that flutter in her belly again. Was it apprehension about leaving Emma? Or being alone with Zach?

"Age!" Emma held her arms out, and Paige pushed her concerns aside to offer her a smile.

She reached for the child, who was squirming to get out of Zach's arms. As he released her, the back of his hand brushed the side of Paige's breast. The contact was both fleeting and accidental, but the accompanying punch of sexual awareness nearly buckled her knees.

"Sorry," Zach mumbled.

She didn't—couldn't—respond. Her cheeks flamed, but the heat in her face was insignificant compared to the fire in her blood.

She wanted him.

There was no way she could continue to deny that simple fact. Maybe she didn't want to want him, but apparently her brain and her body were in complete disagreement where Zach Crawford was concerned.

"Age pay?" Emma asked.

She shook her head. "Sorry, honey. Paige can't play with you right now because I'm going out with Zach."

Emma's little brow furrowed. "Age pay Ack?"

Yeah—in her dreams. But even that thought was enough to make her cheeks flame even hotter, so she kept her gaze focused on the little girl in her arms and hoped that Zach couldn't guess what was going through her mind.

"No, honey, we're going for dinner."

Emma's lower lip jutted out, and Paige braced herself.

But before the tears could start, Zach's mom came in and told Emma that she needed her help to make ice-cream sundaes before they could watch a movie together, and Emma happily trotted off to the kitchen with her.

"Crisis averted," Zach noted, then smiled at Paige.

But that smile did crazy things to her pulse, and as Paige walked out the door beside him, she wasn't sure the crisis had been averted at all.

Zach sensed that Paige was a little apprehensive about being alone with him, so he kept the conversation casual and he noticed that gradually, during the course of the exquisite meal, she began to relax. So much, in fact, that by the time their dessert dishes had been cleared away, she was tapping her fingers in rhythm with the music that was playing.

When she saw him watching her hand and realized

what she was doing, she curled her fingers into her palm. "Emma loves this song," she explained.

"Emma loves it?"

She flushed. "I have it on my iPod," she admitted. "And when she hears it, Emma dances around until it's over, then she says, 'Again. Again.'"

He smiled. "Do you dance with her?"

The color in her cheeks deepened. "Sometimes."

"Will you dance with me?"

She seemed both wary and startled by the question. "What?"

"I said, will you dance with me?"

"Why?"

"Because the way you're tapping your foot to the music suggests you'd rather be moving out there—" he nodded toward the dance floor "—than sitting here."

"Maybe," she allowed, "but—"

"No buts." Zach pushed his chair away from the table and reached for Paige's hand.

She let him draw her to her feet and lead her to the dance floor, thinking that as long as it had been since she'd been out for dinner with a man, it had been a lot longer since she'd kicked up her heels.

"But the song's over," she told him, just as the last notes faded away.

"So we'll stay for the next one," he said, and pulled her closer as the soft strains of an Aerosmith ballad floated over the dance floor.

She shouldn't be attracted to him.

Every logical and rational cell in her brain warned Paige of the folly of falling for someone who could break her heart—as Zach would do if he took Emma away from her. But while her brain clearly understood the dangers, her body didn't care about anything but the yearning that stirred inside whenever he was near.

And he was very near to her now.

His arm was around her waist, and he was holding her close, and she suddenly couldn't imagine why something that felt so good could be wrong.

And so she gave up trying to figure it out and gave herself over to the exquisite sensations that poured through her system like a drug, making her yearn for so much more.

The minute Paige had stepped into the foyer of his parents' house, Zach had wanted to touch her—to hold her close, just like he was doing now.

She fit into his arms, as if she was meant to be there. And her steps matched his effortlessly, as if they'd danced together a thousand times before. And he found himself wondering if they would find such a perfect and easy rhythm if they were naked together in his bed.

Because that was where he wanted to be with her. He wanted to get her away from the crowd, to take her somewhere that they could be alone together and slowly peel away the dress she was wearing.

It wasn't surprising that he felt such a distinctly sexual attraction for Paige. She was a beautiful woman and he spent most of his time in the company of men, so his reaction to her was hardly unexpected.

But his attraction to her was still, he knew, unwise. Because Paige was his daughter's legal guardian, the woman who intended to fight him to maintain custody of Emma—yet that knowledge failed to negate his response to her.

Another couple, obviously too wrapped up in one

another to pay attention to anyone else, bumped into Paige as they moved past. She stumbled against him, her breasts pressing against his chest, nearly making him groan aloud. Well, if she hadn't realized how aroused he was before, there could be no mistaking his body's response now.

Her gaze locked with his, and he saw surprise flicker in those dark-chocolate-colored eyes, then awareness, quickly eclipsed by an answering desire.

Then she looked away. "It's getting late."

"It's not that late," he told her.

"But it's a long drive, so we should be heading back."

"If that's what you want," he agreed.

She looked at him again, and he could see the indecision warring inside of her. "I'm trying to do the right thing here, Zach."

"And why do you think ignoring the attraction between us is the right thing?"

"Because I don't want this," she told him.

"I think it would be more accurate to say you don't want to want this."

"Same thing."

He drew her nearer. "Is it?"

"Zach." Once again, she'd meant to speak his name as a warning, but the breathless tone made it sound more like a plea. Although not even Paige was certain of what she was pleading for.

After a moment, Zach said, "Let's go home."

Neither of them said much on the drive back, but the sexual tension was thick in the air between them. When Paige finally got out of the car, she wanted desperately to put some distance between them. But as they made their way toward the house, she carefully kept her pace steady. She didn't want him to know that she was running. She didn't want him to guess that she was scared—not of him, but of her own feelings.

But somehow Zach sensed her inner turmoil because he paused with the key in his hand and turned to face her.

"We didn't do anything wrong, Paige."

"I didn't say that we did."

"I had a good time tonight," he said. "I especially enjoyed dancing with you. Holding you."

Paige remained silent.

"And I thought you had a good time, too."

"I did," she finally admitted. "I just think we need to remember that we're on opposite sides here."

"I'm not entirely sure that's true. After all, we both want what's best for Emma."

"We just can't agree on what that is," she reminded him.

He stepped closer. "I don't see why that has to prohibit us from being friends."

"I have no objection to us being friends," she said. "I just don't think there should be any more dancing."

"What about kissing?"

Her gaze shifted automatically to his mouth, now hovering mere inches above hers. She hadn't forgotten that long-ago kiss, hadn't stopped wanting more. But she'd learned, a long time ago, that she couldn't always have what she wanted. And that sometimes when a person got what she wanted, she realized it wasn't what she wanted after all.

"Definitely no kissing," she said, but the breathless tone of her voice contradicted her words.

"Because you didn't like it when I kissed you before?"

She raised her hands to his chest, a physical barrier. "Because I did."

She turned to go, but Zach grabbed her arm, preventing her escape.

"Dammit, Paige, you can't say something like that and then just walk away."

"You're Emma's father, Zach. And Emma's mother was one of my best friends."

"I was Olivia's lover," he agreed. "And I'm not going to apologize for that, especially because the little girl we both love wouldn't be here if not for that relationship. But I can tell you honestly that I never felt about Olivia the way I feel about you."

And then his lips crushed down on hers.

And in his kiss she tasted anger and frustration and need. It was a merciless sensual assault that made her pulse pound and her knees weak. She reached for him, her hands curling around his biceps, holding on.

His mouth was hard and impatient, his body was tight and tense. But even as he ravaged her with his kiss, she knew that he was holding on to control, that he wouldn't take more than she wanted to give.

So she gave to him, answering his need with her own. And in doing so, she found that there was more than anger and heat—there was gentleness and affection. With a sigh that signaled both surrender and desire, Paige melted into his arms.

Zach didn't misinterpret her response. His arms came around her, and he yanked her against him so they were pressed together from chest to thigh. The full-frontal contact sent her body temperature through the roof.

His dark, masculine flavor slipped into her blood like a drug, rushed through her veins, leaving her hot and aching and desperately wanting.

She hadn't expected anything like this. Or maybe the reason she'd fought against the attraction for so long was that she'd been afraid of something exactly like this. Maybe, somewhere deep inside, she'd known that her response to Zach would be off the charts.

His tongue delved into her mouth, tangled with hers. His fingers sifted through her hair, tipping her head back so he could deepen the kiss even further.

When he finally lifted his head to say, "Come to my room with me," she responded simply, "Yes."

Without another word, Zach took her by the hand and led her into the house. He wanted her as he couldn't remember wanting any other woman—with a fierce desperation. He wanted to lower his body over hers, into hers. He wanted to take, to devour, to possess.

And as he drew her into the darkness of his bedroom, he knew that he could. He could take her here and now, up against the wooden door or on the hard floor, and she wouldn't protest. And maybe then he'd find some release from the need that burned inside of him whenever he was near her.

But he wanted more than a fast and reckless possession of the woman who had been driving him to distraction for weeks—and she deserved more. So he forced himself to go slow, to savor the moment, the pleasure, the woman.

His woman, he thought, and even as he wondered

where the unexpected possessiveness had come from, he didn't doubt the rightness of the feeling. From this moment forward, she was his.

He stripped away her dress, leaving her clad in only a couple of scraps of sheer black lace, then he lifted her into his arms and laid her back on the mattress. Her hair spilled over the pillow, a coppery halo. Her eyes were dark and fathomless. Her lips were moist and erotically swollen.

He quickly discarded his own clothing, then fumbled around in the drawer of his nightstand. When he came up empty-handed, he swore.

"What's wrong?" Paige asked.

He felt like a complete idiot. He finally had her exactly where he wanted her, naked and willing, and he was completely unprepared to take advantage of the situation.

"I don't have any condoms," he admitted.

She slipped away from him, but instead of reaching for her dress, she reached for her purse. "I do."

"I didn't get the impression that you expected this to happen tonight," he said, when she handed him the small square packet.

"I didn't," she said, obviously shocked that he would even suggest such a thing. "I just believe in being prepared."

"Well, I'm glad you were." He reached for her hand and drew her toward him. "And very grateful."

"How grateful?"

He eased her back onto the bed. "Let me show you."

He lifted her arms over her head, then cuffed both of her wrists with one of his hands. With the other, he flipped open the clasp at the front of her bra. Then he nudged the fabric aside and closed his mouth over one peaked nipple.

She gasped and arched beneath him.

He continued to tease and torment her breasts, moving from one to the other and back again. He took his cues from her, listening to the rhythm of her breathing, letting her moans and sighs guide him.

Keeping her hands pinned, his mouth trailed lower. Sweeping down her torso, dipping into the hollow of her belly, dallying at her navel. She struggled against his hold, wanting—needing—to touch him as he was touching her.

When he finally released his grip on her wrists, she reached for him, desperate to touch him, to feel his warm and solid flesh beneath her palms. She stroked her hands over him, savoring the delicious contrast of smooth skin and hard muscle.

In one quick movement, her panties were stripped away and tossed aside.

Now, she thought and braced herself for the glorious press of his body into hers.

But Zach had other ideas. He parted her thighs and lowered his head, and with the first touch of his tongue to her moist core, she simply and completely shattered.

Her hands slid limply from his shoulders to fist in the sheets.

"Zach." His name was a whimper, a plea.

But he wasn't finished. With his tongue and his teeth, he drove her up again so that she had to bite down hard on her lip to keep from crying out.

She wouldn't have thought it was possible, but somehow the second climax was even more explosive than the first, and her body was still pulsing with the aftershocks of pleasure when he finally rose up over her and plunged into her.

She thought there could be no more, that she had nothing left to give, but as her body moved in rhythm with his, he proved her wrong again.

She'd had sex before. Numerous times, in fact. And with different partners, too. She wasn't ashamed to admit it or embarrassed by the fact that she enjoyed sex. She wouldn't have wasted her time with it otherwise.

But she'd never before had sex with someone who made her want so much, need so much, feel so much. It wasn't just physical satisfaction—although every pass of his hands over her skin made her quiver and yearn. There was a sense of connection with Zach that she'd never felt with anyone else.

When his mouth captured hers again as he shuddered with his own release, she realized that what they'd just experienced was more than a joining of their bodies— it was a mating of their souls.

Or maybe she was just being fanciful.

Zach brushed his lips over hers again. Now that their mutual desire had been sated—at least temporarily— there was more gentleness than passion in his kiss, and the sweetness of the gesture nearly brought tears to her eyes.

She wasn't the type of woman that a man snuggled up to after sex. At least, she never had been before. And she knew that was her fault—or maybe it was more accurate to say it was her design. Because, although she recognized and accepted that she had sexual urges like any other woman, she didn't want or need intimacy. She was a strong, independent woman. She valued her space and her autonomy. She didn't need to cuddle. She didn't want to share confidences or hopes and dreams.

But she had no energy left to push herself away from him, to slip out of the warmth of his arms and into the cold emptiness of her own bed.

Instead, she snuggled close to him. And fell asleep listening to the beat of his heart beneath her cheek.

Chapter 10

When Zach woke up, it was with a sense of content-ment and satisfaction that he hadn't experienced in a very long time. And he knew the soft, warm female pressed against him was responsible for the feeling.

He was tempted to show his appreciation by skim-ming a hand down her back or touching his lips to the top of her head, but he resisted because he suspected that the slightest movement or lightest touch might wake her. And despite the incredible passion they'd shared through the darkest hours of night, he knew that with the light of day might come recriminations and regrets.

He didn't want her to regret what they'd shared, but he couldn't deny that spending the night together changed things between them. And although he be-lieved the change was for the better, he understood that Paige had some issues with his uniform that weren't likely to be resolved by one night of passion. Maybe not even two or three nights, although he was more than willing to give it a shot.

Just the thought had his blood stirring. And when Paige sighed and snuggled closer in her sleep, the stirring became a churning. He closed his eyes and mentally cataloged the morning chores in the vineyard. Though it had been years since he'd worked in either the grape-growing or wine-making aspects of his family's business, the exercise helped him get himself under control. Mostly.

He heard the patter of little feet in the hall and experienced a brief moment of panic as he realized that Emma had somehow managed to get out of her crib and was probably looking for Paige. He wasn't worried that she would come into his bedroom because he'd locked the door, but he did worry that the child might be upset if she couldn't find Paige. Then he heard his mother talking to her, and he relaxed, reassured that Emma hadn't got out of bed on her own and wasn't alone.

He could have pinpointed the exact moment that Paige awoke, because every single muscle in her body tensed. And in that moment the warm and languid woman in his arms was again distant and wary.

"Emma's up," she said, sliding away from him in the bed.

"My mom's with her."

Paige's only response was to toss back the covers and turn so that her back was to him.

He couldn't help but notice that it was a lovely back—her skin was pale and smooth and soft and fragrant. He'd definitely neglected her back last night. But she had so many parts that had demanded his attention—and he'd enjoyed giving it.

Watching her wiggle into her panties, Zach temporarily lost track of the conversation. Although he had to admit that as enticing as it was to watch her dress, it had been a lot more fun to take her clothes off.

"I should be with her," Paige said, scooping her dress off the floor.

He snapped his attention back to the present. "You don't have to be with her 24/7," he told her.

"She's my responsibility. At least until the court says otherwise."

He sighed as her comment brought reality crashing down on his fantasy. "I thought we were going to forget about the custody issue while we were here."

"I can't." She looked at him, those beautiful dark eyes pleading for him to understand.

But he couldn't. Or maybe he didn't want to even try to understand why she was pushing him away. "Were you thinking about it last night while we were naked?" he challenged, needing her to remember what they'd shared, to think about what they could build together.

Her cheeks drained of all color. "No."

"Jesus, Paige, stop feeling so damned guilty. Wanting something for yourself isn't a maternal defect."

She shook her head, obviously not convinced. "I've only known you for three weeks."

"Which, coincidentally, is precisely how long I've known you," he pointed out.

"Men aren't judged the same way."

His eyes narrowed on her. "Do you think I'd somehow use what happened between us last night against you?"

Her silence was damning, and though he wanted to grab her and shake her, to force her to acknowledge that what they'd shared had nothing to do with anything except the way they felt about each other, he knew that any show of anger on his part—justified or not—would only cause her to withdraw from him even more.

"When you have a child, you're not supposed to forget about her when it's convenient for you," she said softly.

Although he knew Paige's comment was directed more at herself than at him, he said, "I'm not trying to forget about her. I'm trying to get you to admit that there's something between us."

"The only thing between us is the unresolved issue of Emma's custody," she insisted.

"If you really believe that, then you're lying to yourself."

The only response he heard was the click of the door closing at her back.

Paige had to talk to someone.

She was so completely confused she didn't know what to think or how to feel. She decided to call Ashley because Megan had never been a morning person and probably wasn't any more so now that she had a baby waking her up at frequent intervals through the night. But the sleepy "hello" that came across the line suggested that she'd miscalculated and awakened Ashley.

"I'm sorry," she said quickly, sincerely.

"Paige?"

"Yeah."

"Where are you?" her cousin's voice was drifting, as if she was still half sleeping.

"I'm in California."

"So why are you calling?"

"Because I slept with Zach."

She heard the rustle of sheets and imagined that her cousin had just bolted upright in bed.

"Okay, I'm awake now," Ashley said. "But you might want to repeat that because I thought you just said that you slept with Zach."

"I did." She closed her eyes. "It was a mistake, of course, but—"

"How was it a mistake? Are you saying you accidentally had sex with the man?"

Paige managed a smile. "No, it was a deliberate decision, just not a very well-thought-out one."

"It definitely complicates things," her cousin agreed.

Paige felt like banging her head against the wall, but settled for leaning back against it. "I never should have agreed to this trip."

Ashley was quiet for a minute before she asked, "Was it lousy sex?"

"What? Why would you ask that?"

"Well, it just makes sense that you'd be more likely to regret getting naked with someone if the experience was…disappointing."

"The experience wasn't disappointing," she said. In fact, just the memories of making love with Zach were enough to send her pulse racing.

"Then why are you on the phone with me instead of dallying in his bed?" Ashley asked.

"I don't know how to dally."

"I'll bet Zach could teach you," her cousin teased.

Paige sighed. "This isn't helping, Ash."

"Well, what do you want me to say?"

"I don't know," she admitted. "I just woke up with Zach beside me this morning, and I panicked."

"That isn't like you," Ashley said.

"I know." It wasn't like her to fall into bed with a man without careful consideration of the consequences, either, but all she'd thought about before getting naked with Zach was how very much she wanted to get naked with Zach.

"Zach's a good guy," her cousin said. "And I think he could be good for you, if you let him."

"If I let him?" Paige frowned. "What's that supposed to mean?"

"It means that you have a habit of shutting out any guy who tries to get too close."

"Well, if it turns out that he is Emma's father, that won't be an option, will it?"

"You still haven't received the test results?" Ashley asked, obviously surprised.

"No. I got a text message from Megan's friend at the lab, but I haven't had a chance to get back to him yet."

"Haven't had a chance?" her cousin wondered. "Or don't want to know?"

Paige sighed. "The truth is, I think I do know."

"You've accepted that Zach is Emma's father?"

"Yeah," she said, because she knew it was ridiculous to continue to deny what was obvious to everyone else.

Ashley was silent for a moment. "Can I ask you one more thing?"

"Sure."

"Had you accepted that fact before you slept with Zach?"

Paige wasn't entirely sure of the answer to that question herself. "Does it matter?"

"It might—if you slept with Zach to establish a personal relationship with him in order to strengthen your connection to Emma," her cousin said.

Paige was stunned by the suggestion. "Do you really think I'm that calculating?"

"I think you're that desperate to hold on to a child you love as if she was your own," Ashley said gently.

While Paige had to acknowledge the point, she could confidently assure her cousin, "I promise you, Ash, I wasn't thinking about Emma while I was getting naked with Zach."

"I'd say that's a very good sign," her cousin said approvingly.

Paige hung up with Ashley and called the lab. When she got Walter Neville's voice mail again, she let out a sigh that was partly relief and partly frustration, then left another message.

Over the past few days she'd gotten in the habit of taking walks when she needed to clear her head or organize her thoughts. Most of the time she walked in the vineyard. There was just something about the dirt beneath her feet, the sun on her cheeks and rows upon rows of grapes all around her that usually made her feel at peace.

Emma seemed to like walking among the grapes, too, and she loved playing peekaboo in the vines, though she'd also developed a fascination for the tiny clusters of baby grapes. Paige had quickly learned to keep a close eye on her to ensure she didn't try to pull them off of the vines.

But no matter how far or how long she walked after Walter had finally returned her call, the feeling of peace that she sought eluded her today. Instead there was only turmoil—in her heart as much as in her head.

If she'd learned nothing else about the Crawfords over the past week, she'd learned that family was important to them. And Emma was family. There was no doubt about that anymore.

She and Emma had been getting along just fine before Zach walked into their lives. Paige had been confident that she could give the little girl everything she needed, that she could ensure she was happy, well-adjusted and loved. But she couldn't give her the kind of family that was Zach's.

She wasn't naive enough to believe that the Crawfords were perfect. She knew that no family was. But she also knew that they were the type of family who stood together and supported one another, and she wanted that for Emma, even if she would never be part of it.

Paige's hasty escape from his bedroom earlier that morning proved to Zach that nothing had changed for her just because they'd been intimate. For Zach, *everything* had changed. From the moment he'd learned of Emma's existence, he'd known that he wanted to be a father to his daughter. Now he knew that he wanted Paige to be part of their family, too.

The example his parents had provided for him and his sisters had made him unwilling to settle for anything less than what they had. Not that he'd consciously been looking for a life partner. And he certainly hadn't expected to get tangled up with Paige Wilder. But when he woke up with her in his arms, he knew that he'd done just that.

The obstacle that faced him now was convincing Paige that they were meant to be together. Forever.

As his mother had noted on their first day in California, Paige kept her feelings carefully hidden. And while he'd managed to anticipate and respond to her wants and needs in the darkness of the night, he was at a complete loss again in the light of day. But what he lacked in the way of a plan, he hoped to compensate for with perseverance.

Stepping outside, he saw Paige with Emma in the vineyard, and he made his way over to them. The child spotted him first, and she tilted her head back to look up at him, her smile as bright as her eyes.

He wouldn't have thought it was possible to love so much so fast, but Emma had proven otherwise.

"Da!" she said and held out her arms, a signal that she wanted to be picked up.

He noted the dirt that was spread not just on her palms but halfway up to her elbows and liberally streaked across her shirt, but he scooped her up anyway. It was only after he'd tucked her little body close to his chest that he registered what she'd said.

Usually she called him "Ack" but this time she'd clearly called him "Da." He looked over at Paige. "Did she just say—"

His throat was suddenly tight, preventing him from finishing the question.

But she nodded in response, and though she tried to smile, he noticed that her beautiful deep brown eyes glistened with tears.

"You heard from the lab?"

She nodded again. "I just spoke to Walter Neville.

The results confirm that you are definitely Emma's father."

Emma, who loved looking at books and had listened to enough stories to garner a basic understanding of what a daddy was, clapped her hands happily to discover that she had one. "Da! Da!"

"That's right," he said. "I'm your daddy."

"Ma!" Emma said and looked questioningly at Paige.

Was it possible that she'd somehow made the leap from "Daddy" to "Mommy" and believed that having one entitled her to the other? Or was she just echoing the two words that she'd often heard together? Paige knew it was more likely the latter, but that didn't ease the ache in her chest.

She shook her head, swallowed around the lump in her throat. "No, honey. Your mama's gone," she reminded the little girl gently. "But you have a dada now."

"Da!" Emma said again.

Zach knew his smile was at least as wide as his daughter's, but when he glanced at Paige, it wasn't joy but heartbreak that he saw etched clearly on her face.

Over the past few weeks he'd come to believe that Paige had accepted what the test would prove. He realized now it wasn't the results that worried her so much as the repercussions.

And although Zach's heart was still overflowing with joy, as he watched Paige make her way back toward the house, he couldn't help but feel a pang of regret that his happiness had caused her sadness.

The past two days had been a roller coaster of emotions for both of them. He'd barely had a chance to catch his breath between the highs and the lows, and he imagined it was the same for Paige. He just wished

there was a way that they could work through everything together, share the joys and the disappointments.

And then he realized that there was—and that the
solution was actually very simple.

In the space of a few months, Paige's life had been
turned completely upside down, but even more so in the
past few weeks. And although she couldn't deny there
was a part of her that wished Zach Crawford had never
shown up at her door, she knew there could be no going
back now. She had to accept the cards that fate had dealt
her, play out the hand and move on.

The best way to do that, she figured, would be to go
back to Syracuse and her job at Wainwright, Witmer
& Wynne and bury herself in work until her memories
of Zach and the pain of losing Emma finally eased—if
they ever did. And the sooner she went home, the sooner
the healing could begin.

She was packing her suitcase when Zach walked in.

Her fingers clutched the blouse she'd carefully
folded, her white-knuckled grip showing no mercy for
the delicate fabric.

She'd known this confrontation was coming, but she
still wasn't prepared for it. She didn't want his platitudes or his pity.

But what Zach said was, "I think we should get married."

Paige stared at him for a long moment, waiting for
him to explain. Because the words, straightforward
though they seemed, didn't make any sense to her.

But Zach didn't say anything else. He just stood
there, waiting for a response, and she finally said, "Is
this about last night?"

"It's not about last night." He smiled. "Or not entirely about last night."

"Because it's the twenty-first century," she reminded him. "And no one expects you to marry a woman just because you've had sex with her."

"I'm aware of that," he said drily. "In fact, I've had sex with plenty of other women before you came along without proposing to them."

"So why me?" she asked him.

"Because it occurred to me that getting married would settle the issue of Emma's custody without having to battle over it in court."

So his impromptu proposal wasn't really about their relationship at all—it was about Emma. And while the realization shouldn't have surprised her, she couldn't deny that she was a little disappointed.

She chided herself for the irrational and emotional response. Of course he was thinking of Emma. Everything they'd both said and done to this point had been about the little girl.

Everything except last night.

She pushed the thought aside. "Have you talked to your lawyer about this?"

"No. Why?"

She hesitated, but knew that she had to be honest with him. "Because the truth is, there probably wouldn't be a battle. With the DNA test confirming that you're her father, you have cause to overturn the court order granted to me."

She'd known that from the beginning—it was precisely why she'd continued to deny that he was Emma's father for so long. Because conceding his relationship to the child would have hastened what she'd finally accepted was inevitable, and she'd just wanted to hold on to Emma a little longer.

As if he'd read her thoughts, Zach said, "I don't want to take Emma away from you, Paige."

She blinked away the tears that stung her eyes. "And I appreciate that, but marriage…" She shook her head.

"What is it that you're opposed to—marriage in general or marrying me?"

"I've never really thought about getting married," she admitted.

"You haven't dreamed of your wedding day since you were a young girl?"

"Maybe I dreamed of it when I was a kid," she said, but thinking back, she honestly couldn't remember indulging in any kind of happily-ever-after fantasies. "But as I got older, the whole falling-in-love thing never held much appeal for me."

"You've never been in love?" he asked.

She shook her head.

"Any long-term relationships?"

She shook her head again.

"None?" he said, real surprise in his voice.

"Why does that seem so unbelievable?" she demanded.

"Because you're a beautiful, passionate woman."

The intensity of his gaze told her that he believed the words he'd spoken, and he almost made her believe them, too.

She'd never cared if anyone thought of her as beautiful or passionate, and she'd never felt as beautiful and as passionate as she did when she was with him. But she pushed the memories and the yearning aside.

"I'm a family-law attorney," she reminded him.

"Maybe I've just seen too many marriages go bad to believe in happily ever after."

"Or maybe your parents screwed up your perception of marriage."

"Maybe. The only thing I really remember about their marriage is the fighting. I was seven when my mom left, and I was relieved, because I knew that I wouldn't have to listen to them yelling anymore."

She hadn't realized until weeks later that the silence could be so much worse.

"Where's your mom now?" Zach asked.

"I have no idea," she admitted. "I don't even know if she's dead or alive."

He touched a hand to her cheek—a gesture of comfort that was somehow more arousing than soothing. "I'm sorry, Paige."

"I didn't tell you so you'd feel sorry for me." She moved away, because she needed a clear head to continue this conversation, and Zach's nearness never failed to cloud her mind. "I just wanted you to understand why I haven't been looking for some idealized, romantic notion of love."

"Does that mean you'll consider my proposal?"

She sighed. "The thing is, if I had thought about getting married, I certainly wouldn't have thought about marrying someone with a career in the military."

"I'm not asking you to follow me around the country," he told her.

She turned back. "You're not?"

"No. If it was what you wanted—if you were planning to marry me because you were desperately in love with me and couldn't bear for us to be apart—" his tone was self-deprecating "—then I wouldn't object. But I understand why you want Emma to have a real home and a stable environment."

"So we would be married, but Emma and I would still live in Syracuse?" She looked to him for confirmation.

He nodded. "Or Pinehurst, or wherever you decided was best for your career and for her."

"It seems as if you've given this a fair amount of thought." She couldn't keep a note of sarcasm from creeping into her voice.

"I'm sure there are a lot of details I haven't considered," he admitted, "but the most important thing seemed to be to ensure that Emma will always be with someone who loves her."

"I can't believe I'm even having this conversation," she said. "It's crazy and impulsive and—"

"We could make it work, Paige," he said, sounding as if he really believed it.

"How do you know?" she challenged.

"Because we've been living together for a few weeks and managed to tolerate one another fairly well."

"A few weeks is a far cry from 'till death do us part,'" she pointed out.

"And because we generate some pretty impressive sexual chemistry together that will undoubtedly help smooth over the rough spots," he continued.

"People don't get married just because they have great sex," she countered, although she found herself thinking that there might be fewer divorces if they did.

"And because we both want what's best for Emma."

She sighed, unable to dispute that one. But she still couldn't help but wonder what he would get out of the arrangement he was proposing.

"I just don't understand why you would choose to marry me. You have to know that I would keep Emma with me for no reason other than that you'd asked."

"Being my wife and Emma's stepmother will help ensure that she stays with you if anything happens to me."

She didn't want to consider the possibility that something might happen to him, that Emma could lose her father as abruptly and tragically as she'd lost her mother. But his casual comment reminded her of the inherent risks in his occupation and reinforced her determination to do what was best for Emma.

"And besides that," he said. "*I* want to get married."

"You do?"

He nodded. "I'm not committed to bachelorhood. I just never met a woman I wanted to spend the rest of my life with. Because whenever I thought about getting married, I thought about what my parents have—that deep and abiding forever kind of love."

"You were lucky to be given that kind of example," she told him.

"I know. And I didn't want to settle for anything less."

"And yet you're willing to marry me." She was still skeptical, still wary and surprisingly tempted.

His only response was a half smile. "So what do you say?"

She'd have to be crazy to accept.

She'd have to be crazier to refuse when he was offering her everything she wanted. To keep Emma. To be part of a family. To be with Zach.

Because after spending last night with him, she knew

that she did want to be with him. That one night wasn't nearly enough.

She took a deep breath, blew it out. "I guess I say—when's the wedding?"

Chapter 11

Neither of Zach's parents batted an eye when he confirmed that he was Emma's father nor when he informed them that he and Paige were planning to get married. In fact, his mom's immediate response was to comment on the opportune timing of the announcement.

Apparently one of the reception halls in the winery had been booked for a surprise fiftieth-anniversary party, but the children who'd planned the event had been the ones surprised when they learned that their parents had flown off to a Caribbean island to celebrate the occasion in private. Which meant, Kathleen explained to Zach and Paige, that the room was available, the flowers already ordered and the caterers arranged. All they needed was a minister.

When Zach protested that they didn't want to make a big fuss over the occasion, his mother managed to look both furious and so incredibly wounded that he immediately excused himself to call Reverend Lamont, the minister who had officiated at all family events dating back to his baptism thirty-seven years earlier.

Confident that her son was taking care of that detail, Kathleen turned her attention to her future daughter-in-law.

"I don't imagine you packed a wedding dress," she said.

The bride-to-be, still reeling from her impulsive acceptance of Zach's proposal, hadn't had a chance to catch her breath, never mind think about what she would wear for the wedding.

"No," she acknowledged. "But I don't need anything fancy."

"I'm not suggesting that you need a cathedral-length train or a hoop skirt, but a bride—even one getting married on only a few days' notice—deserves a new dress for her wedding."

Then, before Paige could even begin to formulate a response to that, Kathleen said, "Let me do this for you, Paige. Please." And there was no way she could refuse.

Of course, she hadn't anticipated that Zach's mother's seemingly innocuous request to go shopping would turn into a capital-e Event. But when Paige met Kathleen in the kitchen the next morning, Lauryn and Jocelyn and Hayden were there, too.

"Wednesday mornings are my day off," Lauryn said.

"I woke up with a sore throat," Jocelyn explained, with a conspiratorial wink that belied her words.

"I'm playing hooky," Hayden said unapologetically.

So the five women piled into Jocelyn's Expedition and headed into town.

It was an ambush, and Paige realized she should have expected it. Because although Zach's mother and sisters had seemed to not only accept his decision to marry but also be thrilled about it, they were obviously just waiting for an opportunity to get Paige alone to demand to know what was really going on.

Except that it quickly became apparent to Paige that what was really going on was simply a shopping trip.

Their first stop was at a little café not unlike the one where Paige had enjoyed countless weekend brunches with Ashley and Megan. While they fueled up on lattes and chocolate croissants, the women talked about various dress options—white versus cream, long versus short, satin versus lace, veil versus hat.

There were so many choices and so many different opinions being bandied about that Paige's head was spinning long before they walked into the bridal boutique.

As Zach's sisters each took off in a different direction in search of the perfect dress for Paige, Kathleen touched a hand gently to her arm. "Are you okay?"

"Yeah, I guess I'm just a little…overwhelmed."

"I never thought—I was so excited about doing this for you, it didn't occur to me that it wasn't my place, that this was something you should be doing with your own mother."

Paige looked away. "My mom walked out on my dad and I when I was seven."

"I'm sorry," Kathleen said.

She just shrugged.

"What about your dad? Will he be coming to the wedding?"

Now she shook her head. "I haven't seen him in fifteen years."

Though she tried to sound nonchalant, she knew that Zach's mother wouldn't understand, as Kathleen's frown proved.

"Why not?"

"He's a busy man."

"Too busy to take a few days for his daughter's wedding?" she asked incredulously.

Paige was embarrassed to admit that he wouldn't take a few hours for her wedding if he was in town, much less leave wherever he was currently posted to witness an occasion that had absolutely no bearing on the security of the nation.

She wished her family was like Zach's, but they weren't. She'd come to terms with that fact years before, but she still didn't know how to explain the reality to her future mother-in-law.

"He's stationed overseas right now," she said, because, as far as she knew, it was the truth. "He wouldn't be able to get a few days, especially not on such short notice."

"Is there anyone else you wanted to invite?"

She shook her head again. She'd called both of her cousins to tell them of her plans, but she knew that it was out of the question for either of them to make the trip to California. "My cousin Megan just had her first child, and her sister Ashley is in the final stages of her pregnancy, so neither of them is able to travel right now."

"Well, no matter," Kathleen said decisively. "Because you're part of our family now."

The tears that she'd promised herself she wouldn't

cry filled her eyes, and Paige had to swallow the lump that sprang up in her throat before she could speak. "Thank you."

Kathleen gave Paige a quick hug.

Then Jocelyn returned, her arms full of something huge and billowy and white, and the moment was broken.

Paige eyed what looked like miles and miles of lace with skepticism, but she gamely agreed to try it on.

Several minutes later she stepped back out into the main part of the dressing area.

"I feel like the abominable snow monster," she said, following the signal of the saleslady and climbing onto the dais in the center of the room.

"You look like an abominable snow monster," Hayden admitted.

"Who picked that out?" Lauryn wanted to know.

Jocelyn sighed. "I did."

Her sisters both stared at her in shocked disbelief.

"It's a Rodney Harbinger," she said, tossing out the name of an up-and-coming local designer who had recently been at the center of all kinds of media attention.

"It's a harbinger of disaster," Hayden declared.

Jocelyn glared at her.

"But part of the fun of shopping for a wedding dress is trying on all kinds of styles," Lauryn said, clearly trying to keep the peace between her sisters. Then she pushed another dress on Paige.

They were in the boutique nearly four hours, during which time Paige tried on eleven different dresses before she found one that actually made her think *This might be it.*

When she stepped out of the dressing room and all

of Zach's sisters breathed a collective sigh, she knew she was right. But it was Kathleen, who had picked out the simple, strapless column of ivory silk, to whom she looked for confirmation.

Her eyes misty with tears, Zach's mother nodded.

Zach was a little worried about how Paige would fare on her shopping trip. Not that he didn't think his mother and his sisters were the best, but all of the women in his family had strong personalities, and for an only child like Paige whose upbringing had been so very different from his own, he wasn't sure she would come away from an all-day outing with the same impression.

But when he sat down across from her at the picnic tables that had been weighted down with platters of burgers and fries and salads to feed everyone who had gathered for the post-shopping feast, she smiled at him, and in that moment, he realized his mother was right.

He had fallen in love with the woman he was going to marry.

He picked up his glass of wine and took a long swallow. He was still trying to get his head around that revelation when Jocelyn spoke up from the end of the table.

"What are you guys doing about a honeymoon?" she asked.

All other conversations around the table ceased, and Paige's panicked gaze collided with his across the table.

Obviously this was a detail neither of them had considered, maybe because they both saw their marriage as a way of giving Emma a stable family and hadn't really looked beyond that. Not that he hadn't thought about it, but he hadn't made sharing a bed a condition of their marriage because he was confident that it would happen naturally.

But to his family—who didn't understand the real rationale behind their hasty union—a wedding required adherence to certain traditions, of which a honeymoon was one.

"Well, actually—" Paige began.

And Zach decided to let her take the lead on this one because his brain was suddenly locked on the fantasy of a honeymoon with Paige. A private villa on a tropical island…or a secluded cabin deep in the woods. He wouldn't care where they were, so long as he could spend hours making love with her.

"—we've decided to wait on that."

"But why?" his middle sister demanded.

"Because Zach only has a few more weeks' leave and we feel it's important to spend that time with Emma."

"I can understand why you wouldn't want to be gone for two weeks," Lauryn said. "But surely you could take a long weekend somewhere."

"Maybe we will," Zach finally spoke. "When we get back to Pinehurst."

"But if you took it while you were here, we could look after Emma," Hayden pointed out.

"Paige has family in Pinehurst," he reminded them.

"So where are you planning to spend your wedding night?" Jocelyn taunted. "In separate guest rooms across the hall from one another in your parents' house?"

"Stop teasing your brother," Kathleen said, setting another platter of burgers on the table.

"But our opportunities are so few and far between these days," Hayden pointed out.

"And if you keep this up, you're going to make Paige have second thoughts about marrying into the family."

"If Paige was that easily intimidated, she would never have boarded a plane to come out here in the first place," Jocelyn declared.

"What about the guesthouse?" Hayden suggested.

"The guesthouse?" Paige echoed, obviously struggling to follow the circuitous conversation.

"For your wedding night," Lauryn explained.

"I think that's a wonderful compromise," Kathleen agreed. "Close enough that you won't worry about being away from Emma but with enough distance to give you some privacy."

Zach didn't know what to say, how to refuse. And the truth was, a little bit of privacy would mean he could spend hours making love with Paige without worry of any interruption.

A quick glance across the table at Paige's flushed cheeks confirmed that she was having similar thoughts and eased some of Zach's concerns about her reasons for agreeing to marry him.

Maybe he'd been thinking of Emma when he proposed, and maybe Paige had been thinking of Emma when she accepted, but there was something more between them than their mutual love for the little girl, which gave him hope it might grow into love for one another.

After dinner, after everyone else had gone home and Emma was asleep and his parents had wandered down to check on things at the winery, Zach and Paige sat out under the stars with a bottle of merlot and Emma's baby monitor.

"Are you sure this is your first marriage?" she asked him.

His lips curved. "I think I'd remember if I'd been married before."

She sipped her wine, taking a moment to savor the flavor, before she asked, "So why are your parents not questioning this?"

"Do you think they should?"

"Yes," she admitted. "Especially considering all the questions they had about Emma."

"They were understandably surprised and more than a little disappointed that I'd fathered a child out of wed-lock."

"So why are they not surprised that you're marrying a woman you've known only a few weeks and who isn't even the mother of your child?"

"Because they like you," he said simply.

Her response was an unladylike snort.

"Or maybe they're just relieved that they won't lose the deposit they paid to the caterers for the anniversary party," he offered as another alternative. "Or maybe they can just tell that we're desperately in love with one another."

"Could you be serious for a minute?" she demanded, annoyed that her heart had actually skipped a beat in response to the mention of "love." He was only kid-ding—she knew that. And yet his words underscored her biggest concern about their impending marriage—that they were doing this for all the wrong reasons.

"I could," he agreed. "But it seems that you're being serious enough for both of us."

"Ashley and Megan both had questions. A ton of questions," she told him.

He refilled their glasses. "What kind of questions?"

"What's the hurry? Why do we have to get married now? Why do we have to get married in California?"

"I should have realized that they would want to be at your wedding."

Paige shrugged. "Of course, that's not possible for either of them right now."

"We could always have another ceremony when we get back to Pinehurst," he offered.

"One wedding is quite enough." She tapped her finger on the base of her wineglass.

"What else is on your mind?" Zach asked.

It was unnerving how easily he seemed to tune in to her thoughts sometimes. On the other hand, his question gave her the perfect opening. She'd debated with herself for hours about whether or not to bring up the subject, but with their wedding only a few days away, she knew she couldn't postpone any longer.

"I think we should have a prenup," she said.

The glint of amusement in his eyes faded. "Why?"

She was surprised that he had to ask. "Because I've been a family-law attorney for half a dozen years and the idea of entering into a marriage without one seems both foolish and reckless."

"It seems to me that making provision for what will happen in the event of a breakdown of the marriage doesn't imply much faith in the marriage."

"The reality is that a large percentage of all marriages end in divorce, even though most couples believe—at least at the time they exchange vows—that their marriage will last forever."

Zach looked as if he was going to say something

else, but then he just shrugged. "Fine. You want a pre-nup, draft one up."

"This is for your benefit as much as mine," she told him. "So why do you seem angry?"

"Because this whole conversation just proves to me that whatever else is between us, we still don't have trust. And without trust, we don't have a hope in hell of making a marriage work."

"I'd trust you with my life," she told him and meant it. "And Emma's life, too."

He tossed back the rest of his wine and stood up. "Just not with your money."

She frowned. "Is that what you think this is about?"

He shrugged. "I don't know what kind of assets you have, but I have to figure that an attorney has a better income than a military pilot."

"What about the winery?" she challenged. "Don't you have any interest in the family business?"

"Well, of course, but—"

"And don't you think it would be wise to take steps to protect that interest?"

"Maybe I'm naive," he allowed. "But it seems to me that a woman who rearranges her life to care for some-one else's child is someone inherently worthy of trust."

Before she could think of a response to that, he'd gone into the house and left her alone with the wine and the stars and an uncomfortable feeling that her mar-riage-of-convenience to Zach Crawford was going to be anything but simple.

She stayed up late into the night, working at her laptop, drafting and revising a prenuptial agreement. But in the end, she realized he was right. More impor-tantly, she recognized that what he was giving her—

his name and legal standing in Emma's life—were a lot more valuable than anything she was bringing into the union. And if, for some reason, their marriage didn't work out, she didn't see Zach going after her condo in Syracuse or her designer wardrobe any more than she would go after his Trenton apartment or his flight suits.

And if getting married without a legal contract felt to Paige like jumping out of an airplane without a secondary chute, it was a leap of faith and one that she was ready to take. Because somewhere between saying yes to Zach's proposal and shutting down her computer, she'd realized that she did want this marriage to work—and not just for Emma.

Because she was falling for Zach.

And while that had definitely not been in her plans, the more time she spent with Zach and the more she discovered about him, the more she realized that he was a man she could count on.

She'd meant it when she'd told him that she trusted him with her life. She wasn't sure she was ready to trust him with her heart, but it was already in his hands.

Chapter 12

Zach didn't have any expectations about how Paige would look when she walked down the aisle. He knew she'd gone shopping with his mother and his sisters and that she'd come back with a dress, but the women had all been careful not to reveal any details about it within his earshot. Not that it mattered to him. He was certain that she'd look fabulous in whatever she'd chosen.

But in all of the conversations they'd had about their wedding and all of the plans they'd made for their marriage, his fiancée had been forthright and practical. So the last thing he expected to see was Paige looking like a bride.

A breathtakingly beautiful bride.

The moment he saw her moving down the makeshift aisle toward him, everyone and everything else faded away.

The ceremony was, thankfully, brief and focused on the exchange of vows and rings. Paige's voice quavered slightly when she recited her part and her hand trembled when he lifted it to slide the diamond-encrusted band onto the third finger, but her gaze remained steady throughout.

She struggled a little when it was her turn to put his ring on his finger, but then it was done and Reverend Lamont finally said, "You may kiss your bride."

Paige was the least nervous about this part of the wedding because this was a part she and Zach had done before. Not as husband and wife, of course, but kissing was kissing, and although she didn't make a habit of kissing in front of an audience, it still seemed less significant than the speaking of vows and giving of rings.

Or so she thought until Zach kissed her.

Because this kiss was more than an obligatory touch of his mouth to hers. It was a soft, lingering kiss that teased just a little and promised so much more.

When he drew back, she was breathless, yearning and terrified. Because while the smattering of applause from their wedding guests echoed dimly in the back of her mind, she knew the kiss hadn't been for their benefit. It had been for her.

It was a kiss that told her she mattered, when she hadn't expected to matter. Not over and above the arrangements they'd made for Emma. But this had nothing to do with Emma.

This was personal, and the realization shook her to the very core. It was a reminder of what they had shared. A promise of what could be.

Then Emma broke the spell, lifting her arms toward Zach and demanding, "Up."

He picked her up, and she kissed his cheeks, first one, then the other, then she leaned over to do the same to Paige. And even those who might have impassively observed the kiss the groom shared with his bride were not untouched by the sweet innocence of her gesture.

The guests erupted into applause again, and Emma beamed.

After the ceremony, pictures were taken in the gardens outside the château. As Paige moved around in response to the photographer's directions, her mind alternately skipped back to the kiss they'd shared and jumped forward to the night ahead with giddy anticipation.

Dinner came after the pictures, and while everything looked delicious, she honestly didn't taste a bit of anything she'd eaten. She was aware only of Zach.

Paige didn't see her aunt Lillian until she escaped to the ladies' room to freshen her makeup in anticipation of her first dance as Mrs. Crawford, and when she did, she stopped dead in her tracks.

Her aunt smiled. "Congratulations, Paige."

"I can't believe you're here," she murmured.

"I can't believe you didn't invite me," Lillian admonished.

"I didn't invite you because you're living in Switzerland now." And because she hadn't expected that she would go out of her way to attend her niece's wedding. Not that Lillian hadn't always been wonderful to her, but because her aunt's acceptance had never quite made up for her father's rejection.

"But I was in Pinehurst visiting with Megan and Gage and the baby when you called to tell her you were getting married," Lillian explained. "She and Ashley both wanted to be here, but they agreed to stay put so long as I promised to come in their stead."

"They shouldn't have asked that of you," Paige murmured.

"They didn't ask, I offered," Lillian told her. "I wanted to be here, to see you married."

"Then I'll tell you that I'm very glad to see you," she said, and impulsively hugged her.

Her aunt seemed surprised but pleased by the gesture of affection, but ever mindful of appearances she said, "Careful of your dress—you don't want to be covered in creases for the rest of the night."

Her admonishment was so typically Lillian, it made Paige laugh, which successfully warded off the tears that had filled her eyes. "I'll be careful," she promised.

Lillian's gaze softened. "You look so much like your mother on her wedding day."

"Really?" Paige was skeptical, and not sure that any resemblance to her mother—a woman who had abandoned her child to an uncaring father—was a good thing.

Her aunt nodded. "Except that you're even more beautiful."

"I don't remember what she looked like," Paige admitted softly. "After she left, he got rid of anything that reminded him of her. I don't even have a photo."

"I should have expected as much," Lillian murmured. "Your father isn't a bad man. He's just...uncompromising."

"That's one word for it," she agreed.

"I have some pictures," her aunt told her. "Of their wedding. Of you and your mom when you were just a baby. Even one or two of you with both your mom and dad. I'll see that you get them."

Although she wasn't sure what purpose they could possibly serve after so many years, Paige was grateful for the offer. "Thank you."

"Now go," Lillian said. "Your groom is waiting."

She met Zach in the middle of the dance floor, just as the music began to play. As they danced together, they shared some more kisses, and with every moment that passed, Paige grew increasingly anxious for the reception to be over and their wedding night to begin.

"What are you thinking about?" Zach asked.

She felt her cheeks heat. "Nothing really," she lied.

He pulled her closer, his lips brushing against her ear as he asked, "Want to know what I've been thinking about?"

She tried not to shiver, not to let him know how much his nearness was affecting her. "Okay."

"Zipper or buttons."

She drew back, certain she hadn't heard him correctly. "What?"

"I've been wondering, since you came down the aisle in that dress, how to get you out of it," he explained. "If it's a zipper, it will be quick. If it's a long line of buttons, it will take longer."

"Now I know why you've been sliding your hand up and down my spine." And her body was tingling in response to the promise of his words as much as the lazy caress of his hands.

"That's part of the reason," he admitted. "The other part is that I just like touching you. Of course, touching you tends to fog my brain, which might be why I haven't been able to figure out the schematics of this dress."

"Or maybe it's because the zipper is over here," she told him, and reached for the hand that was on her back and guided it around to the side.

Zach sucked in a breath as his palm brushed the curve of her breast. Paige smiled, clearly pleased by his reaction.

"Can we get out of here now?" he asked.

"I think we'd raise more than a few eyebrows if we made a beeline for the door at the end of our first dance."

"I don't care," he insisted.

"Well, I do," she told him. "Besides, I promised a dance to the father of the groom."

"Watch that guy," Zach warned. "He's got some pretty smooth moves."

"I have been watching him. He and your mom. They look so happy together, even after forty years of marriage."

"They love each other," he said simply.

Paige didn't know how to respond to that, so she only glanced toward Justin and Kathleen again. Their bodies were close together, their gazes locked on one another as they swayed to the music. And as she watched them, she realized that she wanted what they had—that forever kind of connection.

Could she have that with Zach? she wondered. Could she fall in love with her husband?

His lips brushed against her temple; her heart fluttered.

Yeah, she was pretty sure she could fall in love with him. So maybe the real question was could *he* fall in love with *her*?

A few hours later, they finally said goodbye to their guests, gave Emma hugs and kisses, then headed for the exit.

Paige had been as anxious as Zach was to get away from the crowd so that they could be alone together. And the moment they stepped out of the reception and into the night, her heart started pounding harder and faster.

With every step she took closer to the guesthouse, her anticipation grew. It was ridiculous to be nervous. Even if it was her wedding night, she was hardly a virgin bride. It wasn't even the first night she and Zach would be together.

But somehow, the ring on her finger changed everything.

And when she and Zach had sex tonight, they wouldn't just be having sex, they would be consummating their marriage. It was an archaic concept, but even acknowledging it as such didn't diminish the significance of the act. After tonight, she would truly be Zach's wife in every sense of the word.

Zach's wife.

After almost thirty years spent establishing her own identity, she expected that such a possessive term would annoy her. But the way Zach looked at her and the way he touched her made her feel not like a possession but like someone who was cared about, cherished. And when he made love with her—

She shivered at the memory of what he could do with his hands and his mouth and his body.

He stroked a hand down her bare arm, raising goose bumps on her flesh. "Cold?"

She shook her head. How could she possibly be cold when there was so much heat inside of her?

But he was already shrugging out of his jacket, tucking it around her shoulders. So she snuggled into it, absorbing the warmth from his body, breathing in his scent, already thinking about him taking the jacket off of her again, along with every other scrap of clothing she was wearing.

Anticipation tangled with the nerves in her belly as they rounded the corner and came upon the guesthouse.

There was a soft glow from the window, suggesting that a light had been left on inside. Probably one of Zach's sisters, Paige thought, recalling their efforts to ensure that every detail of their brother's wedding day was memorable.

He dug the key out of his pocket and slipped it into the lock. With a soft click, the dead bolt released and he pushed the door open.

Paige started forward.

"Wait."

She paused in midstep. "What am I waiting for?"

"I'm supposed to carry you over the threshold."

"Why?"

"Because it's another one of those wedding traditions my family is big on—along with the honeymoon we're not having."

"But your family isn't here."

Zach looked around, squinting into the night. "It's too dark to be sure of that."

She chuckled. "Do you really think your sisters are lurking somewhere in the rows of grapes?"

"It wouldn't be the first time," he muttered.

"Now that sounds like an interesting story."

He swept her off of her feet and into his arms. "And not one I'm going to share."

"Hayden will tell me."

"Yeah, she probably will," he agreed, and carried her through the open door. "But not tonight. Tonight is just for you and me."

Except that when they entered the guesthouse, his concern that one of more of his sisters might be watching them proved well-founded because it was apparent someone had been there before them. The light she'd seen from the window wasn't from a lamp that had been left on but clusters of candles set around the room.

"I hear music," Paige said and, entranced, started to follow the sound of the soft notes floating on the air.

Zach, after only a slight hesitation, climbed the stairs behind her.

She'd never been in the guesthouse before, but she would bet that the room from which the music emanated was the master bedroom. The furniture was masculine looking—the wood solid and dark—but the tone of the room was balanced with distinctive feminine touches. Airy curtains at the windows, a collection of little bottles on the bureau, a rose-colored wing chair beneath an antique reading lamp in the corner.

The music was coming from a portable boom box on one of the twin nightstands that flanked the bed, along with a crystal vase filled with pink roses. On the other was a silver bucket in which a bottle of champagne was chilling, two crystal flutes standing at the ready beside it. More candles flickered in here, too, the light casting a decidedly romantic light over the scene.

But it was the bed at the center of the room that caught and held her attention. It was king-size and made up with cream-colored satin sheets scattered with fragrant rose petals.

"Wow," Paige said.

"Apparently my sisters are romantics."

"They're wonderful," she said. "Your whole family has been wonderful—" she sighed "—and I feel like such a fraud."

He tipped her chin up, forced her to meet his gaze. "Why?"

"Because they think this is a real marriage."

"It is real," he insisted. "I've got the paperwork to prove it."

She knew the marriage was legal, but what tugged at her conscience and what she wasn't willing to remind him of now was that neither of them had really meant the vows they'd recited. Neither of them was in love with the other. But she believed they were both committed to the marriage, and maybe that would be enough.

"Well, then," she said. "What do you want to do now?"

She couldn't help it—even as she asked the question, her gaze just automatically slid back to the bed, to the velvety pink petals scattered on the glossy sheets.

Zach's brows lifted. "What did you have in mind?"

She shrugged. "I was thinking maybe a hot bath, some cool champagne, then sliding between those sheets."

"I was thinking the same thing," he said, his hands

cupping her shoulders to draw her closer. "Minus the bath and the champagne."

"We can't let good champagne go to waste," she protested, though not very strenuously.

"We'll have the champagne." He kissed her lightly. "After."

"Never let it be said that I don't know how to compromise," Paige said, drawing his mouth down to hers for another, steamier kiss.

"I wouldn't dream of it." He slipped his jacket from her shoulders. Then his fingertips skimmed over the ridge of her collarbone, down the length of her bare arms and back up again. This time when she shivered, he didn't need to ask if she was cold.

His mouth eased away from hers, his lips trailed kisses along her jaw, down her throat. The bustier that Jocelyn had insisted would be perfect with her dress pushed up her breasts so that they swelled over the top of the bodice. Zach took his time exploring those swells and the valley between them.

Paige wasn't nearly as patient. She tugged at his tie until the knot came loose, then began working at the line of buttons that ran down the front of his shirt, eager to get her hands on him.

She unfastened his belt, pulled it free of the loops and let it fall to the floor. Then she unhooked the front of his pants and released his zipper, stroking her hand down the front of his trousers as she did so. She smiled when Zach groaned, pleased to know that he was as aroused by her touch as she was by his.

After what seemed like an eternity of his hands stroking her body through the fabric of her dress, he zeroed in on the zipper at the side and slid it slowly downward. Then, just as slowly, he peeled the dress away until she was standing in front of him in only her undergarments and a pair of sexy silver sandals.

His eyes skimmed over her hotly, and her skin burned as if from his touch.

"And I thought you looked beautiful in the dress," he murmured, then swept her up into his arms for a second time that day.

But this time she knew it was for her benefit alone, and though it was a foolishly romantic and completely unnecessary gesture, that knowledge didn't stop her heart from fluttering wildly in her breast or prevent a sigh of pure pleasure from slipping from her lips.

"Do you like it?" she asked him.

"Like it?" He couldn't take his eyes off of her.

The sheer lacy undergarment that she wore nipped tight at her waist and lifted her breasts so that they practically spilled over the top. Below, she wore a tiny pair of bikini panties that were just as sheer and lacy.

"Yeah, I like it," he said, unfastening the tie that held the two sides together. "But not as much as I like what's underneath."

This time it wasn't an impulse and it was more than a stolen hour. They had the guesthouse all to themselves—there was no baby sleeping in the next room, no parents slumbering down the hall. There was no one but Paige.

And this time he was going to linger. He was going to listen for the hitch in her breath, the sound of her sighs, the tenor of her moans. She did sigh as his mouth slid over the curve of her breast, gasped when his lips nibbled the already turgid peak and moaned when he suckled deeply.

Yeah, that was what he wanted—and using her responses as his guide, he continued his leisurely exploration.

He could feel her heat and her wetness, and as his tongue stroked over the triangle of lace between her legs, her hips instinctively lifted. His hands slid up the back of her thighs, curved around her buttocks and held her immobile while he feasted.

She whimpered and writhed. And when he pushed aside the scrap of fabric and laved her hot, wet center with his tongue, he savored the essence of her explosion.

This time he was prepared, although he had to find the pants he'd discarded to retrieve the condoms he'd stuffed in his pocket. He made quick work of that task and hastily sheathed himself before rejoining her on the bed.

But the moment he braced himself over her, all sense of urgency vanished.

She looked so beautiful in the candlelight. So perfect.

She reached for him, her hands draping over his shoulders, her legs hooking around his waist. He slipped inside of her wet heat, his groan mingling with her sigh. He began to move, and she matched him, beat for beat, thrust for thrust, faster, harder, deeper.

Her body arched as the climax wracked her body, and he rode the wave with her, then shuddered his release into her.

This time when Paige woke in the morning and found herself wrapped in the warm strength of Zach's arms, she didn't panic at the thought of getting caught in his bed. No, this time her panic had a different origin. It was the realization that she could quite happily wake up like this every morning for the rest of her life.

Maybe that wasn't an unusual thought for a newly married woman, but it was both unusual and unnerving for a woman who'd married for only practical reasons.

She started to shift away from him, needing some physical distance to put her thoughts in order, but his arm clamped tighter around her, keeping her close to his side.

"Where do you think you're going?" he asked in a sleepy voice.

"I thought I'd, uh, take a shower."

"We showered last night," he reminded her.

"That was last night," she said. "And it was before you decided to get creative with the champagne."

Although his eyes remained closed, his lips curved. "I don't remember hearing any protests at the time."

She seemed to recall gasping with shock when he'd dribbled the liquid on various parts of her body, then moaning with pleasure as he'd slowly and thoroughly licked up every drop, but she definitely hadn't protested. "That's not the point."

His hand slid up to cup her breast, his thumb rubbing lazily over her nipple. "I think it's a pretty good point."

"Zach." Definitely a moan rather than a protest.

"Yeah?" His hand moved downward, between her thighs.

Her legs parted for him and she sighed, surrendering to what they both needed. "Maybe we could try the hot tub instead of the shower next time."

"Whatever you want," he promised her.

* * *

When they finally got out of the hot tub, they were both starving. Though Zach thought it was unlikely that the refrigerator would be stocked, he pulled open the door anyway and found a fancy tray done up with meats and cheeses and crackers and fruit.

"Your sisters are the best," Paige said, helping herself to a plump ripe strawberry.

"I'm starting to warm up to them myself," Zach agreed, which made her laugh.

She piled a cracker with a square of Muenster and a slice of kielbasa, popped it into her mouth, then washed it down with a mouthful of springwater. "You're crazy about them."

"I'd be crazy to admit it." He went straight for the Colby, tossed a few cubes into his mouth.

"And they adore you."

He winced at that. "They adore torturing me."

"Because that's what sisters are supposed to do," she informed him, selecting a cluster of green grapes.

"I guess I didn't get the memo on that."

"You're lucky," she said. "I didn't know what it meant to have siblings until I went to live with Ashley and Megan."

"And did they torture you?"

"We tortured each other," she admitted. "But we always knew we could count on one another, too."

"You miss them, don't you?"

"I do. But we have such different lives now. Both Megan and Ashley are married and having babies and—"

"You're married now, too," he pointed out. "Or did you forget that already?"

She blushed. "Of course I haven't forgotten. I'm just still getting used to the idea."

"I think you forgot," he said, feigning indignation. "Obviously I have to figure out a way to remind you."

"What did you have in mind?"

"Let me show you," he said.

After they made love again, they finally, reluctantly, got dressed.

"This has been…incredible," Paige said.

"So why do you sound so sad?"

"Because I wish it was more than just an interlude from the real world."

"Is the real world so bad?" he asked gently, understanding that when she spoke so reproachfully about the real world what she was referring to was *his* world—the military environment in which he worked and lived.

"I guess time will tell."

He kissed her gently. "I meant what I said when I spoke those vows," he told her. "I will always come home to you and Emma."

In fact, he'd meant everything he'd said during the ceremony in which he'd promised to love, honor and cherish her, but he knew she wasn't ready to hear those words just yet.

Which she confirmed when she said, "Speaking of Emma, it really is time for us to be getting back."

Reminding himself that he had no right to be frustrated, he picked up his duffel bag and slung it over his shoulder, then followed her up the path to the main house.

Chapter 13

It surprised Zach how easily he settled into the house on Chetwood Street with Paige and Emma. Of course, he'd been staying there with them before the trip to California, but he'd been a guest then. Now, he was legally Paige's husband and legitimately Emma's father, and he felt as if they really were a family. And he was happier and more content than he could have imagined.

It wasn't the kind of life he'd ever envisioned for himself. A tidy two-story home in the middle of suburbia. A lawn to mow, flowers to tend, windows to wash. It was almost ridiculous how much he enjoyed tackling those mundane day-to-day chores. Or maybe it was the beautiful wife and adorable baby girl who fulfilled him in a way he'd never felt before.

They shared meals together and they spent time with Emma, playing with her, caring for her. And when she

The Baby Surprise

was settled down for the night, he and Paige would go upstairs together and he'd find himself reaching for her, wanting her as he'd never wanted another woman. And she would come to him willingly, even eagerly, and they would make love as if they couldn't get enough of one another.

It was so perfect, he knew it couldn't last.

And he couldn't help but wonder, what was going to happen when he left? Because the one thing both he and Paige had been certain of at the outset was that he would be leaving again.

It was, in fact, the reason they'd married—so Emma would have a mother to care for her when he was away and provide her with the stability that his transient career couldn't provide.

Meanwhile, Paige was still in the process of figuring out her career plan, trying to decide if she wanted to go back to Syracuse and her position at Wainwright, Witmer & Wynne or maybe look at staying in Pinehurst where she would be closer to her cousins and their families. He thought about suggesting Trenton as another possibility, but he knew that would be solely for his own convenience and completely unfair because he wouldn't be home all that often.

But the more he thought about leaving Paige and Emma, the more he found himself having doubts about the life he'd chosen for himself. Or maybe it was simply that falling in love had caused him to reevaluate the choices he'd made before he was a father, before he'd met Paige.

If he was willing to walk away from his career, he might be able to have a normal life with Paige and Emma. He'd never wanted a normal life before. There was no adrenaline rush with normal, no sense of purpose. Except that there was definitely a rush whenever he thought of Paige, and he couldn't imagine any task with more purpose than being a father to his daughter.

Whenever he'd thought of his life before, he'd thought first and foremost of his career. The military *was* his life, a second family when he was so far away from his own.

But he'd given them fifteen years, and as much as he loved flying, he knew he couldn't fly forever. In fact, they were already trying to promote him out of the cockpit. And watching the young guys coming up in the ranks, witnessing their boundless energy and unflagging enthusiasm, sometimes made him feel even older than his thirty-seven years.

He wanted something for himself now. He wanted Paige and Emma and maybe even more children down the road.

Of course, more children was something he definitely needed to discuss with Paige. He had no idea what her thoughts were with respect to kids, except that—by her own admission—she'd been completely unprepared for a child when Emma came into her care. Prior to that, she hadn't given any thought to parenthood.

He didn't know if that had changed at all. Certainly it wasn't anything they'd talked about before they'd gotten married. In fact, there were too many things they hadn't talked about, too much they hadn't known about one another before pledging to spend their lives together, and he vowed to change that.

But every time he tried to broach the subject of their future, Paige would steer the conversation in another direction. And because he was reluctant to force the issue when things were going so well between them, he let her, and the days simply slipped away until it was time for him to say goodbye to his wife and daughter and report back to duty.

She didn't ask how long he would be gone, probably because she knew it wasn't a question he could answer with any degree of certainty. And he didn't ask if she would be there when he came home, because he trusted that she meant to honor the vows they'd exchanged, that she wouldn't disregard a promise as easily as Heather had done.

Paige had known Zach was going to leave. Because she grew up in the military, she understood what the uniform meant to the men and women who wore it. She understood and appreciated the sacrifices they made for their commanders, their comrades, their country.

But knowing Zach was going to leave still hadn't prepared her for the reality of his absence, and she felt the emptiness keenly when he was gone.

Twenty-four hours after he'd said goodbye, she was trying to remember what her life with Emma had been like before he'd ever walked into it. She'd been happy enough then. She certainly wouldn't have said that there was anything missing. But now, everything seemed empty without him.

"Dada," Emma demanded.

"Dada had to go bye-bye," Paige said.

The little girl curled and uncurled her fingers, the toddler version of a wave. "Bye-bye."

"That's right, sweetie. Dada's gone bye-bye."

"Pawk?" Emma said, latching on to her next favorite topic.

Paige managed to smile. "I have some work to do this morning, but maybe we can go to the park later."

Emma clapped her hands together. "Pawk!"

Paige ruffled the little girl's hair and wished there was something that could lift her mood as easily.

Paige was feeling too melancholy to want to be alone with her thoughts, so she called Ashley and Megan and invited them to come over. Now only a few weeks away from her own due date, Ashley hadn't been venturing far but was more than happy to get out of the house for a while—even if it was just to go down the street. Megan had just gotten home from Marcus's first monthly checkup but willingly strapped the baby back into his car seat and came over to join them.

Ashley brought Maddie with her, of course, and the little girl happily occupied Emma while the adults chatted. It was a nice way to spend the afternoon, or so she thought until Megan asked about Zach.

"How long is he going to be away this time?"

"Probably until the new year," she admitted, trying not to think about how many months and weeks and days that would mean and how very much she missed him already.

"That sucks," Ashley said.

Paige just shrugged, feigning a nonchalance she wasn't anywhere close to feeling. "Except for the ring on my finger, it just means that nothing has really changed in my life."

"Uh-oh," Ashley said softly, ominously.

Paige frowned. "What?"

"You've fallen in love with him."

"I have not."

"Then why are you getting all bent out of shape over the fact that he's gone?" Megan demanded.

"I'm not bent out of shape," she denied.

Ashley and Megan exchanged looks.

"Okay, maybe I have feelings for him," Paige allowed. "And maybe they're deeper than feelings I've had for anyone before."

"Well, considering that you're married to the guy, I'd say that's a good thing," Megan noted.

But Paige wasn't so sure and said so.

Ashley shook her head. "Did you really think this marriage would be like a business arrangement with enforceable terms and conditions?"

"Yes."

Megan rolled her eyes. "You had sex with him before you married him, right?"

"So?"

"So obviously there was an attraction."

"I've been attracted to other men before without my feelings spiraling out of control," Paige informed her.

"You didn't live with any of them," Ashley pointed out logically.

"She never dated anyone long enough to make that kind of commitment," Megan noted. "And yet she married Zach after knowing him only a few weeks."

"Because it was the only way I could be sure I wouldn't lose Emma."

"Well, then, I guess you got exactly what you wanted," Ashley said.

And Paige nodded, because it was true.

The problem was, now she wanted so much more.

* * *

Ashley had her baby on Friday.

Megan had gone three endlessly long days past her due date before her labor started, and then it had been both intense and painful. Ashley had her baby three weeks early and after only five hours of labor.

Because Ashley had suffered for years with endometriosis and the doctors hadn't even been sure that she would be able to get pregnant and carry a baby to term, it seemed only fair that her pregnancy and delivery should proceed relatively easily. So when she came out of delivery with bright eyes, glowing cheeks, a radiant smile and a perfect seven-pound, ten-ounce baby girl, neither Megan nor Paige held it against her.

When Zach called later that night, she told him all about baby Alyssa. Of course, he remarked on how different Ashley's labor was in comparison to Megan's only six weeks earlier, and Paige couldn't help but think how much her own life had changed in that same six-week period.

The day Megan had gone into labor, she hadn't trusted Zach to stay alone with Emma for a few hours. Now she was married to him. And missing him like crazy.

Of course, she wasn't ready to admit as much to him, but she did tell him, "Emma really misses you."

"I miss both of you, too," he said, and he sounded so sincere that her heart ached.

"I had a meeting at Wainwright, Witmer & Wynne on Monday," she said, needing to steer the conversation to a more neutral topic before she said something to give away the feelings she hadn't yet acknowledged to herself.

"Are you thinking of going back?" he asked her.

She sighed. "No. These past couple of months with Emma have made me realize how little time I spent with her before. I definitely need to get back to work, but I've decided to explore other options."

"In Pinehurst?" he wondered.

"That's one of the possibilities," she agreed.

"There are others?" he prompted.

"Yes, but I don't want to talk about them until I've figured some things out."

"So what do you want to talk about?"

"It doesn't matter," she said. "I'm just happy to hear your voice."

"Maybe Emma's not the only one who misses me?" he prompted.

She refused to respond to that, telling him instead about a recent conversation she'd had with his mother, updating him on the news from California.

When she'd finally run out of things to say, Zach said, "I really do miss you, Paige. I go to bed at night aching for you, and I wake up in the morning reaching for you. And then I cross another day off of my calendar and curse the fact that the new year is so far away."

She felt the prick of tears at the back of her eyes and sighed. "Zach?"

"Yeah?"

"I miss you, too," she said, because it was easier to be honest with him over the phone, when she didn't have to look into his eyes and worry that he could read the emotion that was filling her heart.

Paige's thirtieth birthday was on the twentieth of July. Although she hadn't wanted or expected anyone to make a big deal about the occasion, Ashley—despite having given birth less than a week earlier—insisted on having her over for dinner, promising that Cam was in charge of the cooking. When Paige and Emma showed up, they found that Megan and Gage and baby Marcus were also there.

The adults ate salmon steaks, grilled asparagus and baby potatoes while Maddie and Emma happily chowed down on macaroni and cheese and the babies alternated between napping and snuggling at their mothers' breasts.

It was a low-key celebration but no less enjoyable because of it. And if Paige found herself wishing, once or twice, that Zach could have been there with her, well, she knew to push such impossible fantasies aside.

Because everyone had babies to tend to, she said good-night early, and when she returned home with Emma, she found a package from her aunt Lillian in the mailbox.

The envelope wasn't very thick, but it felt heavy in her hand, and Paige was as apprehensive as she was anxious to see what was inside. But she took care of Emma's bedtime routine first, giving her a bath, putting her in her jammies, brushing the ten teeth that she now had and just sharing a few minutes of quiet cuddling before tucking her into her crib.

Then she finally went back downstairs and opened the envelope.

There were only five photos in total, among them the wedding picture that Lillian had mentioned, and which confirmed that Paige had inherited many of her features from the woman who had given birth to her. But aside from that, Paige experienced no sense of rec-

ognition in looking at the photo. It was as if she had no
memory of the woman at all, and that realization made
her unbearably sad.

She was about to set the photo aside when her gaze
shifted to the groom, and she found her attention riveted
by a face that was at once familiar and yet so very different from the man she remembered. Familiar in that
the shape of his nose, the line of his jaw and the intensity of his stare were all the same. Different in that she
had never seen him looking so happy before.

He was smiling in the photo. No, not just smiling,
actually grinning, as he gazed down at the woman he'd
just married.

What happened? Paige wondered.

What could possibly have gone so wrong between
them to turn such obvious love into bitterness and animosity?

She flipped through the rest of the pictures—one of
mother and child taken in the hospital probably only
a few hours after birth, a formal portrait of both parents with their baby, a later one of Paige when she was
about three years old, kneeling in the sand beside her
mother and trying to build something that didn't in
any way resemble a castle but over which they were
apparently laughing. And the last, obviously taken a
few years later, with Paige seated on her mother's lap,
a storybook open in front of her, but this time, neither
of them was smiling.

She didn't know if it was just the timing of the candid shot or if their more somber expressions were in-
dicative of the fact that both mother and daughter knew
that their lives had already begun to change and would
soon veer in different directions.

With a sigh, she slid the photos back into the envelope. But the corner of one of them seemed to catch on something, and when Paige opened the envelope wider, she found a folded piece of paper with a sticky note tucked inside. She unfolded the page and her breath caught.

Lynn Mackenzie
216 Eastport Drive
Berkeley, CA

The note was from her Aunt Lillian.

Paige,
After we spoke at your wedding, I dug through some old files to find these photos and came across this address. I don't know if you have any interest in trying to contact your mother or even if Lynn is still in California, but if you want to find her, this at least gives you a starting point.
Lxo

California?
It seemed like too much of a coincidence to ignore.

Zach had adjusted to the routine of being back in Afghanistan easily enough. What he couldn't adjust to was missing Paige and Emma.

He'd been an Air Force pilot for fifteen years, and during that time, he'd never had any trouble keeping his focus. He'd never let anything or anyone distract him from his job. And it wasn't that he was distracted so much as he felt disconnected. He went through the motions but he felt empty inside.

After a particularly long and grueling day, he stripped out of his flight suit and headed to the shower. As he stepped beneath the stinging hot spray, he mentally calculated the time difference to Pinehurst and swore when he realized it was too late to call.

He'd desperately wanted to hear Paige's voice, to have her tell him that she missed him as much as he missed her. Obviously that wasn't going to happen tonight, so he checked his e-mail instead, hoping for a message from her, just so that he could feel less out of touch. He was surprised to find a message from Megan Richmond—and he swore again when he read it through.

It was three days after Paige's birthday before Zach had an opportunity to call. As usual, he couldn't talk for long, but he'd been aching to hear her voice and anxious to apologize for missing her birthday. He'd felt like such an idiot when he'd read her cousin's e-mail and realized he'd gotten married without even knowing his wife's birth date. Worse, he hadn't gotten the e-mail until it was too late for him to do anything about it.

But Paige sounded genuinely pleased to hear from him when she answered the phone, although she immediately passed the phone to Emma so that he could say a few words to his daughter. Of course, Emma didn't say much back except "Dadadadada" and then Paige was on the line again.

"I'm really sorry I missed your birthday," he told her. "I promise I'll make it up to you when I get home."

"It's okay," Paige said, and she actually did sound as

if she was okay about it. "And the flowers were—and still are—absolutely beautiful."

Later he would blame sleep deprivation for the delayed functioning of his brain because instead of realizing that someone—Ashley or Megan or both—had covered his ass for him and responding with something like, 'I'm glad you liked them,' he heard himself say instead, "What flowers?"

There was a moment of absolute silence during which all he heard was the cursing inside his own head.

"You didn't send the flowers?"

He winced, uncomfortably aware that he couldn't change his response now, no matter how desperately he wanted to do so. "I would have, if I'd known it was your birthday, but—"

"It's okay," she interrupted to say again, although she sounded a little less okay this time.

"I'll make it up to you," he promised.

"There's nothing to make up. Really."

But the rest of their conversation after that was brief and somewhat stilted, and when he said, "I miss you, Paige," her only response was "Fly safe."

Paige didn't confront Ashley and Megan about the flowers. She didn't need a confession to know that they had arranged the deception. And although she also knew that her cousins had done so with the best of intentions, the fact remained that she had been duped—and forgotten.

The rational part of her brain argued that she couldn't hold Zach responsible for forgetting something he'd never known, but that didn't soften the ache of rejection that echoed deep in her heart and brought back memories of another birthday that she'd thought long-buried.

"What are you sulking about?" Phillip Wilder demanded.

His voice, always so powerful and authoritative, echoed in her mind, as real as if he was speaking to her now. But the scene that played out in her mind was one that she'd lived seventeen years before.

"You missed my birthday party," she spoke softly, almost apologetically, as if she knew the oversight was somehow her own fault and that she, therefore, had no right to be upset with him.

"Your birthday party?" There was no remorse in his tone, only cold, hard scorn.

She nodded, though it wasn't just that he hadn't made an appearance at the party but that he'd made no mention of her thirteenth birthday at all, as if he'd completely forgotten the significance of the date. And in that moment, she knew that he had.

He shook his head. "I lost three men yesterday, so forgive me for thinking that some things are more goddamned important than cake and ice cream."

And with that parting remark, he'd stormed out of the house again, slamming the door behind him.

Paige hadn't celebrated another birthday until the year she turned sixteen. Of course, she'd been living with Ashley and Megan and Aunt Lillian by then, and Aunt Lillian had insisted that a girl's sweet sixteen required a party. She'd invited all of Paige's friends from school and she'd decorated the living room with flowers and streamers.

Paige had been touched by the effort her aunt had undertaken, but she hadn't been able to swallow a bite of the gorgeous cake that had been ordered to celebrate the occasion.

She pushed aside the memories and glanced at the flowers on the table again.

The were stunningly beautiful.

And they were a lie.

Just like her entire marriage was a lie.

She took the tall cut-crystal vase to the garbage, dumping both the flowers and the container inside. Then she picked up the phone and dialed an all-too-familiar number.

"Wainwright, Witmer & Wynne," Louise said. "How may I direct your call?"

Paige took a deep breath. "Hi, I wanted to make an appointment to see Karen Rosario."

"Certainly," the receptionist agreed. "May I ask what it's regarding?"

She swallowed around the lump in her throat. "Child custody."

Chapter 14

Paige's car wasn't in the driveway when Zach got home, and although he was undeniably disappointed, he knew he only had himself to blame. He should have called from the plane to let her know that he was coming home, to tell his wife that he'd made some decisions that he wanted to share with her. But he'd wanted his arrival to be a surprise—and instead, he surprised himself by coming home to an empty house.

He dropped his duffel inside the door and went to the kitchen to grab a drink. He opened a can of Coke and noted that the message light was flashing on the answering machine. He took another swallow from the can and pressed the button.

"Hi, Paige, it's Karen Rosario. I understand that you canceled your appointment for this afternoon and I was a little concerned about your reasons for doing so. I know you had some qualms about proceeding while your husband is out of the country but, as I explained earlier, I believe that his absence can work in your favor, so please give me a call to reschedule—"

Zach pressed the stop button.

He'd heard enough.

More than enough.

Lord, he felt like such a fool. He *was* a fool. To think about what he'd been willing to do, what he'd done, to prove himself to Paige. To prove that he wanted to be with her and wanted to be a father to Emma. To prove that he loved them both and that nothing mattered to him as much as being with them.

And while he'd been changing his life for the benefit of his family, Paige was trying to destroy it.

Maybe the lawyer's message hadn't been explicit, but the information had been there. Karen Rosario was the lawyer Paige had consulted when they'd been trying to work out custody of Emma, and obviously that was the direction that she'd decided she wanted to go in again.

She'd never claimed to love him. He was the one who'd foolishly believed she had to have some feelings for him, who'd foolishly let himself hope those feelings would grow—that she would come to love him as much as he loved her.

Paige wasn't the type to act emotionally or impulsively. Not usually.

Her marriage to Zach suggested otherwise, but she knew that her decision to accept his proposal was only further proof that nothing had been usual since he'd walked into her life almost three months earlier.

In that moment, everything had changed. And not just

because his existence had threatened her relationship with Emma, but because his presence in her life threatened everything she knew and believed about herself.

Being with Zach made her want things she'd never wanted before—most notably, a future and a family with someone she knew she would love forever. And the love she felt for him—the depth and scope of the emotion unlike anything she'd ever known—scared her senseless.

And so she'd reacted as if she truly were brainless—pushing him away when she wanted to hold him close. Threatening to tear apart the family they'd so recently put together.

She'd had relationships before, of course, but none of any real significance. She'd certainly never been in love before. Maybe she'd come close once or twice, but the truth was, she'd been hurt too many times to let herself form any kind of deep emotional attachments. And as Ashley had so astutely pointed out, whenever anyone had started to get too close, she'd pushed them away.

It wasn't that she didn't want to fall in love and be loved in return—she just didn't know how to let down the protective barriers she'd built around her heart and welcome someone in.

Of course, she hadn't *let* Zach in, either. But somehow he was there. He'd stormed through the barriers without her even realizing it until he was so firmly ensconced that she didn't know how to get rid of him.

Or even if she wanted to.

Zach stayed up through most of the night, waiting for Paige to come home.

She never did.

He tried calling her cell but kept getting her voice mail—and he had no interest in leaving a message.

He finally fell asleep toward dawn and awoke with a start, suddenly thinking about Olivia and the tragic accident that had taken her life. What if something had happened to Paige and Emma? As angry as he still was about the telephone message from Karen Rosario, he knew he couldn't bear it if he lost his wife and daughter.

He couldn't think of anywhere that Paige could be, where she might have gone, but it occurred to him that Ashley or Megan would probably know. Because Ashley was closer, he decided to start there.

She answered the door with a tiny infant in her arms and a genuine smile on her face. "Zach, hi. I thought I saw your truck drive down the street last night, but Paige said you weren't coming home until after Christmas."

He knew he should congratulate her on the new addition, show an interest in the baby, but he was too tired and worried to make idle conversation so all he said was, "Where is she?"

Ashley frowned. "Paige?"

"Yes, Paige. Where is she? Where did she take my daughter?"

Her cousin was obviously puzzled and just a little wary. "Haven't you talked to her?"

"If I'd been able to get in touch with her, I wouldn't be here," he ground out.

She blinked at the harshness of his tone and rubbed a hand soothingly down the baby's back. "She took Emma to California."

He frowned. "California?"

"To see your parents." She touched a hand to his

arm. "Are you okay?" she asked gently. "Has something happened?"

"That's what I'm trying to figure out," he muttered.

"Did you want to come in—"

He shook his head. "No. Thanks. I have to catch a flight to San Francisco."

When Paige and Emma flew into California, Zach's parents insisted on meeting them at the airport. Although she'd been prepared to rent a car—and would have, in some ways, preferred to do so—they'd insisted that there were enough vehicles available for her use that it wasn't necessary. But the transportation issue aside, Paige had to admit that it was nice to be met at the end of a long journey. And when she found herself caught, first in Kathleen's embrace and then in Justin's, she really felt as if she'd come home.

She'd expected that Zach's parents would have a lot of questions about the reasons for her trip, especially considering that only a few weeks had passed since her first visit with Emma. But they didn't ask. Maybe they wanted her to tell them, or maybe they were just so genuinely pleased to have another chance to visit with their granddaughter that the reasons didn't matter.

But on the fourth day of their visit, while Paige was helping Kathleen prepare dinner, her mother-in-law asked, "How are you holding up?"

Paige pushed the masher into the steaming mound of cooked potatoes. "What do you mean?"

"Just that it can't be easy to say goodbye to a man you've only been married to for a few weeks with the expectation that it will be a lot longer than that before you see him again."

"I thought I would be okay with it," Paige told her. "I mean, my father was—*is*—in the military, so I grew up with frequent goodbyes and extended periods of absence."

"But you never had a choice in that, did you?" Kathleen guessed.

"No," she agreed. "But even knowing what kind of demands his career entailed, I chose to marry Zach."

"And now you have regrets?"

"No," she said again, shaking her head for emphasis. "Maybe I did when he first went away. Or maybe it would be more accurate to say I had fears."

"What kind of fears?"

"That he wouldn't come back to me. Not because he couldn't, but because he wouldn't want to."

"Oh, honey." Kathleen put her hand on Paige's shoulder, squeezed it gently. "I know my son, which means that I'm well aware of how difficult and uncommunicative he can be, and I have no doubt that if you and Zach actually sat down together and talked about this, you wouldn't have cause to worry.

"But because that isn't possible right now, let me assure you that because I know my son, I know that, whatever his purported reasons for marrying you, he never would have done so if he didn't love you."

Hope flickered inside her, but was quickly extinguished. She knew that Zach cared about her, but he'd never said anything about love. "Zach married me so that Emma would have a mother and a father," she admitted to his mother.

"I'm sure that was a factor in his decision," Kathleen agreed.

Paige wanted to insist that it was the only factor, but she didn't see any point in arguing with her mother-in-law. But Kathleen must have sensed her skepticism because she squeezed Paige's shoulder again. "Why don't you believe that he loves you?"

"Because no one ever has."

She hadn't intended to speak the words out loud, hadn't even realized that sense of unworthiness was so deeply rooted in her heart until she said it. And it wasn't until she felt Kathleen's arms come around her that she realized she was crying.

Her mother-in-law's warmth and compassion encouraged her to confide her deepest fears and insecurities, and Paige found herself telling Kathleen everything about her past, from her mother's abandonment to her father's banishment and everything in between.

And when she was finally done, when all her tears had been cried and the potatoes were stone-cold, Zach's mom continued to hold her.

It had been so long since Paige had been held, so long since she'd felt a mother's affection, that she wasn't in any hurry to withdraw from the embrace. As Kathleen comforted her, Paige's spirit was soothed and her resolve was strengthened. And she knew that she'd made the right choice, not just in coming to California but in marrying Zach. Because he was the man she would love forever and she wasn't going to give up on their marriage or their family. Ever.

* * *

Zach couldn't get a direct flight to California, which meant that instead of the trip taking seven hours, he was in transit nearly fourteen.

By the time he arranged for a car and made the drive to his parents' house, he was annoyed, exhausted and even more furious with Paige.

And then he found out that she wasn't even there.

"Where is she?"

"I don't know," his mother responded calmly to his impatient demand. "She just said that she had some things she needed to do and asked if she could borrow a car for a few hours."

"Where's Emma?" he demanded.

"She's with Paige." She looked up from the laundry she was folding. "Honestly, Zach, what has gotten into you?"

"I just...I need to talk to Paige."

"Well, she should be back soon. In the meantime, why don't you go down to the winery to see your father? Maybe he can do something about this mood you brought home with you."

Being sent to his father was a revised version of "wait till your father gets home," and as Zach trudged toward the winery, he regretted that he'd taken his anger and frustration out on his mother.

He was halfway between the house and the winery when his mother's little red car came zipping up the driveway. The vehicle slowed as it drew nearer, then stopped right in the middle of the lane.

With the sun glinting off of the windshield, he couldn't see the driver. But even before the door opened, Zach knew it was Paige.

She stepped out of the car, her lips curved.

The smile was like a sucker punch to his gut.

How could she look at him like that—as if she was happy to see him? How could she pretend that everything was okay when she was planning to end their marriage?

Leaving the car door open, she started toward him.

Zach didn't dare let her get any closer because he knew that if he let her touch him, he would be toast. He would give her anything, everything, just to be with her.

But she'd already made it clear that wasn't what she wanted, and he wasn't going to beg.

So he halted her in his tracks by asking, "Where in hell is your phone?"

Paige stopped moving. Her smile faded.

It obviously wasn't what she expected to hear from him, and she stared at him, uncomprehending. "What?"

"Your phone," he practically growled. "I've been trying to call you for two days."

"Oh. Emma dropped it in the toilet."

"Emma dropped it in the toilet?"

"At the airport. It's completely fried, and I haven't had a chance to replace it." Her brow creased. "How did you get here? And why are you angry with me?"

"Maybe because I traveled for twenty-two hours to get home from Afghanistan only to find that my wife and my daughter weren't anywhere to be found."

She took an automatic step back, as if she was afraid of him. Not that he could blame her when he sounded like a madman. But then she dug in her heels and lifted her chin, reminding him that she wasn't easily intimidated.

Her strength of character was only one of the reasons he'd fallen in love with her, and as hurt and angry as he was right now, he couldn't deny that he did love her. And he knew that he always would.

"If you'd let me know that you were planning to come home, I would have advised you of our plans," she said coolly. "And in any case, you've found us now."

"But I still don't know why you're here," he told her, and then couldn't stop himself from asking, "Did you find out that it's easier to petition for divorce in the state in which you were married?"

Petition for divorce?

Paige stared at him, as stunned by the question as she'd been by his unannounced arrival and unexpected distance. And then the words sank in, and her heart plummeted. "Wh-what do you mean?"

"You really should call home every once in a while to check your phone messages. If you had, you'd know that your lawyer is trying to get in touch with you."

Suddenly his distance, his coolness made sense. Except that he didn't even know half the story. "It's not what you think, Zach," she said, suddenly desperate to explain, desperate to make him understand, to erase that cold distance in his tone and the icy disdain in his eyes.

"You mean you didn't go see her about your chances of maintaining custody of Emma if we split up?" he challenged.

She winced. "Okay, I did, but—"

"Jesus, Paige, why don't you just take a knife and carve out my heart?"

The anguish in his voice brought tears to her eyes. She'd hurt him, which was what she'd wanted when she first went to see Karen—to hurt him as he'd hurt her. As everyone she'd ever loved had hurt her by not loving her back. And then she'd gone home after her appointment and spent some time playing with Emma, and she'd realized that Emma would be the one who hurt the most, and as angry as she was with Zach, she never wanted to hurt their little girl.

"I made a mistake," she said, silently pleading for him to understand.

But his gaze was hard and flat and cold when it locked on hers again. "So did I."

She swallowed. "Aren't you going to let me explain?"

"What's to explain? If you want out of our marriage, I have no intention of trying to change your mind."

Of course he wouldn't. Because he didn't care enough to fight for their marriage, to want to keep her with him. No one had ever cared enough.

And suddenly she felt as if she was seven years old again, trying to understand how her mother could just leave. Or fifteen years old and on a plane flying across the ocean because her father had sent her away. And just like both of those times, she felt helpless and overwhelmed and completely alone.

But then she remembered something that Kathleen had said to her. That Zach wouldn't have married her unless he had some pretty strong feelings for her. And although she saw no evidence of those feelings in the man standing before her now, she had to trust that his mother knew what she was saying. She had to trust in Zach.

And if she wanted him to fight for her, to fight for their marriage, she had to show that she was willing to do the same.

"I don't want out," she told him. "But I don't know how to do this."

"Do what?"

"Make a relationship work. Especially a long-distance one."

"So you decided to walk away."

"It was the pattern of my life," she reminded him. "I never learned how to stick things out. Maybe I never wanted to."

"That's clear enough," he said.

"No!" Tears burned her eyes, her throat was tight. "I don't want to walk away this time."

"What do you want?"

"I want to work it out."

"Why?"

"I'm not sure I understand what you're asking," she hedged.

"Is it for Emma?"

She knew that her answer to his question could decide their future, that it was time to put her heart on the line. But he was so cold and distant right now, she was terrified that he would throw it back at her, and she wasn't sure that she was strong enough to handle rejection again. "Of course," she said. "Emma deserves—"

"What about us, Paige?" he interrupted. "You and me. What do we deserve?"

The weary tone in his voice warned that she wasn't likely to get many more chances to tell him the truth about her feelings, so she took a deep breath and tried again. "I don't know what we deserve," she admitted, "but I know what I want. I want to be with you and Emma, to be a family."

Before he could respond to that, a little voice called out from the back of the car. "Da!"

Paige exhaled, torn between relief and frustration

when Zach turned away. He was immediately at the door, reaching inside the car to unhook Emma from her seat. Joy, pure and simple, shone from his eyes when he lifted the pint-size child into his arms.

"There's my girl," he said, his tone filled with all the warmth and affection that had been missing when he'd spoken to Paige.

Emma beamed at him and kissed each of his cheeks.

Zach closed his eyes as he hugged her. "You can't possibly know how much I missed you."

"Dadadadada," she said again.

"Yeah." He kissed the tip of her nose. "Dadda's home."

For how long? Paige wanted to ask. But she stifled the impulse, reminding herself it was enough that he was here now. And so long as he was, maybe they could figure out their future together.

"Pawk?" Emma asked.

He chuckled. "Not right now, honey."

She turned to Paige. "Pawk?"

Paige shook her head. "Grandpa said he'll take you in the pool after supper."

Which was apparently a satisfactory substitute for "park" as Emma clapped her hands together happily.

She knew that she and Zach had a lot of things to work through. She also knew that they weren't going to make any progress right now while father and daughter were so completely immersed in one another. Not that she minded. She would never begrudge Emma any time that she had with Zach. She just wished she knew where she fit in his list of priorities.

* * *

After dinner, when Emma was in the pool with her grandpa, Paige cornered Zach in the living room.

"Do you think we could finish the conversation we were having this afternoon?" She broached the topic cautiously.

"You mean the one in which you were explaining why you went to see a divorce attorney?" he challenged.

Although there was still an edge to his tone, it wasn't nearly as sharp as it had been earlier. She didn't know if that meant he was willing to listen to her explanation now, or if he'd just grown weary of the whole conversation.

"I told you that was a mistake."

He scrubbed a hand over his face. "Maybe I'm the one who made the mistake," he said.

Her eyes filled with tears. "Don't say that, Zach. Please."

"I had unrealistic expectations," he said, sounding resigned.

"What do you mean?"

"Somewhere along the line I started to believe that we were more than two people trying to do what was best for a little girl." He looked at her now, and the icy mask was finally stripped away. "And I fell in love with you."

"You fell...in love...with me?" She was stunned, and thrilled, and filled with cautious hope. She wanted to say the words back to him, to tell him what was in her heart, but he didn't give her a chance.

"I didn't plan for it to happen," he admitted. "But it did, and I thought that maybe, eventually, you might fall in love with me, too. But I knew it wasn't going to happen while I was out of the country, so I came home from Afghanistan and heard the message from your lawyer and—"

"Iloveyoutoo."

Zach stopped talking. He stared at her. He seemed taken aback, though she didn't know if it was by the words or the way she'd blurted them out.

"Okay, maybe I wasn't supposed to shout the words at you like that," she acknowledged, "but I've never actually said them to anyone before."

"I know," he said, his expression wary. "Which makes me wonder why you're saying them to me now."

"Because I do love you," she said and exhaled a sigh of relief when the words came out more easily this time.

"Then can you tell me why, if you love me, you went to see a divorce lawyer?"

She sighed. "Because I'm an idiot."

"I'm not going to dispute that," he said. "Not in this instance, anyway."

"I was hurt and angry and it was an impulse," she admitted. "And then I changed my mind."

"What changed your mind?"

"Realizing that I loved you." She smiled a little, because the words were getting easier to say every time. "And realizing that if I only had five days a year with you, it was better than no days at all."

"Do you really feel that way?" he asked cautiously.

She nodded. "I really do."

He frowned, still struggling to put all of the pieces together. "So why did you come to California?"

"There were a few reasons that I decided to make the trip," she hedged.

"Any particular reason you didn't tell me?"

"Because I didn't think you would find out. I didn't want you to know."

His brows rose. She winced.

"Okay, that sounded bad. But it wasn't a big secret so much as it was supposed to be a surprise." She blew out a breath. "I came to write the bar exam.

"It was your father's idea," she explained. "I mean, he mentioned the possibility of me finding a job in California the last time we were here, and I disregarded the idea because I'm not licensed to practice in California, and then I started to think that maybe I could be."

"You're looking for a job in California?"

"Well, the test results will take a few months yet, but if I pass the bar, I thought *we* might want to consider moving closer to your family."

"But—what about your family?"

"I love both of my cousins dearly, but they have their own families now. And if we wanted to give Emma a brother or a sister someday, it would be nice to be closer to your parents and your sisters, especially if you're overseas."

"You want to have a baby?"

They hadn't talked about having other children and she didn't know how he would respond, but she smiled at the hopeful note in his voice. "I've found myself thinking about it a lot lately, but I'm not sure I could manage two kids—or maybe even more—on my own."

"You wouldn't be on your own," he told her.

"Well, that's why I was thinking we could live here. Not here in this house," she amended. "But somewhere not too far away."

"I'm happy that you would even consider moving to be closer to my family, and I know my parents would be overjoyed. But when I said that you wouldn't be on your own, I meant that I will be with you."

"I know you'd make every effort, but—"

"No," he interrupted. "I won't *try* to be with you, I *will* be with you. I've decided to resign from the military."

"But...why?"

"Because you need me," he said simply.

She was stunned by his response, shocked that he would really take such a step for her and racked with guilt for the same reason.

"I don't need you," she denied. "Emma and I were getting by just fine and we can continue to do so."

"You need me," he said again, "maybe almost as much as I need you."

She was humbled, speechless.

"That stunned you into silence, didn't it?" He grinned and finally pulled her into his arms. "Yes, I need you. But even more important, I want you by my side, every day, for the rest of our lives together."

"Well, I know that Emma would love to have her daddy around full-time."

"What about you?" he prompted.

"I think that 'every day, for the rest of our lives together' sounds a heck of a lot better than the handful of days I was willing to settle for."

"You shouldn't have to settle."

"Then I don't want less than everything," she told him and lifted her arms to link them behind his head. "I love you, Zach."

"I love you, Paige."

She smiled. "I could get used to hearing that."

"I'll make sure you do," he promised.

"If you're really going to be sticking around, can we have a honeymoon?"

He chuckled. "I am so all over that one."

"And a baby?"

He paused, but it was hope rather than hesitation that burned in those blue, blue eyes that locked with hers. "Are you sure?"

"Yeah." She smiled. "It surprised me, too, but the more I thought about it, the more I realized it was something I really want."

"To have a family of your own," he guessed.

"To have *your* baby," she corrected.

He kissed her again. "I think that's definitely something we could start working toward."

"Tonight?"

"You read my mind."

It was later that she finally told him about the last of her reasons for coming to California.

They were lying naked in his bed, and this time Paige didn't feel panicked about anything. She only felt completely and blissfully content.

As Zach stroked a hand down her back, then slowly up again, she snuggled into him, listening to the beat of his heart beneath her cheek and feeling as if all was truly right in her world—or at least moving in that direction.

"I went to see my aunt today," she told him.

"Lillian?"

She shook her head. "Serena. My mother's sister."

"I didn't think you had any contact with your mother's family."

"I didn't—until today. But I had an address in Berkeley, and because I was in California anyway, I thought I would try to track her down. I thought that putting together the pieces of my past might help me build toward the future."

"And did you find any of those pieces?"

"More than I ever would have imagined," she said. "Most importantly, and surprisingly, that Colonel Phillip Wilder isn't really my father."

Zach's hand paused.

"Well, legally he is," she continued, "because it's his name on my birth certificate, but biologically, there's no real connection between us."

"How do you feel about that?" he asked.

"I'm not entirely sure," she admitted. "I was stunned at first, then angry, because if he isn't my father, who am I? But now, I think, I'm relieved. I hated to think that a man could be so ambivalent toward his own child, so it's almost easier to accept that what he felt wasn't ambivalence but resentment.

"According to Serena, when my mother decided to leave her husband, she planned to take me with her. But he came home while she was packing and told her that she could walk out if she wanted but no way was she taking his daughter.

"So she told him that he wasn't my father, and he said he didn't care. He didn't care about that fact any more than he cared about me. It was all about his rights.

"We were living in Germany at the time, and my mother told Serena that she didn't want to leave the country without me, but she believed it would be easier for her to petition to amend my birth certificate and get a court order for custody once she was back in the United States."

"Obviously something fell through."

"After months spent battling bureaucracy and cutting through red tape, just when she thought it was finally going to happen, when she was finally ready to serve all of the required legal documents on her husband, she found out that his unit had been deployed to another country. By the time she tracked him down again, she'd been diagnosed with ALS and decided that she didn't want to bring me to live with her if it meant that I would have to watch her die."

"I'm sorry, Paige. Not just because you lost your mother, but because the last thing you needed after having all of this dumped on you was for me to jump all over your back."

"You didn't know," she said.

"But I should have," he insisted. "And I should have been there with you."

"You're here with me now."

He hugged her tight. "You've already forgiven me, haven't you?"

"I love you," she said simply.

"I like hearing you say that." He kissed the top of her head. "I like it even better when you don't stumble over the words."

She smiled. "The point of all of that was to tell you that I do have a family of my own. Not just my aunt Lillian and Ashley and Megan, but now aunts and uncles and cousins on my mother's side, too."

"So what are you saying—that you don't need my family now?" he teased.

"Maybe I don't need them, but I want them anyway." She brushed her lips against his. "Although not nearly as much as I want you."

"I could happily spend every day of the rest of my life with you just like this," Zach told her, then sighed. "But I think, eventually, I'm going to have to get a job."

"Have you ever thought about getting your commercial pilot's license?" she asked him.

"It's not the kind of job that would allow me to sleep at home every night," he told her.

"Would you be gone for months at a time?"

"No."

"Would you come home to me and Emma every chance you could?" she asked.

"Of course," he answered without hesitation.

"Do you love to fly?"

He sighed. "Yeah."

"Then you should do it," she insisted.

"I'll think about it," he said, and she knew that he already was.

"Because whether we're living in New York or California, we're going to be doing a lot of traveling back and forth," she told him.

"So any airline discount would come in handy," he guessed.

She nodded. "Especially when we're hauling three or four kids around."

Zach's brows lifted. "Three or *four?*"

Paige just smiled.

"Well, then," her husband said, a mischievous sparkle in his blue, blue eyes, "I guess we should get started."

Epilogue

Olivia Lynn Crawford was born nine months later and christened on the one-year anniversary of her parents' wedding.

Since Ashley and Megan had both missed the nuptials, they made sure they were on hand—with husbands and children in tow—for the baby's baptism. Of course, it helped that Zach was able to get them all a great deal on flights through the airline for which he was now working.

And though Paige's cousins had planned to stay at a nearby hotel, Zach's parents had insisted that they could find room for everyone in the main house. It was a tight squeeze, but no one complained.

No one except Zach.

"I was hoping for a more private anniversary celebration," he grumbled to his wife. "I haven't had any time alone with you since the baby was born."

"We'll be alone when the kids go to sleep," Paige said, and she knew that despite his protests, he was as happy as she was to have their family around to celebrate a year that had been filled with adjustments for both of them.

She'd passed the California bar and was job sharing with another attorney who wanted to spend more time with her children. Though she'd worried about going back to work and putting Emma in day care, Kathleen and Justin had alleviated her concerns by offering to watch Emma. They had since extended the offer to include their newest granddaughter.

It was an arrangement that made Hayden as happy as her parents, because the time they spent with the grandchildren was time they weren't interfering in the business, and the winery was thriving under her management. It was also a convenient arrangement for Zach and Paige, since they were living in the guest cottage while they finalized plans for their own home to be built on property they'd purchased a few miles down the road.

As she looked around at everyone who had gathered, she said a silent thank-you to the friend after whom she and Zach had named their daughter, for helping her to discover the true value and importance of family.

For Paige, that included her aunts and cousins and their respective spouses and children, and Zach's parents and sisters and all the connections that flowed from them. But at the heart of her family was Zach, the man she loved enough to follow to the ends of the earth. And the man who loved her enough to understand how much she needed a place to call home.

As if he knew exactly what she was thinking, Zach put his arm across her shoulders and hugged her close. And she smiled up at him, knowing that in his arms, she was finally exactly where she belonged.

* * * * *

SPECIAL EXCERPT FROM

H HARLEQUIN®

Desire

Here's an exciting sneak preview of
Cat Schield's
BECAUSE OF THE BABY...

As **TEXAS CATTLEMAN'S CLUB: AFTER THE STORM**
*continues, two members of feuding families come together
to care for a very special baby born during the tornado...*

"It would be better for you if I was here full-time," Keaton said.

"How do you figure?"

"Have you considered what will happen if Grace is up all night? If I'm here we can take turns getting up with her." He could see Lark was weakening. "It makes sense."

"Let me sleep on it tonight?" She held out her hands for the baby.

"Sure."

Only, Lark never got the chance to sleep. Neither did Keaton. Shortly after Grace finished eating, she began to fuss. During the second hour of the baby's crying, Keaton searched for advice on his tablet.

"She's dry, fed and obviously tired. Why won't she sleep?"

"Because it's her first day out of the NICU and she's overstimulated."

"How about wrapping her up?" he suggested. "Says here that babies feel more secure when they're swaddled." He cued up a video and they watched it. The demonstration looked straightforward, but the woman in the video used a doll, not a real baby.

"We can try it." Lark went to the closet and returned with two blankets of different sizes. "Hopefully one of these will do the trick."

When she was done, Lark braced her hands on the dining room table and stared down at the swaddled baby. "This doesn't look right."

Keaton returned to the video. "I think we missed this part here."

Grace was growing more upset by the second and she'd managed to free her left arm.

"Is it terrible that I have no idea what I'm doing?" Lark sounded close to tears. It had been a long, stressful evening.

"Not at all. I think every first-time parent feels just as overwhelmed as we do right now."

"Thank you for sticking around and helping me."

"We're helping Grace."

The corners of her lips quivered. "Not very well, as it happens."

And then, because she looked determined and hopeless all at once, Keaton succumbed to the impulse that had been threatening to break free all week. He cupped her cheek, lowered his head and kissed her.

Don't miss BECAUSE OF THE BABY...
by Cat Schield
Available January 2015
wherever Harlequin® Desire books and ebooks are sold.

JUST CAN'T GET ENOUGH?

Join our social communities
and talk to us online.

You will have access to the latest
news on upcoming titles and special
promotions, but most importantly,
you can talk to other fans about your
favorite Harlequin reads.

Harlequin.com/Community

Facebook.com/HarlequinBooks

Twitter.com/HarlequinBooks

Pinterest.com/HarlequinBooks